PRAISE FOR R

"*The Professor* is that rare combinat..., ...ills, and heart. Gripping from the first page to the last."

—Winston Groom, author of *Forrest Gump*

"Robert Bailey is a thriller writer to reckon with. His debut novel has a tight and twisty plot, vivid characters, and a pleasantly down-home sensibility that will remind some readers of adventures in Grisham-land. Luckily, Robert Bailey is an original, and his skill as a writer makes the Alabama setting all his own. *The Professor* marks the beginning of a very promising career."

—Mark Childress, author of *Georgia Bottoms* and *Crazy in Alabama*

"Taut, page turning, and smart, *The Professor* is a legal thriller that will keep readers up late as the twists and turns keep coming. Set in Alabama, it also includes that state's greatest icon, one Coach Bear Bryant. In fact, the Bear gets things going with the energy of an Alabama kickoff to Auburn. Robert Bailey knows his state, and he knows his law. He also knows how to write characters that are real, sympathetic, and surprising. If he keeps writing novels this good, he's got quite a literary career before him."

—Homer Hickam, author of *Rocket Boys/October Sky*, a *New York Times* number-one bestseller

"Bailey's solid second McMurtrie and Drake legal thriller (after 2014's *The Professor*) . . . provides enough twists and surprises to keep readers turning the pages."

—*Publishers Weekly*

"A gripping legal suspense thriller of the first order, *Between Black and White* clearly displays author Robert Bailey's impressive talents as a novelist. An absorbing and riveting read from beginning to end."

—*Midwest Book Reviews*

"Take a murder, a damaged woman, and a desperate daughter, and you have the recipe for *The Last Trial*, a complex and fast-paced legal thriller. Highly recommended."

—D. P. Lyle, award-winning author

"*The Final Reckoning* is explosive and displays every element of a classic thriller: fast pacing, strong narrative, fear, misery, and transcendence. Bailey proves once more that he is a fine writer with an instinct for powerful white-knuckle narrative."

—*Southern Literary Review*

"A stunning discovery, a triple twist, and dramatic courtroom scenes all make for a riveting, satisfying read in what might well be Bailey's best book to date . . . *Legacy of Lies* is a grand story with a morality-tale vibe, gripping and thrilling throughout. It showcases Bailey once more as a writer who knows how to keep the suspense high, the pacing fast, the narrative strong, the characters compellingly complex, and his plot full of white-knuckle tension and twists."

—*Southern Literary Review*

"Inspiring . . . Sharp in its dialogue, real with its relationships, and fascinating in details of the game, The Golfer's Carol is that rarest of books—one you will read and keep for yourself while purchasing multiple copies for friends."

—Andy Andrews, *New York Times* bestselling author of *The Noticer* and *The Traveler's Gift*

THE
WRONG
SIDE

ALSO BY ROBERT BAILEY

BOCEPHUS HAYNES SERIES

Legacy of Lies

McMURTRIE AND DRAKE LEGAL THRILLERS

The Final Reckoning

The Last Trial

Between Black and White

The Professor

OTHER BOOKS

The Golfer's Carol

THE
WRONG
SIDE

ROBERT
BAILEY

THOMAS & MERCER

This is a work of fiction. Names, characters, organizations, places, events, and incidents are either products of the author's imagination or are used fictitiously. Any resemblance to actual persons, living or dead, or actual events is purely coincidental.

Text copyright © 2021 by Robert Bailey
All rights reserved.

No part of this book may be reproduced, or stored in a retrieval system, or transmitted in any form or by any means, electronic, mechanical, photocopying, recording, or otherwise, without express written permission of the publisher.

Published by Thomas & Mercer, Seattle

www.apub.com

Amazon, the Amazon logo, and Thomas & Mercer are trademarks of Amazon.com, Inc., or its affiliates.

ISBN-13: 9781542025935
ISBN-10: 1542025931

Cover design by Shasti O'Leary Soudant

Printed in the United States of America

In memory of Winston Groom

PROLOGUE

Sunday, October 16, 2016

Helen gazed up at the huge mansion on the hill. She had pulled her vehicle off Highway 31 so as not to block traffic and had cut the lights. It had become a habit to stop here a few times a month and peer up at the structure where her son lived. She had been up the driveway only once, at the party last November, when they had finally put all their cards on the table.

Since then, she'd "visited" by parking her car off the highway and staring at the house. That was as close as she would allow herself. Like a child reaching her fingers toward a flame, knowing that if she touched the fire, it would burn, but curious nonetheless.

Why had she come here tonight? Helen couldn't answer that one. Her life, which had for so long been one of structure and order, was now off its hinges. Would she ever get back to where she had been? Did she even want to return to her old life?

Her phone, which was lying on the passenger seat, began to ring. Helen gazed at it, seeing the familiar number that she'd known would pop up.

She answered on the fourth ring.

"You've had a busy day." His voice sounded younger to her than his thirty-eight years. She wondered if the voices of adult children always sounded younger to their parents. Helen wouldn't know. She had only one child and had known him for less than a year.

"Very busy."

"Do you think you've got your man?" There was a tease to his tone, which made Helen's stomach quiver.

She didn't answer.

"Did the sheriff's office consider anyone else? Was . . . *I* . . . a person of interest? You looked a bit uneasy at the press conference."

Helen bit her lip, knowing he was trying to rile her. She'd been all-business during her few seconds at the podium. No one could tell she was cracking.

Except my son? My own flesh and blood . . .

She shook her head, not believing her thoughts. *He wants to get a rise. Don't give him the satisfaction.*

"Would you like to come inside? I could make us some coffee. Or tea if you prefer? We could talk about your new case. Hard to believe someone would even think of hurting the princess of Pulaski, much less kill her. And is the culprit the young lad you charged with the crime? Star of the football team, no?" He paused. "What drama. But . . . have you considered the possibility that the sheriff's office might have it wrong yet again? Like they did with you last year. Oh, wait. They actually had that—"

"Michael—"

"Hang with me now. What if Sheriff Springfield and Chief Storm are focusing on the wrong suspect?" He snickered. "Please come inside, Mother. We could talk about the murder. We could even discuss what I was doing at, say . . . one o'clock yesterday morning."

"No," Helen whispered, closing her eyes and leaning her head against the steering wheel. *What am I doing?*

Since the press conference, she'd been driving the streets of Giles County, thinking through the case and trying to figure out what to do. *I should be at the station. Supervising everything and making damn sure nothing gets screwed up. Frannie is probably wondering where the hell I am.*

Her car had finally ended up here, as it had done often in the past eleven months.

"This is silly, Mother." Her son's voice jarred her back to the present, and she lifted her head off the wheel. She opened her eyes and took in a deep breath.

"Are you scared of me?" he continued. The tease in his tone was gone.

Yes. But Helen didn't answer. Instead, after a brief hesitation, she clicked "End" and set the phone down.

Then, sighing and taking a last look at the huge house, she put her car in gear and merged back onto Highway 31.

PART ONE

1

Friday, October 14, 2016

From the tunnel outside the home locker room, the crowd sounded like the low rumble of thunder. How many were there? Sam Davis Stadium held 4,200 people, but for this game, they had allowed another thousand fans, mostly students, to surround the field. Odell Champagne gazed out the opening and shook his head. "Kickoff is still an hour out, and it's already crazy. Can you believe it?" he asked, hearing the wistfulness in his voice. He felt a hand grab his own and then warm breath in his ear that smelled like bubble gum. He smiled.

"Yes," Brittany said, kissing his earlobe. "They're here to see the best football player in the country."

"No, they're not," he said, taking a step forward and pulling her with him. "They're here to see Fizz . . . *the most electrifying band in the Southeast.*" He mimicked public address announcer Earl Morring's broadcaster voice, and she elbowed him in the rib cage. *"With lead singer, Pulaski's very own . . . Brittany Crutcher. Ahhhhh."* He held up their hands together on the last part and started bouncing on his toes.

Brittany rolled her eyes with a smile, and Odell pulled her in close. "We'd have a good crowd if it was just Giles County versus Tullahoma . . . but not like this." He cocked his head toward the opening. "All those kids along the field and already sitting in the stands. They're here for the concert after the game." He grinned at her. "They're here for you."

She shrugged and glanced down, chewing the large wad of gum that she had in her mouth.

"And you know it," Odell said, leaning in and kissing her cheek and neck. Then he pulled back and squinted at her. "How many pieces you got in your mouth?"

"Two," she said.

Odell shook his head. "Looks like double that to me, girl." He knew that Brittany liked to chew gum to relax. He'd seen her take down several packs on concert days. "Nervous about the show?"

"No," she said before taking out her gum and tossing it hard into the trash can against the wall.

"Liar," Odell teased.

Brittany peered up at him. She looked like she wanted to say something.

"What?"

"Nothing." She glanced behind her. "Don't you need to go inside? Won't Coach P. be wondering where his star player is?"

"We can chill for a little while longer." He paused. "So . . . are you going to watch the game?"

"You know we have to rehearse."

"The first half?"

"I have to meet with someone first." She sighed. "About the band."

"Mr. Zannick, right?" Odell snapped the name off like it pained him to say it. He looked away from her, trying to keep his annoyance in check. "I can't believe you're hanging around that criminal. You know what Mr. Haynes thinks of him."

"He's been good to me, O. He . . ."

"He what?" Odell ground his teeth together. "I know he's spent a lot of money on the band, but isn't it obvious what he really wants?"

Brittany pursed her lips. "Last I checked, Mr. Zannick's been good to your momma too. Isn't she working at his club, or did I dream that?"

"And she hasn't been the same since." He took out his phone and held it up. "Been trying to reach her all day long, and she's ghosted again."

"That's not Mr. Zannick's fault. She was disappearing for days before she took that job. O, you've got to move on from your mom. If you don't, she's going to ruin your life like my dad tried to do mine. At least move out of that apartment. I'm sure Mr. Haynes would let you live at his house for the rest of the year. And next year . . ." She playfully pushed him. ". . . you'll be out of here, baby. In Tuscaloosa. Or Knoxville. Or . . . maybe Southern California."

"You know I can't do that."

"Why not?"

"It's different for me, Brit. My mom's all I've got. I can't leave her."

"And you can't save her," Brittany said, touching his chest with her hand and running her fingers up his neck. "You know that, don't you?"

Odell looked away from her. "Brit, please watch the first half. Why in the world do you have to meet with that dude Zannick tonight? It's the biggest game of the year. *The largest crowd in Giles County High School history.*" He again mimicked the PA announcer's voice, but it felt forced.

She didn't smile. "That's not who I'm meeting."

Odell raised his eyebrows. "Who then?"

"It doesn't matter." She started to walk away, but Odell stepped in her way and held out his hands.

"At least watch the second quarter."

She folded her arms and stared past him.

"Brit." He stepped closer to her. "I'm sorry, OK? I shouldn't have brought Zannick up." He reached for her, and she let him pull her toward him. When he kissed her, he felt her heart thumping hard against him. He touched her cheek. "What's wrong?"

She looked down at the concrete floor, and Odell lifted her chin back up. "What is it?"

9

Her eyes glistened, and she pulled back. "You don't need to be worrying about me. How many college scouts are out there tonight? Ten? Twenty? Don't worry about me, and don't think about your mom either. You focus on you, OK?" She grimaced slightly.

"Hey, tell me what's going on. Let me help."

She wiped her eyes. "You can't help me with this, O. No one can. I've done something I can't take back."

Odell felt his body tense. "What'd you do?"

She brushed past him toward the opening, and he followed her, wrapping his arms around her waist. "I love you, Brit."

She turned and pressed her body into his, and he could still feel the thudding of her heart. She hugged his neck and brought her lips to his, then kissed him until he lost himself. Finally, she whispered into his ear, "I love you too, O."

He watched her walk away, feeling his own heartbeat racing with equal parts desire and fear. "Brit?"

But his words were drowned out by the crowd.

"What'd you do?" he asked again into the emptiness.

———

Brittany Crutcher walked as fast as she could across the parking lot toward her car. She was stopped twice by well-wishers and once by a sixth-grade girl wanting an autograph. She signed her name on the girl's T-shirt, smiling at the middle schooler's parents, who both wished her luck. When she reached her Toyota 4Runner, she collapsed into the front seat. She was exhausted, mentally, physically, and emotionally.

What have I done? Then, as if someone had heard her thoughts, her phone dinged to announce a text. Brittany pulled the device out of her pocket, already knowing who the sender had to be. She'd told him she would check in before the game started and had yet to do so. She glanced at the screen, and her fears were confirmed.

Michael Zannick.

Call me, his text said.

Sucking in a deep breath, Brittany clicked on his name and heard the phone begin to ring.

"I've been waiting," he said.

"The game hasn't started yet."

"Will I be seeing you after the show?"

"You're not coming?"

A sigh on the other end of the line. "I'm a pariah at that school— you know that. Besides, I hate crowds, and given our announcement tomorrow, I'd prefer to keep a low profile." He paused. "But I do want to see you tonight. Maybe around eleven o'clock?"

Brittany closed her eyes, biting her lip.

"Not having second thoughts, are you?" he asked.

"No."

"Good," he said. "See you at eleven."

"Michael, I . . ."

The phone went dead. Brittany glared at the screen for several seconds before flipping the device onto the passenger seat. She gritted her teeth. Then she leaned over and pulled a pack of gum out of her purse. She popped two pieces into her mouth and began to chew as the inevitable dawned on her.

No one could help her now. She thought of Odell, now probably inside the locker room, receiving his final instructions from Coach Patterson. What a night this was supposed to have been for him. For both of them. Their classmate Doug Fitzgerald was having a party after the concert, and Odell would expect her to meet him there. The band was all planning to go and blow off some steam, maybe even play a few impromptu songs for their friends. It was their last year of high school. How many more nights like this would there be?

11

None for me, Brittany thought, finally putting the car in gear and pulling out of the parking lot. As cars continued to filter into Sam Davis Stadium, Brittany Crutcher turned right onto Highway 31.

She wouldn't be going to Doug's party. Hell, she wasn't even going to finish senior year. She had one loose end to tie up. Then she would go to Michael's later tonight, and tomorrow morning, she'd be gone. Leaving her parents, her friends, high school . . .

Odell . . .

Her lip trembled.

Tears began to fall down her cheeks. She pressed her foot to the accelerator, willing herself to move forward.

What have I done?

———

Before joining the team, Odell decided to take a walk around the field to clear his head. He knew he needed to focus, but his mind was distracted. He was worried about his mother, who still hadn't responded to any of his calls or texts. He was also concerned about Brittany. Finally, as he peered around the mass of humanity that inhabited the Brickyard, he felt butterflies in his stomach. *This is unbelievable,* he thought, staring up at the stands and seeing every row full.

"Hey, O!" a familiar voice yelled to him from the steps by the home bleachers.

"Yo, Ian, what's up?" Odell walked over and held out his fist to a skinny white kid who wore an Atlanta Braves baseball cap to cover up his long blond hair. Ian Dugan was the lead guitarist of Fizz and a fellow senior at GCHS.

Ian looked up above them and grinned. "This place is lit, huh?"

"Crazy," Odell agreed, still lost in his thoughts.

"You guys ought to be glad you've got a fairly awesome rock and roll band playing after you. Otherwise it would just be a few parents up there hoping to see their kid score a touchdown." Ian held a straight face for a second and then burst into a grin. "Kidding, O. I know a lot of this is for the team and mainly you. Good luck tonight, man."

"Thanks," Odell said, finally beginning to relax. Of the members of the band, Odell liked Ian the best. The guitarist had a dry, sarcastic sense of humor that Odell enjoyed. Ian was also a math wiz who had helped Odell study for a few big tests.

"You going to Doug's party tonight?" Odell asked.

"Wouldn't miss it. After you and the team tear up Tullahoma and Fizz sets this place on fire afterward, I'm going to be in the mood to talk with some ladies."

Odell rubbed his chin. "Playing the rock star card."

Ian's face went serious. "We play the hand we're dealt . . . Mr. Five Star Football Prospect dating the hottest girl at the school."

"Easy." Odell faked throwing a punch at Ian, who fell back as if it had connected.

Odell gazed around the stadium, feeling the energy building with each passing second. "You're right about one thing, man. This place is lit, and it's definitely not just because of the game." He crooked an eyebrow at Ian. "How near are you guys to getting a deal? Brit's been pretty quiet about it lately, but I'm hearing rumors."

"My sis says we're close, man. We'll be inking with a label soon."

Odell rocked his head back in acknowledgment. He'd met Ian's sister, Cassie, several times at the band practices he'd attended. He knew she had been pushing Fizz hard to do more events with the one tonight being the biggest yet. "Awesome," Odell managed. Smiling wide, he elbowed his friend in the rib cage. "Then what you gonna do? Play Clash of Clans all day long when you're not touring?" Odell had heard Ian talk about his "gaming room" when the two studied together.

"I'll do whatever the hell I want," Ian said.

"And ditch that scholarship to Tennessee?"

"*Half* scholarship," Ian corrected. "And you're damn right. Rock and roll is, was, and will always be the dream. And with Brittany on lead vocals, we can't be stopped. You're going to be working out next year at whichever school you sign with and listening to Fizz on your earbuds."

"I hope so," Odell said. "Hey, I got to run. Thanks for the comic relief."

"Odell Champagne, can I have your autograph?!" Ian screamed after him. Odell waved him off as he walked away.

"See you at Doug's later?" Ian yelled.

Odell held his right thumb up and trotted back to the locker room. As he did, he peered up at the growing crowd and thought about Brittany, Ian, and their band. He knew that the guitar man was right.

Fizz was going all the way.

Still . . . *what is bugging Brit?* Odell wondered as he walked toward the tunnel. Pausing at the opening, he took out his phone one last time, hoping for a return message from his mother. There was none.

Odell breathed in a large gust of the chilly October air and placed his right fist into his left hand, steeling himself.

Game time, baby.

2

Les Patterson had never actually played football. His asthma hadn't allowed it. But he'd loved the game since he was a kid, and he bled Tennessee orange. He'd been ten years old in 1982 when the Vols broke the streak against Alabama. Les and his dad had stormed the field when the clock struck zero, and they'd watched the goalposts come down inside Neyland Stadium. In high school, he'd been the equipment manager for the Lincoln County Falcons when the legendary John Meadows had roamed the sidelines, and he had soaked up the lessons of the famous coach, who'd retired with almost three hundred wins. During college, he'd been a statistical analyst for Tennessee head coach Phillip Fulmer. After two years as a graduate assistant, he'd gotten his teaching certificate and had taken the job as junior varsity assistant coach at Giles County High, eventually being named head football coach in 2011. Since being hired, he'd earned several winning seasons and one county title.

But this year, the goals were higher. *State,* he thought, as he glanced around the crowded locker room and heard the steadily rising roar of the capacity crowd outside. When Odell Champagne had transferred to GCH, Les's team had gone from being competitive to dominant. And tonight they had a chance to send a message that this year's state championship was going through Pulaski.

"Take a knee," Les said. His voice was hoarse from the effects of a bad cold and a week's worth of interviews. His stomach had also tightened into a knot. He'd have to pop another antacid before kickoff.

Had there ever been a game in Pulaski as big as the one his team was about to play? Not only were the stadium and school grounds overflowing with people, but Giles County vs. Tullahoma had been selected as the ESPN high school game of the week. And finally, there was a by God rock concert set to start thirty minutes afterward on the fifty-yard line.

No, there had never been a contest quite like this one, and Les doubted there ever would be again. That was why he had called in reinforcements for his final few minutes with the team.

"Gentlemen, you've had a good week of practice," he began. "You've worked hard, and I'm proud of you. You've handled the press coverage and all of the hype about as well as I could have hoped. At this point, I don't have anything left to offer you. If the line blocks and Odell runs the way we know he can, they can't stop us. They have a solid QB, but they haven't played a defense like ours . . . or an outsider linebacker like Odell." He stopped himself. He didn't want to focus too much on one player, even though that was all ESPN had done this entire week. Other talented boys were on the team, but there were few players, if any, in the whole country who could compare to Odell Champagne.

"Before we head out on that field, I've invited someone to say a few words. A man who has played on the biggest of stages, both on a football field and in life." He paused. "And you all know him." Les nodded at his assistant coach, Ronnie Davidson, who was standing by the door to the locker room. Without hesitation, Davidson opened the door.

"Gentlemen, give it up for the greatest Bobcat. Number 41, Bocephus . . . Haynes."

——

He strode into the room to a cacophony of yells, whistles, and a couple of spirited *hell, yeah*s from the team. Bocephus Aurulius Haynes wore dark jeans, a flannel button-down, and a brown bomber's jacket. At six feet, four inches tall and a shade over 240 pounds, Bo was almost as big as the door itself, and for a few moments, he stood in the opening, making eye contact with as many of the players as he could. After a couple more seconds, the cheers subsided, and the only sound was the rumble of the swelling crowd outside. As Bo approached the middle of the room, the smell of sweat, leather, and Old Spice deodorant filled his nostrils, and he almost smiled as the memories of his own gridiron glory came flooding back to him. Bo had been all-state at Giles County High and a preseason all-American his junior year at Alabama before a knee injury had ended his career.

He shook hands with Coach Patterson, who took a couple of steps backward, gesturing for Bo to speak when ready.

"Thank you, Coach P.," Bo said, running a hand over his smoothly shaved head. For several more seconds, Bo peered at the team. The expressions he saw were a mixture of determination, fear, and anxiety. All natural emotions to experience when adversity came knocking.

Outside the four walls of this enclosure were at least five thousand screaming fans. Some had come to watch a football game. Others wanted a good seat for the concert that would take place immediately after the game. The only thing that was certain was that the large majority of the kids in this room would never again play in front of a bigger audience in their life.

"My advice to you is simple," Bo finally said, keeping his baritone voice low. Several of the boys scooted closer to hear better. "First, do your job. Whether you're the third-string offensive lineman or . . ." Bo's eyes landed on Odell Champagne. ". . . the starting tailback. Focus on your role on each play and concentrate *only* on that. If you do, then you'll give yourself and, most importantly, this team its best chance to win." Bo paused. "Second, play as hard and fast as you can." His face broke into a grin. "I've got a phrase I use around my law office when I start working up a case. It's kind of become my philosophy for life. T. J., tell them what it is."

A lanky kid stood and looked around the room. "Wide ass open," T. J. Haynes said, nodding at his father.

"Wide ass open," Bo said. "Each one of you has an internal motor that determines how fast and hard you play. And each of you knows that sometimes you take it easy and don't push yourself. You take plays off. You get lazy, and that engine inside of you barely gets hot. And that kind of half-ass effort gets you beat. On the football field and in life." He paused and moved his eyes from one player to the next. "Wide ass open means pushing your motor full throttle. One hundred and ten percent effort, all you got, everything you have, and a little more until the whistle blows. A down in football lasts anywhere from five to fifteen seconds. If you play wide ass open, as fast and hard as you can go, for every one of those seconds, four quarters, forty-eight minutes, you'll give yourself the best chance to win." Again he stopped, this time pointing toward the wall. "And that team in the other locker room will *hate* having to line up against you." Bo paused for a full five seconds, feeling the adrenaline resonating through the room. *"Do you hear me?"*

"Yes, sir!" the team screamed in unison.

"What?"

"Yes, sir!"

"All right then," Bo said, taking a final look at the players. "Go get it."

3

Bo stayed behind in the hallway outside the locker room as the Giles County High Bobcats took the field. He slapped T. J. on the helmet and his nephew Jarvis on the shoulder pads as they filed out, feeding off the energy of the team. Bo was dog tired after a week on the road taking expert depositions in Little Rock, Arkansas, but wild horses couldn't have kept him away from this game. The last player out of the room was Odell. He stopped when he noticed Bo.

"Nice speech," he said, holding out his fist, which Bo bumped with his own. Then the young man's brow furrowed. "Have you seen my mom?"

"No, but I just got here."

"I haven't seen her all day, Mr. Haynes. She should have gotten off work yesterday around nine, and since then she's been off the grid. I'm worried she's on another bender. Would you mind calling her?"

"Will do," Bo said.

Odell peered down at the concrete. Bo grabbed his face mask and raised it until he was looking into the player's eyes. "You keep your mind on the game." Bo pointed toward the field. "On those hundred yards out there, you hear?"

Bo put his hands on the side of the kid's helmet as Odell nodded. "Focus on what you can control, son. You can't fix your mom. Only she can do that. All you can do is to own yourself. Own you . . . and go get it out there. Dog and bone, right?"

Odell's face finally broke into a pensive smile. "Dog and bone."

"And remember, I'm going to need you in the morning out at the farm. I got a special project that T. J. and Lila are helping me with. I want you there too."

"Yes, sir," Odell said. "I'll be there."

As Odell ran out of the tunnel, Bo grabbed his cell phone and searched his contacts for Sabrina Champagne. He dialed her number and waited. Five rings and no answer. Then he sent her a text. Sabrina, you at the game? Odell's worried about you. He put the phone back into his pocket. Then he stepped out of the tunnel himself and gasped at what he saw.

The bleachers on both sides were filled to capacity, the sound of cheers deafening as the Bobcats took the field to the school fight song. Had there been this many people when Coach Paul "Bear" Bryant had come to watch Bo play in the mid-1970s?

No, Bo thought. Of course, the new "Brickyard," what the locals affectionately called Sam Davis Stadium, had a few more seats than the old one. *And there wasn't a rock concert happening right after my game either.*

Bo smiled up at the crowd, seeing signs for the home team mixed in with other posters for the band Fizz. The group's lead singer was Pulaski's own Brittany Crutcher, and rumors were swirling that she and her bandmates were on the verge of signing with a major record label.

"Incredible, isn't it?" a familiar voice whispered in his ear.

Bo turned and saw Chief Deputy Sheriff Frannie Storm appraising the bleachers. Frannie had light-brown skin and was in her early thirties. She'd made all-state in basketball at Giles County High and little all-American at Lipscomb University and had played a few years in the WNBA before injuries had led her into a career in law enforcement. At just over six feet, she was a thin woman whose demeanor typically radiated intensity. Tonight, however, even in her khaki uniform, Frannie seemed more relaxed.

"Yeah," Bo said. "I've never seen so many folks in the Brickyard."

"Not even when the Bear came to see you play?" She turned and pierced him with mischievous brown eyes, but Bo knew they could turn predatory on a dime. He had always gotten along well with Frannie, whose aunt Ellie had been Bo's legal assistant for twenty years. Yet a case last year had strained the relationship between cop and attorney. Since then, Bo had felt an awkward tension when he was in the chief deputy sheriff's presence. Even now, under the surface of the good tidings, he felt an uneasy vibe.

"I was just thinking about that night, and the answer is no," he managed. "This is a lot bigger."

"Maybe if the Jackson Five had been playing after the game, you'd have rung in a few more folks."

"Maybe," Bo agreed. "Is it true about Fizz? They about to go big time?"

Frannie cocked her head. "That's what everyone's saying."

Bo looked down at his feet and then back at Frannie. "You on duty tonight?"

"Unfortunately. We've got a slew of deputies flanking the stadium and a few in the stands for crowd control."

"Expecting trouble?"

"No. But we want to be ready if it comes."

Bo frowned. "Speaking of trouble, Odell said he hasn't seen his mother in twenty-four hours. Let me know if you see Sabrina, would you? He's worried she's been drinking again."

"I swear," Frannie said, speaking between clenched teeth. "That woman needs to be in rehab or jail. We should have locked her up after the last public intoxication charge, but the sheriff wouldn't do it. I *guaran damn tee* you that her sorry butt would be behind bars if her son wasn't God's gift to football. And now that she's working at the Sundowners . . ."

"It's not the boy's fault," Bo said.

"I know that. But if we keep enabling his mother, we aren't doing Odell or anyone else any favors."

For a moment, he looked at her, admiring the chief's intensity and the wisdom of her words. Then he smiled.

"What?" she asked.

"Pulaski is lucky to have you, you know it?"

She smirked. "Whatever." She gestured toward the field with her right hand. "How's T. J. liking football?"

Bo crossed his arms. "He's enjoying it."

"Remind me again why you would let him risk his future in round-ball to play this violent game." Frannie's tone was sharp, sarcastic.

"It's his senior year. He didn't want to have any regrets for not playing the game that . . ."

". . . his daddy was so great at," Frannie said. "I can understand that. But if he gets hurt out here, he'll regret that a lot worse. He's got basketball offers from Vanderbilt and UT, right?"

"Yeah. Still waiting for the one he really wants."

"Bama?"

Bo nodded. "I'd be fine with the other schools, but he—"

"Wants to play where his daddy played," she said.

Bo peered down at the turf. "And his mom." Subconsciously, he rubbed his thumb over the third finger of his left hand, where a wedding ring had been for over two decades. His wife, Jasmine, whom he'd called "Jazz" since the day he'd met her in Tuscaloosa, had run track at the University of Alabama. She had died almost three years ago, but there were still moments each day when his heart ached for her. The milestones reached by his kids in particular were tinged bittersweet because he couldn't share them with their mother.

Bo felt a light touch on his arm. He glanced up at Frannie, whose eyes had softened.

"I'll see you, OK? I hope T. J. plays well, and I'll let you know if I see Sabrina."

"Thank you," Bo said. He felt a lump in his throat as he looked out on the field and saw T. J., who was running pass patterns with the other receivers. He was wearing Bo's number, 41, which the school had brought out of retirement this year so T. J. could wear it. For his first year playing football, T. J. had excelled, earning a starting position. He'd caught seven touchdown passes already, with the season only half over. He seemed a lock for all-county. Though Bo was proud of these accomplishments, he was prouder of the man his boy was growing into. It was hard to believe that T. J. was a senior. In less than a year, he'd be off to college.

Bo turned and glanced at the swell of students who were standing along the home sidelines below the bleachers. He squinted, looking for Lila, but didn't see her. Somewhere, his daughter was standing with friends, probably talking more about Fizz than the football game. He took out his phone and shot her a quick U ok? text, which she responded to almost immediately with a thumbs-up emoji. Then, seconds later, she added, Saw you talking to Frannie . . . followed by a smiley face.

Bo sighed at the phone and put it back in his pocket. His kids were both beginning to give him subtle and not-so-subtle hints that they were OK with him dating again, but he'd taken no steps in that direction. As he again thumbed his ring finger and gazed around the packed stadium, he felt a cloak of sadness envelop him. It was an incredible night.

For his kids. For Giles County High. For the town of Pulaski.

But for Bocephus Haynes, like so many evenings in the past two and a half years, the night felt empty, hollow. He loved his children and was proud of the new life he, T. J., and Lila had carved out in Pulaski. He was also thrilled for his hometown, which carried the stain of being the birthplace of the Ku Klux Klan but was now hosting a dual event celebrating two teenage African American superstars. It was a great time to be alive, and he knew he should try to enjoy the moment. But still, as he turned toward the home team stands and hoped his cousin Booker T. had saved him a seat, Bo couldn't escape the melancholy that had built a fort in his heart.

He missed his wife.

4

Odell Champagne stood on the goal line and ground his teeth together. Gone were his worry over Brittany and concern for his mother. For the next forty-eight minutes of play, his anxiety would be replaced by one overriding emotion.

Rage.

He could literally feel his body hum with it in the seconds before the start of a game. He knew that many folks might say what he was experiencing was adrenaline, but Odell knew better. Adrenaline came and went, like the rush of losing your stomach on a roller coaster or the fear-soaked danger of being chased by a security guard after stealing a loaf of bread from the store.

The rage Odell felt on a football field was different. It never went away. It gave him energy and strength, heightening his senses, making him feel unstoppable.

Who did he have to thank for this trait? Odell shot a glance toward the home stands, to the section reserved for the team's parents. He knew his mother wasn't there, that Mr. Haynes wouldn't be able to get her on the phone.

What was she high on tonight? Coke? Pot? Gin? Who the hell knew? Odell wished he could stop caring, but he would *never* abandon his mom. He would *never* emulate the actions of his father, the true source of his fury.

Fuck you, Billy . . .

Even in the silence of his thoughts, Odell couldn't bring himself to say *Dad* anymore. He gripped his hands into fists and squeezed.

As the kicker for Tullahoma booted the ball into the October air, Odell Champagne loosened his hands. The world narrowed into a tunnel that held only one hundred yards of green grass.

5

Three miles away from the stadium, in downtown Pulaski, Kathy's Tavern was quiet. That wasn't surprising for a Friday night in the fall, where traffic tended to pick up after the football game was over. Cassie Dugan stood behind the bar, counting the bills in the register and keeping an eye on the restaurant's lone patron. Clete Sartain was an eightysomething-year-old man who typically spent a couple nights a week belly up to the bar, drinking Natural Light from the can and telling stories about his time as a forklift operator at the SunDrop Bottling Company. He had a snow-white beard, and each December for as long as Cassie could remember, he'd been Santa Claus in the annual Christmas festival downtown. Clete was normally gone by this time of night, and rumors circulated that when he wasn't at Kathy's, he liked to spend his time at the infamous Sundowners Club, the county's lone strip joint. Cassie didn't know whether to be sickened or impressed by the gossip, but she half hoped it was true. If it was, then that would be a surprise, and surprises were few and far between in the life of Cassie Dugan, who'd spent the better part of the last decade pouring draft beer and whiskey at Kathy's.

She shut the register and decided to inquire if there was a reason for Clete's extended hours. She ambled toward her customer and glanced at the back of the restaurant. Most Friday nights there would normally be a band playing later, but there would be none tonight. Not with Fizz performing at the Brickyard. Cassie smiled to herself, knowing that she was partly responsible for that development.

"Clete, why are you still here?"

The old man looked up at her and extended his can of Natural Light in a toast. "I didn't want to watch the game alone at home, so I thought I'd hang out here. That OK?"

Cassie gazed up at the big-screen TV that adorned the wall behind the bar. "I guess. But you can't loiter without ordering anything. Can I get you a cheeseburger?"

"Yes, ma'am," Clete said. "And keep a steady stream of Nattys heading my way too. Now scoot, Cassie. I don't want to miss kickoff."

"You're not going to make me drive you home again, are you, Clete?"

He shook his head, glued to the screen.

Cassie rolled her eyes. "So are the Bobcats gonna win State this year?" she asked, peering up at the television and hearing the jingle of the door announce a new customer.

"As long as Odell Champagne stays healthy, they can't be beat. That kid is the best football player to ever play for Giles County High."

"Better than Bo Haynes?" Cassie asked, feeling her stomach tighten as she recognized the guest who'd taken a seat at the table closest to the bar.

Clete chuckled. "I think even Bo would say Odell was better."

"Huh," Cassie said, striding toward her newest patron and feeling butterflies. "Surprised to see you. Shouldn't you guys be warming up?"

Her guest, who wore a cap to cover her head and was chewing gum, put her finger over her mouth.

"Don't you shush me, Brittany," Cassie said, plopping down on the chair opposite her guest. "And don't think that cap is stealthy." She turned. "Hey, Clete, look who's here."

Clete glanced up from his can and squinted. "Oh, hey, Brittany. Shouldn't you be at the Brickyard?" Clete sipped his beer and turned back to the screen. "Your boyfriend is already lighting it up. Look at that run." He pointed at the screen and then banged his fist on the bar.

Brittany sighed. Then she ripped off her cap, revealing thick locks of dark-brown hair that fell to her shoulders. "I miss not being recognized."

"No, you don't," Cassie said. "And don't ever say that around me again, you hear me? I'd have given my left boob to be where you are. Fizz is about to go platinum, and Clete's right about Odell. He's incredible. You should be at the game supporting him."

Brittany peered down at the table and took a drink coaster and began to fiddle with it. Fidgeting with her hands was one of a number of nervous habits the girl had, including chomping on gum like there was no tomorrow. If she didn't have any gum, she would no doubt be gnawing on a straw or a pen. Brittany was always a little amped up before a concert, but something was off here. She should be at the stadium with the rest of the band.

"What's wrong, Brit?" Cassie asked.

Brittany glanced at her and then back at the table, where she continued to twist the coaster between her fingers. "I had a meeting this morning with Joanie Newburg."

Cassie felt her heart flutter. *"Joanie Newburg?"*

Brittany looked up and slowly nodded. "She's with the record label—"

"ELEKTRIK HI," Cassie chimed in. "I've reached out to Joanie several times. Why didn't you tell me about this? I should have—"

"They made an offer."

Cassie had to blink a few times before what the singer had said registered. When it did, she squealed so loud that Clete spilled beer down his chin and neck.

"Damnit, Cassie," Clete hissed. "You girls keep it down over there. And bring me another damn beer when you have a second. I've spilled most of this one."

Cassie pulled her chair around the table so it was right next to Brittany. "Details, please. I need details."

"One album. Twelve songs."

"Do they have a—"

"Bob Vogt is the writer."

Cassie squelched another squeal. "He's *perfect* for the band's sound. I love what he's done for Morgan Sperry and Clutch."

Brittany nodded, saying nothing.

"What about the money?"

Brittany spoke so soft that Cassie could barely hear her. "Five hundred thousand advance. Another hundred and fifty K for an option on the next album."

Cassie blinked her eyes in wonder. When she and Ian were forming the band, selecting a lead vocalist had been a grind. There'd been several false starts, good singers who just didn't have *it* . . . whatever *it* was. They could sing well enough, but nothing stood out.

Finding Brittany had been the last piece that made everything work. She'd started as a toddler in the Bickland Creek Baptist Church, but her pipes were the most versatile Cassie had ever encountered in person. She could belt out Aretha Franklin and make your heart pound. She could croon high like Michael Jackson and pull off the husky rasp of Janis Joplin. She made every cover song her own and had allowed the band to expand into originals. They'd finally reached pay dirt with "Tomorrow's Gone" over the summer, their first song with radio airplay.

Cassie thought of all the concerts she'd arranged throughout the college towns of the Southeastern Conference. Tuscaloosa, Auburn, Knoxville, Athens, Oxford, Starkville, Fayetteville, and Gainesville. The numerous shows in Nashville, hoping to get noticed. Praying to take that last step. And now, finally . . .

"Do you have the offer in writing? If not, we need to get it. Nothing's final until we have a signed—"

"Cassie—"

"And we probably need to get the contract looked at by a lawyer. Bo Haynes owes me a favor or two for providing information on cases. I can—"

"Cassie, please—"

"Joanie Newburg!" Cassie squealed yet again. "I can't believe it. The band has worked so hard—"

"They don't want the band," Brittany said, her voice tinged with angst. "Only me."

Cassie felt the wind go out of her stomach. She stared at Brittany open eyed. Then, as shock turned to anger, she narrowed her eyes into slits.

"I'm sorry, Cassie," Brittany said. "That's what's wrong. If I sign with ELEKTRIK HI, then I break up the band. I break up Fizz."

"Then don't sign." Cassie spat the words. As she glared at Brittany Crutcher, it all finally dawned on her. "You've already done it, haven't you?"

Brittany started to cry. "I leave for LA in the morning." She stifled a sob. "I'm sorry."

"*Tomorrow?*"

Brittany nodded.

Cassie swallowed and found it hard to breathe. She gripped the sides of the table and tried to steady herself. "This is Michael Zannick's doing, isn't it?"

Brittany averted her eyes. Cassie grabbed her shoulders and shook her.

"It was the only way I could get the deal."

Cassie shook Brittany again. "I've told you how that man screwed me over. He used me for information and introductions to the key players in this town and then spat me out like that gum in your mouth. He'll do the same to you, and you have a lot more to lose than me."

"Hey, now. Easy over there, Cassie."

Cassie turned and saw Clete Sartain gazing at them with bloodshot eyes. "I'll have your beer in one second."

"OK then," Clete said, turning back to the television, but Cassie knew the old coot was still watching out of the corner of his eye.

Cassie looked at Brittany. "How could you do this to us?" she asked, her voice quivering. "To the band? To me? Michael doesn't care about anyone but himself."

"He knew the right people and got an offer. He also gave the band a lot of money, and all you've done with the funds is get us gigs in college towns."

"*Every band* starts like that. *Every band.* R.E.M., Hootie and the Blowfish, Dave Matthews . . ."

"That's not the way the music world works now. I made it to the finals of *America's Got Talent*, Cassie. I should've had a contract by now. Almost all of the other contestants that made the finals are with labels, and none of them signed with their band." She took out her gum and stuck it onto the coaster. "Fizz is holding me back, and Mr. Zannick finally convinced me of that. This is my shot. It's been over a year since the show, and I'm losing my window. Can't you understand?"

"No," Cassie said, getting to her feet and feeling a wave of nausea roll over her that she swallowed back. She spoke in a low tone that she was confident no one else but Brittany could hear. "All I understand is that you are an opportunistic little bitch, and . . . Michael Zannick is the perfect manager for you." Cassie paused. "You fucking him too?"

"*No*," Brittany said. "The only person who's done that at this table is *you*, and I don't want to be you. I wanted a recording contract, and you couldn't get it done."

"We were getting close," Cassie said.

"No, we weren't." Brittany glanced around the tavern. "You're a bartender, Cassie, not a manager. When it was obvious you weren't going to take us any farther than being a college cover band, I sought out someone who could."

Cassie glared at Brittany. It was all she could do not to slap her. "He'll want something in return for his good deed. I know him, Brittany. Michael Zannick doesn't do things out of the goodness of his heart. And if you don't give it to him . . ."

"I can handle him," Brittany said, biting her lip.

"You know what he did to Mandy Burks last year."

"The charges were dropped."

"Doesn't mean he didn't rape her."

Brittany smirked. "You're such a hypocrite, Cassie. Zannick's past didn't stop you from dating him. Why should it stop me from having a business relationship?"

Cassie folded her arms, knowing Brittany was right. "Do your mom and dad know?"

Brittany shook her head.

Cassie hooked a thumb toward the television. "How about your boyfriend? Have you told him?"

Brittany's lip began to quiver. "I wrote him a note. I . . . couldn't face him."

"Gonna leave him high and dry, just like us."

"It's not like that, Cassie, and you know it. This is my chance."

"What about the band? Do any of them know?"

"Not yet. I wanted to tell you first. Even with what I've just said, I . . . I appreciate all you've done for me." She paused, tears forming in the corners of her eyes. "And Fizz will live on without me. Maybe with you as the lead?"

Cassie snorted. Her singing days were long over. She'd failed in that pursuit a decade ago. She'd tried out for *American Idol* and had done well, advancing past the first couple of rounds but eventually being told that her sound wasn't unique. "A thousand other women can sing that song just like you," Simon Cowell had said after she'd performed "I Will Remember You," by Sarah McLachlan. And though she hadn't quit singing, her spirit was broken after her failure on the talent show.

She'd never again believed she could make it, and belief, above all else, was what you had to have as a performer.

"Get out of here, Brittany," Cassie said, leaning over and pulling the girl up out of the chair. She looked into Brittany's scared eyes and again wanted to slap her. "If you fuck up tonight for Fizz, I'll break your neck," she whispered. "And before you leave for LA, you've got something that belongs to me, and I want it back."

Then, knowing that the bar's only other patron was watching them, she kissed the girl's forehead. "All right then!" Cassie's voice rose so Clete could hear. "Y'all knock them dead tonight. I've got Julie covering my shift, and I'll see you at the stadium at nine sharp." Cassie took a couple of steps back. "Opening song is at nine thirty, and I've already run through the lights with Earl Morring. I trust you're prepared to sing the number?"

Brittany wiped her eyes, nodding. Then she walked to the door and spoke without looking at Cassie.

"I'll never forget what you've done for me."

As the door closed, Cassie whispered, "Neither will I."

6

Odell Champagne had many strengths as a player. His size at five feet, eleven inches and 215 pounds was ideal for a running back. He had breakaway speed—his forty-yard time was a blazing 4.42 seconds—and was a danger to score from any position on the field. And he was strong, bench-pressing over three hundred pounds and squatting five hundred, which allowed him to break tackles at will.

But if Odell had to identify his greatest talent, none of those traits would be it. His number one asset was more cerebral, possessed by every hall of fame running back.

Vision.

Odell saw holes open up where, a half second earlier, there were none. As he took the toss sweep from the quarterback on fourth down and one with three minutes to go in the game, Bobcats trailing by three and pinned deep in their own territory, Odell bolted toward the right hash. Out of the corner of his left eye, he saw a cutback alley. He planted with his right foot and cut hard to the left up the middle.

And the floodgates opened.

———

The Bobcats' play-by-play announcer, Earl Morring, almost hyperventilated on the radio broadcast of the game.

"Champagne cuts back and there's a hole. Odell is in the open field and no one's going to catch him. He's at midfield. To the forty . . . the thirty . . . the twenty . . . the ten . . . the five . . . TOUCHDOWN, BOBCATS! Odell Champagne does it again."

Color commentator Chuck Turner, also breathless, added, "The kid never ceases to amaze. Biggest play of the season. Fourth and one. Fourth and the ball game. Fourth and the season. And Champagne takes it eighty-three yards to pay dirt. Earl, have you ever seen a player like Odell Champagne?"

"Not in this lifetime, Chuckie. Oh my, and the Brickyard is going absolutely bananas."

———

Odell handed the ball to the referee like he did after every touchdown. *Act like you've been there before,* Billy had told young Odell when he was playing Pop Warner ball in Town Creek, Alabama. *Don't make a production out of it.* Billy Champagne hadn't been much of a father, but that was one piece of advice that Odell had adopted. As his teammates jumped all over him, Odell chest bumped T. J. Haynes. Then he looked to the home stands. *Where are you, Brit?* he wondered. He knew she was probably warming up for the concert but hoped she'd at least caught that play on TV.

Coach Patterson slapped Odell on the helmet. "Attaboy, O." Then he gathered the team. "Two and a half minutes, boys. One hundred and fifty seconds. Let's not give them an inch, got it?"

"Yes, sir!"

"Odell, what does this team do?"

He looked at the coach and then the rest of the team. "Finish!"

"What?" Coach Patterson yelled.

"Finish!" they all chanted in harmony.

———

Tullahoma never had a prayer. With the crowd going nuts, their kick returner bobbled the kickoff and returned the ball only to the fifteen-yard line. Three incomplete passes later, they were staring at fourth and ten. Odell had hung back and played coverage on the first three plays, but he wouldn't be doing that on this one. He knew the left tackle couldn't block him. When the ball was snapped, he was in the offensive backfield in a split second. He hit the quarterback with his right shoulder with a textbook tackle, and the ball came loose.

———

"Fumble!" Earl Morring's voice blasted over the radio. "Sack by Odell and now he has the ball. Odell Champagne is going to score again as the clock strikes zero. Ball game. Bobcats are still undefeated."

"My goodness gracious," Chuck Tanner chimed in. "My goodness gracious," he repeated, his voice reverential. "What a player."

———

Odell again handed the ball to the referee as his teammates swarmed him and the students who had been watching from the sidelines stormed the field.

It was pandemonium, but he felt calm. The only times in his young life when Odell Champagne had felt completely at peace were on a football field.

And when I'm with Brit, he thought, knowing he would be with her soon.

7

Brittany Crutcher watched the television from the band room inside the confines of Giles County High School. Her heart was beating fast, and she was still distracted by her confrontation with Cassie. She hadn't told Fizz's makeshift manager everything. *I lied to her,* Brittany thought. The deal she'd struck with Michael Zannick over the past few weeks had indeed come with strings.

Brittany wasn't proud of the things she'd done, but the ends had justified the means. Zannick, true to his word, had delivered a recording contract.

"O sure can ball," Ian said, slapping his hands together as he watched the tube. Ian was Cassie's younger brother, a senior at Giles County High and Odell's best friend in the band. As the lead guitarist for Fizz, Ian looked the part with his curly blond hair, which fell below his neck, like a blond-headed Slash from Guns N' Roses. He turned from the television and peered at Brittany with inquisitive eyes. Then he waved his hands at her. "Earth to Brit. What's up?"

"I'm sorry," she said, rubbing her hands over her arms and glancing up at the television. It was hard for her to even look at Odell. Behind his rough exterior, there was a sweetness. A tenderness that she hadn't expected when they'd started dating over the summer. She thought of how he'd gone to Exchange Park with her to watch her sister, Gina, coach one of the softball teams for younger kids. He'd never complained and seemed to enjoy interacting with the kids, showing them how to throw a ball or get in the right batting stance. Despite his toughness

---

on the field, Odell had a vulnerable side that was an incredible turn-on. He also had a silly sense of humor, and she enjoyed his endless ribbing of her about her gum chewing. For some reason, he couldn't understand her other craving for boiled peanuts, which Odell thought were beyond nasty. During band practices, he liked to play the Chicago Bulls theme music and introduce each of them like he was the public address announcer, closing with, *"And from Pooooolaski, Tennessee, a five-ten senior with a voice to die for and a ridiculous and unhealthy love for boiled peanuts, Ms. Britt . . . ney Crutcher."* Brittany thought of how he had come up with a corny intro for each member, saving some of his best stuff for Ian, whom he called, *"Lead guitarist, above-average tutor, and maniacal gaming warlord, Ian . . . Dooooooooooooogan."*

Brittany suppressed a smile, knowing that Ian gave as good as he got. She would miss seeing the two of them talking smack to each other.

She held back her tears and thought of Odell's hands, which were strong and marked with calluses but felt so soft on her skin. So right . . .

How could she explain her actions to him in person?

She hoped he'd understand when he read the note. She'd snuck into the locker room and slipped it inside his locker when she'd arrived at the stadium, right before she'd seen him in the tunnel.

Brittany looked around the small space and noticed that the rest of the band was watching her. "I guess I'm nervous," she added, forcing a laugh.

"Child's play, Brit," Ian said. "These folks are going to love us. This is home."

"I know. I just . . ." She looked at Ian and then to keyboard player Teddy Bundrick, a short, plump albino kid affectionately called "Teddy B." by everyone in the band. And then she turned to the drummer, Mackenzie Santana, whom they all called "Mack." Mack was a Latinx girl with black hair trimmed short on the sides and spiked on top and a birthmark on her forehead. She was the loudest of the group and scowled back at Brittany.

"You just what, girl?"

"Nothing," Brittany said.

"Tape it up, sister," Mack said, stretching her arms over her head. "Showtime in thirty minutes."

Brittany knew she had to tell her bandmates about the ELEKTRIK HI deal, but now wasn't the time. Not before the biggest concert they'd ever had. She wouldn't do that to them. She loved them all too much for that.

"Showtime," she repeated.

8

At 9:30 p.m., the stadium lights at the Brickyard abruptly shut off. The crowd, which had been at a low murmur in the half hour after the game, burst into loud screams and applause.

In the press box above the field, Cassie Dugan began an internal countdown.

Ten . . .

Justin Cross was a thirty-five-year-old Giles County lifer and the head of the school grounds crew. He'd winked at Cassie when she'd connected with him before the game to go over the lighting plan for the concert. Five years ago, Justin had taken Cassie on a few dates, but things had never gone past first base. He was a bad kisser, and his breath had reeked of Grizzly chewing tobacco.

Nine . . .

Frowning at the memory but relieved that Justin had, so far, not screwed anything up, Cassie embraced the darkness. And the noise.

Eight . . .

The crowd that the television crew had estimated at 5,400 at kick-off had to be well over 7,000 now, the biggest audience Fizz had ever played in front of.

Or ever will, Cassie thought.

Seven . . .

She'd arrived in time to see the last few minutes of the game, which had been electric with intensity as Odell Champagne scored not one but two touchdowns to ice the win.

Six . . .

Cassie had checked in with the band, kissing her brother, Ian, on the cheek and asking if everyone was ready.

Five . . .

She hadn't even looked at Brittany.

Four . . .

Then she'd gone about her preparations, making sure that Earl Morring was ready to do the spotlight.

Three . . .

He'd said he was, but now would be the acid test.

Two . . .

The noise had reached a nervous frenzy.

One . . .

Cassie snapped her fingers at Earl. "Now!"

Out of the darkness, the spotlight shone on Ian's electric guitar on the stage on the fifty-yard line, and he burst into the opening chord of "China Grove," by the Doobie Brothers.

Everyone knew the song by now. Everyone knew the beginning. And it was impossible to hear it and not feel chills. Fizz covered several tunes by the Doobies, but this one was Cassie's favorite. It gave her brother a chance to shine and showed off Brittany's pipes right off the bat.

If the stadium was loud before, the Brickyard had now reached DEFCON 1. Cassie began to move her head back and forth, playing air guitar and mimicking her brother. The bleachers literally shook below her as the fans began to bounce up and down. Kids and adults alike reached their hands toward the sky, many with their eyes closed as if they were praying. Cassie thought of her favorite old movie, *Footloose*, and Ren McCormack's speech to the town that dancing was good. That King David himself had leaped and danced before the Lord.

Cassie had heard some folks describe a Fizz show as part rock concert, part revival. She wasn't sure they were wrong.

Steady drumbeats from Mackenzie Santana followed along with the energy from Teddy B.'s keyboard. The noise level, if it were humanly possible, seemed to rise even higher. Cassie snapped her fingers again at Earl, and the spotlight shifted to the left-hand corner of the stage.

The scene took Cassie's breath away.

Brittany Crutcher wore white spandex pants, a black tank top, and a red bandana over her head, her thick brown hair falling out underneath. A bass guitar was strapped around her shoulder. Illuminated by the spotlight, her skin glowed a golden brown, and she held her left hand high into the sky, making the rock and roll symbol with her index and pinky fingers. She moved her head back and forth to the side along with the guitar beat, keyboard, and drums. Cassie felt her heart pounding, and she looked below her to the student section, where all the kids continued to bounce on the balls of their feet.

She took her phone out of her pocket and sent a text to Justin Cross. Now.

Three seconds later, the lights to the stadium came back on, and Cassie blinked against the brightness as Brittany's vocals sliced through the air.

The sound was hard to pinpoint, but Cassie's immediate thought was a deeper-voiced version of another Brittany. Not the pop queen Britney Spears, but Brittany Howard from nearby Athens, Alabama, who'd found fame with her band the Alabama Shakes and played everything from the *Late Show with David Letterman* to *Saturday Night Live* over the last few years. But Brittany Crutcher's voice had more of a rasp that allowed her to pull off many songs originally done by male vocalists, including almost all of the Doobie Brothers' hits and the harder rock sound of the Black Crowes.

Despite how betrayed she felt by the young woman, Cassie couldn't help but tap her toes to the beat as the song entered the chorus. It was the magic and power of music. Like a gifted athlete, a talented singer could carry a person away to another place, if only for a little while.

Cassie Dugan smiled at the spectacle, thinking of all the great performers whose personal lives had been train wrecks. Few lived happy, normal lives.

And so many barely lived a life at all. Icons like Buddy Holly and Selena, shooting stars. Here for a sizzling second and then gone.

Cassie crossed her arms and pressed them hard against her chest, glaring down at Brittany. *She's everything I've ever wanted to be,* Cassie thought, knowing that her time as the pseudomanager of a popular band was about to end.

Tomorrow, the news would be out. Fizz might be larger than life right now, but tomorrow . . .

"Tomorrow's gone," Cassie whispered, shaking her head at the irony. "Tomorrow's Gone," Fizz's flagship song, the first and only one played on the radio. There should have been more. There would have been many more.

But she ruined it. She and Michael . . .

"Great show, Cassie," Earl said. He was standing close to her, and she could smell his cheap aftershave. Unlike her interactions with Justin Cross, she'd done a little more than kiss Earl when they'd gone out two years ago, and she tried not to gag at the memory. Depression began to settle in Cassie's veins. "Maybe after the concert," Earl continued, "we could—"

"Fuck off, Earl," Cassie said, shooting him a glare. "Just concentrate on that spotlight, will you?"

"Yes, ma'am." He whispered, "*Bitch,*" under his breath, but Cassie barely took notice. She felt numb all over.

Brittany had been the final and most important piece. With her as lead vocalist, Fizz could have been as big as the Alabama Shakes or the Black Keys. Maybe even bigger.

She still will be, Cassie thought, leaning her hands against the glass window of the press box and feeling sick to her stomach. *She just won't be bringing us along.*

44

Cassie glanced at Earl Morring, who grinned. When he did, she noticed his yellow, cigarette-stained teeth. *And I'll still be stuck in Pulaski.* Cassie closed her eyes and felt hate in her heart. For herself.

For Pulaski.

But mostly, for Brittany Crutcher.

"Tomorrow's gone," she whispered.

9

Odell held the note in his hand and reread it for the hundredth time in the last hour. Outside the locker room, he could hear the pounding of feet on the bleachers and, over the cheers, the sound of his girlfriend's powerful voice.

Ex-girlfriend, Odell thought, gazing down at the yellow sheet and finally crumpling it up. He wanted to throw the note away, but instead he stuffed it into the front pocket of his jeans.

Everyone leaves, Odell thought, gazing around the now-empty space and then down at the tile floor. His father had left when he was five and a half years old. Walked out the door of their shack in Town Creek and never came home.

His mother had left too. Not physically, but in every other way she'd been gone for a long time. Odell barely remembered the woman she'd been when he was kid. Fun, always laughing and cutting up.

And now Brittany was leaving him too. Normally the rage he felt on the football field dissipated once the game was over. But it had returned with a vengeance once he'd found the note.

He stood and punched his locker, causing a small dent. Then he punched it again. And again.

Why did everyone he love leave?

He screamed and kicked the locker several times. Then he sat on the bench, rubbing his now-bloody hands roughly over his face and blinking at the tile.

Not Brittany too. He stood from the bench and walked into the bathroom, then cleaned the cuts on his knuckles until the bleeding stopped. He peered at himself in the mirror.

"Make her stop," he whispered. *You know she loves you.* He gripped the porcelain sink and closed his eyes. His heart was beating fast, anger cloaking his every fiber.

He'd been in Pulaski for six months. Everyone had been nice—the coaches, his teammates, and even the neighbors who looked the other way when his mother stumbled up the steps to their apartment. That's how people acted when they wanted something from you. Odell was great at football. As long as he delivered on the field, everything would be fine. He'd be a hero. The sins of his past—the theft convictions, the juvenile assault charge, the expulsion from Town Creek High—all of it would be swept under the rug.

It had been that way his whole life, and he presumed college would be no different. Big man on campus, hell. If he ever tweaked his knee or lost a step, he'd be thrown out with the breeze. Like a piece of meat that had started to rot.

That's all I am and all I'll ever be.

But things had been different with Brittany.

———

They'd met during summer workouts. Brittany didn't play a sport but was jogging on the track while the football team ran bleachers. A few of the team members, like Doug Fitzgerald, whistled at her, but most of the boys were in awe, including Odell. There'd been a lot of talk on the team about the girl who'd made the finals of *America's Got Talent.* When the team was done, Odell decided to run a few laps and trotted up beside her. As he was about to introduce himself, he felt his stomach lurch, and for a moment, he thought he was going to be sick. Because of the excessive heat, a session on the bleachers often caused him to hyperventilate or, worse, have a case of the runs. With the excitement of approaching Brittany making him light headed, he worried that a bout with the latter was coming on. *Are you kidding me?* he thought, cursing his timing. He clammed up, and for a whole lap, he prayed to God he could control his stomach until he got inside the locker room. Finally, she broke the ice.

"Am I supposed to be impressed?"

He cocked his head at her while they ran. "About what?"

"About the great Odell Champagne, can't-miss five-star prospect, wanting to run with me? What's next? Do we just go off behind the bleachers? Is that how it worked in Town Creek?"

"You're talking crazy, girl," Odell managed, holding his stomach tight with his right hand. "I just wanted to run."

"Bullshit," she snapped. "You ran the bleachers twenty times. I can tell by your voice that you need some water. The last thing you need to do is run more." She mercifully slowed to a walk, and he did the same, breathing in the hot June air, which did nothing for the volcano burning inside his stomach.

"My name's Brittany Crutcher," she said.

"I know," he said.

"If you knew who I was, why'd you run a whole lap and not speak?"

Odell grimaced. "Because I was nervous."

"Oh, give me a break. Big football star too scared to talk to a girl."

"No, it's not that," he said, shaking his head and deciding what the hell. He'd tell her the truth. "I was planning to say something, but my stomach started cramping up on me, and I was afraid I might . . ." He trailed off, and his face felt as hot as the tip of a lit candle.

"Afraid you might what?" A huge smile spread across her face, and she let out a tiny giggle.

Odell rubbed the back of his neck and shook his head. Finally, he giggled too. "Shit my pants."

This time, she belly laughed. When she finished, Brittany touched his hand. "What are you doing tonight, Odell Champagne?"

———

They'd gone to the movies in her car and, when the flick was over, parked at Martin Methodist College and had gone for a long walk around the campus. They'd ended up sitting under the gazebo by the art center for over an hour. Odell wasn't sure why it was so easy to talk with Brit, but it was. Maybe because of the embarrassing initial encounter, he knew he could be straight with her. Or perhaps it was because she had the same fate as him. Brittany was a monumental singer. That was all anyone ever saw with her. Brittany Crutcher. Lead singer of Fizz. Record labels were in her future, like an NFL contract was in Odell's. She too had issues with her parents, the opposite of Odell's. She hadn't been abandoned. She'd been suffocated.

We need each other.

Odell opened his eyes and stared again at himself in the mirror. He was kidding himself.

Brittany didn't need him. She'd left him without even the decency of a conversation. She'd had every opportunity in the tunnel before the game to tell him about her recording deal, that she was leaving him behind, and she hadn't.

All he'd gotten was a damn note.

He squeezed the sides of the sink, tried to calm down, but it was no use. This wasn't how it was going to end. He wouldn't let her do that to him.

Odell finished washing his hands and walked out the door of the locker room and into the chill of the night. As he made his way to the field, people began to part. He slapped fives and fist-bumped kids he barely knew, finally ending up standing between T. J. Haynes and Jarvis Rowe, his only real friends on the team.

"Where you been, O?" T. J. asked.

"Needed to chill a little, man. Tough game. Pretty sore."

"You going to Doug's party?"

Odell had planned to hang around after the concert and go to the party with Brit, but those plans were now dashed. "Yeah, sounds good. Can I get a ride?"

"You know it," Jarvis chimed in, elbowing Odell in the side with his massive arm. "Your girl on fire tonight, man."

Odell tensed but managed a nod. "She always is."

"You going to see her later?"

Odell glanced up at the stage and stuffed his hands in his pockets, feeling the crumpled note. "Yeah," he said. "I'm going to see her."

10

For Brittany, the cheers were like gasoline in her depleted tank of energy. As she looked out over the Brickyard to the student section and saw the kids jumping up and down on the bleachers, she felt a current of adrenaline run through her. This was all that really mattered, wasn't it? She was a performer. A singer. Whether with Fizz or by herself, she was most free on the stage. Moving and singing to the music. There was something pure and innocent about it. Every time she sang in front of people, she was six years old again and standing at the front of the Bickland Creek Baptist Church, bursting into that Easter favorite "Up from the Grave He Arose" as the men, women, and children in the pews called out, "Amen." It was her spiritual center. The place where she felt one with God and the universe and herself.

Amen, she thought, feeling a deep sense of peace. Everything drifted away as Ian Dugan's electric guitar sizzled behind her. The deal she'd made with Zannick. The meeting that morning with Joanie Newburg. The solo contract she'd signed with ELEKTRIK HI. The problems she was having with her parents, especially her father. And, finally, the note she'd written Odell.

For most of the day, especially when talking to Cassie, she'd felt like Judas Iscariot. But now, as she began to belt out the chorus to the band's most popular song, she let go of her worries. Her doubts. Her fears.

"Yesterday's forever . . . ," she sang, gazing out over the crowd, most of whom were now swaying back and forth, their lit cell phones all held up in the encore gesture. ". . . but tomorrow's gone."

Amen, Brittany thought again.

Amen.

PART TWO

11

The body was found on the back row of a school bus. The deceased had on gray joggers and a blue long-sleeve T-shirt. Her feet were covered by a pair of stained socks, one of which had slid down her left foot several inches to expose her heel.

On the ground beside the face of the victim was a pink wad of bubble gum.

Chief Deputy Sheriff Frannie Storm swallowed hard and turned away from the corpse. She gazed out the dust-covered window of the bus and tried to control her breathing.

"You OK, Chief?"

Frannie turned to the voice, which belonged to Ty Dodgen, a young deputy in the department. "You recognize the victim, Ty?"

He shot a glance at the body, and Frannie followed his eyes. The dead girl's head, neck, and shoulders were on the floor of the bus directly in front of the seat. Only her feet stretched into the aisle.

"Jesus H. Christ," Ty whispered. *"Brittany . . ."*

Frannie felt warm tears falling down her cheeks. Seven hours ago, she'd watched this young woman play the largest concert in Giles County history. Brittany Crutcher had owned the stage, lit by the spotlight that shone on the fifty-yard line of Sam Davis Stadium. What had blown Frannie away was that, despite the singer's growing fame,

Brittany had hung around to sign autographs and take pictures with the kids who'd waited around for her after the show.

She's dead, Frannie thought, still not quite believing it as she stared at the body. *Brittany Crutcher is dead.* During her career in law enforcement, Frannie had never had to investigate the murder of someone she knew. She bit her lip and tried to fight off the emotions swirling inside her.

How was she ever going to break this news to Israel and Theresa Crutcher? The Crutchers were longtime members of Bickland Creek Baptist, the largest Black church in Giles County. Frannie had attended Bickland Creek since birth, and her parents and aunt Ellie were close to the Crutcher family.

Brittany had sung in church last Sunday, and Frannie's lip trembled at the memory. "'Amazing Grace,'" she said, her voice hoarse.

Frannie took in another deep breath and exhaled, her breath forming smoke clouds in the close confines of the unheated bus. It was a little chillier than normal for mid-October; the temperature couldn't be much over forty-five degrees. She blinked and forced herself to concentrate on her work. There was a large purplish hematoma on the victim's forehead. Otherwise, Frannie couldn't tell much. The T-shirt appeared to be stained, but it was hard to determine whether the marks were blood or something else. There were fragments of glass on the floor and on the seat above the body. In addition to the scent of the dead body, Frannie also thought she could smell a hint of stale beer.

"Call the crime lab," Frannie finally said, her tone firm as she noticed dried blood on Brittany's nostrils and upper lip. "We need a forensic team here ASAP."

"Yes, ma'am," Ty said, turning and walking down the narrow corridor of the bus. When he reached the end, he looked back at her. "Do you want to try and talk with the caller again?"

Frannie blinked and gazed down at a white Styrofoam cup that lay on its side on the black rubber flooring. There were still a few drops of coffee visible around the cup's rim. At a shade after four in the morning, sanitation worker Daryl Hitchcock had arrived at the transportation yard on Eighth Street to begin cleaning the buses. At a little after five, after finishing four of them, he'd fixed himself a cup of Folgers from the Keurig machine in the small office and walked to the next bus in the row. He'd placed his mop and bucket at the foot of the steps and, as was his practice, planned to do a visual of the inside of the bus to assess the damage. Typically he'd see the remains of spilt sodas, wrappers, and other trash to go along with everyday dirt and dust. But after opening the door and trotting up the steps, he'd smelled a strong odor coming from the back. He'd been halfway down the corridor when he'd seen a socked foot sticking out into the aisle. He'd taken one more step forward but stopped in his tracks when he'd seen Brittany's lifeless eyes gazing up at him.

Daryl had dropped his Styrofoam cup of coffee on the floor and stumbled backward down the corridor and then the steps, collapsing on his knees outside, gasping for breath. After struggling a few seconds to regain his composure, he'd pulled out his cell and called 911.

That was all the information they'd gleaned from him when Frannie and six other officers, including Ty Dodgen, had arrived at the scene at 5:32 a.m. Daryl had begun to hyperventilate as he told the story and was now being attended to by a paramedic.

"Yes," Frannie said. "We need to get an official statement from him, but right now, I want to see if the search of the perimeter has turned up any leads." Upon arrival, Frannie had ordered four of the officers to do a sweep of the entire yard and surrounding area up to a half mile in all directions.

"Yes, ma'am," Ty said. Then he walked down the steps of the bus. As he did, another officer was coming up to them. Even from twenty paces away, Frannie could hear the wheezes of the man's breathing.

"Chief," Deputy Bradley McCann called, pointing his thumb over his shoulder. "The dogs found a broken beer bottle on the northern end of the yard." He coughed and swallowed back another wheeze. "There appears to be some blood on what's left of it."

Frannie felt gooseflesh break out on her neck and arms. Her brain filled with questions. As she began to stride toward the front of the bus, she started to ask McCann for more information, but the deputy's labored voice drowned her out.

"The dogs found something else."

12

"Oh no," Frannie said, gazing down at the figure shaking on the ground below her.

He wore a gray hoodie covered with dirt and lay in a thicket of trees and brush on the edge of the school bus yard. His legs and arms were curled in the fetal position, and his brown eyes were wide, as if he'd just woken up.

Two German shepherds barked above him.

Frannie stared into the man's frightened eyes and then peered up at Ty Dodgen, Bradley McCann, and the rest of the small group of officers that had huddled around them. She saw recognition in each of their eyes. "All right, quit staring and do your job. Deputy McCann, we need photographs of everything you see here, got it?"

"Yes, ma'am," McCann said. He'd already gathered his crime scene camera and began to snap photographs of the man on the ground.

Frannie peered closer and noticed that the man was gripping tight to a piece of clothing with both hands. She shone her flashlight at his chest, her throat tightening when she recognized the sweatshirt. The fleece pullover was black with gold block letters embroidered across the front.

"GCHS," Ty Dodgen said out loud, the intensity in his voice palpable. Beside him, Deputy McCann snapped several rapid-fire pictures of the article of clothing. "Too small to be his."

"It's not his," Frannie said. She'd seen Brittany at a Wednesday-night supper at Bickland Creek two weeks ago. She'd been seated with her mother and younger sister. She'd worn jeans and the same pullover that Frannie now saw being clutched by the man below her.

"She was a senior, wasn't she?" Ty asked.

Frannie nodded. "Had a full ride to Belmont on a music scholarship, but the word on the street was that Fizz was about to sign a recording deal." The chief took a step closer to the man and squatted, making sure to tread lightly, as she didn't want to do anything to upset the scene. In a couple of hours, crime scene technicians would be combing every square inch of this space for DNA and other evidence. She squinted at the sweatshirt and saw what appeared to be droplets of blood on the front.

Frannie rose up and looked behind her. Two deputies were leaning over an object on the ground. She walked over to them and crouched so she could see what they were examining.

The silver-and-blue Bud Light label was intact, as was the entire base of the bottle, but the stem of the longneck had been cracked; all that remained was a shard of jagged glass. A reddish-black substance covered the sharp edges and had also dripped onto the label.

"All right, let's step away," she instructed, and the two deputies backed away from the bottle. "For God's sake, don't touch it or disturb it in any way. That very well could be the murder weapon."

Frannie peered back at the man on the ground, who'd been rolled onto his bottom. Officer McCann had pulled the hood off his head, and Frannie shone her flashlight at him as McCann took more photographs. She thought through her next move, noticing a six-pack carton of Bud Light longnecks on the ground. The beers appeared to be full and unopened. Finally, she lowered the spotlight and knelt, looking at the man, whose eyes were unfocused.

"Odell, I need you to let go of the sweatshirt," she said, her voice soft but firm.

He glanced at her and then at the article of clothing in his hand.

"Now," Frannie ordered.

He held it out toward her. His arms were shaking.

"Just let go of it, all right?"

Odell Champagne, who'd scored three touchdowns for Giles County High in last night's ESPN high school game of the week against Tullahoma, dropped the sweatshirt and watched it fall to the ground. He let out a hollow sob and rolled over on his side again, covering his face with both arms.

Frannie turned to Officer Dodgen. "Get him up and take him down to the station for questioning."

"Chief." Dodgen's face was pale. "This case—"

"I know," Frannie said, sighing and glancing east as the first traces of sunlight began to peek over the horizon. "The press is going to descend on us like vultures." She paused and turned to Deputy McCann. "We need photographs of the inside of the bus. Every conceivable angle of the body, the seat above the corpse, the corridor, the gum near the victim's face. Everything. Got it?"

"Yes, ma'am. On it." He began to lumber back toward the bus with the camera.

Frannie let out a deep breath, trying to keep herself calm. "OK, Ty. Cuff Odell and get him down to the department. We can hold him for trespassing for now." She squinted at the deputy. "I don't want anyone talking to him until I get there, you hear?"

"Yes, ma'am," Dodgen said, removing a pair of handcuffs from his belt buckle. "Have you notified the sheriff?"

Frannie had already started walking back toward the bus. "He's in Knoxville at a seminar and is on his way." She looked over her shoulder at the young deputy. "But you can guess what his first instruction was."

Dodgen gave a weary nod. "Have you called her yet?"

Frannie took her cell out of her pocket. "Calling now." She hovered her thumb over the contact list, but before she could click it, a blood-curdling scream rang out from the direction of the bus.

"Oh no," Frannie cried, feeling her heart and stomach constrict. *No* . . . She stuck the phone back into her pocket. The call would have to wait.

She began to run.

13

When Frannie arrived back at the bus, she saw Bradley McCann and two other sheriff's deputies, Greta Tice and Jack Moran, trying to restrain a large Black woman. "Is that my baby in there?" the woman asked, tears streaking both of her cheeks. Her eyes darted behind the uniformed officers to the steps leading up into the school bus. "Brittany!" She wailed the name, and the sound pierced Frannie Storm's soul.

Theresa Crutcher wore a lavender peacoat over a pair of black pants. Even in her current state of disarray, she still resembled the Sunday school teacher who'd taught Frannie and every other fourth-grade kid at Bickland Creek over the past twenty years. Frannie gently placed her hand over the woman's neck. "Mrs. T., please try to be calm. I'm so very sorry."

"Is that my baby girl in that bus?"

Frannie braced herself for what was about to come. There was no harder job for a law enforcement officer than breaking the news of a loved one's death. It would have been difficult enough to have knocked on Theresa's door to share the awful information. Having to do it in this manner, almost unbearable. "Yes, ma'am. It's Brittany."

For two seconds, there was a pause, as if the ocean had calmed before the rising of a tidal wave. And then there came a moan that seemed to begin low. Theresa Crutcher fell forward into Frannie's arms, the chief slowly bending her knees until they touched the hard asphalt. She gripped the grieving mother tight as the sound of Theresa's moan increased until it became an anguished cry.

Frannie began to cry again and spotted the first of what she knew would be dozens of television news vans pulling to a stop on Eighth Street. She peered up and saw sixteen-year-old Gina Crutcher standing behind them. "Gina, come here!" Frannie called out, and the teenager did as she was told. Unlike her slender older sister, Gina had a sturdier build that resembled that of her mother. Her face was blank. She appeared to be in the first stages of shock.

"I need you to take your momma home."

Gina blinked and gazed past Frannie to the school bus. "My sister in there?"

"Yes, Gina, she is."

"Is she dead?" The question carried no emotion, and Frannie again surmised that the young girl was overcome.

"Yes."

Gina's face registered a slight grimace. Nothing more.

Frannie stood and put her hands on the teenager's shoulders. "Listen to me. Drive your momma home and don't leave her side. I'll come by as soon as I have things under control."

Gina's face was ashen, but she managed to nod. "You know who did this?"

Frannie peered behind the girl, seeing Deputy Dodgen leading Odell Champagne toward a police cruiser in handcuffs.

"Is that Odell?" Gina asked, her eyes following Frannie's.

"Just take—"

Before Frannie could finish, Theresa was off the ground and walking with purpose toward the officers.

"Theresa, stop!" Frannie ran to catch up, and deputies Tice and Moran did the same.

"You do this?!" Theresa asked, beginning to run herself.

Frannie got in front of her right before she reached Odell and Dodgen.

"Did you do this?" Theresa repeated, looking around Frannie at Odell, who was peering at the ground as the officer opened the side door of the patrol car. Several flashes went off, and Frannie noticed a photographer on the curb snapping pictures as if his life depended on it. "Clear out of here right now," Frannie yelled, snapping her fingers at Officer Tice. "Greta, you tell those reporters and photographers to stay away from the crime scene unless they all want to be arrested for obstruction of justice."

While Frannie was distracted, Theresa stepped around her and lunged forward toward the patrol car. She grabbed the front of Odell's hoodie and shook him. "Why would you hurt Brittany? *Why?*" Her chest heaved, and her voice began to shake. "Israel w-w-was . . . *right* . . . about you."

Frannie wrapped her arms around Theresa and pulled her from Odell, cocking her head back at Ty Dodgen. "Go!" she said. "Now."

Dodgen nudged Odell into the back seat of the patrol car and closed the door. Then he ran around the front of the car to the driver's side. Seconds later, the vehicle lurched forward down Eighth Street and out of sight.

Frannie pulled Theresa toward Deputy Moran as camera flashes lit up the night again. "Take her to her daughter's car and escort them home." Frannie looked around them and saw Gina still looking up at the school bus. She hadn't moved since Theresa had bolted toward Odell.

Frannie walked toward the girl, cursing under her breath. Things were getting out of control.

As more police sirens pierced her ears, she retrieved her phone. After entering the security code, she saw her contacts list and immediately recognized the one she wanted. While her other contacts all carried a first and last name, this one simply had a title.

The General.

Feeling a mixture of adrenaline and dread pulsing through her veins, Frannie pressed her thumb down on the military title and then, perusing the menu of options, clicked the one for the cell number.

The call was answered on the second ring. "What's going on?" The woman's sharp voice radiated confidence and authority.

"General," Frannie said, hearing the anxiety in her own tone and trying to remain calm. "There's been a murder. I need your help."

"Where are you?"

"The Eighth Street bus yard."

There was a pause and then a rustling sound, as if a jacket was being put on. "I'm on my way."

14

At 6:05 a.m., a black Crown Victoria pulled to a stop behind two of the news vans.

A woman got out of the car wearing faded jeans, a brown leather jacket, and cowboy boots. Her jet-black hair was tucked under a navy cap.

Helen Evangeline Lewis had been the district attorney general for the Twenty-Second Judicial Circuit, which included the counties of Giles, Maury, Lawrence, and Wayne, for over twenty years. An oddity of Tennessee law was that the head prosecutor was called "General" during court proceedings. For most prosecutors, the title dropped the second they were out of court, but not for Helen Lewis. Frannie had rarely seen anyone address Helen without using the military title, and as she watched the woman approach, she saw and heard several reporters try to sneak in a question.

"General Lewis, can you comment on the suspect in custody?"

"General, is it true that the victim is Brittany Crutcher?"

Helen ignored the media blitz and walked in a beeline straight for Frannie. It wasn't often that Frannie saw the General in casual attire. The prosecutor typically wore a black suit and heels to court. Still, even without the formalities and dress of the courtroom, Helen Lewis oozed self-assurance and confidence as she strode toward Frannie. The chief deputy sucked in a quick breath and found herself straightening her posture.

Frannie Storm was six feet, one inch tall and 140 pounds of lean, athletic muscle. There were few women or men whose presence gave her a rush of adrenaline, but Helen Lewis was one of them.

"Talk," Helen snapped, brushing past her and walking toward the bus.

"The victim is Brittany Crutcher. You've probably heard of her."

Helen stopped and turned on Frannie. "The singer?"

Frannie nodded. "Made the finals of *AGT* last year. Lead singer of Fizz. They played the Brickyard last night after the game. Did you go?"

"No."

Frannie waited for more, but the General added nothing. Helen Lewis had never been much for small talk or sharing any details of her personal life. "The victim is eighteen years old," Frannie continued. "A senior at Giles County High School." Frannie paused. "And I know her family well."

The General crossed her arms. "Do you think your personal feelings will affect your ability to investigate the case?" There wasn't an ounce of empathy in Helen's tone, and Frannie gritted her teeth.

"No."

"Good," Helen said, climbing the steps of the school bus. Frannie followed, feeling anger and a twinge of embarrassment burning within her. Helen stopped walking when she reached the body, and at the sight of Brittany's corpse, Frannie forced any thoughts other than those of the case out of her brain.

After several seconds, Helen let out a ragged breath. "Damnit," she hissed. "Those reporters already knew the identity of the victim. How?"

"Probably because they recognized Brittany's mother and sister."

Helen turned and peered up at Frannie. The General's eyes were the blue-green color of the Gulf of Mexico. They bore into Frannie's with unveiled exasperation. "Those two were here?"

"Yes. Theresa Crutcher, Brittany's mom, and Gina, her sister, arrived about twenty minutes ago, around the same time as a couple of news crews. Theresa had to be helped to her car by two deputies. She was screaming Brittany's name, and she had an altercation with the suspect we have in custody . . ." Frannie trailed off.

"How did the family learn about what happened so fast? Did you call them?"

"No."

"The press hounds also mentioned a suspect."

"We found a man on the north end of the bus yard. He'd been sleeping or was passed out, holding a sweatshirt that wasn't his size."

"The victim's?"

"I'd stake my life on it," Frannie said. "There was also a bloody broken beer bottle on the ground a few yards away."

"Did you recognize him?"

Frannie nodded. "He's almost as high profile as the victim."

Helen's face was blank. "Who?"

"Odell Champagne."

For a long moment, the two just looked at each other. Finally, Helen grunted. "Dating the victim, I presume." It wasn't a question.

"Yes."

"And you said the victim's mother confronted him."

"Yes."

Helen shook her head. "Frannie, how could you let that happen?"

Frannie's face burned. "There was kind of a lot going on."

"That's no excuse."

"I know," Frannie said. "We had to take him in, and Theresa Crutcher saw him. Some reporters started snapping pictures, and things got out of hand for a few minutes."

"How in the hell did the media pick up this story so soon?" Helen asked. "It's six o'clock in the morning. When did you get the call from dispatch?"

"Five twenty-five. We got here a little after five thirty."

Helen smirked. "Somebody in your office tipped them."

69

Frannie ground her teeth and felt a hot flash of anger resonate down her chest. "Not a chance. No one in my department would leak any information about a murder investigation."

Helen's gaze narrowed to a glare. "If you say so. My experience with your department has been a little different."

Frannie bit her lip but held the General's eye. "You should speak for yourself. The only moles in this county that I'm aware of have come from the DA's office."

For a long second, they both peered at each other, the friction unmistakable. During her first few years as a sheriff's deputy, Frannie had enjoyed a healthy relationship with Helen. In fact, she had considered the prosecutor a mentor. The General had carved out a legendary career in a male-dominated job, just as Frannie was seeking to do. In cases they'd worked together, Helen had seemed to take extra care to explain to Frannie the significance of evidence and how it could be used or not used in the courtroom. Frannie was a fast learner, and the pair had developed into a strong team.

But everything had changed last spring when Butch Renfroe, the General's ex-husband, was murdered in his home, and Frannie became the lead investigator on the case. The evidence quickly and overwhelmingly pointed toward Helen as the prime suspect, and she was eventually charged with capital murder. After a grueling trial, the jury found Helen not guilty when her attorney uncovered new evidence at the last minute that shone light on another suspect. Since her acquittal in October and reelection in November, Helen had been at best aloof around Frannie and at worst downright rude. For her part, Frannie had avoided the prosecutor because she still had serious questions about Butch Renfroe's murder, which remained unsolved despite the theories and facts introduced by Helen's counsel during the trial. Mercifully, they hadn't worked on a case of any significance since the General's trial, but that was about to change in a big way.

If Odell Champagne killed Brittany Crutcher . . . Frannie finally looked away from Helen's cold stare. Brittany's presence as the victim, given her age and status as a budding rock star, would make this a huge case. But Odell's involvement would take it to another level. Football was king in the Deep South, and Odell was a talented prospect. He had scholarship offers from every big school in the country. *He also has a rap sheet . . .*

"I don't think it was your office or mine who tipped the press," Frannie finally said, jerking her head toward the front of the bus. "Daryl Hitchcock is who found the body, and his sister works for the *Vine*."

Helen raised her eyebrows. The *Vine* was short for *Casimir's Vine*, the town's local online news blog.

"My bet," Frannie continued, "is that Daryl called or texted her while he was waiting for us to get here."

"Fucking cell phones," Helen said, exasperation leaking into her tone. "Have you notified Melvin?" she asked, and they both gazed back down at the body.

"Should be here any minute," Frannie said. "What about crime scene techs? Did you follow up with the TBI?"

"Yes," Helen said. "They got Ty's message, and a crew is on its way. They should be here in less than an hour."

Frannie let out a ragged breath of relief. Despite her issues with the General, she was grateful for Helen's experience and knowledge. "Let me show you where we found the suspect," Frannie said, turning away from the body and striding back down the bus.

"I realize the media may jump to conclusions, but it's a little early for us to be using that label, don't you think?" Helen asked, following closely on Frannie's heels. "Wouldn't *person of interest* be a better word? At least until we talk with him?"

Frannie didn't stop walking, nor did she turn around. "Not when he was found literally a tenth of a mile from the body and a few yards away from the presumed murder weapon, holding a sweatshirt the victim wore to Wednesday-night church supper." At the bottom of the stairs, she waited for Helen to reach the ground. "And not when you have Odell Champagne's criminal background and reputation," Frannie continued, rage radiating through her body. "Do you feel me?"

For a moment, Helen squinted as if she was going to say something in protest. But then her eyes softened ever so slightly. "I do. Very much so. But until I have a chance to question him, he is a person of interest only. If we make what's perceived as a rash and hasty decision based on perception and innuendo instead of cold, hard evidence, then any defense lawyer worth his or her salt is going to stuff that fact right up our collective asses at trial." Helen paused and took a step closer to Frannie. "Do *you* feel me?"

Frannie gazed down at the asphalt, knowing that the General was right, angry with herself for losing her cool. All she could manage was a nod.

"Good," Helen said. "Now . . . let's finish our inspection of the scene."

15

As Helen followed the chief deputy sheriff toward the north end of the bus yard, she could feel goose bumps on her arms that had nothing to do with the October cold. Helen had always been able to disguise any misgivings she was having about an investigation or how a trial was going with a calm, cool exterior—it was one of her gifts as a prosecutor. But now, as she walked behind Frannie Storm, she was having a hard time keeping her emotions at bay as she thought of Brittany Crutcher's dead body.

Other images also popped into her mind. The ones that kept her up at night.

The dark cemetery. Her ex-husband's headstone. The bottle of whiskey in her hand. The smell of the alcohol in her nostrils and the taste on her tongue. A familiar voice, speaking behind her, telling her that he knew everything she had done. That he understood that one mistake shouldn't define a person's life.

"We found him here," Frannie said, mercifully breaking through Helen's hypnotic and torturous thoughts.

They had reached the far end of the yard. An approximately fifteen-yard area had been enclosed with yellow tape, and within that space, a smaller semicircle of about ten feet had been marked off with red tape in a patch of high grass beneath two trees. "In the red," Frannie added.

Helen narrowed her gaze and leaned forward. She saw a carton full of bottles on the ground within the red circle. "What's that?"

"A six-pack of Bud Light."

"Champagne's?"

"Well, we wouldn't want to jump to conclusions or any-thing . . ." Frannie's voice dripped of mock sarcasm that Helen fig-ured she deserved. ". . . but yeah. The officers that led him to the cruiser said he reeked of beer. We're planning to ask Odell if he'll consent to a blood test to confirm the presence of alcohol. Perhaps we'll find something else."

"Do you suspect he was on other drugs?" Helen snapped her eyes up at Frannie.

"No, but we could confirm their absence."

"Where'd you find the broken bottle?"

Frannie turned and pointed to a smaller spot within the yellow boundary tape, also marked in red, about ten yards to the left of them.

"Is it still there?"

"We haven't moved anything but Odell. We didn't want the CSI guys fussing at us for disturbing the scene."

"Good," Helen said, noticing that two deputies were guarding the boundaries of the crime scene. Helen stepped over the yellow tape and walked toward the smaller red circle. She knelt and saw the blood-caked stem of the longneck.

"That's definitely blood," she said, squinting and cocking her head, noticing that more blood covered both sides of the beer label. Then she looked back at the larger red semicircle in the thicket of brush where Odell Champagne had been found. "You said he was asleep or passed out? How do you know that?"

"Because the officers that found him had to jostle him awake."

"Anything else about his appearance that stood out? Did he seem surprised? Scared? Guilty?"

"He was dressed in a gray hoodie that was filthy. Other than that, he just looked in shock. As if he wasn't sure what was going on."

"Did you find any belongings? A bag? Satchel? Shaving kit?"

"No."

"Did we get photographs of Champagne's position while he was here?"

"Yes. From every angle. And Deputy McCann has already taken crime scene photographs of the entire bus with multiple shots of the victim."

"Was there anything else of Brittany's near Champagne other than the sweatshirt?"

"No."

"Anything out of the ordinary with the body other than the hematoma to the forehead and stains on her T-shirt?"

Frannie rubbed the back of her neck, and it was obvious to Helen that the chief was thinking about what she'd seen. "Yes," she said. "Brittany didn't have on her shoes. She was wearing Birkenstocks . . . you know, the slip-on sandals—"

"I know what Birkenstocks are," Helen snapped.

"Anyway, we found them at the other end of the bus near the driver."

"Indicating that maybe she threw them?"

"That's my gut instinct," Frannie said. "She felt threatened and threw her shoes at her attacker."

"All right," Helen said, beginning to walk in the direction of her Crown Vic. "That's interesting. Is Champagne in the holding cell?"

"Yes," Frannie said, catching up to her in two long strides. They both stepped over the yellow crime scene tape at the same time. "You want first shot or me?"

"You," Helen said. "I want to watch his face. See if I can read anything on it."

"Good," Frannie said as they approached a group of deputies huddled together drinking coffee. Frannie barked some instructions, but Helen continued to walk toward her car. She sucked in a breath and quickened her pace as she waded through the press vultures again. They seemed to have doubled since her arrival a half hour ago. Questions were hurled at her, but all she heard was a rushing sound. Like a freight train in her ear. It had been almost a year since she'd been acquitted for Butch's murder. Eleven months since her reelection. In that time, she'd yet to process what she'd done or the ramifications of her new life. She'd gone through the motions of being the district attorney general but hadn't tried a case. She hadn't faced the heat or stress of a murder investigation, much less the pressure of a jury trial.

But I will now . . .

Brittany Crutcher was an African American teenager. A talented singer in a beloved local band. Helen didn't know her, but Pulaski was, as Frannie had said, a small town, and Brittany's murder would be the talk of the county. The populace would expect justice.

Can I deliver it?

Helen groaned as she sat down in the driver's side of the Crown Vic. She cranked the ignition and again heard the man's voice at her ex-husband's grave site, playing, as it often did, in her mind.

I believe that good people make terrible mistakes in this world . . .

"I can't do this," she whispered, gazing across the growing army of reporters to the school bus.

As she put the car in gear and eased it forward, she didn't feel like she was going to the sheriff's office to question a person of interest. She felt like she was running.

Helen gripped the wheel tight with both hands. *I've been running for eleven months . . .*

16

At 6:55 a.m., Israel Crutcher was in the middle of his preoperative inspection of the surgical suite, making sure all the anesthetic equipment and monitors were in place for the procedure. Once he satisfied himself that everything was where it should be, he planned to visit with his patient, a forty-three-year-old schoolteacher named Josephine Gilgenast, and go over the anesthesia aspects of her surgery, which was a total abdominal hysterectomy.

Israel had been a certified registered nurse anesthetist for eighteen years, but even now, he still got an adrenaline rush on the morning of a procedure. It wasn't unlike how he used to feel before taking the football field for the Giles County Bobcats. That was probably why Israel had been drawn to surgery. There was a focus you had to have that got his competitive juices flowing. Nodding as he did a final sweep of the area with his eyes, he strode out of the OR and headed toward the room where his patient was waiting. At the nurse's station, he applied hand sanitizer and grabbed Ms. Gilgenast's chart, reviewing the particulars relevant to anesthesia. As he perused her history, he felt a squeeze on his arm.

"Israel, you have a call."

"Take a message, Judy," Israel said. "I need to do my assessment of Ms. Gilgenast, and I don't want to be the reason for any holdup. I'm not in the mood for an ass chewing from Dr. Royer."

Israel had been the CRNA for hundreds of surgeries performed by Dr. John Royer, the dean of OB-GYN in Pulaski, and it was typical for

Israel and the nurses to banter about which of them might get cussed by the physician, who was as brilliant as he was ornery. But when Judy didn't say anything, only squeezed his arm harder, Israel looked up from the chart.

The nurse had tears streaming down her cheeks, and her eyes were red. "Please, Israel. You need to take the call."

Israel handed Judy the records and walked around the counter to the phone. As he did, he saw two other nurses gazing at him with concerned eyes. Feeling a knot in his stomach, he grabbed the phone. "Yeah," he said.

"Daddy, it's Gina." Her voice was soft and monotone.

"Hey, baby girl. What's wrong?" A long silence filled the line, and Israel tapped his foot with impatience. "Gina, I have a procedure to do. What's—"

"Something's happened to Brittany." The volume behind the words was louder, but his youngest daughter still spoke in her typical uninflected tone.

Israel swallowed and gazed back at Judy, who had both hands covering her mouth as she watched him. As he moved his eyes around the nurses' desk, he saw that they were all watching him. Beyond them, in the hallway, Dr. Royer was talking with Chad Mead, another CRNA. In Israel's analytical mind, he knew that John was already preparing to do the surgery without him. *Adapt and overcome.* He could almost hear the crusty surgeon's voice in his ear.

"What's happened?" Israel managed to ask, his voice hoarse.

"You need to come home, Daddy," Gina said. "Momma's really upset, and there are a bunch of folks out on the lawn." A pause. "I'm scared."

"Gina, what—?" Israel stopped when he noticed that the surgery suite was deathly quiet, all eyes still on him. *No,* he thought. *Please, God, no . . .*

"I'm on my way," he said, hanging up the phone.

He walked around the desk without making eye contact with any of them, knowing they were all still staring at him. He brushed past Dr. Royer, nodding at his longtime colleague, who mouthed the words, "I'm sorry."

Israel heard nothing.

A minute later, he was outside the hospital. He started to run toward his car, visions of Brittany coming to him like daggers crashing into his heart. Her first steps taken in the backyard by the swing. A few years later, walking into kindergarten holding her momma's hand. So shy, his oldest daughter had been then. Her first solo at the church. The range of her voice even at six years old had made the whole congregation stand and cheer. Things had been so good between them then.

"No," Israel choked the word out as he started his car. Ten minutes later, he pulled into his driveway. Neighbors approached him, their eyes wet with tears, but Israel avoided them. Not wanting to believe.

He barreled into the house and saw Gina sitting on the couch, looking at her phone. "Where's your momma?"

Gina shot to her feet, but before she could say anything, Theresa emerged from the bedroom. Her hands and arms were shaking, her face and cheeks puffy and red.

"Tell me she's OK," Israel said, forcing the tremble out of his voice.

Theresa continued to cry and walked toward him. She tried to grab his hands, but he pushed them away.

"Tell me that Brittany is OK," Israel said. *"Tell me."* He gripped the back of a chair to steady himself and glanced out the window, where the crowd of people and cars was growing.

"She's . . . g-g-gone," Theresa managed.

He glared at her, seeing the brokenness, feeling something shatter inside him. *"How?"*

Theresa crinkled up her face and gazed down at the ground.

Israel grabbed her shoulders and shook her. *"How?"* he repeated, feeling anger and despair burning within him.

She bit her lip and met his eyes. "She was killed," Theresa said, speaking through clenched teeth. "Our baby . . . was murdered."

Tears finally flooded Israel's eyes. "Are you sure?"

Theresa leaned close to her husband's ear. "Odell did it. You were right about him."

Israel pulled back and stared at his wife, who nodded, repeating the words in a whisper. *I saw them arrest him. I saw him taken away.*

17

Odell barely noticed when the door to the holding cell slid open. He continued to gaze at the yellow cinder block walls, seeing and hearing nothing. In the furthest reaches of his brain, he knew he was in shock. He'd checked out and wasn't ready to check back in.

"Odell?"

He didn't acknowledge the tall uniformed woman who took the seat across from him. He continued to stare at the wall, not wanting to move, much less speak.

"Odell, my name is Frannie Storm. I'm the chief deputy sheriff of Giles County. I'd like to ask you a few questions about what you did last night . . . and this morning. Do you hear me?"

Her words came in and out as if they were being spoken with a vacuum cleaner running in the background. Odell said nothing.

"Odell, can you tell me what you did last night after the game?"

When Odell said nothing, he felt the woman's hands press into the table that separated them. "Did you see Brittany Crutcher last night?"

He glanced at Frannie, his first indication he was aware of her presence.

She crossed her arms. "Did you see her?"

Odell returned his eyes to the cinder block wall. His head ached.

"Odell, can you tell me anything about what happened last night? Why did you end up at the bus yard?"

Odell took a breath. He closed his eyes, then opened them.

"We found the note, Odell."

His eyes darted to Frannie without any conscious thought.

She nodded. "We know about the breakup." She paused. "Did that make you angry? When did you receive it? Before the game? Afterward?"

He swallowed and felt nauseous.

"Do you mind if I read it out loud?"

Odell glared at her.

"OK." She held up her hands. "I won't." She leaned her elbows on the metal table and met his eyes. "Odell, Brittany is dead. She was murdered, and you were found a couple hundred yards from her body." She licked her lips. "The sooner you tell me what you did last night, the sooner you might be able to leave."

Odell's heart began to pound in his chest. He gritted his teeth, trying to will himself not to vomit. Visions bounced into his brain. Riding with Jarvis and T. J. to Doug Fitzgerald's keg party. How many beers had he had? He looked at his knuckles, which were still skinned from punching his locker the night before. He felt his jaw, which stung from something. Had he gotten into a fight at Doug's? Everything was a blur.

All he'd wanted to do was kill the pain of the note. He'd sent Brit several texts, hoping to connect with her before she left town. Asking her to meet him at the bus yard. He remembered arguing with someone at the party and then hitching a ride home. He'd gotten a six-pack along the way, but from where? Then he was at the bus yard, climbing up the steps of the bus. Knowing she was in there and feeling anger at her abandonment. Her betrayal. In his nostrils, he could smell the scent of bubble gum. And then . . .

Brittany . . .

Odell placed his face in his hands and finally checked back in. His body began to shake, and he leaned over and vomited on the concrete floor. Then he wailed and punched the sides of his face with both fists. His chest heaved, and an anguished sob finally escaped his mouth. And then another.

He felt a hand patting his back and then heard the swooshing of the doors open and close. He smelled the lemony scent of some type of cleaner and saw the head of a mop moving over the concrete floor. He wiped his eyes and leaned back in his chair.

The female cop's eyes were kind, her face wrinkled up in a grimace that looked like concern. "I'm going to get you a Coke and some crackers. Is that cool?"

He nodded and leaned forward over his knees, visions of Brittany dancing through his mind.

A minute later, a red can of Coke and a package of saltine crackers were placed on the metal desk. Odell opened the package and held a cracker to his mouth, but he couldn't eat. He took a small sip from the can and coughed several times.

"Odell, are you OK?" the cop asked.

He shook his head.

"Please tell me what happened. The Crutchers deserve some answers, don't you think? You saw how upset Mrs. Crutcher was."

Odell hung his head. He remembered Theresa Crutcher's fierce eyes. *Israel was right about you . . .*

Finally, Odell looked across the table at the officer and tried to control his breathing. He'd been in cells like this before, questioned by the police for things he hadn't done and things he had. He knew that, regardless of how nice she was acting, this woman didn't give a damn about him. He took a deep breath, and the faint smell of bile combined with floor cleaner filled his nostrils. He gagged but stopped himself from vomiting again.

"Odell—"

"I'm not going to say anything until I see my lawyer."

He saw the officer's face tense. "OK then," Frannie said. "Who might that be?"

Odell Champagne knew only one lawyer in Pulaski. "Mr. Haynes," he said. "Bocephus Haynes."

18

Helen stood by the window and peered through the one-way window at Odell, who'd buried his face in his arms. "What do you think?" she asked, still watching the detainee and trying to keep her voice calm. Since Odell's mention of his attorney's name, Helen's heart rate had increased, and she could feel the beginning of a headache.

When Frannie didn't respond, Helen turned and peered at the chief deputy sheriff, who was sitting at the conference room table. "Frannie?"

"I don't know," Frannie finally said, sighing and shaking her head. "What do *you* think?"

Helen folded her arms. "Too early to tell. Hard to say if his reaction was more sadness, shock, or regret over what he's done."

"Or a combo of all three."

"Or that," Helen agreed. "Did you notice the abrasions on his knuckles?"

"Yes."

"Could one of or both of his fists have caused the hematoma on the victim's forehead?"

Frannie grunted. "It's possible, I guess. Odell is a strong kid. But I'm not sure a punch to the forehead could create those kinds of cuts on his hand either. It's like he hit something more sharp edged."

"Could have punched something else beforehand and then lit into Brittany. Or he could have hit her with the beer bottle until it broke." Helen paused, thinking it through. "We need to see the results of the forensics . . . but I'd bet a gold nickel that Champagne's prints are all over the base of that bottle."

"And I'd bet another that the blood on the bottle will match Brittany's."

"Any word from Melvin?"

"As soon as the crime lab guys finish up in the bus, the body will be transported to the morgue, and he'll start the autopsy. He said he'd call when he was about to begin."

"I want to be there for that."

"Me too," Frannie said. She stood and walked over to the window next to Helen. "The breakup note gives Odell motive."

"Yep," Helen agreed. "And, barring a surprise with the autopsy and the forensics, it sure looks like he had the means and opportunity."

"Damnit," Frannie whispered. "This is just . . . *awful.*"

"I know. But we can't make any decisions based on assumptions. We've got to nail down everything and make damn sure we're right. Once we arrest this kid for Brittany's murder . . ." Helen trailed off, knowing that Frannie was on the same page and didn't need a primer about the press scrutiny that the case would receive.

"I have a couple deputies rounding up the other members of Fizz," Frannie offered. "And several more are checking in with the football team. If he isn't going to tell us where he was, then hopefully we can get that information from some of his friends."

"Good deal. Do we have someone analyzing the victim and Champagne's phones for text messages, calls, and social media activity?"

"Dodgen's on that. He's the techie in the department."

"All right," Helen said, stretching her arms over her head and gazing again through the glass at Odell. "We need to talk with both sets of parents. His and hers. Get everything we can get. Since you know the Crutchers, you take them." She pointed at the plexiglass window and turned to the chief. "Do you know anything about his home situation?"

"It's bad," she said, squinting at Helen. "His mom's a train wreck. He was looking for her last night before the game."

"Find her," Helen said, walking toward the door.

"What are you going to do?"

Helen looked at Frannie. "I'm going to speak with his attorney."

19

At 9:30 a.m. on Saturday, Bocephus Haynes turned into the gated entrance. He punched in the digits for the security code and waited for the ancient wrought iron barrier to swing open. It was still a bit odd not to see the gold-plated *W* that had adorned the gate for as long as Bo could remember. Now the only marking for the property was a billboard on Highway 64 designating with an arrow the "Future Home of the Roosevelt Haynes Farm for Boys and Girls."

Bo continued up the gravel drive, inspecting the progress of construction. The plantation-style home that his biological father, Andy Walton, had called "the Big House" was still sitting on its perch at the end of the drive. When he was a young boy growing up in a shack on the other side of this farm, Bo had thought that the Big House had to be the largest home in the world. Now, as he slowed to a stop and gazed at the covered front porch, he felt that everything about the place looked and seemed smaller. Part of this vibe, he knew, had to do with the fact that everything seemed larger to a child, especially a kid who'd grown up in as tiny a home as Bo had.

The other reason the mansion appeared less impressive was that the foundation for three other structures had been poured to the right, left, and behind it. Each of these outbuildings had also been framed, and though none of them was as large as the former home of Andy Walton, their collective presence seemed to diminish the size of the Big House. It gave Bo great satisfaction to think that a new era was being ushered in with the boys' and girls' home, one that couldn't erase a complicated past but would transform this land into something good.

Bo parked his silver Chevy Tahoe and climbed out of the front seat, breathing in the cold, fresh air and stretching his arms over his head. He looked out over the empty rows of corn that had been harvested last month. Though his vision for the land was to house troubled teens, he hadn't wanted the place to stop being a farm. His cousin, Booker T., had made sure that the corn was planted last spring, and the harvest had come in right on time in September.

Bo yawned, tired from the events of the last week, which had taken him across the states of Tennessee, Georgia, and Arkansas for depositions of expert witnesses in a products liability case. His joints were also sore and stiff, and he pressed one leg, and then the other, against the back bumper of his truck. Bo wasn't quite as limber in middle age as he'd been as a linebacker for Coach Bryant at the University of Alabama in the late '70s. Driving long hours at a time, even in the spacious Tahoe, and sleeping in hotel rooms, with their stiff mattresses and hard pillows, caused his muscles to ache for the comfort of home. He'd gotten to his house late last night after the concert and finally had a good night's sleep, albeit only six hours of it.

Bocephus Haynes had never been much of a sleeper. Ever since he was a small boy, his motor had always run hot, and he only knew one speed.

"Wide ass open," he said out loud, beginning to pace the construction site and thinking about his trip, which had been productive. Mediation was set for next week, and based on the results of the depositions, Bo felt there was a strong chance that the case could settle for north of seven figures.

His client, Darren Mullins, had been rendered a paraplegic when the forklift he was operating rolled over on top of him after he'd made a tight turn in the plant where he worked. Bo smiled, knowing that the money from a settlement would allow Darren to put his two girls through college and provide for his medical needs for the rest of his life. The funds would also allow him to go back to school and find a way to earn a living that didn't involve manual labor.

As Bo walked through and around the concrete slab and wooden boards that would one day be dorm rooms housing boys and girls who had no other home, he breathed in another deep gust of air, knowing that it wasn't wise to count his chickens before they hatched. The prospects of a successful mediation were promising, but a settlement wasn't a done deal.

There were few, if any, sure things in the practice of law.

Still, if he was honest with himself, he knew things were rolling. Since his successful defense of General Helen Lewis eleven months ago in a murder trial that had garnered national attention, his caseload had doubled. His do-everything office assistant, Lona Burks, was being engulfed with calls about new cases every day, and it wouldn't be long before Bo would have to take on a partner, something that would have been unheard of this time last year.

Bo shook his head as he ran one of his thick hands over the wooden framing of the building behind the Big House, which was slated to be a cafeteria and game room, feeling grateful for his new life. Still, there was an ever-present melancholy.

Why couldn't Jazz have lived to see him reach this point?

The sound of gravel on tires jogged him from his reverie, and he glanced up to see a black Jeep Wrangler easing up the drive. Bo's face broke into a grin, and he strode toward it. Before the car had even come to a full stop beside his Tahoe, the passenger-side door shot open, and a white-and-brown English bulldog bounded toward him.

At six years old, Lee Roy now weighed close to seventy pounds, and the effort of sprinting twenty yards caused him to wheeze as he pressed both paws onto Bo's stomach. "How's my big boy?" Bo asked, rubbing the dog behind the ears and looking past it to the two teenagers walking toward him with sheepish grins planted on their faces.

"You're late," Bo said, raising his voice in mock anger and then grinning. "Couldn't get your sister out of bed?"

"It wasn't my fault this time, Daddy," Lila said, flashing the same brilliant and mischievous smile that her mother used to shoot Bo when he fussed at her about her credit card bill. Lila was dressed in faded jeans and a flannel button-down, her black hair pulled back in a ponytail. She was fifteen years old and, to Bo, still his little girl. But since he'd reenrolled both kids at Giles County High School in January, Lila had grown at least three inches and was now five feet, nine inches tall, the same height her mother had been. Before long, Bo knew she would be going on dates with boys. He cringed at the thought.

"She's right," T. J. said, shaking his head. Thomas Jackson "T. J." Haynes was a couple inches shorter than Bo with a sleek and slender build that made him one of the top shooting guards in southern Tennessee. And not a bad wide receiver either. He'd had four catches for eighty yards in last night's win over Tullahoma. "Wasn't her this time. We swung by Odell's place to pick him up, and no one answered the door. I tried to call him, but it went straight to voice mail. We waited a couple minutes, then left."

"Huh," Bo said. "Did you text him?"

"Yeah, that too. He still hasn't responded." T. J. peered down at the grass.

"What is it?" Bo asked.

"Nothing."

"Don't give me that. Something's wrong. Spit it out."

T. J. stuffed his hands into his pockets. "We went to a party last night at Doug Fitzgerald's. Things got kind of . . . out of hand."

"What does that mean?"

"It means there was a lot of drinking," Lila blurted.

"Lila!" T. J.'s eyes darted at his sister.

Bo frowned. He knew kids in high school drank alcohol and did all sorts of other things they shouldn't do. Teenagers had been doing that for eons, and Bo himself had drunk a little in high school, though he wished he hadn't. "Well," he said, choosing his words carefully. "That true?"

"Yes, sir," T. J. said.

"Did you drink any?"

"No, sir," T. J. said, holding Bo's eyes. "But a lot of the kids did . . . including Odell."

"That doesn't explain why he wasn't at home this morning."

"He wouldn't leave the party with me and Jarvis. Said he wanted to stay out and find Brittany." T. J. grimaced. "I've never seen Odell like that. He had a lot to drink and was really loud. And . . ." T. J. trailed off.

"And what?"

T. J. shook his head. "Nothing. Just worried about him."

Bo rubbed the back of his neck and gazed out at the farm. He was also worried. An athlete with as much to lose as Odell Champagne shouldn't be out drinking at parties. As he'd told T. J. a hundred times and had also instructed Odell, an athlete was a target. And Odell couldn't afford to get in trouble, not with his background. The drinking was troublesome and disappointing, but it wasn't the only thing that bothered Bo.

Odell had never blown off a day working at the farm. In the past few months, the kid had spent almost every Saturday and Sunday out here. Not only was he strong and able to hold his own with the yardwork and construction labor that Bo had assigned him, but Odell also had a keen perspective for what the farm should be. He'd spent a lot of his life alone, raising himself, and Bo had begun to rely on the young man's judgment.

One particular moment stood out. While helping Bo and T. J. paint one of the property's many fences, Odell had said that he'd never been to summer camp. Kids in Town Creek would go to camp and swim, hike, and sit around fires and tell stories. He had a couple friends who were always talking about how much fun they had. "This place could be like that," Odell had said. "A place where kids like me can learn to do stuff they wouldn't ordinarily get to do." Then he'd paused and said something that Bo hadn't forgotten. "But I hope it's more, Mr. Haynes. I know you want it to be a lot more. I think this farm should feel like a home and not a housing project. Kids need someone to look up to . . . someone to let them know when they get out of line . . . and someone to hug on them when they're hurting." He looked around the massive expanse of land and then peered at Bo with sad eyes. "That's all I've ever wanted." As he continued to paint, he added, "I hope you're bringing in some good folks to work here. That's what these kids are going to need most. Someone good in their life." He glanced at Bo again. "People like you and your boy here." Then he smiled and painted the side of T. J.'s arm. The two flung paint at each other until they were both covered in it.

Bo had let them play, but he'd taken Odell's message to heart. He was actively involved in interviewing potential counselors and foster parents who would work and live at the farm. He agreed with Odell that even more than the facilities, making good personnel choices would be critical.

Until today, Odell had never missed a day of work. Bo had paid him for his time, and in the process, Bo and his children, especially T. J., had grown close to the troubled teen, whose upbringing wasn't that different from Bo's own difficult childhood. Bo thought back to the game last night and Odell's angst over his mother. He took out his phone, realizing that Sabrina Champagne had never responded to his text or called him back. He typed out a quick U ok? text to Odell and pressed send. Then, pushing aside his worries, he wrapped an arm around each of his children. "I missed you guys. I'm sorry I was gone for so long. Hope y'all were good for your grandma."

"We were," Lila said.

Juanita Henderson was the children's grandmother on their mother's side. Things hadn't always been good with Jazz's parents, especially in the year after her death. There had been a custody battle, and for a short period of time, Juanita and Ezra Henderson had been granted temporary custody of the children. But last November, just a few weeks after his victory in General Lewis's trial, Bo had won his petition to regain custody. Since then, things had begun to thaw, at least with Juanita. When Bo had asked her to stay with the kids while he was gone, he'd expected her to say no, but she'd agreed without hesitation. He only wished that things could be the same with Jazz's father, Ezra, but Bo doubted a flamethrower could melt Ezra's frosty, bitter feelings toward him.

"Good," Bo said.

"I'm glad you're back, Daddy," Lila said. "I'm sorry we didn't get to talk much last night, but wasn't the concert awesome?"

"Both the game and the show were amazing," Bo agreed. "I can't remember a night like that in Pulaski . . . ever."

"So why couldn't we sleep in today?" Lila asked.

Bo squeezed his daughter's neck and glanced at T. J. "You bring what I asked you?"

T. J. nodded. "Yeah, Dad, but why—"

"You'll see," Bo said, leaning down and petting Lee Roy again behind the ears and then walking with a brisk pace toward his truck. "We're going to do something I should have done a long time ago."

———

An hour later, Bo and T. J. were both drenched with sweat, each of them having removed their pullovers.

"Remind me again why we didn't use a chain saw," T. J. said.

Bo chuckled and gazed up at the top of the oak tree. Then, peering over at Lila, he held out the ax and winked. "You ready for a couple more swings?"

His daughter wrinkled her face and wrung her hands. "Remind me again why we didn't bring gloves," she teased. Lila had made a couple of early attempts, and then her hands had begun to ache, and Bo had made her stop. Softball tryouts would be held soon, and he didn't want to do anything to hurt her batting prowess. T. J., meanwhile, needed to bulk up a little for football and basketball, so Bo felt that chopping down a tree with an ax would be good for him.

But this wasn't about a workout or what was good for anyone, Bo knew, turning back to the tree that had been the site of two different murder scenes, forty-five years apart.

Bo's life had been defined by these two killings. In 1966, as a five-year-old boy, he'd watched the man whom he'd thought was his father lynched by ten members of the Ku Klux Klan. When the leader of the mob had given the instruction, the horse Roosevelt Haynes was sitting on had been kicked, and Roosevelt's neck had snapped from the force of the drop and the tightness of the noose. Bo had tried to stop what was happening and had received a kick in the face for his trouble.

Four and a half decades later, the leader of the mob, Andrew Davis Walton, a man who'd remade himself into a powerful investor after his days in the Klan were numbered, had been shot and killed at the Sundowners Club. His body had later been displayed here, a noose also around his neck. The corpse had been set on fire, and the tree had almost perished in the blaze. Amazingly, it had survived, though char marks from the flames could still be seen around the trunk, and some of the lower branches were likewise damaged.

The limb of the tree where both hangings had occurred hadn't survived the blaze. Bo looked at the spot where it had been and closed his eyes. He hadn't witnessed the second killing, though he'd been charged with murder for it.

During the trial, the charges had eventually been dismissed, and the true killer of Andy Walton had emerged along with a truth long buried. Though Roosevelt Haynes had acted as Bo's father, Bo's biological father was Andy Walton. The impetus for both Roosevelt's and Andy's murders was an affair between Bo's mother and Andy.

So much tragedy, Bo thought, hanging his head and then feeling his daughter's hand grip his forearm.

"You OK, Daddy?"

Bo nodded and let out a long, deep breath of air. Then, forcing a smile, he extended the ax to her. "One more swing?"

She smiled and took the ax. Then, she got into her batting stance and took a mighty whack at the tree, adding another couple of inches to the gap they'd made in it. She handed the tool back to her father. "You should be the one who takes it down, Dad."

———

Ten minutes later, after one more mighty hack, Bo watched as the tree teetered and began to lean. As it fell toward the pond where he had swum as a boy, Bo felt tears form in his eyes. Was it possible for a person to ever get closure in life and truly move on? Or was acceptance more important? Did bad things eventually become absorbed into a person's soul, acceptance taking the place of the pain?

Bocephus Haynes wasn't a philosopher and didn't want to be one. He was a lawyer, and he liked to think he'd risen above his past to make something of himself. His obsession with the events that happened in this clearing had strained his marriage and made his children's lives more difficult than they ever should have been.

But here they were, together again. He wiped his eyes and glanced at his two kids, who were also crying. He'd finally told them the story of his childhood over the holidays last year, leaving out no details as to their heritage. Despite their teasing over the ax, they both knew the pain this place on the farm had caused their father.

"I love you guys," Bo whispered.

"Love you too, Dad," T. J. said.

Lila walked over and hugged him. "Love you too, Daddy." She pulled back from him. "Have you thought about what you want this part of the farm to be?"

Bo gazed around the clearing that led to the thicket of trees and then to the pond that fronted the trees. He pointed to his left. "I'd like to put a barn there. A gathering place where the kids can have parties and dances." He grinned. "Ice cream socials, if that's still a thing. A place where kids can worship God or pray to whatever higher power they believe in. I want this place to be filled with laughter and fun . . . and peace." He paused. "Maybe put some picnic tables over by the pond and fill the water up with bream or crappie so the kids can fish."

He gazed down at his daughter. "How'd that be?"

"Sounds wonderful. When's it all going to be ready?"

Bo peered around the vast property, knowing that they were ahead of schedule. "Maybe by the end of the year? Christmas if we're lucky."

"You should have a big kickoff party," Lila suggested.

"Yeah, Dad," T. J. said. "Maybe get a band or something. Maybe you could ask Fizz to play."

"Sounds good," Bo said, wiping sweat from his forehead. In the distance, he saw a vehicle approaching. He hadn't invited anyone else to this get-together, but as a black Crown Victoria got closer, his stomach tightened. He knew only one person who drove a car like that.

"What's the General doing here?" T. J. asked.

Helen Lewis strode toward them, her face tense. *Something's wrong,* Bo thought.

"Hey, Lila," Helen said, reaching out and squeezing the girl's hands. "I'm sorry, but can I have a second with your dad?" She pierced Bo with a hard look, all business.

"OK," Lila said.

Bo approached, and Helen took a few steps closer to the vehicle and away from the kids. "What's up?" Bo asked.

"Brittany Crutcher was murdered last night."

Bo opened his mouth, but no words came. He thought of the young woman he'd seen on the stage at the Brickyard last night. Her band's performance had been captivating, giving Bo, who had been dog tired, a much-needed shot of adrenaline. He thought of all the bleachers that had been filled with kids, teenagers, and adults, young and old. How long had it been since he'd been to a concert where even he was jumping up and down to the beat? Or where he'd seen others do the same, no matter their color or age? Brittany's range and the energy of her voice had been as impressive as anything he'd heard in a long time. He'd watched her grow up in the Bickland Creek Baptist Church, singing in the choir when she was just a first grader and wowing the congregation then as she had most of Pulaski last night. He felt a wave of despair rush over him. "What?" was all he could manage to say.

"Her body was found this morning on the back of a school bus at the transportation yard on Eighth Street. She had a large bruise on her forehead. Blunt force trauma is the likely cause of death, but the coroner hasn't completed his autopsy."

Bo blinked. He lived on Jefferson Street, about a half a mile from the transportation facility. He remembered hearing police sirens that morning while he ate his breakfast. "That's terrible. Do you have any leads?"

"That's why I'm here," Helen said.

Bo's whole body tensed, and he glanced to his right at his son.

Helen reached out and touched his arm. "No one suspects T. J. of anything. But we have Odell Champagne in custody."

"Odell?" Bo raised his eyebrows.

Helen nodded. "He was found in close proximity to the body as well as the presumed murder weapon. I can't give you any more details right now, but he appears to be the prime suspect."

Bo peered down at the grass, thinking about what T. J. had said earlier about something being up with Odell last night. "Jesus," he whispered. He looked at Helen. "General, I still don't understand why you're here."

"We're interviewing all the football players, so we need to get a statement from T. J. Can you bring him down to the station?"

"Of course," Bo said, again looking at his children. They both had worried expressions on their faces. It seemed as if all of the good vibes of the past two hours had dissipated in a second. "Is that all?"

"No. Odell won't talk to us without his lawyer present, and . . ." She paused. Bo could feel the anxiety in the General's tone and demeanor. ". . . he says that's you."

20

Twenty minutes later, after dropping Lila and Lee Roy off at home, Bo and T. J. walked into the Giles County Sheriff's Office. Frannie was waiting for them.

"He's here to give a statement," Bo said, squeezing his son's shoulder. "I'd like to be present when he does."

"Of course," Frannie said, her voice clipped. Gone was the relaxed vibe from the night before. This was the Frannie Storm Bo had grown accustomed to seeing.

"I'd like to speak with Odell first."

Frannie frowned. "OK. T. J. can wait in my office until you're through."

"No questions until then, promise?"

"Promise," Frannie said, taking T. J.'s arm and leading him down the hallway to her office. When she returned, Bo grimaced. "All right then, take me to him."

Frannie entered digits into a box on the wall, and a metal door slid open. Bo followed her into a narrow corridor that led to an attorney consultation room. Bo was no stranger to the place. He'd been here many times as an attorney and once as a detainee.

"Has an arrest been made?" Bo asked, as they both faced the door behind which Odell Champagne was waiting.

"No," Frannie said, and Bo thought he heard a trace of torment in the chief's tone. She looked at him with eyes that radiated pain. "But the evidence is piling up."

21

As Bo stepped into the tiny square attorney consultation room, Odell shot to his feet. "Mr. Haynes, I'm sorry. I should have called first, but—"

"Sit down," Bo said, pointing at Odell's chair. "Now."

Odell did as he was told. Bo took in his surroundings. A metal desk and two plastic chairs were inside. He shook his head at the familiarity of it all.

Five years ago, he'd been the client during these meetings when he was on trial for the murder of Andy Walton. And last year, he'd had countless sessions with the General during her capital murder case. Since then, Bo had steered clear of the jail and all but resolved not to take any more criminal assignments. *Yet here I am again . . .*

Bo took the other seat and crossed his legs, looking the boy up and down. He was wearing the orange jumpsuit of a pretrial detainee. His clothes were probably being examined for DNA evidence and fingerprints. Odell's eyes were bloodshot, his feet bouncing under the table. Bo's gaze fixed on the boy's hands.

"Your knuckles are all busted up. Why?"

"I punched my locker a few times after the game."

"And why the hell would you do that? You'd just iced the win with two touchdowns."

Odell peered down at the desk.

"Look at me, son. I want to hear it straight. I can't tell if you're lying unless you look at me."

Odell slowly raised his eyes. "I'm not lying. I punched my locker last night after the game. I was angry . . . because Brittany broke up with me. She left me a note saying she'd signed a recording contract and that she was leaving for LA in the morning. We'd been hanging out together right before the game. We were in the tunnel looking out on the field, watching all the people that had already shown up. I knew something was going on with her, but she wouldn't tell me. She told me she loved me. That was the last thing she ever said to me." His red eyes glistened. "I found the note in my locker. I'm not sure when she put it in there."

"What did it say?"

"That she was leaving. She'd gotten an offer from ELEKTRIK HI—that was her dream record label—and she couldn't turn it down. She was leaving in the morning and didn't want there to be a sad goodbye." He stopped again and wiped his eyes. "She wanted us to have a clean break and wished me luck with football." His mouth curved into a sad smile. "She said it wouldn't hurt her feelings if I took the Southern Cal offer."

"Did the note say why she was leaving so quickly?"

"The studio wanted to start recording tracks as soon as possible. The contract was a solo deal, and she knew the rest of the band was going to be really mad at her. She also knew her dad wouldn't understand, and she didn't want any arguments or fights."

Bo felt a tickle in his chest at the mention of Brittany's father. Israel Crutcher had been a teammate of Bo's in high school, but they hadn't been friends. "Did the note say anything else?"

"Yeah. 'When opportunity knocks, you have to answer.'" He snorted. "She actually wrote that. And that she knew I'd understand."

"But you didn't understand."

Odell shook his head. "No, sir."

"And so you lost your temper and tore up your locker." Bo couldn't hide the disappointment in his tone. He'd cautioned Odell many times during their visits on the farm or at the house that the true test of a champion was how he or she dealt with adversity. It was the same advice he'd given his own son. Words of wisdom that had been passed down to him by his college football coach, Paul "Bear" Bryant, and by his law professor and best friend, Professor Tom McMurtrie. Keeping your cool was essential. On the football field and in life. An emotional outburst served no purpose except to defeat you. And the advice went double for Odell Champagne. The kid had a rap sheet. Theft convictions. An assault charge. He'd been kicked out of Town Creek High School for fighting. He was under the microscope all the time. He didn't have the luxury of flying off the handle when things didn't go his way. Bo had told him all of this multiple times.

He glared at the young man, now hoping that Odell's worst offense last night was beating the hell out of his locker. *"Answer the question."*

"Yes, sir. I guess I just lost it."

"Where's the note?"

Odell glanced toward the door to the outside. "Cops have it."

Motive, Bo thought, remembering what the General had told him at the farm. *He was found in close proximity to the body as well as the presumed murder weapon.*

"What'd you do after the game?"

Odell shrugged. "Watched the concert."

"Who were you with?"

"T. J. and Jarvis."

Bo's stomach tightened at the mention of his son's name. "What happened during the concert?"

"Nothing really."

"And afterward? Did you see Brittany at the Brickyard?"

"No, I left with T. J. and Jarvis. We went to a party."

"At Doug Fitzgerald's house?" Bo remembered what his son had told him.

Odell nodded. "Yeah, we were there for a few hours."

"Did you drink any alcohol?"

Odell looked down at the table.

"Eyes on me," Bo snapped. "Did you?"

"Yes, sir. Doug had a keg. I had a few beers."

"How many is a few?"

He sighed. "I don't know. Five maybe. Could have been more."

"Was Brittany at the party?"

"No. I texted her and asked her to come, but she didn't respond."

"Did you send her any other texts?"

"Yes," Odell said.

"How many and what did they say?"

"I can't remember how many. I was angry. At some point, I asked her to meet me at the bus yard."

Bo felt his stomach clench again. *The murder site . . .* "Why the bus yard?"

"Because that's where . . . the first time, you know." He paused and glanced up at the ceiling. This time, Bo didn't scold him for looking away. "Over the summer, Brittany had gone to see one of the young girls from church play softball at Exchange Park. Brittany's sister, Gina, coached the team, and I had actually been to a few of the practices with Brit. Anyway, I met her there, and it was cool, you know. We both signed autographs for the kids. When it was over, she said she wanted to take a walk. It was a nice night, and we ended up at the bus yard. That was a place where she and the band would hang out sometimes and blow off steam." He paused. "When none of the others were there, we went into one of the buses, and . . ."

"All right then," Bo said, his voice soft. "Back to last night. Did Brittany say she would meet you?"

Odell shook his head. "Not at first."

"What does that mean?"

Odell groaned. "It means I thought she was going to blow me off . . . and when she didn't respond, I texted some ugly things."

"Like what?"

Odell hid his face behind his hands. "Like 'Eff you.' I know I said that." He let his hands drop to the table. "I can't remember anything else. Things got out of hand at the party. Jarvis tried to take me home, but I wouldn't let him. We ended up wrestling around on the ground for a while. Anyway, I wouldn't give in, and he and T. J. left."

Bo pressed his lips together. T. J. hadn't told him about any fight with Jarvis. "What then?"

"Everything's kind of hazy after that. I hung out some with Ian Dugan. Ian's in Fizz, and he was pretty drunk too." Odell paused. "We did a few shots, and then I got a ride back to my apartment."

"Did you tell Ian about the breakup with Brittany?"

"Yeah."

"What about Brittany signing a solo deal?"

Odell shrugged. "I think I did. I was mad at her, and I'm pretty sure I said something about it."

"Who took you to your apartment?"

"I can't remember. Ian was too drunk to drive, so it must have been someone else at the party. All I remember is that the car was small. It wasn't a truck or an SUV. Anyway, I wanted to see if my mom was home yet, but she wasn't." Odell's eyes went wide. "Mr. Haynes, have you heard anything from my mom?"

"No."

Odell began to wring his hands, and Bo reached forward and touched the boy's shoulder. "I'll find her, O. I promise."

"I wonder if she knows I'm . . ." Odell's voice began to shake.

"I'll find her," Bo repeated. "But if I'm going to be able to help you, I need you to finish telling me what happened last night. You got to your apartment. Then what?"

"Mom wasn't home. Ian and the other folks were going to ride around for a little while, but I didn't feel like it. They left, and I think I must have passed out for a little while. Tired from the game and the alcohol. When I woke up, I saw that Brit had texted."

"What did she say?"

"That she was at the bus yard and wanted to see me before she left town."

"When did she send the text?"

"I don't know."

"What did you do?"

"I went to the bus yard."

"How did you get there?"

"Mom still wasn't home . . . so I walked."

"You walked?"

He nodded. "Actually, I ran most of it, even though I'd had some drinks. Our apartment is off College Street. It's only about a mile and a half."

"Any stops along the way?"

Odell looked down at the table.

"Odell?"

"I went into Slinky's gas station and got a six-pack of Bud Light."

Bo knew the place, having stopped there for gas and the occasional six-pack himself many times. "And the clerk sold it to you?"

The sad smile came back to his face. "The guy recognized me when I pulled down my hoodie. I'm Odell Champagne, remember? Best player at Giles County High. Told me I played a hell of a game and said the beer was on the house." Odell grunted. "And to be careful."

"Yeah," Bo said. "I wish you'd followed that advice. And I damn sure wish you would have remembered who you were. Go on."

Odell took in a deep breath. "When I got to the transportation yard, I saw a sweatshirt on the ground by one of the buses. It was Brittany's. I knew it from sight, and I also picked it up, and it had her scent." His voice began to quake. "She always smelled like bubble gum. I thought . . ." His voice cracked.

"What did you think?"

"I thought she was playing with me," Odell said. "I walked up the steps of the bus. I saw one of her feet dangling in the aisle. I said something . . . I can't remember. Something like, 'I see you, girl,' but she didn't say nothing back. Then I noticed one of her sandals was on the floor. When I got up close to her, I saw the bruise on her head and . . . and the broken bottle. I looked into her eyes, and there was no life . . ." Odell let out a sob and placed his face in his hands.

Bo reached his hand out again and placed it on the boy's shoulder. He spoke in a tone just above a whisper. "Then what happened, son?"

Odell gazed up at Bo, tears streaking his face. "I don't know." He held out his palms. "I can't remember nothing after that. All I know is I woke up a little while later with dogs barking down at me."

Bo leaned back and crossed his legs, thinking through everything he'd heard. There were a lot of missing pieces, but Odell's story was plausible. It explained his presence at the murder scene and the evidence that Frannie indicated was piling up against him. Finally, he stood and looked down at the boy. "Odell, are you telling me the truth?"

"Yes, sir. I swear to God."

"Did you kill that girl?"

"No, sir. I loved Brittany. I w-w-would never have hurt her."

Bo held his eyes for several seconds and turned toward the door.

"Mr. Haynes, are you going to represent me?"

Bo paused and spoke without looking at him. "I've known the Crutcher family for a long time, son. I . . ."

"You're all I got, Mr. Haynes. If you don't help me, I've got nobody."

"That's not true. The court will appoint you a lawyer if you can't hire one."

"Mr. Haynes, please . . ."

Bo finally turned and looked at him. "Odell, I've put my family through a lot in these last few years. I'm not sure I can put them through a case like this."

Odell started to say something but then closed his mouth. He wiped his eyes. "All right, go on then. I don't need you."

"Odell, I didn't say no."

"I don't need nobody. You go on and leave me too. Just like my daddy. Just like my momma. Just like Brittany was going to do."

"If I can't take the case, I'll make sure that you have a good attorney."

Odell smirked. "Don't sweat it, Mr. Haynes. I got no chance without you. If you say no, I'll represent myself."

Bo crossed his arms. "That would be a huge mistake."

Odell grunted. "My whole life is a mistake."

Bo started to leave, but Odell's anguished voice stopped him. "Mr. Haynes?"

"Yeah, son."

"Please find my mom."

22

Bo sat rigid in Frannie's office as he listened to T. J. describe the events of the previous night, which were consistent with what he'd said at the farm except for two small details. One was the skirmish that Jarvis and Odell had gotten into, which ended with the two wrestling on the ground and several of the partygoers, including T. J., having to break them apart. While this was bad, the other missing piece stung worse.

"T. J., before you and Jarvis left Doug Fitzgerald's house, did Odell say anything about Brittany?"

T. J. glanced at Bo, who nodded firmly back at him. "Tell the truth, son."

"He was drunk, Ms. Frannie. He wasn't thinking right."

"T. J., I know that Odell is your friend, but I need to know what he said about Brittany."

"He said she'd broken up with him and that she'd done it with a note. He'd pulled out a wadded-up piece of paper and shown it to us."

"Did he read it?"

"No, he just held up the paper."

"What else did he say about Brittany?"

"Right as we were leaving, after he and Jarvis got into it, I told him he needed to tighten up. That he was Odell Champagne, five-star prospect. I tried to loosen him up and told him there would be other girls."

"What did Odell say?" Frannie asked.

"He said not for him. And that there was no way he was going to let her leave him like that."

"Anything else?"

"Yes, ma'am." T. J. cleared his throat and stared at the floor. "He said no one was going to treat him that way and get away with it."

———

Out in the hallway, Bo told T. J. to go to the car. Once he was out of earshot, he peered at Frannie. "Where's the General?"

"At the morgue waiting for me. The autopsy of Brittany's body is about to begin." She paused. "Do you want me to have her call you?"

"Yeah," Bo said. "Thanks." He started to walk away, but her voice stopped him.

"Bo?"

He turned.

"I'm sorry," she said. "Really. I wish T. J. wasn't involved."

"I know," Bo managed.

For a while, she peered at him with an expression he couldn't read. "Are you going to represent Odell?" she asked.

Bo looked past her to a spot on the wall. "I don't know," he said, feeling the weight of the decision that faced him beginning to bear down on him. "What do you think I should do?"

She touched his arm. "Can't answer that one for you, Counselor." She started to walk away, and Bo called after her.

"Frannie, given Brittany's fame, I know there'll be pressure to make an arrest. Please don't rush it. That kid in there . . ." Bo gestured with his head toward the door that led to the jail. ". . . has a future."

"So did Brittany," Frannie said, her voice as cold as December. "And that *grown man* in there may have taken it."

"He's eighteen," Bo said, hearing the plea in his voice.

Frannie leaned her head forward and glared at him. "So was she."

23

On the covered porch behind his house, Bo flipped the burgers and took a long pull on his bottle of beer. Four hours had passed since he'd left the jail, and he'd tried to bring some normalcy to the day by inviting Booker T. over to watch the Bama football game and eat dinner. As the Tide scored yet another touchdown in a contest long since decided, Bo glanced at T. J., who was staring off into space, not even watching the screen.

There would be no normalcy tonight, and he wondered when it would return. But damned if he wasn't going to try. He pointed with his spatula at the TV that hung above the outdoor fireplace. "Coach Saban sure does have things rolling in Tuscaloosa," he announced, giving his head a jerk. "He's turned the third Saturday in October into a cakewalk. The Alabama–Tennessee game used to mean something."

"Don't act like you don't enjoy pounding the Vols every year," Booker T. said. "And it's a streaky series. It's bound to go the other way soon." Then he shook his head too. "But forty-nine to ten is some kind of butt whipping. Who does Bama play next week?"

Before Bo could answer, T. J. chimed in, his voice soft. "Texas A&M. The rumor is that College GameDay is coming to T-town."

"Is that so?" Booker T. asked, taking a sip from his own bottle and shooting a wink at Bo. Booker Taliaferro Rowe Jr. was Bo's first cousin and one of the largest human beings Bo had ever encountered. At six feet, six inches tall and over three hundred pounds, Booker T. was one of the few people in Bo's life who towered over him and pretty much everyone else who got around him. "Well, maybe you can get your dad to take you down for the game. Maybe set up a meeting with the basketball coach, huh?"

"Maybe," T. J. said, with no enthusiasm in his voice. He rose from his seat. "Dad, I'm going to go up to my room and play Xbox. That cool?"

"Sure, son," Bo said. "You mind peeking in on your sister?"

"Will do."

Bo watched him leave and then peered at his cousin. "Tough day. Lila's been in her room all afternoon crying."

"Tell me about it. I couldn't even get Jarvis to come over here, and he loves your burgers." Booker T. shook his head. "Been in his room since he left the station."

"Did the sheriff's office really interview the whole team?"

"Pretty sure," Booker T. said. "A lot of them saw Odell last night, and all of them were at the concert. Makes sense they'd be questioned."

Bo nodded his agreement. "We were at the clearing when we learned the news."

"And . . . did you take down that tree?" Booker T. asked.

"Yes."

"All three of you?"

"We took turns," Bo said.

Booker T. smiled. "About damn time." He paused. "How did it feel?"

"Good," Bo said. "Right."

"That entertainment barn is going to be perfect there. I'm meeting with the architect for that on Monday."

"We still looking good to open by Christmas?" Bo asked.

"Maybe not open, but we'll be through with construction. I'm betting by early January of next year, we'll have our first group of kids." Booker T. rubbed his hands together. "This is a real good thing you're doing, Bo. Real fine."

"It was your idea," Bo said.

Booker T. grinned. "Oh yeah. I almost forgot. Hey, those burgers almost ready? I could use some nourishment."

Bo smirked and was about to say something about his cousin's girth when his cell phone began to ring. He took it out and didn't recognize the number on the screen. Normally, he might chalk the call up as a solicitor, but given the events of the day, he decided to answer.

"Hello."

"Bo, this is Frannie." Her voice was anxious.

He felt a shiver run up his arms. "What's wrong?"

There was a pause and the sound of her saying something that Bo couldn't make out to someone who must be near. Then Frannie spoke into the microphone. "I've found Sabrina Champagne."

24

Fifteen minutes later, after telling T. J. to watch things at the house, Bo and Booker T. pulled into the Sundowners Club on Highway 64. Frannie Storm was waiting by her police cruiser with a scowl on her face. Next to her, wearing what appeared to be a blanket, was Sabrina Champagne. Bo hopped out of Booker T.'s pickup and walked over to them while his cousin hung back in his truck.

"Bocephus Haynes," Sabrina said, slurring her words and opening up the blanket. Bo looked away in time not to see anything. "My, what I would like to do to you."

Frannie's voice penetrated the air like a laser. "Ms. Champagne, if you do that again, I'm going to book you for indecent exposure and prostitution, do you hear me?"

Sabrina giggled and hiccuped. "Yes, ma'am. Aye, aye, Chief." She did a mock salute, and her blanket almost came off again.

Bo looked at Frannie. "Where—"

"In the VIP room upstairs. She was giving a 'private dance.'" Frannie put the quote symbols up with her index and middle fingers. Bo knew what that meant. He'd had plenty of dealings with the Sundowners Club over the years, and he knew the VIP rooms were used for a lot more than dancing. Frannie leaned close to Bo and spoke under her breath. "I haven't said anything to her about Odell."

"How can I help?"

"I don't know what to do with her. I don't want to take her in. Not with everything else going on. And I can't drop her off at her apartment because the crime scene techs are over there now."

"Surely you don't want me to bring her to my house."

"Yeah, baby," Sabrina chimed in, collapsing into Bo's arms. "Take me to your house, and I'll make it worth your while, Bocephus."

Frannie sighed. "Do you have any other ideas?"

"I can probably let her stay at my office," Bo said, thinking out loud. "Or maybe get her a hotel room. Or—"

Sabrina Champagne let loose a shriek that cut Bo's words off in an instant. As she began to fall to the ground, Bo and Frannie caught her around the waist. She yelled again.

"Sabrina, what's wrong?" Bo asked.

"My stomach," she said. "It's killing me." She screamed again and bit down on her arm.

Bo moved a hand to her forehead and pulled back at the heat. "I don't think this is an act," he said. "Feel."

Frannie touched Sabrina's forehead. "She's sick," Frannie said, and Bo thought he heard a touch of relief in her tone. "She didn't say anything about her stomach hurting inside the club."

"Well, I'm no doctor," Bo said, "but it feels like she has a fever, and if she's been on a bender for a few days, she probably needs to be in a detox unit. I can take her to the hospital if you'd like."

"I'll take her," Frannie said.

"OK, I'll help you get her in your cruiser." He reached down and lifted Sabrina Champagne into his arms in a princess carry.

"My stomach," she said, grimacing and then coughing into his face. Bo almost gagged as he breathed in the scent of rum and smoke.

"Easy now," he said, placing the woman in the back of Frannie's vehicle. When he straightened up, he noticed another police car pulling into the gravel lot. A male officer rolled down his window. "Everything OK, Chief?"

"I need you to follow me to the Hillside ER."

"Yes, ma'am."

She looked at Bo. "Thanks for coming."

Bo nodded. "Thanks for finding her."

"At least she'll be safe at the hospital."

"And out of trouble," Bo added.

"Let's hope," Frannie said and then climbed into her car.

———

Bo watched the two police cars leave the lot and heard footsteps behind him. "Well, cuz, why do all roads in Pulaski eventually lead to this dump?"

Bo knelt and picked up a handful of gravel and slung it across the space, watching the pebbles light upon the highway. "Seems that way, doesn't it?" He looked at Booker T. "Come on, let's go. I'll heat up those burgers."

"No offense, Bo, but this little scene kinda made me lose my appetite."

"Ditto. Sabrina can seem so normal at times. Almost charming. And then she goes off the deep end."

"Working here ain't helping."

"How long has that been going on?" Bo asked. Odell hadn't mentioned that his mother had taken a job at the Sundowners.

"Couldn't be long. When did she get fired from Hitt's Place?"

"Late August," Bo said. "I got her that job, and the owner called me and said she'd do great for a few days and then show up two hours late with no excuse. He couldn't have that, and I didn't blame him for firing her."

"So she's here a month and already turning tricks in the VIP room."

"You heard that?" Bo asked.

"I had the window rolled down. Heard the whole thing. She's lucky as hell Frannie found her and not one of the other officers. Otherwise she'd be in a cell right next to her son."

For a moment, both men were quiet. Finally, Booker T. asked the question that had hung in the air between them since the press conference. "So, you going to represent the kid or not?"

"I don't know," Bo said.

"If they're still holding him, there must be some pretty strong reasons."

Bo said nothing, knowing his cousin was right.

"Bo, you don't owe the kid this," Booker T. said. "I know you like Odell and probably see a bit of yourself in him, but you don't owe him a defense to murder. We've known Israel and Theresa Crutcher since we were kids. I realize you and Israel ain't close, but still. You really gonna help someone charged with killing his daughter?"

"If he's charged, the kid is innocent until proven guilty."

"I know that. And some other lawyer should argue it for him. Not you."

"He told me today that he won't let anyone else represent him. That he'll go it alone if I say no."

"Then he's a damn fool and deserves his fate."

Bo squinted at his cousin. "Cold."

"Truth," Booker T. said. "If you represent Odell Champagne, you're gonna be on the wrong side of your friends, your church, and your family. You think Lila and T. J. want you involved in this mess?" Booker T. waved his hand around the gravel lot of the Sundowners. "Look where it's already taken you."

"Frannie called me because she knows I'm close to Odell, and I mentioned that he was looking for his mother at the game last night. This has nothing to do with representing him."

More silence between the two, the only sound coming from a country number being played from the speakers inside the Sundowners.

"When are you going to decide?"

"I don't know," Bo said.

Booker T. took a step toward Bo and placed his meaty index finger in Bo's chest. "Well, my advice is simple and loud and clear. Don't do it." He opened the door to his truck. "And your ass better be at the visitation for Brittany tomorrow. If it's not, I'm gonna whip it."

"We'll be there," Bo said, climbing into the passenger seat. As the truck pulled onto Highway 64, Bo asked, "Have you seen Israel yet?"

Booker T. peered out over the steering wheel and nodded.

"How was he?"

Booker T. grimaced. "How long's it been since you've seen Israel? The reunion?"

"Yeah," Bo said.

Booker T. scoffed. "Two of the most successful Black men in Pulaski, and y'all haven't spoken in that long."

"That's a two-way street. Me and Israel have been like oil and water since high school, and you remember what happened at that reunion." He paused. "You didn't answer my question. How was he when you saw him?"

Booker T. shook his head. "Israel's always been kind of moody. Never been the easiest person to talk with."

"He's an asshole," Bo said, feeling guilty for the words the minute they came out of his mouth. They were now on Highway 31, the lights of downtown Pulaski visible in the distance.

"A lot of folks say the same about you, cuz."

Bo glared at Booker T., knowing his cousin was probably right. "Will you quit beating around the bush?"

"Israel's in a bad place. I went over there last night, and he didn't say a word to me. Didn't even grunt. Just sat on the porch and looked over the railing. I'm worried about him. Underneath that cold exterior is a damn furnace." Booker T. glanced at Bo. "Know what I mean?"

117

Bo did. Several times in high school and once as an adult, Bo had seen Israel Crutcher's fuse blow. When his temper was sufficiently provoked, he could be downright scary.

Like me, Bo thought. "I know," Bo said.

"I'm worried he might do something."

"Like what?"

"I don't know, but Brittany was Israel's whole world. His pride and joy. In these last few years, about the only time I've seen him smile was when he was talking about her."

"Anything else going on with him?" Bo asked. "Financial problems? Marriage?"

"I'm really not sure. But I'm worried that losing Brittany is going to send him over the edge."

"You and him always been friends," Bo said. "And you've been through a lot this past year too. Why don't you try to talk to him again?"

Booker T. gripped the steering wheel, not looking at Bo. "I've tried. I hope what I'm seeing is just trauma, which would damn sure be natural given what's happened."

"But you don't think so," Bo said.

Booker T. turned his head to Bo. "No, I don't."

A minute later, Booker T. turned into Bo's driveway and pulled his truck to a stop. He took in a deep breath and exhaled. "So much for chilling on your back porch with some burgers, beers, and SEC football."

"My heart wasn't in it anyway."

"Mine either. But I could've done without that scene at the Sundowners."

"You and me both," Bo said, slapping him on the shoulder. He stepped out of the truck and looked back at Booker T., who'd rolled the window down. "Thanks for coming."

"Don't take this case, Bo," Booker T. pleaded. "I don't want to have to be bailing your ass out of trouble every night."

"Seems to me that you got that backward, dog."

Booker T. guffawed and put his truck in reverse. Seconds later, the pickup lurched forward toward downtown. For a moment, Bo looked around the yard and then to the brick house that he'd bought this past November. For almost twenty years they'd lived on Flower Street, just three blocks away. Lila had hoped that they could buy their old house back, but that wasn't possible.

This is best anyway, Bo thought, sticking his hands in his pockets and gazing past the houses and trees to downtown Pulaski. He could see the top of the Giles County Courthouse, which was partially lit by streetlights and the full moon above. As with his old house, Bo could walk to court or to his office, which was a block from the courthouse, if he so desired.

Bo was grateful for the new beginning that coming back to Pulaski had offered him and his family. But as he trotted up the steps to the house and took a last look back at the courthouse, he felt an ominous vibe in his bones. The murder of Brittany Crutcher was one of the worst crimes he'd ever heard of in Pulaski, and there'd been a few in his lifetime. And if Odell Champagne was charged . . .

Bo took in a deep breath and exhaled, watching his breath turn into smoke in front of him. The case would garner national media attention, given the celebrity status of the victim and the athletic notoriety of the defendant.

A damn circus. Did he really want to be a part of it? Was it fair to T. J. and Lila to put them through another controversial case? So far, their transition back to Pulaski had been smooth, but this case could make for rougher waters. T. J. was already involved as a potential witness.

He didn't want to think about it anymore, at least not tonight. As he took a last look at downtown Pulaski, Bo couldn't help but feel sorry for his snakebit hometown, which could never seem to rise out from under the shadow of its painful history. Most of all, though, as he stepped over the threshold and peered up the stairs to where his kids were getting ready for bed, he felt terrible for Israel and Theresa Crutcher. Bo figured that the loss of a child would be the worst pain a person could ever endure.

He shut the door and leaned his back against it. Closing his eyes, he said a silent prayer for the Crutcher family.

Then he thanked God for his own children. And for the new life they'd made.

Please, Lord . . . don't let me screw this up.

25

Israel Crutcher sat in a plastic chaise longue chair and gazed up at the full moon. He held a half-drunk pint of Jim Beam in his hand and brought the bottle slowly to his lips, taking a long sip and closing his eyes as the bourbon burned his throat going down. Despite the cold of the night, he felt hot. Feverish.

He still wore the scrubs he'd donned that morning. He was slated to be the on-call nurse anesthetist for the weekend and had wanted to be ready if he were needed. Truthfully, he hadn't wanted to think about what he was going to wear. He didn't want to think at all.

But the only communication that came from the hospital was from the director of surgery, Peg Morton, who'd told Israel that he'd been replaced for the weekend and given a week's furlough to grieve the loss of his daughter. He'd argued with her, saying he hadn't asked for any time off, but Peg wouldn't budge. Lives were at stake every time a surgery was done, and the complications of anesthesia could be fatal. "You need a break, Israel. We are all devastated by Brittany's death, and we know you are too. And with everything else you've had going on . . ."

She hadn't completed the thought, and Israel hadn't pushed her. He knew his life had been a hot mess for the past few months, and Pulaski was a small town. The surgery suite was its own little Peyton Place too.

Israel took another sip of bourbon and moved his eyes around the hotel pool. The Comfort Inn on College Street would never be confused with the Ritz-Carlton, but it was comfortable and clean. He'd been a guest here since the Fourth of July. Since *the incident*, as Theresa called it. He had thought things would blow over in the days and weeks that followed.

They hadn't.

Israel felt his eyes begin to burn with fresh tears, but he made no move to wipe them. He wasn't a crier and despised any type of weakness or vulnerability. He liked to be in control. It was what had drawn him to anesthesia. The doctor did the surgery, but nothing worked if anesthesia wasn't properly induced and monitored. The whole operation was at the mercy of the CRNA, who really had more control than the anesthesiologist, who acted primarily as a supervisor during the procedure.

But control was fleeting and unattainable when it came to people and families. Free will was a bitch, and Israel, after directing his daughter's singing career since she was nine years old, had found himself being replaced, first by that street-smart barmaid down at Kathy's Tavern and then by someone much more dangerous.

Israel had felt Brittany was going through a stage. She was headstrong and stubborn but not stupid. She would see that she couldn't trust the new people in her life.

But patience was never Israel Crutcher's greatest virtue, and he'd lost all sense of it this past Independence Day.

And now I'm here, he thought, taking a long pull on the bottle.

And Brittany's gone.

———

After finishing off the pint, Israel trudged back to his room on the second floor, taking the stairs to avoid any contact with people. He slid his card in the slot and stepped into the small space before taking a seat on the bed. He grabbed his phone, which he'd purposely left on the nightstand so that he could sit by the pool in peace. How long had he been down there? An hour? Two? He had lost all track of time. The day, just as every second had been since learning of Brittany's death, had been a blur.

He gazed at the screen and sighed. Fifteen text messages. Two missed calls. Most of the messages were from friends at the church, though there was one from Theresa, reminding him about their meeting with Pastor Coy in the morning to go over the details for Monday's funeral. There was also a message from Gina, who said she missed him and added a dagger of a request. Please come home, Daddy. Please. Momma is about to break. She needs you. We all do. Especially now. His youngest was far more comfy expressing her emotions with a text than in person, and he was touched by her concern.

Israel felt heat behind his eyelids, but he typed his reply as if on autopilot. I wish I could baby girl. It was the same response he'd given Gina every time she'd asked him to come home.

The first missed call was from a number he didn't recognize. *Probably a solicitor.* The second was from his friend Booker T. Rowe. Booker T. had also left a text, asking if he needed anything. Israel didn't respond to either. Everyone asked if there was anything he needed, but there wasn't.

All I need . . . all I want is Brittany back. Ain't nobody gonna do that for me.

He squeezed his eyes closed and saw Brittany as he'd seen her last night at the Brickyard. Owning the stage as she always had.

Everyone said the sky was the limit. That she'd win a Grammy before it was all said and done. But for Israel, especially now, it was hard for him not to picture the ten-year-old girl who seemed to smile brightest when she had her father's approval. Her first singing competition had been a southeastern regional talent contest in Huntsville, Alabama. All of the kids had, for the most part, sung old traditional numbers. Slow songs that were either uplifting, sad, or both. His Brittany had belted out "Listen to the Music," by the Doobie Brothers, and had run away with first prize, the audience bowled over. He and Brittany had

Robert Bailey

celebrated by sharing a pizza and root beers at the Mellow Mushroom. They'd both been so happy. Israel could never have imagined a universe where he wasn't close with his daughter.

Fresh tears streamed down Israel's cheeks. After the concert last night, he'd gone down to the field to speak to her while she and the band were putting up their gear. All he'd wanted was to tell her how well they'd played. But when he tapped her shoulder, she turned and peered at him with eyes dripping with disdain. "What do you want?" she said.

Israel almost flinched from the coldness in her tone and demeanor. "You were great," he managed.

"Thanks," she said and then went back to putting her guitar in its case, ignoring him. If there was any shred of the little girl who'd had pizza and root beer with him as a ten-year-old—the girl who'd talked to him as if he were the only person in the world—it was gone.

Israel had felt anger then, as he did even now. In his hotel room, not even a full day removed from his daughter's murder, and he was still mad about the slight. The disrespect.

There had been more, but Israel couldn't remember, only that his last words to his daughter had been spoken in haste and anger.

Israel placed his elbows on his knees and rubbed his face hard with both hands. Then he shot off the bed and began to pace the confines of the small hotel room, his heartbeat racing. He'd hoped the pint of bourbon would relax his nerves, but the liquor had only seemed to amp him up more.

Finally, he went to his suitcase and felt underneath the underwear and socks until his hand wrapped around the cold steel of the pistol. He took out the weapon and walked back to the bed. He checked the chamber and confirmed that it was loaded. He cocked the gun and put the barrel into his mouth.

This is what I deserve . . .

Israel gazed at his reflection in the mirror across the room. *Do it,* he told himself. *Do it.*

124

Three hard knocks on the door jarred him. His finger continued to hover on the trigger. *Just do it.*

He blinked his eyes and again peered at himself in the mirror.

Three more hard knocks. Then a female voice. "Israel? You in there?"

Theresa.

"Damnit," Israel whispered, his finger still on the trigger. *Do it,* he told himself again.

"Israel!"

He stood and glared at himself in the mirror. Then he placed the handgun in the bottom drawer of the nightstand and walked on unsteady legs to the door. He turned the handle and saw his wife of thirty-two years. Her eyes were red from crying, but her voice was strong, firm.

"They need us down at the sheriff's office."

Israel tried to speak, but his heartbeat was racing. He leaned his elbow against the opening, thinking about what he had almost done, the metallic taste of the handgun still in his mouth.

"Israel, what's going on?"

He walked back into the room and sat on the bed, taking several deep breaths.

"Have you been drinking?"

He folded his arms tight around his chest. He'd been so close to shooting himself, to stopping the pain.

"Israel, talk to me."

He let out a long breath and blinked, trying to focus. "Wh-why do they need us?" he managed.

"They want to update us on the investigation."

"Have they charged that thug yet?"

"I don't know. They just want to talk with us. I tried to call, but you weren't answering the phone, and you didn't respond to any of my texts. What have you been doing?"

Israel gazed down at the carpeted floor and rubbed his eyes.

"From the smell of things, I'd say you've been drinking."

"Theresa—"

"I'm not going to fuss. I'm done fussing at you. But Frannie wants us down at the station, and I'm on the way. I thought you'd want to be a part of it."

Feeling slightly more with it, Israel managed a nod. "How many times did I warn her about that that boy?"

"Just get ready," Theresa said. "That talk doesn't help . . . even if you were right. Looks like there's a pot of coffee going in the lobby. I'll get you a cup."

"Theresa—"

She was already walking away.

Israel closed the door and went into the bathroom. After splashing some water on his face and brushing his teeth, he thought he looked presentable. Before leaving the room, he took the gun and returned it to his suitcase, again hiding the weapon under some of his clothes.

He looked around the prison cell of a room, which had been his home the past three and a half months. *Odell Champagne,* he thought, remembering his cautionary warning to his daughter. *You're better than him, Brittany. He's trouble, and getting wrapped up with him will bring trouble on you.*

But none of his advice took. He felt another wave of anger roll through him, but then he sighed in disgust. It didn't matter.

Nothing mattered anymore.

26

At 10:30 p.m., Frannie Storm sat across a large mahogany desk from Sheriff Hank Springfield. They were in his office, having just adjourned their meeting with the Crutchers.

"So how do you think they took everything?" Hank asked, rubbing his bloodshot eyes.

"There're still in shock," Frannie said. "As you would expect family members to be with a crime like this."

"They barely said a word. To us or each other."

"They're devastated. Neither of them can believe their daughter is gone or that a universe exists where their child could be taken from them in such a horrific way."

Hank took a sip of coffee from a Styrofoam cup. "I agree, but I sensed something else was going on. The deputies that searched the Crutchers' home said that there was no sign of Israel living there. You know them pretty well, don't you?"

"All my life," Frannie said.

"Well, are they separated?"

"I don't know. I go to Bickland Creek Baptist Church and have since I was a little girl. The Crutchers have been members as long as I can remember. Theresa and the two girls would attend every Sunday, and Brittany sang in the choir. Israel rarely came with them. I didn't think much of that because Israel is a CRNA at the hospital and has always worked long hours. He obviously wouldn't be the only spouse who stayed at home while the other went to church."

Hank folded his hands into a tent and peered at them. "Did you catch a whiff of the smell coming off him?"

"Alcohol of some kind."

"Bourbon," Hank said. "And by the look of his eyes, he'd had quite a bit."

"He's in mourning, Hank. How would you react if something like this happened to one of your girls?" Frannie knew that Hank had three daughters, the oldest being sixteen, but she immediately regretted the comment when she saw his eyes widen as if he'd been slapped. "Look, I'm sorry." She stood and walked over to the window of the office. She was exhausted, having worked nonstop with little rest since the discovery of the body.

She was also irritated. *Where the hell is the General?*

Since attending the autopsy with Frannie, Hank, and Melvin Ragland that afternoon, Helen had vanished. Frannie had wanted her to be there for the meeting with the family. She'd also hoped to go over the evidence again with her before shutting down for the day. Plus they were still waiting on the coroner's final report; Melvin had said he'd be finished with it late tonight or first thing in the morning. In a case of this magnitude, Helen typically liked to jump in early.

But the General had left the sheriff's office immediately after the autopsy and hadn't checked back in.

"Frannie, you OK?"

She looked over her shoulder at the sheriff, who was peering at her with concern. "Yeah, Hank. This case hits close to home. Like I said, I've known the Crutchers my whole life. I watched Brittany grow up." She hesitated. "And the General doesn't seem engaged. She should be here."

"She's been through a lot in the last year, and this is her first murder case since . . ." He trailed off.

"I know all that, but it's not good enough," Frannie said. "Not for me and certainly not for the Crutchers."

"She's a lot more involved than most prosecutors. When I worked in the Nashville PD, it was rare for a prosecutor to get involved at all until after the arrest. The General has spoiled us with her attention to detail all these years. Maybe she's decided to take a step back and let us do our jobs."

"Maybe," Frannie said, closing her eyes and leaning her forehead against the cold glass of the window. *But I'm not buying it.*

27

On the second floor of the Giles County Courthouse, the lights were on in the circuit courtroom. Helen Lewis sat in the back row of the jury box, shoes off, holding Deputy Ty Dodgen's summary of Brittany Crutcher's cell phone usage in her hand. She'd already read the report several times and still couldn't believe it.

Helen rarely worked on Saturdays. It was her one free day of the week. Before being charged with the murder of her ex-husband last year, she'd liked to spend Saturdays shooting her various guns at Doug Brinkley's range. Though she still did that on occasion, the stress relief that she used to get from shooting was gone now. In truth, every time she pulled the trigger, she saw Butch's face in her mind.

She pushed off her seat, gazing across the courtroom at the witness chair, which, in the historic Giles County Circuit Courtroom, faced the jury head-on. Then to her right, where she had prosecuted cases against alleged criminals for over twenty years on behalf of the state of Tennessee. Finally, she moved her eyes to the defense table, where she'd sat almost a year ago.

It was an unenviable position, being the defendant in a murder trial. And if she had to guess, Odell Champagne was about to be in this seat very soon. Based on Dodgen's cell phone summary, the last person Brittany had texted was Odell, saying that she was at the bus yard and wanted him to meet her. Odell Champagne, who was mad at Brittany for breaking up with him, telling T. J. Haynes that he wasn't going to let her get away with it. Odell, whose fingerprints were the only ones identified on the broken beer bottle at the scene and who had been found a tenth of a mile from the body.

At the autopsy, coroner Melvin Ragland had said that the cause of death was clearly a blunt force trauma to the forehead, which fractured the victim's skull. His preliminary opinion was that the beer bottle was the instrument used but that he would have a final report to them soon. Certainly the base of the bottle was hard and blunt enough to have done the deed.

Assuming the bottle was the murder weapon, Odell became the perfect suspect.

"Motive, means, and opportunity," Helen whispered. "Jealous boyfriend kills his ex in a fit of rage," she continued, walking around the jury box and into the well of the courtroom, gazing back at the twelve chairs as she would if she were giving her opening statement.

She could prove this case. There wasn't a doubt in her mind. And based on the texts she'd received from Frannie Storm, the pressure was mounting for the department to make an arrest. When it did, Odell would need a lawyer.

Would Bo defend him? She wasn't sure. He'd told her that he was done with criminal work after her case, but it would be hard for him to turn away from Odell. If Bo didn't represent the kid, who would? It was doubtful that Odell or his mother could afford a good attorney, and an appointed counsel would be no match for Helen.

She gazed at the burgundy curtains that covered the windows, which had always made the courtroom feel like its own opera house or theater. What a drama it had been last fall when she'd stood for the jury's verdict and the foreman had looked at her and said, "Not guilty."

"Karma is a bitch," Helen said out loud, knowing that your past decisions always caught up to you. Most of hers had last year, and she was still paying for them.

How can I prosecute anyone for murder when I'm a murderer myself?

It was one of the many questions that had dogged her since reelection. And it was probably why she'd shied away from trial dockets, letting Gloria do most of the heavy lifting. She'd told her assistant that she was training her to eventually take the mantle. Helen knew that with her endorsement, Gloria would have a strong chance to win the job in the next election cycle. Helen couldn't be the district attorney general forever, and she wanted Gloria to be ready when it was time to pass the torch.

Maybe it's time now . . .

Helen walked down one of the aisles, peering up at the ancient balcony. Outside on the streets of downtown Pulaski, the honk of a car horn startled her, followed by several other horns. Helen blinked and collapsed into one of the spectator chairs. She felt restless, uneasy, as if she could hear a clock ticking out the time she had left in her job.

Karma is a bitch, she thought once more. Then, hoping that perhaps the information would change, she again peered down at the piece of paper she was holding. While Odell's texts certainly set up the scene for why he should be charged, there was something else in Brittany's cell phone usage that Helen couldn't get around. Something that caused a chill to hide in her heart. While Odell's name appeared frequently in her call and text log, another name appeared more. In fact, outside of Odell and a group text with the band, there was only one other person Brittany had communicated with on her iPhone in the twenty-four hours before she died. Six calls ranging in time from ninety seconds to ten minutes along with ten text messages, the last one coming at 11:17 p.m. on Friday.

Helen ran her fingers over the name and the number that had called her as well quite a few times in the last eleven months.

"Michael," she whispered, shutting her eyes and feeling the walls of her life beginning to close in on her.

28

Bo tried to go to sleep, but it was useless. His mind raced with questions about Brittany's murder and whether he should represent Odell.

He'd texted Frannie before getting in bed. She'd said that Sabrina Champagne was in the ER with the expectation that she would be admitted to the detox unit. She'd thanked him again for his help, and he'd decided to ask what was on his mind. Has Odell been charged?

No, but I'll let you know when he is, had been her cryptic response, *when* being the operative word.

Bo finally gave up on sleep at four thirty in the morning. He checked on the kids, making sure they were still asleep, and let Lee Roy out to use the bathroom. Then, after putting on some sweats and sneakers, he headed out the door, locking it behind him.

The air was cold and crisp as he began to walk briskly up Jefferson Street. The sun had yet to begin its ascent, and the only illumination came from a few lamp poles and the occasional house light. After about a half mile of walking, Bo stretched his legs and began to jog.

As his feet clapped against the pavement, Bo thought about Odell. The kid had been in Pulaski all of six months. During that short time frame, Bo had taken a genuine liking to him. Odell did remind Bo of himself, as Booker T. had said. Bo had grown up without parents, raised by his aunt and uncle, and he sympathized with Odell's plight. That was why he'd offered him work on the weekends at the farm and, from time to time, advice on how to deal with his mother's alcoholism and drug problems. *You can't fix her, son. All you can do is love her. But you don't owe it to your mother to drown with her.*

He'd been a mentor to the kid, and now Odell needed him. *My kids need me too,* Bo thought. Sometimes, he knew, doing the right thing was difficult to figure out. Booker T. had said he was going to be on the wrong side of things if he took Odell's case, but what was the right side?

As he reached Eighth Street and ran past Exchange Park, where T. J. had played Little League baseball, Bo thought back to his time in the attorney consultation room with Odell. Had Bo believed him?

He still wasn't ready to answer that question. When the school bus yard came into view, he slowed his pace. Gazing out over the place, he squinted and saw the yellow crime tape that surrounded a bus on the south side of the yard. Bo stopped and took in from afar the site where Brittany's body had been discovered almost twenty-four hours ago. Questions flooded his brain.

Was she killed here?

Or was the body moved here after the murder?

Why here? Why would someone dispose of a dead body on a school bus? Was there a message?

Bo stopped and placed his hands on his hips, moving his eyes over the yard. Though there was a light above the garage, it didn't cast much of a glow. Bo doubted that any passersby would have been able to see anything at this time of day, much less earlier in the night. And if the garage had any video cameras, he doubted they would reach the south end of the yard, where the body had been found.

Were these details planned out by the killer? Or were they just pieces of luck? Perhaps there was a video that Bo wasn't aware of that did show something. Bo glanced to the south toward College Street and saw the traffic light. He knew traffic signals had video cameras, and he suspected the prosecution would get them.

The defense attorney for Odell would want to see those too.

There was also a strip mall kitty-corner to the bus yard that might have video possibilities. Bo wondered if the sheriff's office had requested those yet.

He forced his feet to move and picked up his pace to run up the hill on Madison Street, passing the dormitories and school buildings of Martin Methodist College. Bo saw a male student exiting one of the residential houses carrying an athletic bag over his shoulder. The student was Black. Behind the young man, two other men exited the same house, both white, both carrying gym bags. Bo waved at them, and they returned the gesture. This was the Pulaski that nobody saw but those who lived here. For nonresidents, Pulaski meant only one thing.

He slowed his pace when he reached downtown and stopped when he came to a plaque attached to a nondescript brick building on Madison Street. On Christmas Eve, 1865, six Confederate soldiers had formed what, according to the legend, was originally supposed to be a "social club" in an upstairs room of this building. The marker that commemorated the founding of the Ku Klux Klan had been turned backward in the early '90s by the building's owners, who had tired of all the nuts who liked to come to Pulaski to pay homage to the "founding fathers" of the world's foremost hate group. Now all a person could see was a black-and-green slab.

Many times in his life, Bo had gravitated toward this archaic reminder of Pulaski's tragic roots. In times of sadness and even after a victory, the tablet served as a reminder that his work wasn't done. That the quest for justice was never over. It was constant. Unmerciful. Steady as November rain and as unrelenting as a dog after a bone.

Wide ass open, Bo thought, shifting his gaze from the plaque to the Giles County Courthouse. The sun had finally begun to rise, and the golden dome on top of the architectural marvel of a building shone bright.

Bocephus Haynes wasn't a history buff per se, but his late wife had been. Jazz had watched the History Channel every night, and she had agreed with the adage that history oftentimes repeated itself.

As Bo thought about his own trial for murder, and the impending case being brought against Odell Champagne, he wondered if it was about to happen again. Was Odell's criminal background going to cloud the judgment of the sheriff's office and eventually a jury? Bo knew the kid had made mistakes in Town Creek, but look at the heartache Odell had endured to get to where he was. He was on the brink of signing a major college scholarship. One of the best running backs in the whole country. Would he really have thrown it all away because a girl broke up with him? Odell obviously loved Brittany. Was it possible that he killed her in cold blood?

Do I believe him?

The murder of Brittany Crutcher was counter to everything Bo knew about the recent history of Odell Champagne. *He was trying to make a new life . . .*

He turned his gaze away from the courthouse in the direction of his new house. *Like me,* Bo thought. He sighed, knowing that regardless of how you sliced it, race would again be at the forefront of another tragedy in Giles County. Could a Black man get a fair trial in Pulaski? The charges against Bo for the murder of Andy Walton had been dismissed before a jury actually had to make a decision.

Would I have won if my case had gone the distance?

But this case would be even more complicated, because Brittany, the victim, was a Black woman. Bo knew that, historically, the lives of Black women had been undervalued by the legal system. How many perpetrators, white and Black alike, had gotten off with a lighter sentence for a brutal crime against a Black female? He thought of the movie *A Time to Kill,* based on the novel by John Grisham. In Jake Brigance's closing argument, he asked the jury to imagine the Black teenage victim as being white in order to get their full attention. The scene had made

Bo mad, as why would a white life matter more than a Black person's? But to a mostly white jury in the Deep South, this was a sad reality. When Bo had mentioned Odell's position as a teenager with a future to Frannie yesterday, she'd rightfully called him on the hypocrisy of his words. *Brittany had a future too . . .*

She was also a celebrity, which was the final and perhaps largest complication of all. Bo had seen at least a dozen news articles online that night detailing her trip to the finals of *America's Got Talent* last year, the prominence of Fizz, and its first big song. And of course, Brittany's murder and various possibilities for who did it, all mentioning that her boyfriend, football star Odell Champagne, was being held in custody. Most of those articles mentioned Odell's expulsion from Town Creek High and his prior convictions for theft.

Bo took in a deep breath and exhaled, watching his air turn into smoke and rise into the morning sky. He peered again at the blank slab, behind which were words celebrating an organization that perpetuated hate crimes against Black people. Then his eyes drifted up to the historic courthouse, and he thought of the circuit courtroom with its balcony that had once been reserved for "colored" people.

Could a person ever escape the past? Bo lowered his eyes again to the green-and-black slab.

Could a town ever be fully clean from the stink of its sins?

29

When Frannie arrived at the sheriff's office at seven o'clock Sunday morning, she had to fight through a troop of reporters to get to the entrance.

"Chief, has an arrest been made? Will Odell Champagne be charged with Brittany Crutcher's murder?"

"If Champagne is arrested, how will that affect his standing for next week's game against Marshall County?"

"Is it true that Brittany Crutcher had signed a solo recording deal with a major record label?"

"We're hearing rumors of a press conference this afternoon. Can you confirm the time?"

Frannie pushed through the entrance and walked with purpose down the hallway, noticing that Sheriff Springfield had a throng of people in his office, including the mayor of Pulaski, Dan Kilgore; a couple of county commissioners; and recently appointed city attorney Reginald "Sack" Glover. Frannie tried to control her breathing. She hadn't slept much last night, but the interaction with the press and seeing the brass of the town all in Hank's office had fired up her tank of adrenaline.

When she stepped inside the investigative war room, county coroner Melvin Ragland was waiting for her. The coroner was a thin man who, regardless of the weather, always wore a short-sleeve white button-down shirt, clip-on tie, khaki pants, and brown penny loafers. He had on an ancient brown sports coat with patches at the elbows. Two pens rested in his shirt pocket.

"Blunt force trauma to the front of the skull," Melvin said, sliding several stapled sheets of paper across the conference room table. "Time of death between one a.m. and three a.m. Saturday morning."

Frannie took the report and began to flip through the pages. Subconsciously, she grabbed her phone to buzz the sheriff but then remembered the mob of folks in his office. "Damnit, Hank," she whispered.

"When I got here, he was with the mayor and the other dignitaries," Melvin said.

"I know." Frannie groaned. The pressure was officially beginning to mount.

"Coach Patterson was here earlier too."

"What was he doing?" Frannie snapped.

"Don't shoot me," Melvin said, holding up his palms. "Just the messenger. But I imagine he's wondering if his star player is going to be able to practice this week. They play at Marshall County this Friday."

Frannie ground her teeth and tried not to react. One of the press horde had asked about Odell's status for the football game too. It boggled her mind that a female student was dead and football was actually a concern in anyone's mind. Alas, this was Tennessee. *Friday Night Lights* wasn't only a Texas thing. "Has Hank seen this report?"

Melvin nodded.

Frannie took a seat at the table. "You told us after the autopsy that you believed that the beer bottle was likely the blunt instrument that proximately caused the victim's death. Is that still your opinion?"

He nodded again. "Yes, it is. After further examining the hematoma to the victim's head and the resulting internal and external damage to the bones in her skull, I'm even more convinced that the beer bottle was the object utilized to cause the damage. Additionally, there were tiny fragments of glass found in the victim's eyebrows, hair, and T-shirt, which would appear to be an exact match for the glass of the beer bottle, as were the specks of glass found on the floor of the bus. Obviously, we'll want confirmation from the crime lab that the blood and other DNA on the Bud Light bottle is a match for the victim, but I can't imagine it not being so." He paused and, as he'd done so many times in front of a jury, delivered his opinion with firm conviction. "My opinion is that the broken bottle is the weapon that proximately caused Brittany Crutcher's death."

Frannie stared up at the ceiling. "Odell Champagne, in a fit of rage at being dumped by his girlfriend, hit her over the head with a beer bottle, shattering the glass . . . fracturing her skull." She paused, and her voice shook with emotion and fatigue. "Extinguishing one of Pulaski's brightest lights."

"You're the investigator," Melvin said, "but that would certainly be my conclusion."

30

Helen parked in her reserved spot at the Giles County Sheriff's Office and pushed through a sea of cameras. As Helen walked inside, a familiar and unwelcome visitor greeted her.

"Well, hello, General." Sack Glover smiled at her, showing all of his bleached white teeth. He wore a charcoal suit, his thick red hair sporting a fresh sheen of gel, no follicle out of place. How in the hell the powers that be selected this snake in the grass to be the town's city attorney she would never know. She'd thought Sack's political days were numbered after he unsuccessfully served as interim district attorney general for her trial last year, but the bastard was a survivor. When Sam Fees stepped down, Sack, as usual, knew the right people and slipped into the job.

"Sack," Helen said. "Enjoying the drama?"

"Terrible situation," he said, his frown so obviously fake that Helen wanted to slap him.

"I'm sure you're here making everything better."

He looked past her for a second at the gathering media storm. The look of excitement in his eyes was unmistakable. More than anything, Sack Glover loved the camera. "We need to make an arrest, General. The Crutcher family deserves justice." He paused and nodded toward the entrance. "And the public's watching. I don't want Pulaski to be dragged into any more bad publicity. We had enough of that last year with your trial."

"You mean your handling of it?"

He crossed his arms. Before he could say anything else, Helen stepped forward, violating his personal space.

"And what do you mean, *we*? You aren't in the sheriff's office, and you damn sure aren't in mine."

"Pulaski, General. I represent this town, and I don't want to see it get a black eye. With Hoshima bringing new jobs, everything was going so well. And Brittany Crutcher was going to make us famous all over the world for being something besides the birthplace of the Klan. She'd already started to make her mark last year with the *AGT* show, but signing with a major record label was going to take her all the way."

"You know about that."

"The sheriff was kind enough to share a few facts. We're holding a press conference this afternoon at three. An hour before the visitation. I told him that it would sure be nice if we could announce that Odell Champagne had been charged with Brittany's murder."

"That sure he did it, are you?"

"Aren't you? Prints on the murder weapon, found near the body, and she'd just broken up with him. Why, that would be a slam dunk for any prosecutor, much less the by-God General herself."

"Glad you think so," Helen said, pushing past him. Sack was so smarmy that she felt like she'd been doused with slime just being around him for a few minutes.

"I'd like to work together with you on this one, Helen," Sack said, walking along beside her. "Hank has invited me and Dan to the press conference."

Helen's fuse was about to blow. "Great. Glad to know our murder investigation is getting the full three-ring treatment."

Sack frowned. "Why do you hate me so bad, General?"

Helen couldn't resist. "Because you're the one thing in life that I detest more than anything else."

He smirked. "And what's that?"

"A dumbass," Helen said. "A most remarkable dumbass."

142

———

Helen had barely opened the door to the war room before she started letting them all have it. "Why in the unmerciful hell did you think it was a good idea to involve Sack Glover in my investigation?" She glared at Hank and then Frannie. "Are you both too stupid to breathe?"

Frannie returned Helen's glare with one of her own, letting her know who the culprit was. Helen walked toward Hank, who was sitting at the end of the conference table, and stuck her index finger in his chest. "Have you lost your ever-loving mind?"

Hank Springfield's face turned cherry red, but he managed to keep his voice under control. "General, do you realize the scrutiny this case has gotten? The producer of the damn *America's Got Talent* show called me last night. Somehow got my cell phone and wanted a damn update. They're doing a tribute to Brittany on their social media pages. The front desk has messages from CNN, Fox News, and every local news outlet in the state of Tennessee. Did you see the cavalry outside?"

"Yeah, Hank, I saw. Dealing with the media is part of the job. Don't you remember the Andy Walton murder case five years ago? But one thing we don't do is invite more craziness. By letting Sack Glover be a part of this, you've invited Barnum and Bailey to the circus. It was dumb, and we don't have the time or energy for dumb. Got it?"

"General . . ." Hank's voice trailed off, and he turned away from her. "I don't know what to do. On one hand, I've got Coach Patterson and the football boosters on my ass to let Odell out if we aren't going to charge him, and on the other, I've got the mayor, the county commission, and the city attorney breathing down my neck to arrest the kid."

"And we don't make decisions in this office or in mine based on any of that bullshit." She looked around the room, where Frannie and Deputies Dodgen and McCann were standing at rapt attention. "We make decisions in here based on the evidence and only the evidence. Does everyone understand that?"

"Yes, ma'am," Frannie said.

"Yes, General," Dodgen said.

"Yes 'um," McCann added.

"Hank?"

The sheriff let out a long sigh and turned back to her. "General, the evidence screams that Odell Champagne is guilty of murdering Brittany Crutcher."

Helen thought of the cell phone call summary she'd reviewed last night in the circuit courtroom. *Karma,* she thought again. "I agree," she finally said. "Melvin emailed me his autopsy report, and based on that combined with the prints from the broken bottle and bus, we have more than enough to charge him." She turned to Frannie. "Chief, you're being awful quiet."

"I think we should wait," Frannie said. "The last high-profile case we were all involved in we may have charged too soon." She locked eyes with Helen, who was touched by the concession but also anguished.

You had it right, Frannie, she thought.

"Wait for what?" Hank asked.

"We haven't finished all of our fingerprint analysis, and we haven't scratched the surface of interviewing all of the victim's friends and teachers. We also need to complete our search of her home and put together a complete timeline of everywhere Brittany went last Friday night and Saturday morning."

"Frannie, none of that's going to change what we already know," Hank said.

"What about the phone records then?" Frannie challenged. "I'm sure you've all figured out who Brittany was talking to a lot the day she died."

"Zannick was her manager," Deputy Dodgen said. "I fielded a call last night from a lady named Joanie Newburg with the ELEKTRIK HI record label in Los Angeles. She'd flown down for a meeting with Brittany and Michael Zannick on Friday at his Z Bank office. When Newburg arrived back in LA, she learned of Brittany's death. She was reaching out for information, as she'd heard nothing yet from Zannick."

"So he obviously had reasons to be communicating with her," Hank added.

"At eleven o'clock at night?" Frannie asked.

"She'd finished her concert with Fizz at the Brickyard. Might have just been checking in," McCann chimed in.

"He checked in a lot that day."

"What are you getting at, Frannie? Do you honestly think Zannick could have killed her?" Hank asked.

"I don't know," Frannie said. "But this office charged Zannick with the rape of a teenage girl last year. Any defense lawyer up to snuff, and especially one as talented as Bocephus Haynes, is going to seize on any connection between Brittany and Zannick."

"She's right," Helen said, trying to play her role, but her insides were churning. *Karma.*

"The rape charges against Zannick were dropped by *your* office, Helen," Hank said. "Do we really want to fight another losing battle against that millionaire?"

Despite her anxiety, Helen felt anger engulf her at the sheriff's response. "Hank, this isn't about winning and losing. It's about justice for Brittany Crutcher. You understand that, don't you?"

"Yes, General, I do. But the clock is ticking." He glanced at Frannie. "Chief, unless something changes dramatically, I plan to charge Odell Champagne this afternoon and will make the announcement at three p.m."

"Nice to know you're taking your orders from Sack Glover," Helen said.

"I don't take orders from anyone," Hank said. "But in this case, I think Sack and Mayor Kilgore are right. We have to fish or cut bait, and we all agree that Champagne is guilty." He slapped the table with his hands and stood. "We're done here," he said, walking toward the door. "General." He looked at Helen. "Chief." He turned to Frannie. "I expect you both to be at the press conference."

145

31

Odell awoke to the sound of the cell door swooshing open. He was lying on his cot adjacent to the small table. A man walked into the cell followed by the female cop from earlier. Odell recognized the man from news stories on television and online. *The sheriff*...

"Mr. Odell Jerome Champagne," the man said.

"Yes, sir." He sat up on the cot.

"My name is Hank Springfield, and I'm the sheriff of Giles County." He glanced at the lady officer, who continued to look at Odell. "It is my duty under the laws of the state of Tennessee to place you under arrest for the murder of Brittany Crutcher. You have the right to remain silent..."

Odell didn't hear any of the rest. He put his face in his hands and began to weep. In his mind, all he could see was the corridor of the bus. How angry he'd been. And then...

... *Brittany.*

32

Bo was at the Curry Center when the call came through. He was lifting weights with T. J. while Lila ran on the treadmill.

"We just charged him," Frannie said on the line, pausing for a split second. "First-degree murder."

Bo closed his eyes and then opened them. "That sure seems quick. I didn't think a charge would be made until at least Monday or Tuesday."

Silence on the other end. Did she agree, or was she keeping things close to the vest? Either way, Bo figured Frannie was smart not to say too much.

"Thanks for the heads-up, Frannie."

"There's a press conference at three to announce the news."

Bo felt a tingle of anger run through him. "Big event for the department. Showing everyone you've got your man."

"The press is all over us, Bo. We were going to have to present some kind of communication to the media today."

"Much better to announce success than say you're still investigating the crime."

"No comment."

"You really think Odell killed her?"

More silence and then a tired sigh. "Yes, I do."

———

Frannie clicked the phone dead and walked down the hallway of the department to the front window. She saw the microphones being set up, and Sack Glover was already there, granting solo interviews to several reporters. She thought about Bo's question. *Do I really believe Odell killed Brittany?*

She felt a growing depression consume her. What she believed was that the General could prove Odell's guilt in front of a jury. Regardless of whether Bo Haynes appeared for Odell, Frannie believed that the General would win. The evidence was too strong.

But that's still not an answer to the question . . . What had the General herself said? It wasn't about winning and losing. It was about justice for Brittany Crutcher's family.

Are we doing that? she wondered, as a growing horde of media gathered in front of the microphones.

"Ready?" Hank asked as he took his place beside her.

She tried to keep the melancholy out of her voice. "Ready."

33

Bo, T. J., and Lila got home from the gym a few minutes before three. The kids wanted to see the press conference, too, so they all stood in front of the TV on the back porch, waiting. On the screen, the Tennessee Titans were locked in a tight game with the Cleveland Browns. As Marcus Mariota, the quarterback for the Titans, dropped back to pass, the screen switched from the ball game to a local reporter. A young woman spoke directly to the camera.

"We have breaking news from the Giles County Sheriff's Office regarding the murder of local singing sensation Brittany Crutcher. Sheriff Springfield has called a press conference, which we'll take you to now." The screen then shifted to the front of a building, where several people stood side by side next to a microphone. Bo knew them all and felt a rush of adrenaline at the spectacle of seeing both the mayor and city attorney, Sack Glover, sharing the podium with the sheriff, Frannie, and the General.

Sheriff Hank Springfield was a youthful-looking man of about forty years of age with clean-cut brown hair. Though Hank wasn't the sharpest tack in the box, Bo had always thought him honest and fair. Hank cleared his throat and spoke into the mike. "A few moments ago, my office charged the suspect we'd taken into custody with the murder of Brittany Crutcher. The defendant . . . is a name most people in this county will recognize." Hank paused. "Odell Jerome Champagne."

Bo shot his kids a glance. T. J. and Lila both stared wide eyed at the tube.

"Now," the sheriff continued, "Chief Storm is going to discuss our investigation and take a few questions."

Hank stepped back from the microphone, and Frannie took his place.

"Mr. Champagne was taken into custody shortly after we discovered the body of the victim. Based on our investigation, the evidence is clear that he's the perpetrator of this heinous crime." Frannie paused and moved her eyes around the media gathered in front of the microphone. "At this time, we cannot reveal any details, but I'm happy to take a couple of questions." She pointed to a reporter who couldn't be seen on camera.

"Chief, is there any evidence of motive?"

Frannie's face remained stoic and calm, giving away nothing. As Bo watched her through the television screen, he was impressed with her poise, her confidence. "As I've said, we cannot disclose any further details."

"What about Mr. Champagne's history?" a male voice asked. "He was expelled from his last school, wasn't he? Did that play a role in his arrest?"

"No," Frannie said. "It did not. The only facts that were considered were those that relate to this crime."

"Chief, Mr. Champagne is one of the best football players in the country. Will he be able to play while the case is pending?"

Frannie's eyes narrowed. "Mr. Champagne is being held without bond. That's my only response to that question."

"Chief, Brittany Crutcher was a beloved figure in this town. She and her band played the largest concert in Giles County history last Friday night. Can her killer get a fair trial in Pulaski?"

Frannie blinked and then glanced to her right. "My answer is, of course, yes, but I believe it would be instructive to hear from General Helen Lewis on this one. General?" She gestured with her hand, and the camera zeroed in on a woman with jet-black hair, black suit, and black heels.

The General is in full regalia, Bo thought. Taking slow and deliberate steps, she approached the microphone. "Yes, I believe that Mr. Champagne can and will get a fair trial in Giles County."

"General, is the state going to ask for the death penalty?"

Helen's eyes narrowed, but she didn't hesitate. "We haven't decided on the punishment we will seek, but, given the defendant's age and the facts in front of us now, I do not think capital punishment would be appropriate or allowed under the laws of the state of Tennessee." She paused. "Rest assured, however, that we will seek the highest punishment applicable. The victim and her family deserve justice."

"General, there are rumors that local attorney Bocephus Haynes was seen yesterday at the jail. Is Mr. Haynes the defendant's attorney, and if so, how will it be for you to prosecute a case against Mr. Haynes? He was, after all, your attorney in the murder case against you this past year."

"No attorney has made an appearance for Mr. Champagne," Helen said.

"Did you want to comment on the rest of the question?" the same reporter pressed.

"No."

"General, I notice that Mayor Kilgore and Mr. Sack Glover are here today. Can you comment on their presence?"

"No," Helen repeated, glancing at the mayor and the city attorney. "They can do that if they wish. I have no further comments at this time."

Bo couldn't contain his chuckle. *I bet the General hates this circus as much as I do.* Helen stepped away from the mike as more questions were hurled toward her.

"Was this a crime of passion?"

"Mr. Champagne was dating the victim, wasn't he?"

Sack Glover pushed his way to the podium and held out his palms. "To answer your question, the mayor and I are here as a simple show of support for the sheriff's office. We also want the Crutcher family to know that the whole town is behind them and wants justice for Brittany. This is a difficult time, and in times of crisis, a town has to be unified. Pulaski is—"

"Thank you, Mr. Glover," Frannie said, stepping in front of Sack and cutting him off. For a moment, it almost looked like the city attorney was going to object, but then he smiled and waved at the camera. "As the General said," Frannie said with a firm tone as she peered into the camera, "we're through answering questions today but will have regular briefings as the case moves forward. Thank you."

The television screen went blank for a second and then returned to Nissan Stadium in Nashville, where Titans tailback Derrick Henry took the handoff from Mariota and barreled up the middle for three yards. Neither Bo nor his kids paid any attention to the ball game.

Bo looked at Lila, who had tears in her eyes.

"Come here, honey," he said, wrapping his arms around her.

"This is so awful," she said. "I loved Brittany . . . but I can't believe Odell could have done this."

"I know," Bo said, moving his eyes to his son, who'd taken a seat in one of the rocking chairs with a blank look on his face.

"You OK?" Bo asked.

"I can't believe it," T. J. said. "I'm going to be a witness against my best friend."

Bo looked down at the floor. *And I may be his lawyer . . .*

34

What am I doing? Helen thought, leaning her head against the steering wheel and closing her eyes.

Since the press conference, she'd been driving the streets of Giles County, thinking through the case. *I should be at the station. Supervising everything and making damn sure nothing gets screwed up. Frannie is probably wondering where the hell I am.*

Her car had finally ended up here, on the edge of the highway in front of Michael Zannick's mansion, as it had done often in the past eleven months.

"This is silly, Mother."

Her son's voice jarred her back to the present. Helen took her head off the wheel. She opened her eyes and took in a deep breath.

"Are you scared of me?" he continued. The tease in his tone was gone.

Yes. But Helen didn't answer. Instead, after a brief hesitation, she clicked "End" and set the phone down.

Then, sighing and taking a last look at the huge house, she put her car in gear and merged back onto Highway 31.

35

Michael Zannick watched his mother's car pull onto the highway, still holding his cell phone to his ear. Finally, after a few more seconds, he flung the device on the recliner he'd been sitting in when he'd noticed the Crown Vic cut its lights thirty minutes earlier. He'd found himself watching the window more and more in the last few months. He would pretend to work, watch TV, or surf the internet while glancing through the blinds every few moments to see if she was paying him a "visit."

It was pitiful, he knew, and he loathed his own weakness. Still, he found that he couldn't stop himself.

Besides, he figured the next time that he saw his mother, she wouldn't be on a "visit." She'd be here in her official capacity. He and Brittany had tried to keep a low profile about their relationship, but Brittany's recording deal and the person who'd negotiated it would be revealed. He'd become a person of interest or an important witness.

Who knew more about the final two weeks of Brittany's life than him? *Or the last day . . .*

Zannick wasn't a heavy drinker, but he had consumed more liquor in the last thirty-six hours than he had in the last year. He could understand why weaker souls drank alcohol or popped antidepressants to take away the pain. Especially now, as he thought of Brittany prancing around this same den last week, wearing silk pajamas, talking about all the things she was going to do after she signed with ELEKTRIK HI. They'd devoured a take-out pizza from Domino's and watched *Creed* in the very den in which he was now standing.

Zannick couldn't remember a time in his life when he'd ever been truly happy. But his month-long "affair" with Brittany had been close.

Of course he'd known she was using him, and not just for his money and influence. One of her goals was more juvenile, indicative of her age.

Getting back at Daddy, Zannick thought, standing again to look out the window. At this time of night, there were few cars on Highway 31.

Zannick turned his head and peered around his empty mansion. He'd been using Brittany too. He'd been prone to obsessions his whole life, and after his grand plan to obtain revenge on his mother had blown up last fall, he'd needed something else to fixate on.

Brittany had filled the bill quite nicely. She was young, talented, and ambitious. Zannick had noticed her potential immediately upon watching her sing at Hitt's Place bar in early June. He'd asked Fizz to play at his Fourth of July party and had begun to talk with Brittany during a break. It was loud, and he'd invited her out on his patio. He listened to her talk about her band and the gigs they'd lined up. Even outside, Zannick had to lean close to her to be able to hear. Apparently, he'd gotten closer than Brittany's father appreciated.

He never saw the punch before it connected with his jaw. When he looked up, he saw a man hovering over him and telling him to stay the hell away from his daughter. The man grabbed Brittany's arm, but she resisted, punching his shoulder with a closed fist.

By the time that Israel Crutcher slapped his daughter in the face, there was a group of people on the patio. A hush of silence followed the blow, and then Brittany's mother stepped in between Israel and Brittany and told Israel that he needed to leave. Zannick's security detail also arrived and gave the outraged father the same order, albeit with a bit more force, as they escorted him off the premises.

Zannick hadn't pressed charges and, to his knowledge, neither had Brittany. He offered to manage her career the following day and, as a show of good faith, contributed some money to her band. Brittany finally accepted his offer in mid-September on the one-year anniversary of her advancing to the *America's Got Talent* finals, making him promise to keep their arrangement secret. After moving out of her parents' home, Brittany had also started staying over at his house a couple nights a week.

He had rather enjoyed the drama of it all. Brittany was eighteen, so there was nothing illegal about her shacking up with Zannick, though they weren't really "shacking up" in the technical sense of the word. However, given the fact that he'd been charged with the statutory rape of a fifteen-year-old girl the previous year—an allegation that had almost cost the town of Pulaski the Hoshima auto-manufacturing plant and sent Zannick to prison for ten years—he knew people would be outraged if they learned that a teenager was staying at his home, albeit one of legal age. Why else had Israel Crutcher gone berserk when he'd seen his daughter with Zannick on the Fourth?

Zannick didn't care. He wasn't from Pulaski, and he enjoyed shocking people. He also relished the company. He'd been dating Cassie Dugan, an attractive local bartender, for about a year off and on, but he'd broken it off this past Christmas. He was prone to lose interest in people, and Cassie was boring. She was using him, too, but her motives were obvious. She wanted what all women that dated him seemed to want. Not so much money in and of itself as security for her family.

Zannick needed more and found it with Brittany. Ironically enough, he'd used Cassie to set up the Fourth of July gig at his house, as Cassie was moonlighting as the manager of Fizz.

Unlike Cassie, Brittany could care less about security. She was using him as a stepping-stone to her career and for revenge.

That made things more exciting.

And more volatile, Zannick thought, remembering his encounter with Brittany Friday night. She'd been feeling guilty about signing the contract he'd brokered with ELEKTRIK HI and was having second thoughts about leaving her band and boyfriend behind. When he'd said it was too late to change her mind, she'd gotten upset and threatened to break the agreement anyway. He'd told her he expected to see her at Abernathy Field in the morning with her bags packed and ready to fly to LA.

"No," Brittany had said. "I won't do it." Then she had stormed out of the house and slammed the door.

Zannick couldn't remember what he'd said as she was leaving, but to say that he'd lost his temper would be an understatement. He did not like being played for a fool.

He walked into his kitchen and opened the refrigerator. He gazed at the carton of Bud Light, which now had five bottles instead of six, and groaned.

He hadn't taken Brittany's rejection well.

36

At 6:30 p.m., Bo, T. J., and Lila met Booker T. and his son, Jarvis, out in front of the Crutcher home. By this time of night, most of the guests had either already left or were filing out.

"Thanks for coming," Booker T. said, squeezing Bo's shoulder.

"How's the family?" Bo asked, nodding up toward the house.

"Theresa's holding it together pretty well. She's weepy but hanging in there. Able to talk with people and even laugh at some of the funny memories of Brittany. Gina barely acknowledged me or anyone else. Just stands next to her parents with an empty look."

Bo shook his head. "Has to be hard."

Bo and Booker T. soon shook hands with and hugged an older couple from Bickland Creek Baptist Church, who'd just paid their respects.

"What about Israel?" Bo asked as the couple walked away.

Booker T. sucked air between his teeth and gave his head a jerk. "He ain't right."

"What do you mean?"

"I mean the things I told you last night . . . they're getting worse."

Bo stuffed his hands in the pockets of his trousers. "You want me to try to talk to him if the opportunity presents itself."

Booker T.'s eyes narrowed. "Yeah, but I doubt you'll have to wait for an opening."

"Why's that?"

"Because he wants a word with you."

Bo raised his eyebrows. "What?"

"That's what he said. He asked if you were coming, and when I told him I thought you were, he said, 'Good. I'd like to talk to him.'"

Bo swallowed. When was the last time he'd had any kind of conversation with Israel Crutcher?

"Be easy," Booker T. said. "He's hurting bad."

———

Five minutes later, Bo and his kids were inside the house, waiting behind an old man named Maurice Daniels, whom everyone called Mo. Mo operated a barbershop out of his house and cut hair for most of the Black men in Pulaski. In front of Mo was a younger African American couple who had a couple toddlers in tow and an older white woman in a navy floral dress whom Bo didn't recognize.

"Bocephus, when are you goin' come see me again?" Mo asked. Bo remembered that the old man called everyone by their proper and full name.

He smiled and rubbed his bald head. "Not much you can do about this, Mo."

"I bet I could shave it smoother than you," Mo said with a twinkle in his eyes. "Could also give your face a cleaner look too. Now that you're back in town, it's been hurting my feelings that you haven't been by. I've cut your boy's hair a couple times." He nodded at T. J., who had his hands in his pockets, fidgeting with his car keys. They had driven separately in case Bo needed to stick around and speak longer with the family. He again felt a twinge in his stomach as he thought of what Booker T. had told him. *Israel wants a word with you . . .*

"Thomas Jackson, I told you to ask your daddy to come see me." Mo's raspy voice interrupted Bo's thoughts. "Did you ask him?"

T. J. glanced at Bo and then back at Mo. "I'm sorry, Mr. Daniels. I must have forgotten." He was now looking at something on his iPhone.

Mo waved him off. "Teenagers don't remember nothing these days. Too busy with their heads glued to those dang devices."

"Tell me about it," Bo said as they all moved up in line while the woman in navy walked past, her eyes red with tears. Bo nodded at her, and she returned the gesture. "Hello, Bo."

"Hi," Bo said as the woman walked past him. He looked at Mo. "Who was that, Mo? She looks familiar but—"

"Miss Little. She's been the choir instructor over at Giles County High forever . . . probably since the early '70s . . . and teaches voice on the side. She was Brittany's first and only voice coach."

Bo hadn't sung in the choir in high school, but now he remembered. "Joyce Little," he whispered. "She was the cheerleading sponsor when I was in school." He shook his head. "Back in the Stone Age."

"Back when you got a decent haircut from your neighborhood barber," Mo teased, squeezing Bo's arm as the young couple finished paying their respects in front of them. "Come see me, Bo. Ol' Mo ain't going to live forever, and I'd like to catch up with you. Got a lot of stories to tell you, and I'd like to hear a few of yours."

"Will do," Bo said, thinking that there probably wasn't a person in town who knew more about the goings-on in Pulaski, good, bad, and ugly, than Mo Daniels.

Bo watched the ancient barber, whose own hair consisted of two patches of white fuzz on the sides and a slick bald area down the middle, and couldn't help but smile. As Mo leaned down to kiss Theresa Crutcher's cheek, Bo's smile dissipated as he caught his first glimpse of Israel Crutcher.

Israel wore a black suit, white shirt, and dark-burgundy tie. He was around six feet tall and probably a shade over 180 pounds if Bo had to guess. To Bo, Israel still resembled the lean muscled starting quarterback of the Giles County Bobcats.

He gripped Mo's hand and nodded several times. Then, as the barber walked away, Israel straightened his shoulders and glared up at Bo, who stepped in front of his children.

For a moment, there was an awkward silence as Bo and Israel peered at each other. The tension in the air was palpable.

Finally, Bo moved his eyes to the other two family members.

"Theresa, I'm very sorry," Bo said, leaning over and hugging the woman's neck.

"Thank you for coming, Bo," Theresa said, her voice a whimper. Back when they were all in high school, Theresa Crutcher had been quite a looker. She'd had long legs with a curvy figure and an infectious laugh. Booker T. and Bo had both had crushes on her, but Theresa had only had eyes for Israel. Though she was still attractive, age, stress, and fatigue had drawn circles underneath Theresa's lids. Her brown hair, which she'd worn long and natural as a teenager, was now cut short and braided. Bo pulled back from her and turned his attention to the girl in between Theresa and Israel.

Gina Crutcher had short hair like her mother and wore a conservative black dress. She had a square, sturdy build, and when Bo leaned in to hug her, he could feel the muscles in her arms and upper back tighten.

"I'm sorry for your loss, Gina," he said.

She stared at him but said nothing. Her eyes were dull, as if perhaps she had taken an antidepressant. "Well . . . I'm sorry," Bo repeated.

Finally, he turned his gaze again to Israel and extended his hand. "Israel, I'm sorry. I truly am."

Israel Crutcher had dark bags under his eyes, and Bo could see red lines shooting out from the irises. Israel opened his mouth to say something, but no words come. All he could manage was a nod.

"Booker T. said you wanted a word with me."

Israel blinked, as if coming out of a trance. When he spoke, his voice sounded dry and weak. "You got time?"

Bo nodded.

Israel whispered something to Theresa, who shot a disapproving glace at her husband and then shook her head as if to say, *Whatever.*

Bo turned behind him and noticed that there were only a couple other guests in line. Maybe Theresa was angry that Israel was ducking out early. Or maybe there was something else in play? Booker T. had mentioned it was possible the Crutchers were having marital problems.

After whispering to T. J. to take his sister home, Bo followed his old teammate through the house, admiring the artwork and photographs of the children on the walls. There was an oil painting of the Bickland Creek Baptist Church over the mantel in the living room, and Bo wondered if maybe Theresa had created it. There were several family pictures with the girls at different ages and impressionistic portraits of Gina and Brittany as kids, both signed by Rebekah Mims, a local artist beloved by the town.

Pictures of Brittany in various stages of childhood were displayed everywhere, including a shot of her with the other finalists of *America's Got Talent*. In the framed photograph, Brittany wore a black cocktail dress and a charm necklace with a purple stone, her smile radiant. Bo remembered this night. He and the kids had watched her sing "Blue Bayou," by Linda Ronstadt. They'd thought she should have won. Glancing around the home, which had been shattered by Brittany's murder, he thought of his own home, where images of Lila were everywhere. *And Jazz . . .* he thought. *Still . . . Jazz.*

Bo's feet felt heavier as he entered a small study and Israel closed the door behind them. Inside the office, Bo saw a rectangular wooden desk. Behind the desk were several framed photographs of Israel's football-playing days. One had him wearing his Tennessee Chattanooga Moccasins number 18 jersey with the classic Heisman Trophy–type pose. His right arm was held straight out to fend off a tackler, football tucked under his left. Bo approached the frame. "Did you play quarterback at UTC?"

"Nah, they moved me to corner. Not many Black quarterbacks back then. I was lucky to play QB1 at GCH."

Bo moved his eyes along the wall, and his gaze held on a picture he had in his own home. He leaned close and read the engraved words below the photo. GILES COUNTY BOBCATS. 1977 STATE CHAMPIONS. When he saw his own face in the picture, he touched it with his index finger.

"Seems like a million years ago, doesn't it?" Bo asked.

"Sometimes," Israel agreed. "And other times, it seems like it all happened yesterday."

"Hell of a team," Bo said.

"No," Israel said. "We had a good team . . . and we had one once-in-a-lifetime player. 'Number forty-one, Bo*cephus* Haynes.'" He imitated a PA announcer's voice, and his agitation seemed to be giving him energy. Israel's tone was now much stronger. "Led the team in rushing. Led the team in tackles. Punted when we had to punt and, if the field goal was too long for Robby Harlan, damned if Bocephus didn't kick for us too."

"You were good too, Iz. Full ride to UTC. Booker T. played college ball as well."

He smirked. "Bear Bryant didn't come to Pulaski to see me or Booker T. Maybe he would have if more of us had been given a chance. But by God, if we had the ball, Coach Waites was giving it to you. About wore you out before state."

"What did Herschel Walker say? 'That ball ain't heavy.'"

"You could have been better than Herschel. You ever think that maybe your knee would have held up at Bama if you hadn't had such wear and tear in high school? If you hadn't played every single snap for three years."

Bo ground his teeth, finding it hard to believe that Israel could still manage to be jealous of him after all this time, in the midst of mourning his daughter's death. Perhaps seeing Bo again was a distraction and he could air out all the old grievances, keeping his mind off his daughter's murder. Or maybe Israel was just that damn petty. Bo didn't know, but he wasn't about to engage his old teammate.

"Maybe more of us would have made Division One if Coach Waites hadn't given you the ball so much," Israel continued. "And maybe I would have played quarterback in college if I had been throwing more and not handing the ball off to you so much. I was good enough to play in the league." He sighed. "And maybe if I'd played in the NFL, then I could have been a doctor instead of a CRNA, and maybe, just maybe, if all that had played out, then I could have gotten my family out of Pulaski, and maybe my baby girl would be alive now and not dead. Maybe she wouldn't have been killed by a bad seed that GCH should have never let in the school." Israel plopped down in his chair and gestured at the seat across from him. Bo lowered himself to the edge of the cushion and leaned his elbows on his knees.

"You said you wanted a word with me, Israel. I'm sure it wasn't to rehash ancient history."

Israel looked down at his desk. Bo saw that the man's hands had begun to shake. He grabbed his left hand with his right, and his eyes shot up at Bo. "How long's it been since we've seen each other?"

"You know how long," Bo said.

Israel's face wrinkled into a bitter smile. "The reunion nine years ago."

"Yep," Bo said. "Remember how that ended?"

Israel's eyes darkened. "With your face on my fist."

"I think it was the other way around."

"As I recollect, the fight was broken up before it even got started."

"That what you want?" Bo asked, leaning back and crossing his legs. "You want to fight? Will that make things better for you?"

Israel looked past Bo to the far wall. "Ain't nothing ever going to make things better for me. My Brittany is dead. You hear me? My baby girl is *dead*."

"I wish I had the words."

164

"There are no words—you know that," Israel snapped. "You been through a lot of hell in your life. You've had people you care about killed. Words ever help you?"

"Ain't nothing helps but time."

"Time heals all wounds. Is that it? You goin' throw clichés at me now. That all you got?"

"Nothing heals the hurt, Iz. But time has a way of scabbing it. Protecting you against the pain. I hate to throw out another cliché, but life goes on. Whether you want it to or not."

"Not for me," Israel said. "Not until there's justice for my baby."

For a few long seconds, there was silence as Bo let the other man grieve. Finally, he cleared his throat and spoke in a low voice. "Why did you want to talk with me, Iz?"

Israel coughed and wiped his eyes. "You know General Lewis pretty well, don't you?"

"Yes. She was my client last year, and . . . I consider her a good friend."

"Did you watch that press conference?"

Bo nodded.

"What do you think about them not seeking the death penalty?"

"Well . . . capital punishment isn't available in all murders. There have to be aggravating factors. A crime of passion . . . if that's what this is . . . wouldn't necessarily allow for the death penalty. I suspect the defendant's age is a mitigating circumstance."

"What the hell does that mean? He's an adult."

"He's eighteen—barely an adult and still in high school."

Israel let out a ragged breath and shook his head. "There's no way that I'm going to let my daughter's killer breathe air."

Bo sensed his old teammate's agitation and helplessness. "I would advise that you not take the law into your own hands. It'll end up bad for you, Iz. You want to give your family another tragedy to deal with?"

"He killed my girl," Israel said.

"If he did, the General will make sure that he goes to prison for a long time."

Israel blinked his eyes. "Will the General give my baby justice?"

"She's one of the finest attorneys I've ever been around and the best prosecutor, bar none."

"Some folks around town think she got away with murdering her ex-husband."

Bo bit his lip. He'd heard some of the same rumblings. "She was found not guilty."

"Ain't the same thing as being innocent. A good lawyer such as yourself can exonerate a guilty client. Don't tell me you haven't done that before. And you still haven't answered my question. Will General Lewis give my baby the justice she deserves?"

Bo's ponderings from his long and tormented walk that morning came back to him. *Is justice even possible in this crazy world? In this town . . .*

"Do you believe the sheriff's office has charged the right person?" Bo asked.

"You all lawyer now, aren't you, Bo," Israel said. "Answer a question with a question."

"I'm sure the General wouldn't be part of charging Odell if there wasn't some evidence suggesting his guilt. Did you know Brittany and Odell were dating?" Bo knew he was now interrogating Israel but couldn't help himself. He *was* a lawyer, after all, and Israel had opened the door to questions by asking about the General.

"Yeah, I knew. And I told her he was bad news. Brittany had the world by the tail. Why would she bring that kind of trouble into her life?"

"Did Brittany have any enemies?"

Israel hung his head and rubbed his face with his hands. "The sheriff's deputies have asked us all these questions. I'm not aware of any. But there's something that hasn't come up in our talks with the police that bothers me."

"What's that?"

"You know that rich boy who moved here from Boston and brought the Hoshima plant with him? You filed a lawsuit against him last year, didn't you?"

Bo felt a cold chill run up his spine. "Yes."

"I'm pretty sure he'd become her manager in the last few weeks."

Bo couldn't believe his ears. "Israel, you're telling me that Brittany was involved with Michael Zannick?"

"Yeah."

"Was their association only business?" Bo could hear and feel his heartbeat racing.

"I don't know," Israel said, gazing down at his desk again. "But I think there was more to it."

37

Bo trudged down the steps of the Crutchers' home a few minutes later. Though exhausted from the length of the day and the lack of sleep he'd had the night before, he was also wired on adrenaline. *Zannick,* he thought, imagining the slight-looking entrepreneur as he'd seen him at the mediation last November, when Zannick had settled the civil assault case Bo had filed against him on behalf of Mandy Burks for $1.5 million.

He bought his peace.

The rape charge brought by the district attorney general's office had been dismissed by Gloria Sanchez, Helen's assistant, while Helen's own murder trial was pending.

He got away with raping a fifteen-year-old girl . . .

Though he'd obtained a big settlement for Mandy, it still stuck in Bo's craw that Zannick had essentially skated clean. Even $1.5 million was a drop in the bucket for him. Zannick's avoidance of harsher consequences was a bone of contention for Bo's assistant, Lona Burks, who also happened to be Mandy's mother. Though Lona had begrudgingly accepted Zannick's settlement offer, she'd never let Bo forget that the wealthy business magnate had gotten off with a slap on the wrist.

As he reached the last step, Bo looked up in time to avoid colliding with a uniformed officer heading up the stairs.

"Hey, Frannie," Bo said, and she turned as she reached the landing and peered down at him.

"Bo," she said, her face stoic.

"Something wrong?"

"I need to update Israel and Theresa on the case."

"Have there been any developments?"

She narrowed her gaze. "Until you enter an appearance in the case . . . that's none of your business."

Bo held her eye. He knew he deserved the response, but he still didn't appreciate the frigid demeanor, especially after he'd helped her last night with Sabrina Champagne. As she wheeled toward the front door, he decided to poke the bear. "Hey, Frannie. You sure you got the right person this time?"

She looked over her shoulder at him. "I'm not positive I didn't have the right person last time."

"You don't believe that," Bo said.

Frannie ground her teeth so hard that Bo could hear them. "Regardless of what happened before, Odell Champagne is guilty of murdering Brittany Crutcher."

Bo took a step forward. "Maybe you're right. But let me ask you something."

Frannie turned to face him and planted her hands on her hips. "What?"

"Did you know that Brittany was being managed by Michael Zannick?"

"Yes," Frannie said without hesitation. "We know all about their relationship."

But Bo saw what he thought was a combination of irritation and fear cross over her face.

"A bit interesting, don't you think?"

"No comment," she replied.

38

An hour later, Frannie strode into the lobby of the Giles County Sheriff's Office. Her conversation with the Crutchers had been tense and heartbreaking as she relayed the findings from Melvin Ragland. Before she'd left, she'd asked them whether Brittany had any kind of relationship with Michael Zannick.

Theresa and Israel had seemed put off by the question. Theresa had said she wasn't aware of any relationship, but Israel had finally disclosed that it was his understanding that Zannick had become Brittany's manager shortly before her murder. That had provoked an argument between husband and wife, causing Theresa to walk out of the room. By the time Frannie had reached her cruiser, she was reeling. Had Brittany been keeping secrets?

So far, none of the people they'd interviewed had mentioned anything about Michael Zannick, but Brittany's cell phone was littered with calls and texts from the businessman.

Zannick was a secret, Frannie had thought as she'd sped back to the sheriff's office. *Did Brittany have other secrets? What else don't we know?* The timeline that they were constructing for Brittany's last twenty-four hours had a pretty big gap between the time the concert had ended at 11:00 p.m. and her death. After a search of Brittany's 4Runner, they'd found a receipt in her purse that revealed that she'd stopped at the SunTrust ATM on West College Street at 12:41 a.m. and had withdrawn $200, but that was really the only stop they'd been able to confirm. *Cash for the trip to LA?* Frannie wondered. Based on Brittany's text messages, it appeared that she'd probably visited Michael Zannick's home before getting the money, but Zannick had refused to grant an interview.

We need to know more.

As Frannie had parked her car and thought back to Bo's needling on the steps in front of the Crutchers' home, another question had popped into her brain.

Am I about to screw the pooch again?

When she reached the war room and saw the General sitting between Deputies Dodgen and McCann reviewing crime scene photographs, her doubts and fears turned into unadulterated hostility. "Where have you been?"

Helen looked up from the picture she was holding with a scowl on her face. "Are you talking to me?"

"Yes, *you.* I've been trying to get ahold of you since the press conference this afternoon."

"I'm here now," Helen said. "I've been in this room for a while. Waiting for *you.*"

"Why didn't you return any of my calls or texts?"

"Because I've been busy. I have other cases to work. A couple are set for trial on Monday. Those files took a back seat when you brought me into this investigation."

"You like being involved from the beginning. That's always been your MO. Or maybe that's changed now that you've gotten away with murder yourself." Frannie immediately regretted saying it, but she was too stubborn to reel it back in. She looked around the room, and the two other deputies gazed down at the floor.

Helen stood from her chair. "I think the rest of you need to clear out. I'd like a word with Chief Storm in private."

Once they were alone, Helen stepped so close to Frannie that she invaded her personal space. "That's your mulligan, Frannie. I'm going to give it to you, because, overall, I like you and think you have the makings of a great investigator. But if you ever cross the line like that again, you're gone. You understand? I'll see to it you're fired."

"Only the sheriff can fire me," Frannie said.

"And Hank pisses in his pants when I'm in the least bit of a bad mood. He does whatever I tell him, so you watch yourself."

For a long moment, the two women glared at each other, venom in their gazes, neither backing down.

"So what's going on?" Helen asked, her voice low.

"The victim had a secret."

"What?" Helen asked.

"Brittany was keeping a rather large secret from her family and . . . I suspect from Odell too."

Helen crossed her arms. When she realized what the skeleton in Brittany's closet must be, Helen felt a cold shiver on her neck and arms. "Her new manager?"

Frannie nodded. "Israel knew, but Theresa says she didn't. Given Brittany's talent and ambition, it's not surprising that she would seek out a wealthy benefactor to finance her next career steps. Someone with enough money and influence to break through a few doors. All logical. But this particular person happens to have a history of showing a bit too much interest in teenage girls."

"Michael Zannick," Helen said, barely getting the words out.

"Yep," Frannie said. "He's going to be all over this case."

39

On Monday morning at 8:30 a.m. sharp, Bo parked in front of his office on First Street. He cut the ignition and gazed up at the golden shingle that hung above the door. **BOCEPHUS HAYNES, ATTORNEY AT LAW** was stenciled in black letters on the sign.

Bo had opened his firm a few months after passing the bar exam. Initially he had leased the space, which was in an ideal location two blocks from the courthouse. But after his first big wheels verdict in the early '90s, he'd bought the building. In the beginning of his legal career, he'd cut his teeth on criminal defense and workers' compensation cases. Eventually, though, through hard work, persistence, and good fortune, he'd been able to attract several personal injury cases where his clients had suffered catastrophic damages. Two large jury verdicts and a seven-figure settlement later, Bo had become one of the most sought-after plaintiffs attorneys in southern Tennessee.

Over the course of the past five years, through his own trial for murder, the discovery of his true heritage, and Jazz's death, his career and life had teetered on the cusp of disaster. He'd almost lost everything. But his defense of General Helen Lewis had helped him climb back to the top.

Bo opened the door to the building and saw the familiar sight of his secretary/receptionist/paralegal, Lona Burks, typing furiously on the computer with a phone receiver tucked between her neck and shoulder. She had strawberry-blonde hair tied up in a ponytail and wore a brown blouse and faded jeans. Catching Bo's look of amusement, she rolled her eyes. "Yes, we should file this week, Ms. Martin. I'm putting the finishing touches on the complaint now, and Bo will finalize it tomorrow." Her voice was sharp, energetic. Seconds later, she hung up the phone and sighed. "That woman is going to be the death of me."

"Stella Madeline Martin," Bo said. "Personal representative of the estate of Jerome Martin, who was killed when the brakes on his sport utility vehicle locked up on I-65, causing him to rear-end the pickup truck in front of him and killing him instantly when the airbags on said vehicle didn't deploy." Bo stopped as Lona turned her rolling chair to face him and crossed her arms. "Our first case against Hoshima since they moved to town," he continued. "Has their general counsel responded yet to the demand letter?"

"You have a message to call her."

"Good."

"You think she'll want a quick settlement?"

"I do, even though the model is different from the one they're manufacturing here. I'm sure the folks at Hoshima don't want bad press before they open up the plant."

Lona grinned, keeping her mouth closed to hide the caps that were the product of years of methamphetamine abuse. In a prior life, Lona Burks had been a stripper and drug addict. But she was four years clean, raising a teenager daughter on her own, and one of the hardest-working people Bo had ever been around. Even after the Zannick settlement, which would have led most people to retire and lead the good life, Lona hadn't missed a day of work. She'd set up a trust account for Mandy and deposited most of the proceeds there, keeping enough to buy a new house. Bo was grateful for her decision to stay on.

"Thought any more about taking on a partner?" Lona asked.

"Already got a partner," Bo teased. "You just have to get through law school."

Lona's grin curved into a smirk. "Not funny. Seriously, Bo, look at this place . . ." She waved her arms around her desk, which was stacked high with file folders. "Three new files this week. Five complaints we're about to drop. You have the Mullins's mediation on Thursday." She stopped and wrinkled her eyebrows. "What's your gut on that one?"

"Hard to say . . ."

"Bo?"

"Don't want to jinx it, but that case isn't going to get any better for the defendant come trial. I bet we resolve it."

She leaned her arms forward on the desk. "How much?"

Bo cocked his head to the side in mock thought. "One point two million."

Lona whistled under her teeth. "What would that be? Three seven-figure settlements in the last six months? You certainly can afford to take on a partner." She glanced around the cozy reception area. "Ever think about upgrading the office? Maybe using the upstairs for something other than storage or moving to a bigger spot?"

"I like where we are," Bo said. "It's a lot more important for me to be mobile than big. Have you heard from the other member of our team?"

"Nothing since he left for the Keys."

Bo snorted. "That was over a week ago."

"You know how Hooper is."

Bo did. His private investigator kept odd hours, was an Uber driver for fun, and did his investigative research from his own waterfront office in Decatur, Alabama, when he wasn't traveling. But he'd been a valuable asset since Bo had first hired him to help with Helen's case last year. "If he calls in, tell him I need to speak with him."

"You want to sic him on Hoshima? Dig up some more dirt on its airbag and brake problems?"

"Nah, he's gotten enough for me on that one already." Bo rubbed the back of his neck as the Odell Champagne case played in his mind. Brittany Crutcher was being managed by Michael Zannick. Hooper had done a full profile on Zannick during the General's case. Bo tilted his head, knowing he was putting the cart before the horse. *I haven't even taken the case yet.*

"Something wrong?" Lona asked.

"Nothing," Bo said, letting his hand fall to his side and walking toward the hallway that would take him to his private office.

"Anything you want me to tell Hooper if I get him?"

Bo paused in the opening between the reception area and hall. "Just that I may need his help on a new case."

"O . . . K. Something you want to tell me?"

Bo looked over his shoulder at her. "Your daughter goes to Pulaski Academy now, doesn't she?"

"Yeah, Mandy transferred there in January. Couldn't have done it without the settlement."

"When she was at GCH, did she know Brittany Crutcher?"

Lona's face clouded over. "Yeah, actually, they had sort of become friends, because Mandy's interested in music. Terrible what happened to Brittany. Mandy's devastated. You know the Crutcher family?"

"Yeah," Bo said. "I played football in high school with Brittany's dad. Look, I may . . ." He trailed off.

"May what?"

"Never mind. Make sure Hooper calls me if he touches base."

Bo started walking, but her voice stopped him.

"Well, that explains it," Lona said, frowning and ripping a yellow sticky note off her desk and holding it up for him.

Bo snatched the note, tensing when he read the words. "Sabrina Champagne." There was a number on the sticky that he didn't recognize.

"Thought we were done with criminal work," Lona said.

When Bo looked up from the note, he saw that his assistant was still frowning and had folded her arms. "This would be a rather unpopular case to take, don't you think? Could hurt our caseload."

"We'll manage," Bo said. "Besides, I haven't taken the case yet." Before she could say anything further, he strode down the hall and into his private office. He closed the door and leaned his back against it. Things were going so well with his law practice. With his life.

You shouldn't walk away from this case, he thought. *You should run.*

40

Three hours later, Bo sat at the kitchen table of the Crutcher home. A chicken salad sandwich on wheat had been placed in front of him, even though he'd begged off lunch. Theresa stood by the refrigerator dressed in a green bathrobe. Glasses covered her face, her hair pulled up in a bun. She wore no makeup, and her eyes were red from crying or lack of sleep or both. To say that Bo felt guilty for being here, dredging up more memories of this woman's pain, was an understatement. His face burned with shame, but if he were going to get involved in this case, he had to know the answers to certain questions. And he figured Theresa would be the most reliable source.

"I'm sorry to impose like this," Bo said, gazing up at her as she stared down at the tile floor. "You didn't have to make me lunch." Theresa had started preparing the meal once Bo was seated and had set it in front of him before he could protest.

"Please eat it," Theresa croaked. Her voice sounded as tired as she looked. "People from church have brought so much food—there's barely room in the fridge to hold it all. I'm going to have to start throwing it out soon." She snickered. "So funny how all anybody knows what to do is to bring food. I got chicken salad. Fried chicken. Six different kinds of mac and cheese. All sorts of pies and cakes." She choked back a sob. "I got everything but Brittany. Ain't no amount of food or crying or talk is going to bring my baby back."

Bo forced himself to take a bite of the sandwich and washed it down with a sip of sweet tea. "It's good. Thank you so much."

"You're welcome," Theresa said, plopping down on the seat beside him. "You know, you're the first guest we've had other than the visitation. People leave food on the steps, but they don't come in. We're pariahs now. People say they're sorry, and I'm sure they are. But they don't want to get too close. They don't want what happened to us to happen to them."

"They probably aren't sure what to do."

"Maybe." She squinted at him. "So why're you here? I was surprised to see you last night, and now here you are again."

"I was paying my respects last night like everyone else. But Israel told me something that kinda bothered me."

She gazed at him with dull eyes. "That when he took you to his office?"

Bo nodded. "He wanted to know if I thought the sheriff's office would give Brittany justice." Bo chose his words carefully. "And he was upset that the death penalty probably wasn't going to be an option."

"What does that even mean? Justice goin' dig my baby out of the ground and breathe life into her? And if they put Odell to death, is that going to bring her back?"

Bo pulled back from the table. "Theresa, don't you want your daughter's killer to be found and punished?"

"They found him," Theresa said. "I saw Odell out there at the bus yard. He couldn't even bring himself to look at me. Guilty as hell. Israel tried to warn Brittany off that boy, but she was too stubborn. My baby was so damn stubborn."

"Had you ever seen Odell act inappropriately around Brittany?"

Theresa shook her head. "No. But that don't mean anything. I had barely seen Brittany either."

Bo felt another tickle in his brain. "What? Wasn't she living here?"

Theresa continued to stare at him. "No. She moved out of the house in July. The only time I saw her was at church or her music gigs."

Bo crossed his arms. "Why did she move out?"

"Because she was eighteen years old and tired of living by rules. Her band's events were keeping her out later and later, and we wanted her home at night."

Bo sensed he wasn't getting the whole story by Theresa's rehearsed tone. She must have told this same story to the sheriff's office several times. "That the only reason she moved out?"

She blinked and stood from the table, then approached the kitchen counter. "You want some coffee?"

"Theresa, was something else going on that caused Brittany to leave the family?"

Theresa opened a cabinet and got out a package of coffee, then pulled one of the K-Cups out and placed it in the Keurig machine.

"Theresa—"

"She and her daddy weren't getting along."

"Did that have anything to do with Michael Zannick taking over as her manager?"

Theresa placed her hands on the counter and watched as dark liquid began dripping into the mug below the Keurig. The kitchen took on the smell of french roast. For a moment, there was no sound other than the gurgling of the coffee machine. Seconds later, she placed the mug on the table in front of Bo's plate. "All lawyers need a little more coffee, right?" She forced a smile, and Bo held his gaze on her.

Something was off here. It was the Monday after the visitation. Yet Theresa was alone in the house. He wanted an answer to his question about Zannick, but he could wait. "Theresa, isn't Brittany's funeral this afternoon?"

She again turned away from him, walking over to the sink next to the coffee maker and slowly washing her hands.

Bo stood and approached her. "Theresa?"

"There's a service at Bickland Creek at three p.m. Pastor Coy is officiating. Then, when that's over, there'll be a private burial at Maplewood Cemetery." She paused. "Family only."

"Theresa, where's the rest of the family?" There'd been no sight of Gina or Israel since Bo's arrival. And while he was grateful for being able to speak with Theresa by herself, it didn't make sense that she was alone.

"Israel's probably at the hotel." She suppressed a sob. "Gina . . . I don't know. She's been in denial about her sister's death. She's excused from school today for the funeral, so I suspect she's up at the Curry Center working out or shooting ball."

Bo cocked his head. "Why is Israel at a hotel?"

Theresa gripped the counter, not looking at him. "We're separated, Bo. Have been since July."

Bo was stunned. *Israel moved out the same time as Brittany . . .* That couldn't be a coincidence. Yet Booker T. had said nothing to him about it, and he was one of Israel's best friends. "I'm sorry. I . . . didn't know."

She wiped her mouth and took a plastic cup that had been sitting on the counter and placed it under the faucet. After it was half-full, she took a long drink. "We haven't told anyone. Not even our closest friends. Israel hardly ever went to church with me anyways, and that's about the only social activity we did anymore." She chuckled. "Our life was our kids. We still both attended Brittany's band's events and went to Gina's basketball games. We sat together as if nothing was wrong." She took another sip from the cup. "I doubt anyone noticed anything different."

"But something was wrong? What?"

She finally turned and peered at him. "Did you really come over here to talk about our marriage? I thought you wanted to ask me something."

"I already have," Bo said.

"Well, if that's it, I'd like you to leave. I need to get myself cleaned up for the funeral."

"Theresa, I'm sorry. I did have one other question."

She crossed her arms. "What?"

"Where was she living?"

"She said she was staying with her friend Tasha, who's a freshman at Martin. She has an apartment off campus."

"Did you believe her?"

"Yes, but . . ." Theresa paused.

"But what?"

"But nothing. Please go, Bo. You're starting to upset me."

"Theresa, did you tell all of this to the police?"

She averted her eyes. "Leave. *Now.*"

Bo held his ground. "If you and Israel want justice for Brittany, you're going to have to shoot straight with the authorities. Otherwise, you may never know the truth."

"The truth?" She stepped toward him. "The truth is that Brittany's boyfriend, who your son is good friends with, hit my baby with a bottle of beer and killed her." She held her hands up to her face. "None of this other mess matters. Me and Israel's marriage. Brittany moving out. Yeah, our family was in shambles, Bo. You want me to say it? And maybe we're to blame for Brittany being out late at night and not here at home. Maybe we drove her into trouble's path. Maybe all of that's true." She leaned forward and placed her hands on her knees, beginning to sob. "You think I don't agonize about that all day long?"

Bo felt an ache in his heart, and the guilt that had cloaked him when he'd started the conversation with Theresa was back with a vengeance. "Theresa, I'm sorry. Israel mentioned some things last night, and I was following up. I only want what you want."

She pulled herself up. "No, you don't. You ain't been to my house in years, Bocephus Haynes. You're exactly what Israel says you are. A prima donna who only cares about himself. You blew up your whole family, too, and it was a much bigger mess than ours." Her eyes blazed with fury. "Maybe if *you* had been a better man, then Jazz wouldn't have been put in harm's way. Maybe she'd be alive today. You ever think that?"

"Every day," Bo said. "Every damn day." He turned and walked toward the opening that led to the front door, stopping under the archway. When he spoke, he didn't look at her. "Theresa, do you know of anyone who might have any additional information about Brittany's relationship with Michael Zannick?"

"I get it now. Old Theresa is slow on the uptick, but I understand what you're doing now, Bo. You're going to represent that killer, aren't you? You aren't trying to help us. You're investigating your new case."

He peered at her over his shoulder. She was still standing by the sink, arms folded, eyes burning with fury. "Theresa—"

"I want you to leave my house. I don't know why Israel involved you in this, but get gone. *Now.*"

41

Bo waited for Frannie in a conference room at the sheriff's department. He'd driven straight there after leaving the Crutchers. He'd told the clerk at the front that he needed to talk with the chief and had said it was important.

Less than two minutes after his arrival, the door to the room swung open. In stepped Frannie, wearing her khaki uniform with "Chief Deputy Sheriff" embroidered on the lapel. She didn't sit down. "What's up?" she asked.

Bo folded his hands into a tent and peered up at her. "I just left the Crutcher home."

"Been spending a lot of time over there. Didn't realize you and Israel were such good friends. I thought y'all were anything but."

Bo looked down and tapped his fingers on the conference room table. "Israel and I were teammates at Giles County High. We weren't good friends, then or now. But he said something to me last night at the visitation, and it's been bothering me ever since."

"You mean about Brittany being managed by Zannick? Bo, there's no evidence linking Zannick to this crime. Everything points to Odell."

"It wasn't that. Israel asked me if I thought the sheriff's office would give his daughter justice."

Frannie took a seat across from Bo. "The answer to that question is yes."

"Is it? Frannie, if Brittany Crutcher was involved with Zannick, doesn't that change the dynamic a little?"

"Yes, it does," Frannie said. "Does that make you happy, Bo? Yes, Michael Zannick's presence is going to be a dark shadow over this case. He managed Brittany. They were spending a lot of time together in the days and weeks before her death. And according to Brittany's roommate . . ." She glared at him. ". . . yes, we know she wasn't living at home. We know she was estranged from her dad, and we now know that Israel and Theresa Crutcher have separated. It's one big fat mess."

"You were about to tell me what her roommate said. Is that Tasha?"

"Tasha Ferguson." She paused. "Why am I telling you any of this?"

"Because you're a good chief deputy sheriff." He leaned forward. "If I take the case, I'll be entitled to this type of information."

"After the arraignment and not a second sooner."

Bo smiled. "Please."

She rolled her eyes and tapped her fingers on the table. "Tasha said she wasn't spending every night at the apartment."

"Did she say where Brittany was going?"

"No."

"Do you think she was with Zannick those nights?"

"We don't know. He's refused to speak with us."

Bo felt another checker piece fall off the board in his mind. "That's kind of a warning."

"He's rich, Bo. Wealthy people don't like cooperating with police investigations. They're too busy making money."

"He was her manager and helped her sign a major record deal hours before she was killed. Sounds to me like he might have something to hide."

Frannie pursed her lips. "That's a possibility. But it doesn't change all of the evidence we have against Odell."

"What if Odell was framed? What if someone else wanted Brittany dead because they were jealous or mad or both, and framed Odell for her murder, knowing full damn well that he couldn't get a fair trial here or any damn where else because of his background . . . and the color of his skin?"

"Conspiracy theories. If you take the case, good luck with that, Bo. The victim happens to be Black as well—did you forget that?"

"I didn't forget," Bo said. "And I want her killer to be punished as bad as you or anyone else. But I'm not sold on Odell being the murderer. I know that kid, Frannie. He's worked for me. I've been trying to help him."

"Then you should probably take his case," Frannie said. "But it sounds to me like you've been suckered by a con man. A kid who's been in trouble his whole life. Multiple theft convictions. An assault charge that was dropped because he was a football star, and finally an expulsion. The truth is that GCH should have never let Odell in school with his history. But he was good at football, and you know how that story goes."

"You're being shortsighted," Bo said, feeling anger burn through him as he slowly raised himself to his feet. "I seem to remember representing a client who was framed for murder a few months ago and obtaining an acquittal. That was your case, just like this one."

"And let me ask you, Bo. Did Butch Renfroe receive a fair shake? No one has been charged for his homicide. For all intents and purposes, it's an unsolved crime. A cold case. Is that what you're hoping to do here? To muddy the water with your skills so that another victim goes without justice?" Frannie also stood.

Bo kept his voice firm. "All I want is the truth."

Frannie cleared her throat. "This conversation is over. If you want to know any more about the evidence in this case, you'll need to ask the district attorney general. And you'll need to enter an appearance for the defendant." She grabbed the handle and opened the door, stopping for a moment and peering back at him.

"You know, I worshipped you as a child. My aunt loved being your secretary, and I grew up hearing stories about the great Bocephus

185

Haynes, the only Black lawyer in Pulaski. I thought you were a hero to this community." Bo didn't say anything as she pointed her index finger at him. "Aunt Ellie would be sick to her stomach at what you are doing. Brittany Crutcher was a member of your church. *Our* church. She was the daughter of your old teammate. A young Black woman with tremendous talent trying to make good in this town and in the world. Taking Odell's side will pit you against your community and your friends and everything you've stood for your whole life. You prepared to do that?"

Bo let the question hang in the air.

"And at the end of the day," Frannie continued, exasperation creeping into her voice, "all any of this Zannick talk is going to do is provide Odell Champagne even more motive for killing Brittany. Good luck with that."

Then she slammed the door in his face.

42

The funeral of Brittany Crutcher was officiated by Reverend Coy Holland. The Bickland Creek Baptist Church was filled to capacity, with some attendees watching from a television set in the parking lot outside. Cassie Dugan sat next to her brother, Ian, and the rest of the band in the second row directly behind the family. She gripped her brother's hand tight and dabbed her eyes with a handkerchief.

Reverend Holland began the ceremony with the familiar words of Psalm 23.

"The Lord is my shepherd; I shall not want."

As he continued, Cassie glanced down the pew to Teddy B. and Mack. Both had tears in their eyes but managed a nod. She returned the gesture.

"Relax, sis," Ian whispered beside her.

"He maketh me to lie down in green pastures: he leadeth me beside the still waters."

Cassie had never sung lead for the band. It didn't feel right. Especially not after what she'd done.

"He restoreth my soul: he leadeth me in the paths of righteousness for his name's sake."

But how could she refuse Brittany's mom's only request of the band?

"Yea, though I walk through the valley of the shadow of death, I will fear no evil: for thou art with me; thy rod and thy staff they comfort me."

Up until Friday night, Cassie Dugan had felt like she'd lived a good life. There wasn't a doubt in her mind that she was going to heaven. She'd see her dad and grandmother again in eternity.

"Thou preparest a table before me in the presence of mine enemies . . ."

Now, she figured she might not end up on the streets of gold. Why had she done it? Why?

". . . thou anointest my head with oil; my cup runneth over."

Behind Reverend Holland, Cassie tried to focus on the acoustic guitar that her brother would be playing in a couple of minutes. They had rehearsed this version of the song in her garage last night. It was good—she knew it was—but it all felt wrong.

"Surely goodness and mercy shall follow me all the days of my life . . ."

Cassie wiped her eyes again, wondering if the Lord would be merciful to her on Judgment Day.

". . . and I will dwell in the house of the Lord forever."

As Reverend Holland asked the congregation to pray silently to themselves, Cassie, Ian, Teddy B., and Mack slowly walked toward the pulpit. Teddy B. and Mack stood solemnly on either side while Ian and Cassie sat on stools between them. Ian strummed the opening bars, and Cassie began to sing. For most of the song, she kept herself under control, but when she got to the chorus, she couldn't stop the tears or the slightest of cracks in her voice.

"Yesterday's forever . . . *we love you, Brittany* . . .

. . . but tomorrow's gone."

43

Chief Deputy Sheriff Frannie Storm walked into the district attorney general's office without knocking. She'd come here immediately after the funeral.

"Where is she?" Frannie asked, looking at Trish DeMonia, Helen's longtime receptionist and assistant.

When Trish didn't immediately respond, Frannie pushed past her desk toward the General's private office and grabbed the knob.

"She's not—"

But Trish's words were drowned out when Frannie slammed the door shut. For a moment, she had to get her bearings. Gone were the familiar adornments and trophies of a prestigious legal career that had covered the walls of the office for as long as Frannie had been in the sheriff's department. Instead, the walls were barren. The desk was also empty except for a piece of paper. Frannie snatched it up and saw the familiar letterhead of the district attorney general's office.

> To Whom It May Concern:
> I hereby announce that I will be taking an indefinite leave of absence as the district attorney general for the Twenty-Second Judicial District. My decision is due to personal reasons related to my health and is made with the recommendation and suggestion of my physician. It is my hope that my assistant, Gloria Sanchez, be made acting district attorney general in my stead.

Gloria is an accomplished prosecutor in whom I have
the utmost confidence and respect.
Very Truly Yours,
Helen Evangeline Lewis

After taking a few moments to read and reread the letter, Frannie
walked out of the office, still holding it in her hand. "Is this for real?"
she asked Trish.

The veteran staff member nodded. "She cleaned out her office this
morning. I've sent the original of that letter to Judge Page." Harold Page
was the dean of the judges in the Twenty-Second Judicial Circuit, and
it would be up to him to appoint an acting district attorney general.

"Do you expect him to select Gloria as the General recommended?"

She handed Frannie another piece of paper. "He already has."

Frannie snatched the page and held it up—an administrative order
issued by the Honorable Harold Page, appointing assistant prosecutor,
Gloria Sanchez, as the interim district attorney general for the Twenty-
Second Judicial District.

Frannie looked from the page to Trish, whose face was pale, her eyes
red. "This come as a shock to you?"

"I still can't believe it," the secretary managed, her voice shaky.

"Did she tell you anything else besides what's in her letter?"

Trish clasped her hands together. "She said she was exhausted. That
she'd been tired since the election and that the last couple of days had
taken too much of a toll. That the Crutcher case deserved better than
what she could offer."

Frannie stared at Trish but saw no sign that the assistant was lying
to her. She looked again at Helen's letter. *This is crazy.* She started to
walk back into the General's office but hesitated when she heard footsteps entering the reception area behind her. She turned and saw Gloria
Sanchez striding toward her. The young prosecutor had an olive com-
plexion, brown hair, and a wiry frame. She stopped when she was a

couple of feet away from Frannie. For a long moment, the two women sized each other up. Gloria had started in the DA's office around the same time Frannie had joined the sheriff's department. Though Frannie wasn't friends with many of her colleagues, she had always liked Gloria, and they'd sometimes worked out together at the Curry Center after hours.

"Hell of a day you're having . . . *General*," Frannie said, a slight tease in her voice.

"I could say the same about your weekend," Gloria fired back, a tired smile forming on her face. "We have a lot of work to do."

44

At 9:00 p.m., Helen sat in the front seat of her Crown Vic, gazing up at the mansion on the hill. Her phone rang several times. She looked down at the screen, seeing the digits she knew by heart. This time, she didn't answer. She didn't want to talk with him, didn't want to talk with anyone. Eventually, she pulled back onto Highway 31 and drove back toward town, parking near Maplewood Cemetery.

Earlier today, Brittany Crutcher had been laid to rest right here. Helen hadn't gone to the funeral service at Bickland Creek Baptist Church. After boxing up her things and drafting her leave of absence letter, she'd fled downtown Pulaski and driven to her house. After unloading all the boxes, she'd packed her suitcase without much conscious thought. She didn't want to stick around for the onslaught of questions. If they wanted to talk with her, they could call.

Then, after leaving her house, she'd driven the back roads of Giles County for hours, thinking everything through one last time, always coming to the same conclusion.

She knew she had done the right thing. There was no way she could prosecute Odell Champagne for murder. Not with Bo possibly serving as his attorney. And not with . . . *my son as a person of interest.*

Helen stared out at the two and a half acres of land that marked the final resting place for thousands of sons and daughters of Pulaski. Many times over the past three and a half months, Helen had climbed over the fence that enclosed the cemetery and sat beside her dead ex-husband's grave. She would apologize to Butch and ask God to forgive her. And, many times, she'd gotten drunk.

Tonight, she wouldn't go inside. Though Brittany's burial had been several hours ago and Helen didn't see any people or cars around, she couldn't take the chance of being seen here at night. After all, it was a crime to be at the cemetery after dark.

Helen managed a bitter laugh. Given what she'd done and gotten away with, it was ludicrous for her to worry about a trespassing-after-dark charge. And yet she did. Her whole life had become an ironic farce.

She said one last prayer for forgiveness.

Then, hating herself and who she had become, Helen Evangeline Lewis left Pulaski.

45

Bo stared at the woman on the bed, who drifted in and out of consciousness. "Sabrina," he whispered. "It's me, Bo. I'm here."

When she didn't look up, he moved his eyes around the small room, glancing at the different monitors that kept track of her blood pressure, oxygen saturation, and heart rate. A nurse came in and placed a cold washcloth on Sabrina's forehead.

Bo stood to allow more room. The number that Sabrina had given Lona was to the hospital. She'd been admitted to the detox unit of Southern Tennessee Regional Health System, formerly known as Hillside Hospital, on Saturday evening after Frannie had brought her to the emergency room. The only visitors she'd given permission to see her were her son and Bo.

As the nurse was leaving, Bo saw that Sabrina's eyes were now open. He sat down and took her hand. "Hey, you OK?"

"Bo?"

"Yeah, I'm here."

"You came." Tears formed in the corners of Sabrina's eyes.

"You called me." He paused, again glancing around the hospital room. "How are you feeling?"

"Shaky. Very shaky."

"What happened to you on Friday? I called and texted you at the game."

She grimaced. "The game . . . I missed the game."

"That's not all you've missed," Bo said.

"He didn't do it," she said, closing her eyes. "He couldn't have hurt that girl."

"How do you know about it?"

"Chief Storm has been up here a couple times. She asked me some questions about Odell and said they'd searched my apartment." She pointed toward the door. "Plus, there's a TV room they let us go to. Seems like there's a news story about that girl's murder every time I go in there."

"Did the sheriff's office find anything at your place?"

"Chief Storm didn't say."

Bo pushed his chair back and crossed his legs. The room had a sour stink to it, a mixture of sweat and vomit and unwashed bodies. He didn't want to be here any longer than he had to be.

"What have the doctors said?" Bo asked.

"Pancreatitis," she said, coughing the last syllable out. "And alcohol addiction. They want me to go to rehab."

"You should."

"Can't afford it," Sabrina said. "My insurance won't cover it. Besides, rehab ain't gonna work on me."

"You won't know unless you try."

"Easy for you to say. Everyone thinks they can fix me. All I got to do is go to rehab and listen to some shrinks. Group therapy." She chuckled. "My name is Sabrina Champagne, and I'm an addict."

"Treatment has worked for a lot of people."

She coughed. "Not me. Tried it three years ago when we were in Town Creek. Bradford for ninety days. All I got out of that was three months' worth of smoking two packs of cigarettes a day. So now I'm addicted to that too."

"What did Odell do while you were gone?"

"Stayed with his aunt in Trinity, Alabama."

Bo crossed his arms. "Does Odell know you're here?"

Her lip began to tremble again. "Yes. I called the jail and left my number, and he called me here yesterday. He told me that he'd asked you to represent him but that he hadn't heard from you yet."

"I don't know if I can," Bo said. "I've known the Crutcher family all my life."

"He didn't kill that girl, Bo," she whined. "He's innocent. You have to know that."

"Whether I represent him or not, he'll get a fair trial."

She snickered. "Will he? A Black transient from Town Creek? You're smarter than that, Bocephus Haynes."

"Why did you ask me to come here?"

She leaned over the bed and grabbed his hand. "Help my baby, Bo. Please. Help him."

Bo wriggled out of her grasp, trying not to gag from the smell. "I told Odell I would think about it, and that's what I've been doing."

"Thinking ain't going to help my boy."

"You think you're helping him, Sabrina? Have they told you why you have pancreatitis?"

Her eyes again went misty.

"Because you're drinking yourself to death, right? How is that helping your boy? You're addicted to alcohol and drugs, but you won't get help."

"Bo, my husband abandoned me when Odell was five years old. I've raised him entirely on my own."

"And you carry that badge with you wherever you go. It doesn't excuse your drinking and drug use. You can't use that as a crutch your whole life." Bo gritted his teeth. "I know that times were hard. I mean, I can only imagine. But Billy leaving you is no excuse for throwing your whole life away."

Sabrina began to sob. Bo swiveled and headed for the door. He couldn't take any more.

"Please, Bo. I'll get help, I promise. I'll try. I'll fight the insurance company and find somewhere to go. Please represent Odell."

"I don't believe you," he said, opening the door and hesitating for several seconds. "But for Odell's sake, I hope you prove me wrong."

46

Have you decided yet?

Bo peered at his phone and shook his head. Booker T. had sent him several similar texts since Saturday. Bo had answered them all the same. He started to type out *No* again but then stopped himself. He took another sip of beer and looked up at the TV screen, where a rerun of *Cheers* was playing.

After leaving the hospital, Bo had gotten fast food for the kids and asked T. J. to watch Lila, saying he needed some time to clear his head. He'd gone for a long walk, eventually ending up at Kathy's Tavern, one of downtown Pulaski's oldest, most successful watering holes.

He'd ordered a Yuengling in a bottle and a cheeseburger, the house specialty. For the past hour, he'd been lost in his thoughts as the Monday Night Football crowd began to filter out after the game was over. Other than Bo himself, the only other person in the place now was Clete Sartain, who sat on a barstool in the corner, stroking his white Santa Claus beard and sipping Natural Light from a can. Bo and Clete went way back, but they'd already exchanged pleasantries and both were happy to drink alone. Finally, Clete patted Bo on the back and headed for the door himself. "Hope you figure it out, Bo."

Bo called to him over his shoulder. "Figure what out?"

"Whatever the hell is on your mind," Clete said, not turning back to look at him.

Bo couldn't help but smile, and looking over the bar, he saw that the bartender was also smiling. "Old Clete is something else, isn't he, Cassie?"

Cassie Dugan was a thirtysomething-year-old woman who'd been tending the bar at Kathy's ever since she turned twenty-one. She wore her customary football season outfit, which consisted of cutoff jeans, a UT Vols number 19 jersey with the name "Manning" on the back of it, and a Tennessee Titans cap covering her brown hair. She was an attractive woman whose good-natured personality made her a favorite of patrons. She was also a great source of information and had aided Bo with key nuggets over the years. More importantly, she was the de facto manager of Fizz, and Bo had watched her sing at Brittany's funeral earlier today. As he finished his third beer, he admitted to himself that Cassie was the real reason he was here. Even trying to clear his mind, he was, in actuality, working the case.

"They broke the mold when they made him," Cassie agreed. "Another beer, Bo?" She grabbed the empty Yuengling and flung it into a garbage can.

"No, Cassie. Maybe some ice water if that's OK."

"Coming right up."

Cassie took a Styrofoam cup out of a box and filled it with ice. Then she poured the water while peering at Bo. "Haven't seen you in here in a while."

"Too long," Bo said. "Kids seem to have something every night."

"So what brings you this way? Not our famous cheeseburger, I presume."

"The burger was awesome as always, but . . . no. That's not why I'm here."

"Big surprise," she said, her voice oozing pleasant sarcasm. "But I don't know of any big local cases of yours. Everything you had going that I'm aware of since the General's trial has settled, hasn't it?"

Before he could agree, she leaned over the table and whispered, "Did you hear that she left today?"

Bo creased her eyebrows. "Who?"

"The General. She quit the DA's office. Boxed up all her things. Said she was taking a leave of absence for personal reasons."

Bo could hardly believe his ears. He considered the General a friend, and she hadn't mentioned that she was leaving. Two days ago, when she'd found Bo on the farm, she had been very much still working. *What the hell happened?* "So who's going to—"

"Gloria Sanchez was appointed this afternoon. You like her?"

Bo suppressed a smile. He was always amazed at how quickly news traveled in Pulaski and, specifically, how fast that Cassie accumulated it. She was like a human sponge.

"Gloria is OK. Smart and fair from what I've found."

"I've heard she's a bitch," Cassie said, taking another Yuengling out of the cooler and popping the top.

"I said I didn't—" He stopped when he saw her take a sip of the beverage.

"Don't mind if I do," Cassie said, taking three dollars out of her wallet and putting it in the cash register. "Wouldn't want you to think I was filching."

"I would never think that."

"Been a long day."

Bo nodded. "You sang beautifully at the funeral."

Cassie took a sip and looked away. "Thank you. I . . . still can't believe she's gone, you know?"

"You knew her well, didn't you?"

Cassie shrugged. "Thought I did."

Bo felt the hair on his arms tingle. "What do you mean?"

Cassie took another sip of beer. "Don't get me wrong. I loved Brittany like a younger sister, but she was doing things that she wasn't telling me and the band about."

"Like?"

"Like signing a solo recording contract with ELEKTRIK HI and using Michael Zannick as her manager."

Bo raised his eyebrows. This wasn't new information, but he acted like it was. "Solo?"

"Yep. I'd been shopping the band to record labels for months. I was positive that Fizz was going to land somewhere soon. Especially after 'Tomorrow's Gone' got some play on the radio. I wrote that song, you know."

"I didn't know."

"Yeah, I did. I also named the band." She took a sip of beer and gave her head a jerk. "We always played our best. Never took a night off. If we were a soda, we were never flat. We always had—"

"Fizz," Bo said. "Clever."

"I thought so. Some folks said it was cheesy, but for me, it was perfect. And when we found Brittany, everything seemed in reach. She was our X factor." Cassie paused, and a sad smile appeared on her face. "I almost had my own record deal, did you know that? I tried out for *American Idol.* I made it past the first few cuts, and there was some interest from a couple labels, but nothing ever developed. I didn't have the vocal range that Brittany did." She drank some more of her beer. "Hell, no one did. She was . . ." Cassie's eyes watered, and she looked down at the bar. ". . . incredible."

"I'm sorry," Bo said, running a thumb over the rim of his cup. "When did you learn about her solo recording deal and that Zannick was managing her?"

"Here," Cassie said. "Friday night a couple hours before Fizz played the Brickyard. She came here and told me in person."

"Were you mad?"

Cassie took a long pull from the bottle. "I was furious. I felt like she had pulled the rug out from under us."

Bo took a sip of water, watching the bartender. What she was describing would have provided a healthy motive for murder. He thought about asking whether the sheriff's office had questioned her but decided against it. "Did anyone else in the band know what she'd done? How about your brother, Ian?"

Cassie scratched her head. "I'm sure Ian knew something was up. After the concert was over, I texted him and told him not to leave the stadium without getting our grandmother's necklace from Brittany. I explained that I'd told Brittany I wanted it back and to make damn sure he got it and that I would explain everything over the weekend. I'm sure he thought that was weird, because I'd given that piece of jewelry to Brittany to wear for good luck before *America's Got Talent*, and it had been on her neck almost every second since."

"What did he say?"

"That he'd get it."

"Did he?"

Cassie finished the remains of her beer and threw the bottle in the trash can. Then she turned toward the cash register and opened a drawer, pulling out a thin chain with a purple stone. She held it out for Bo to see.

"Beautiful," he said.

She stuck out her chin. "Brittany was born in February, same as my nana. The birthstone is amethyst, which, for my money, is the most striking purple you'll ever see. I gave it to her for luck," she said, her voice quaking. "She died a few hours after giving it back. I know this is crazy, but I can't help but think the necklace would have somehow protected her if I hadn't asked . . ."

The emotions were too much, and Cassie slammed her fist on the table. She returned the necklace to the drawer and snatched a fifth of Jack Daniel's off the shelf. She poured herself a shot. When she reached into her purse for her wallet, Bo waved her off.

"Let me get this one, Cassie, and pour me one too."

She poured another shot and handed it to Bo. "To Brittany," she said, her voice cracking.

"To Brittany," Bo whispered, drinking the whiskey but keeping his eyes on Cassie, who threw back the shot glass and grimaced as she swallowed the liquor. Then she grabbed another Yuengling from the cooler.

"Put that one on my tab too," Bo said. "And grab me one as well." He knew he was drinking too much, but alcohol was a good way to keep someone talking. Besides, he'd walked here.

"So . . . ," she said, taking a swig of beer. "Based on all these questions, I would say that you must be Odell Champagne's lawyer."

"Nothing gets by you."

She mockingly tapped her index finger against her temple. "Like an iron trap."

Bo laughed. "You mean a steel trap."

"Whatever. Just drink your beer if you're going to make fun of me. So . . . are you his lawyer?"

"Not yet," he said. "I'm thinking about it."

Cassie cocked her head and sipped from the Yuengling. "Based on what I'm hearing, you should crank the *Mission: Impossible* music."

"What are you hearing?"

"Found at the scene, right next to a broken beer bottle with her blood all over it."

Bo's hands tensed around his bottle. *No wonder they've already charged him.* "How'd you hear that?"

"A couple reporters at the scene were in here drinking on Saturday night, and one of them let it slip." She smiled. "And Melvin came in yesterday and confirmed it."

"Melvin Ragland, the county coroner?"

Cassie pointed her bottle at him. "Comes in here every Sunday after church for a cheeseburger, fries, and a Dr Pepper. I asked him if my intel was true, and he said it was. Swore me to secrecy." Cassie winked, and Bo returned the gesture.

"Did you see Odell and Brittany together much?"

She nodded. "Oh, yeah. He was at all our local events. He enjoyed watching the band practice too. Everyone in Fizz really liked O, especially my brother, Ian." She shook her head. "I still can't believe it, you know?"

"Do you know if Ian was hanging out with Odell on Friday night?"

"Not sure. Ian went to that party that everyone went to after the game—he told me that."

"Doug Fitzgerald's house?"

"Yes," she said. "That Fitzgerald kid is a crazy bastard. I've had to kick him out of here several times trying to order beer with a fake ID." She whistled through her teeth. "Idiot."

"How did Ian get home after the party?"

She wrinkled up her nose. "Beats me."

"Does he have a car?"

"Yeah, but as I recollect, he had a friend drive him back to Fitzgerald's house to get it Saturday because he'd been too drunk to drive home."

"Where does Ian live?"

"With me. Our dad died years ago, and Mom is in a nursing home." She took a sip of beer and peered down at the bar.

"Do you remember Ian saying anything about the party when he got home that night? Or maybe the next morning?"

"No. He knows I don't approve of him drinking or anything involving Doug Fitzgerald."

Bo took a sip of his own beer, turning over her answers in his mind. "Did Odell ever act violent around Brittany?"

"Never. He adored her."

"Was she afraid of him?"

"Not to my knowledge," Cassie said. "Course I'm learning now that I didn't know everything there was to know about Brittany. Somehow the person who collects all the dirt in this town didn't realize that Pulaski's most famous young citizen was messing around with its richest, most eligible bachelor."

"She and Zannick had a personal relationship too?"

"Brittany said no, but . . ."

"But what?"

"But I dated Michael Zannick. I think I know him about as well as anyone around here." She sipped her beer, cleared her throat. "Michael wasn't helping Cassie out of the goodness of his heart. You know as well as I do that he has a thing for young girls."

"Mandy Burks."

"Exactly." She took another long pull from the bottle. "What was the real story there anyway? He always told me that Mandy had played him and that he didn't rape her."

"I believe Mandy," Bo said, not hesitating for a second.

"Me too." She finished the rest of her beer and threw it in the trash. "You want to know what else I believe?"

"Sure," Bo said.

"I believe that it's closing time," she said. "And I'm drunk . . . and very lonely." She stared at him, and Bo felt something stir in his loins. It had been a long time since a woman had looked at him like Cassie was now.

Bo slid off his stool and took a step back from the bar.

"What?" she asked. "Not attracted to me?"

"It's not that," Bo said. "It's just . . . I know you're hurting right now because of Brittany, and . . . I haven't been with a woman in a long time." He rubbed the third finger of his left hand, fumbling for the right words.

She walked around the bar and grabbed his hand. "You're sweet, Bo. You've always been good to me."

"I like you, Cassie," he said. "Just not in—"

She pressed a hand to his lips. "I understand. Now . . ." She grabbed the closing sign from behind the bar. ". . . if you'll excuse me, I need to lock up."

Bo took out his wallet and placed three twenties on the bar to cover his meal and their drinks. Then he turned and headed for the exit. As his hand grasped the doorknob, he felt Cassie's touch on his shoulder. "Cassie—"

"You know you asked if Brittany was afraid of Odell?" she whispered. She was so close that Bo could smell the whiskey and beer on her breath. "She wasn't afraid of him, but I think she was afraid of someone else."

"Zannick?" Bo asked.

She nodded and leaned close to him, whispering into his ear. "Let me know if you ever change your mind about my offer."

Bo took a step back and watched as the door closed behind him. Seconds later, he heard the dead bolt click.

———

Inside the bar, Cassie Dugan poured herself a shot of whiskey and popped the top on another beer. She sat on the barstool that Bo had vacated and stared at herself in the mirror on the wall. *Is this what I've come to? Hitting on older men at closing time?* She glared at her reflection. Then she took the shot and chased it with a long swallow of beer.

She'd always been fond of Bocephus Haynes. Truth be told, she'd like to hook up with him. But her flirting tonight had been desperate. Deceptive. She'd wanted to end the questioning and not have it seem like she was hiding anything.

She chuckled. If there was anyone who might understand if she confessed the truth, it might be Bo.

But I can't. There was too much at stake. Cassie drank down the rest of the beer. She threw the bottle toward the trash can, but her aim was off, and it crashed into the wall.

As the sound of the glass shattering into pieces filled the confines of the empty space, Cassie Dugan put her head on the cold mahogany bar and began to cry.

47

Bo didn't sleep the rest of the night. Instead, after walking home, he sat out on his covered porch with Lee Roy until the sun began to rise. He watched the stars and moon through the opening under the porch, his mind racing, his body wired and tense from the events of the day.

He thought of Odell, going to sleep for the third night in a row in a jail cell. Odell's mother, Sabrina, coming in and out of lucidity in the detox ward of old Hillside Hospital. He thought of Israel Crutcher, staying in a hotel, mourning his daughter, and still holding a forty-year-old grudge against Bo. And Theresa, who'd kicked Bo out of her house that morning. General Helen Lewis, his client and friend, who'd resigned without telling Bo. He envisioned Brittany Crutcher, a shooting star, whose life had been violently taken. But by whom?

Odell?

Zannick?

Someone else?

He wondered what his mentor, Tom McMurtrie, would have thought of this case and what the Professor's advice would have been if cancer hadn't taken him two and a half years ago.

Finally, he thought of Jazz. He imagined her sometimes looking down on him from her perch in heaven. He wondered what she would have thought about Cassie Dugan's advances on him a few short hours earlier. He laughed, thinking that Jazz would have said that he'd run like a scared puppy. "I'm not ready," Bo whispered, and then, as he often did when he thought of his wife, he cried.

Eventually, as the sun had begun its ascent, Bo's body finally gave out, and he closed his eyes.

———

He didn't open them until he smelled the strong scent of coffee filling his nostrils. When he did, he saw a mug with smoke steaming off the top of it and his daughter standing over him.

"I bet you could use this."

Bo reached out and grabbed the mug with both hands, taking a sip and then standing from the rocking chair, his back, neck, and legs sore and stiff.

"Breakfast is ready," Lila declared.

When he went into the kitchen, Bo forced a smile and plopped down at the head of the table. Noticing that both of his kids were eye-balling him, he asked, "What?"

"We think you should do it," Lila said, putting a plate of eggs and bacon in front of him.

"Do what?" Bo asked.

"Represent Odell," T. J. said.

Bo rubbed his tired eyes. "You know that if I take this case, it's going to be a very unpopular decision in our church and with a lot of your friends."

"You've always taught us to do the right thing," T. J. said. "Well . . . sometimes doing right can put you on the wrong side of your friends."

"This ain't only our friends. Odell is charged with killing the most popular person in this town. Brittany Crutcher was going to put Pulaski on the map far and wide for her music."

"And Odell was on his way to being a football star," T. J. said. "Like you."

"What if he's guilty?" Bo asked. "And son, you realize that you're going to be a prosecution witness in the case. Representing Odell would put me on the opposite side of you too."

"No it won't," T. J. said. "All I'm going to do is tell the truth."

"Dad," Lila said, her voice quieter than T. J.'s. She was standing by the refrigerator. "Do you believe that Odell is innocent?"

Bo thought back to his encounter with the young man in the consultation room on Saturday and then everything he'd heard since, especially last night with Cassie Dugan. Brittany wasn't afraid of Odell; the only person who'd frightened her was Zannick.

"Yes," he admitted.

"Then do what you think is right," she said. "We can deal with whatever you decide."

"That how you feel?" He turned to his son.

T. J. nodded. "If it makes a difference to you, I think Odell is innocent too. I haven't known him that long, but my gut feeling is that the cops have it wrong. Odell was mad about the breakup, and he was blowing off steam at Doug's party. He got drunk and said some things he didn't mean." T. J. shook his head. "I've seen how hard Odell works. On the farm, on the football field, and even in the classroom. He was really trying for a fresh start here."

"That doesn't mean he couldn't have lost his temper and hurt Brittany," Bo said.

"I know that, but I don't see him doing it. He made some mistakes Friday night. He drank way too much, shouldn't have gotten into it with Jarvis. He should have left the party with us. But you have to understand something, Dad. Odell was, like, super protective of Brittany. I never saw him so much as raise his voice at her." He paused and looked at Bo. "There's gotta be something that they're missing."

Bo took a sip of the scalding-hot coffee and looked at T. J. "Thank you, son. Your opinion does make a difference to me." Then he felt emotion getting the better of him. "I love you guys. With all my heart."

"Love you too," Lila said.

"Your momma sure would . . ." Bo couldn't get the rest of it out, and his lips began to shake. He looked down at the table and tried to compose himself. As he placed a forkful of eggs in his mouth and tried to chew, he felt his daughter's hand take his own.

"She'd be proud of you too, Daddy."

48

Bo didn't wait for pleasantries when he entered the office and saw Lona behind her desk, the phone again crooked between her shoulder and neck. "Need you to draft up a notice of appearance for me in a new case, and I want it filed this morning," he said.

"Yes, sir," Lona said, still holding the receiver. "What's the case?"

"State of Tennessee versus Odell Jerome Champagne."

Lona dropped the phone, and it clanked onto the desk. Five seconds later, the busy signal rang out from the receiver, but she took no notice. "Are you serious?"

"As a heart attack. I want you to also draft up a request for discovery and a motion for an expedited preliminary hearing. I want them filed at the same time as the notice of appearance and courtesy copies hand delivered to the district attorney general's and to the sheriff's department, attention Chief Deputy Sheriff Frannie Storm."

Lona took the phone and placed it on the hook and turned to face her computer. "Just when I was thinking things might slow down a tad."

Bo stuck out his chin. "You know how we roll around here."

She placed her hands on the keyboard. "Wide ass open."

PART THREE

49

Hate.

Bocephus Haynes had been motivated by it his whole life. Hate for racism. Hate for inequality. Hate for injustice.

Now, though, he and his client were on the receiving end of the same hate.

He gazed out the window of his office and saw protesters lining First Street. They were an eclectic group of Black and white citizens, many of whom were holding "JUSTICE FOR BRITTANY" banners containing a photograph of the murdered singer.

"Happy?" Booker T. said, standing next to his cousin with his arms folded.

"I didn't ask you to be here," Bo fired back, moving his eyes around the mob. He recognized the Reverend Coy Holland in the crowd, not carrying a sign but holding hands with two of the older parishioners of the Bickland Creek Baptist Church. Bo knew them. Regina Humphrey and Jesse Strong, both in their eighties. They'd welcomed Bo and Jazz to the church three decades ago and prayed with the young couple when they were having trouble having a baby. They'd been to Jazz's baby shower when she was pregnant with T. J.

Now they're here. Two people I've known most of my life. Protesting against me.

Booker T. turned and glared at Bo, flexing his pectoral muscles. "You're my cousin, and outside of my kids and Thelma, you're the only family I got. I don't trust the police escort you have coming. I want those folks out there to know that if they take a shot at you, they're probably going to hit me too."

"They probably won't hit anything but you."

"Not funny," Booker T. said, glancing down at his watch. "It's eight thirty-two a.m. When does the preliminary hearing start?"

"At nine," Bo said, feeling butterflies in his stomach.

"So when are these sheriff's deputies going to be here?"

"Any minute," Bo said.

"Remind me again why you didn't drive to the courthouse a couple of hours ago," Booker T. grumbled.

"Because I kind of like my Tahoe and don't want it to be destroyed."

"Bullshit. You're doing this for the cameras, aren't you? Hero lawyer, Bocephus Haynes, facing down the threats of an angry assembly and pushing through the crowd. What courage in the face of adversity."

"Go to hell," Bo said, but he wondered if maybe there was some truth to what Booker T. was saying. The townspeople who would eventually sit on the jury to decide this case would likely see this spectacle.

"Here come the troops," Booker T. said.

Bo opened his eyes and saw the uniforms pushing through the crowd. They were wearing helmets and carrying batons. "*Jesus*," he whispered, praying that there would be no violence.

Seconds later, a deputy was let in the office by Booker T. and took off his helmet. "Ready, Mr. Haynes?"

Bo looked at his cousin and then at Lona, who was watching from behind her desk. "Good luck," she managed.

Bo turned back to the officer. "Let's get on with it."

50

Booker T. exited the office first with Bo and three deputies right behind him. The crowd parted for Bo's gigantic cousin, which allowed enough space for Bo and the officers to make a beeline for the waiting police cruiser. Seconds later, they were in the car and edging their way down First Street toward the courthouse. Bo watched through the window until Booker T., with the assistance of two more officers, safely made his way back into the office. Then he turned his attention toward the courthouse, where another swell of people was marching on the south side of the building.

The cruiser parked between two other police vehicles, and Bo exited the vehicle and walked toward the basement entrance of the building, surrounded by uniforms. When he entered the courthouse, Chief Frannie Storm was waiting for him.

"You OK?" she asked, nodding for the other deputies to give them some space.

"Fine," Bo lied. "Thank you for the escort."

Frannie scoffed. "The last thing we need is the type of negative press an attack on you would bring." She gestured toward the exit. "But this town is angry, Bo. And a lot of folks don't understand what you're doing."

"All I want is the truth."

"Wrong." Frannie took a step closer to Bo and lowered her voice. "All you want is the publicity. This case was supposed to be about

Brittany Crutcher. About proving the guilt of her killer and giving him a just punishment. But you've turned it into a circus."

"It became a circus the minute Odell was arrested, and you know it," Bo said.

"Do you really believe he's innocent?"

"I do," Bo said, without hesitation.

She shook her head. "Let's see how you feel about it at the end of today."

———

In the state of Tennessee, anyone charged with a felony was entitled to a preliminary hearing, where the state was held to the minimum burden of showing probable cause that the defendant committed the crime with which he or she was charged. Assuming the judge found that the prosecution had met this low burden, which His or Her Honor almost always did, the case would then be bound over to a grand jury.

For a criminal defendant, the preliminary hearing was a chance to see a sneak preview of the state's case. Though some defendants waived their right to a prelim, most, on the advice of counsel, used it as a discovery device to learn as much as they possibly could about the state's evidence.

As Bo entered the historic circuit courtroom, he felt the rush that always accompanied the commencement of a hearing or trial. It was one of the reasons he enjoyed what he did. Few jobs, he suspected, could capture the same sense of competition and intensity he had felt on a football field, but being a trial lawyer was close.

Being the defendant in this situation was a different feeling—one Bo also knew—and he could tell, as he took a seat next to Odell, that his client was scared to death. The boy looked at Bo with wide eyes. "Do I look all right?"

He was wearing a charcoal suit that Bo had bought for him with a white button-down shirt and maroon tie. In some ways, Bo felt like he was looking through a time capsule at a smaller version of himself. "You look great," Bo said.

"Thank you for the threads," Odell said.

"Remember what I said," Bo whispered into his client's ear. "Don't let them see you sweat. Every single facial gesture of yours today could be captured by a potential juror that will decide your fate when we try this case in a couple months. Keep your emotions in check. All we're doing today is seeing what they have. Understand?"

"Yes, sir."

Bo gazed around the courtroom, which was packed wall to wall with people and reporters. Even the ancient balcony, which originally had been where the Black visitors were required to sit but was now more of a museum attraction, was full to capacity. *Crazy,* he thought. His eyes shifted to the prosecution table, where Gloria Sanchez was reviewing a stack of documents, likely the witness statements her office had gathered over the past thirty days.

Since entering his appearance, Bo hadn't been privy to any of those statements, as there was no discovery in a criminal case in Tennessee until after the indictment was handed down. He didn't know what the prosecution had. All Gloria had told him was that Bo would be begging for a plea deal after the prelim. Chief Deputy Sheriff Frannie Storm, who was sitting to the left of Gloria, had been similarly tight lipped. She had reiterated what Bo already knew. If Helen Lewis were still the district attorney general, there was no way she would have turned over any discovery materials before the indictment. Why should Bo expect any different from the new General?

So Bo had done what he could do. He'd met with Odell several times, and he believed he had a solid timeline of what his client could remember from the night of the murder. He'd also met with several of the football players, though many chose, at the request of their parents, not to speak with him. He'd also done as much work on his other cases as he could. He knew the Champagne murder case would go into full-court press mode as soon as this hearing was over. Given the notoriety of both the victim and the defendant, he figured the court would move with all deliberate speed through the necessary hoops before trial.

Bo hadn't come to any sort of fee agreement with Odell. He knew the kid couldn't pay him, and Sabrina, true to her promise to Bo, was now in a rehab facility in Madison, Alabama. He hoped, for Odell's sake, that therapy would take this time. Odell would need his mother as the case neared its conclusion. One person Bo hadn't heard from was Odell's father, but he was planning to rectify that situation soon. If he was going to have any chance of obtaining an acquittal, he felt he needed to know as much about his client as possible.

"Who's that?" Odell's voice brought Bo back to the present. He looked at his client, who nodded toward the door to the judge's chambers, which had opened. A short, buff man whose skin had darkened orange from years of tanning bed use stepped into the courtroom. Ricardo "Sundance" Cassidy had been the court bailiff for the past decade, and he and Bo had always been friendly to one another. Sundance cleared his throat, and his deep voice echoed over the courtroom, cutting off all other noise.

"ALL RISE! Court is now in session. The Honorable Harold Page presiding."

Bo and Odell stood and watched Harold Page stride to the bench. His Honor was the dean of the judiciary branch of the Twenty-Second Judicial District, which comprised the counties of Giles, Maury, Lawrence, and Wayne. He was now seventy-five years old and, by the look of his slouching shoulders and droopy eyes, was showing his age. The judge sat down and motioned with his hands for everyone else to do the same. Bo and Odell sat, but Bo remained on the edge of his chair, knowing that he'd be back up in a matter of seconds.

"State of Tennessee versus Odell Jerome Champagne," Page called out in an even raspier voice than usual. "Are the parties here?"

"The state is here," Gloria Sanchez said, rising again and nodding at the judge.

"The defendant is present," Bo said, standing and buttoning his coat. Behind him, the sound of rustling and murmurs filtered through the crowd. Bo turned and saw hundreds of sets of eyes all locked on him. Most of the spectators were Black, and at least to Bo, they all had scowls on their faces, none worse than the man and woman on the first row behind the prosecution table. Israel and Theresa Crutcher sat bolt upright with their daughter Gina between them. Israel's gaze burned with intensity as he locked stares with Bo. Since entering his appearance, Bo had only had one encounter with Israel, but the memory sent a cold chill down his spine.

———

It was the day after he'd filed all of his opening paperwork. Lona had already left, and Bo was working late. When he came out to the reception area looking for a document, Israel had been standing in the doorway. He took a step closer to Bo and spoke in a chilling voice, his tone dripping with contempt. "I asked you at the visitation if you thought General Lewis would give my baby girl justice."

"Iz—"

"Shut up. Let me finish." He took another step into the room, and now the two men were only a couple feet apart.

"You said you thought she would." He snickered. "And now look at how things stand. The General has quit and left town. And you . . . *you* . . . you're representing the motherfucker who killed my daughter."

"I believe Odell is innocent."

"You didn't come to my house the other night to pay no damn respects. You came to interview me, didn't you? Just like you interviewed my wife the day of the funeral. If it ain't true, then deny it."

Bo knew that wasn't exactly true, but he also knew that a denial would sound weak and misleading.

"Thanks for not bullshitting me," Israel said, taking another step. He was so close now that Bo could smell the other man's aftershave and the liquor on his breath.

"Iz, why don't you go sleep it off."

"I ain't going to sleep nothing off." He reached out with both hands and pushed Bo hard, causing Bo to stagger backward until his legs hit Lona's desk.

"I'm going to give you that one, Israel. You come at me again, you best believe that I'm going to come back at you."

"You're a fraud and a publicity hound," Israel said, his voice cracking with anguish. "The exposure you're going to get in this case is worth its price in gold, right? Bocephus Haynes again in the spotlight. This time representing the football star charged with murdering the rock star. You trying to go nationwide, ain't you? Why the fuck did you move back here if you were going to betray the people who've had your back your whole life?"

"You've had my back, Iz? When? I seem to recall you only trying to stab me in the back over the years. And where were *you*, Israel, when my world was turned upside down? Did you even come to Jazz's funeral? No, you didn't. I bet you loved every minute of my troubles these last five years."

"You ain't my friend. Haven't been for years. Why should I mourn your wife's death?"

"I mourned your daughter."

"No, you didn't. You're using my baby girl's murder for your own personal gain, you conceited prick." Israel reached out to push Bo again, but this time Bo swiped Israel's hands away, causing the other man to stagger against the wall.

"You do that again, and I won't be so easy on you. You're drunk, you're hurting, and I get it, OK? I understand. But you aren't thinking clearly right now, Israel, and I am. There's something that don't smell right about Brittany's murder."

"How can you be so sure that you're right and the cops are wrong? What about Frannie?"

"Frannie's good people," Bo said. "But she's wrong here."

Finally, Israel chuckled. "You doing this for revenge, aren't you? To get me back for all the times I didn't worship you like all the other Black folks around here."

"You need to go home, Israel," Bo said, moving closer to the other man, left foot in front of his right in a fighter's stance.

Israel squeezed his hands into fists and glared at Bo.

Bo stared at the other man but resolved not to strike unless Israel made another move.

Finally, Israel stumbled toward the door. When he opened it, he looked back at Bo, his eyes steel, voice hard. "If you come to my house ever again for anything . . . I'll kill you." He paused. "And if you use your bullshit skills to put my daughter's killer back on the street, I'll kill both of you."

———

Bo finally broke eye contact with Israel as the banging of the judge's gavel brought him back to the present. He turned, and Judge Page was standing and leaning over the bench. "There will be no further outbursts in this courtroom. If there are, I will have the room cleared and will have any violators arrested and held in contempt." Page then glared down at Bo, sending a clear signal as to who His Honor felt was the true person to blame for all the unrest.

Bo glared right back. He'd tried cases before Harold Page for the greater part of twenty-five years and never liked the former prosecutor turned judge. Page was a conservative arbiter who tended to slant his rulings toward the state in criminal cases and the defendant in civil cases. More times than not, that meant he was ruling against Bo and his clients. Bo could handle the judge's leanings, but over the years, Page had seemed to take a particular fondness for giving Bo the screws. Drawing Harold as the judge on this case, as opposed to the fair-minded Susan Connelly, was the first break in the case, and it was a bad one. Hopefully that wouldn't be a sign of things to come.

His Honor moved his eyes to the prosecution table. "General Sanchez, are you ready to begin?"

"Yes, Your Honor," Gloria said.

51

The first witness for the state was county coroner Melvin Ragland, whom Bo had questioned at least a dozen times in court over the past two decades. After being sworn in, Melvin testified that in his opinion, based on his education, experience, and training as well as his thorough autopsy of the victim's body, Brittany Crutcher's death was proximately caused by blunt force trauma to the forehead, which fractured her skull.

Bo was used to the methodical language of the coroner, but he wasn't surprised to hear sniffles from behind the gallery. He forced himself not to turn around and placed his foot over his client's to keep it from tapping. Then he wrote a message on his notepad and pointed at it so Odell could see. *Stay cool.*

Melvin then opined that the instrument that had caused the injury to Brittany's skull was a glass bottle of Bud Light, which had shattered upon impact with the victim's head and was found in the bus yard approximately two hundred yards from the victim's body.

Finally, based on the condition of the corpse and the time at which it was discovered, Melvin testified that the estimated time of death was between 1:00 and 3:00 a.m. Saturday morning, October 15, 2016.

After saying she had no further questions, Gloria placed a copy of the autopsy report in front of Bo and took her seat.

"Cross-examination?" Page asked Bo.

"No, Your Honor."

Bo felt his elbow being nudged, and without looking at his client, he leaned forward and whispered, "I'll save my cross for trial. All we want to do today is see what they have, and I doubt Melvin knows anything more than what's in this report." He tapped his index finger on the pages Gloria had just given them.

The next witness for the prosecution was Chief Deputy Sheriff Frannie Storm, who provided a summary of the sheriff's office's investigation, highlighting each piece of evidence that pointed toward Odell as the killer. She described the discovery of the broken and blood-streaked bottle of Bud Light by the police dogs and finding the defendant lying in the grass a few feet away from the bottle, clutching the victim's sweatshirt. She confirmed that the only prints on the broken beer bottle belonged to the victim and the defendant, further finding that the only identifiable prints on the back seat of the bus where the victim's body had been found belonged to Odell and Brittany. By the time General Gloria Sanchez said she had no further questions, the state had easily produced enough evidence to get past the "probable cause" standard for Judge Page to bind the case over to the grand jury. They'd put Odell's fingerprints on the murder weapon and placed him at the scene of the crime, which showed that he'd had the means and opportunity to do the deed. They would need more at trial, but not today.

Presuming that Frannie was the state's last witness, Bo figured he needed to ask the chief deputy sheriff some questions if he hoped to discover anything else about the prosecution's case.

He started with the physical evidence. With respect to everything beyond fingerprints, the sheriff's office was waiting to hear back from the crime lab in Nashville. Hair fibers found on the victim's and the defendant's clothes as well as the seat on the bus where the body had been discovered were being tested. The lab was also examining blood droplets and saliva taken from the bus, broken bottle, and clothes of the victim and defendant. Those results should be back within the next thirty to forty-five days, Frannie stated.

Next, Bo obtained the names of every person interviewed by the sheriff's department, which included all the players, coaches, and trainers on the football team and a significant number of other high school students who'd attended the party of Doug Fitzgerald the night of the murder. Bo didn't waste his time asking for summaries of the interviews, which would be hearsay for Frannie to describe.

Bo did score one small but significant point. "Chief Storm, there's no evidence from any witness establishing that such person saw Odell Champagne kill Brittany Crutcher, isn't that correct?"

"Yes."

Frannie's testimony was predictable with two glaring exceptions. First, she confirmed that her office had attempted to interview Michael Zannick. However, Zannick continued to refuse to give a statement.

"Don't you find that odd?" Bo asked, genuinely surprised.

"No," Frannie said. "Mr. Zannick is a busy man. If his testimony is needed at trial, he will be subpoenaed."

The second surprise came in the form of the last witness identified by Frannie.

"Have you provided the name of every person that the sheriff's office has spoken to?" Bo asked.

Looking at what appeared to be an investigative report, Frannie answered, "There is one more name."

"Who?" Bo asked.

"Ennis Petrie."

———

There was another rustling from the gallery at the mention of a name that every single person in the courtroom knew. In a former life, Ennis Petrie had been the sheriff of Giles County, Tennessee, for over twenty years. One of the most prominent citizens in the community. Untouchable. But in 2011, during Bo's trial for the murder of Andy Walton, it had come out that Ennis was one of ten members of the Tennessee Knights of the KKK who'd murdered Roosevelt Haynes in

1966. He'd pled guilty to conspiracy to commit murder but was let out on parole early in 2015.

"Quiet!" Judge Page bellowed, banging his gavel. "There will be quiet in this courtroom." Bo waited for the noise to die down, trying to overcome his own shock. "Why did you interview Mr. Petrie?"

"It had come to our attention that Mr. Petrie was familiar with the area of the bus yard."

"Familiar with it?" Bo asked.

Frannie pursed her lips. "Yes. Mr. Petrie had been seen by more than one bus driver sleeping in a bus at night. Because of that, we sought him out."

"Did you find him?"

"Yes."

"What did he say?"

"Objection, Your Honor," General Sanchez said. "Hearsay."

Judge Page creased his eyebrows. "I'm inclined to sustain the objection, General, but I must say that I'm a bit surprised that you would raise it."

Gloria peered across the courtroom at Bo. "Judge, I'd be happy to let Chief Storm describe what Mr. Petrie saw. But I'd prefer for the court to hear it directly from the witness himself."

Bo felt a tickle of fear pass through him. He'd figured that Gloria was done calling witnesses. Most prosecutors would stop with Frannie, not wanting to telegraph any more of their case to the defense. Gloria, however, had decided to make a splash.

"OK, the objection is sustained," Judge Page said. "Bo, do you have any further questions for Chief Storm?"

"No, Your Honor."

"Very well," he said, gesturing for Frannie to leave the witness chair. "General, call your next witness."

"Your Honor," Gloria said, her voice firm, confident, "the state calls Ennis Petrie."

———

Bo tensed as he watched the former lawman enter the courtroom. Gone were the accoutrements of his career in law enforcement. Ennis wore a pair of tattered jeans, a faded flannel shirt, and a pair of work boots. As sheriff, he'd been a plump man with thinning reddish-blond hair and a similarly colored mustache. Since his parole, Ennis was thin and wiry, his face shaved clean and his hair cropped down to where there was an uneven stubble on the top of his head. Bo's history with Ennis was complicated, as the onetime sheriff had assisted Bo with key information during his defense of Helen Lewis last year. *Trying to make amends,* as Ennis had put it. Bo hadn't seen him since Helen's acquittal.

Gloria didn't waste any time once Ennis was sworn in. "Mr. Petrie, on the night of October 14, 2016, did you have cause to see the defendant, Odell Champagne?"

"Yes, ma'am." His voice was soft but firm. Unshakeable. One of the traits that had made Ennis an effective officer.

"Please tell the court how that came to be."

"I was out for a walk," he said. "I walk a lot at night. I live and work pretty close to the bus yard, so I pass by that area quite frequently."

"Have you ever slept in one of the buses at night?"

A wry grin came to Ennis's mouth. "I might have to take the Fifth on that one, General."

There was a smattering of laughter from the gallery, and Gloria also grinned.

"What time did you pass by the bus yard on October 14?" she asked.

"It was after midnight, so probably technically on October 15."

"Why were you walking so late?"

"I had gotten off my day job at the Mexican food truck on Industrial Boulevard around six p.m. Then, after the Little League games at Exchange Park were over, which was I guess around ten, I

Robert Bailey

cleaned the bathrooms, concession stand, and emptied the trash in the dugouts. That's my second job. Anyway, I wasn't tired, and I enjoy walking around Pulaski at night." He paused. "It's about the only exercise I get and . . ." He trailed off.

"And what?"

Ennis looked at Bo. "And when you've done the things that I've done in my life, people aren't always that friendly when I walk during the day."

"You said you saw the defendant. What did you see?"

"I was heading down Eighth Street back toward the park. I was walking along the road because there was no traffic, and I heard footsteps behind me. I turned around, and I saw the defendant walking toward me. He would walk a few steps and then jog a little. He was holding what looked to me like a six-pack of beer and appeared to be talking to himself."

"Was anyone else with him?"

"No."

"How far were you from the defendant when you saw him?"

"When I first noticed him, I was probably fifty yards away, but as he continued up Eighth Street, he was moving faster than me, and he eventually passed me. We were on opposite sides of the street, so maybe ten yards apart. I was probably as close to him as from me to Judge Page."

"Did he notice you?"

"If he did, he didn't show it."

Gloria walked toward the edge of the jury railing, which, when the case was tried, would be where the twelve men and women who would decide the case would sit. "Describe his overall demeanor."

"Pissed," Ennis said. "Angry. Intense. He beat his chest with his fist a couple of times, and he was moving fast." He rubbed his chin. "He seemed to be zigzagging a little, too, so I'd venture to say he'd probably been drinking."

Bo saw Gloria's face flush red, and he knew that Ennis had just said something off script.

"You said he was talking to himself," she snapped, crossing her arms. "What did you hear him say?"

"I couldn't make any of it out."

"Did you see him do anything else?"

"No. He turned into the bus yard, and I kept heading toward the park."

"Do you have an idea when you saw him enter the bus yard?"

Ennis rubbed his chin. "Had to be after one in the morning."

Gloria turned toward Bo. "No further questions."

52

"Cross-examination, Mr. Haynes?"

Despite His Honor's poker face and grim demeanor, Bo could see the slightest trace of amusement in the judge's eyes. "No, Your Honor," Bo said, forcing himself not to look at his client, and waited.

"Does the state have any more witnesses?" Page asked.

"No, Your Honor. The state believes that it has clearly shown through the testimony of Chief Storm and Mr. Petrie that, on the morning of October 15, 2016, there is probable cause to believe that the defendant, Odell Jerome Champagne, committed the crime of first-degree murder in wrongfully causing the death of Brittany Crutcher."

"Anything further from you, Mr. Haynes?"

"No, sir."

"OK, then, I agree with the General and do find that probable cause exists to believe that the defendant is guilty. This case is hereby bound over to the grand jury." Page looked out over the gallery and then banged his gavel. "Court adjourned."

———

Bo waited at the defense table until all of the visitors were gone. As officers came over to escort Odell back to the jail, he grabbed his client's forearm. "Were you talking to yourself and beating your fist against your chest while you walked to the bus yard?"

Odell's eyes drooped, a look of defeat plastered to his face.

Bo put a hand on his shoulder. "All right then. Get some rest, and we'll talk about it tomorrow."

———

As he was packing up his briefcase, Bo felt fatigue closing in on him. The stress of the day along with the hard road ahead had zapped his energy. Bo needed to process today's events and make a plan.

After Bo had suggested that Odell rest, Odell had said, "Yes, sir," but his eyes had been vacant. Since his arrest over a month ago, the kid had lost ten pounds. Because the court hadn't granted him bail, he was going to have to spend every day until the conclusion of the trial at the jail. That would be tough on anyone, but especially a teenager. Bo worried if Odell could stay mentally strong through the winter. *Can I?* Bo also thought, clicking his satchel closed. He was about to say his goodbyes to Frannie and Gloria, but then he saw Judge Page emerge from his chambers without his robe on. "Good, I'm glad all of you are still here." He let out a tired cough. "And that everyone else is gone. Can you all join me in my office?"

———

Bo was the last to drag into Judge Page's chambers, and he took the lone remaining chair on the opposite side of the room from Gloria and Frannie.

Judge Page reached under his desk and brought out a bottle of Macallan Scotch whisky. He poured a healthy portion into a Styrofoam cup and took a sip, wincing as he swallowed the alcohol. He didn't offer anyone else a drink.

Page pulled his spectacles down so that he could look them all in the eyes. "I brought you all here because I'm very worried about this case and the effect it's going to have on the town. You all saw the ruckus outside the courthouse this morning, and I suspect it's only going to be worse for a trial." He paused and moved his eyes to Gloria and Frannie before settling on Bo. "I would encourage you to try and work out a deal."

Bo crossed his legs and cleared his throat. "Well, Judge, I'm all for talking settlement, but it seems like that's a bit premature. Odell hasn't even been indicted yet."

"I'll assemble a grand jury tomorrow morning," Judge Page said. "Shouldn't be long before an indictment is issued and we're holding an arraignment. Then trial. All of that activity is likely to be going on during and shortly after the Christmas holidays. Not the ideal time to try any case, much less one with the emotions that this one brings. I want us to see if we can nip this one in the bud."

"Who's 'we,' Your Honor?" Bo asked.

Page held out his arms. "All of us."

"Well, I haven't gotten any kind of offer from the state yet."

"We're prepared to make a proposal," Gloria said, hesitating for a half beat before adding with a flourish, "Twenty years without parole."

Bo glanced at Page, who was watching him closely, then back to Gloria. "I'll run it by my client."

"You do that, Bo," the judge said, peering down his nose at Bo. "Given what I heard a few moments ago, that doesn't sound like a bad deal."

It doesn't, Bo thought. "I'll let Odell know," he said.

"The other reason for this little hearing is that I'm going to impose a gag order on all counsel until after the trial. No communication with the press about the case. Does everyone understand?"

"Yes, Your Honor," Bo said, and Gloria and Frannie echoed him.

"One last thing," Page said, taking his glasses all the way off and setting them on his desk. "I want you all to know that I received a death threat last week related to this case. I informed the sheriff's office, and they upped security today because of that. I trust you noticed, Mr. Haynes."

Bo nodded. He thought of his children. T. J. was at basketball practice while Lila was on the soccer field. T. J. would drive them home later. If someone was crazy enough to threaten the presiding judge, he or she wouldn't hesitate to go after Bo. *Or my kids . . .* He swallowed, and his mouth felt dry.

"We've upped security at the courthouse," Frannie chimed in. "And we're working with Pulaski PD to have officers patrolling the downtown area at night. Your house will be specifically watched, Mr. Haynes."

"Thank you, Chief Storm," Bo managed.

Judge Page stood and rubbed his hands together. "I tell you all that not to scare you but to provide a warning. This case . . . has touched a lot of people, and some folks are pretty angry about it." He looked at Bo. "Watch your back."

"Yes, sir," Bo said.

53

As Bo was walking down the courthouse steps, he felt a hand on his arm. He turned and saw Frannie Storm.

"You got time for a cup of coffee?"

Bo glanced at the sky. The sun was beginning to set in the west. "A little late in the day for caffeine for me."

"Then how about a drink?"

For a moment, Bo hesitated, thinking of his kids. Given what Judge Page had just said, he needed to call T. J. and tell him to come straight home with his sister after practice and lock the door. "I need to make a phone call and check in at the office, but then I'm free."

"Meet you at Hitt's Place in thirty minutes?"

"See you there."

———

A half hour later, Bo took a seat next to Frannie at Hitt's Place on Bennett Drive. The bar, which was located in a small strip mall in the industrial part of Pulaski, was the self-proclaimed home to the "coldest beer in town" and tended to attract a younger crowd, with many of the students at Martin Methodist doing their weekend partying there.

On a Wednesday night at five o'clock, the crowd was fairly thin with only a couple other patrons enjoying happy hour. "Sorry, but I started without you," Frannie said.

Bo saw a glass of brown liquid over ice. "Bourbon?"

She nodded. "Southern Comfort."

Bo wrinkled his nose.

"Not your brand?"

"A little sweet for me."

A waitress came over, and Bo ordered a Yuengling in a bottle. Seconds later, she was placing the beer in front of him. Bo held it across the table. "To death threats," he said, and Frannie managed a tired laugh, clinking his bottle.

"I'm surprised you agreed to meet me."

"Well, it looked like you had something on your mind, and . . . you've always, for the most part, shot straight with me."

She took a sip of whiskey and grimaced. "Look, there aren't many times when I side with Judge Page, but I agree with what he said back in his office. We need to resolve this case, Bo. For the Crutchers. For the town. For *all of us.*"

"Frannie, I'll pass along Gloria's offer, but there's no way I'll recommend that Odell take it."

"Bo, I realize you feel an attachment to Odell, but think about this for a minute. He was guilty of three misdemeanor theft charges in Town Creek, Alabama. *Three.* My understanding is that those convictions will come into evidence to impeach him. Anything that shows dishonesty or untruthfulness, right?"

"You thinking about going to law school?" Bo forced a smile, knowing that Frannie had correctly summarized the state's ability to use Odell's prior convictions against him.

"So if he's crazy enough to take the stand, then we'll be able to show he's a liar and thief."

"He stole food, Frannie. To feed himself and his mother. Sabrina would go on benders for days, just like she did before the Tullahoma game. Her job status was always volatile."

"How's she doing in rehab?" Frannie asked.

"Fine, I guess. I need to check in with her."

She took a sip of her drink. "What about the assault charge against Odell his sophomore year in Town Creek? Or his expulsion for nearly beating a kid to death after football practice."

"That charge was dismissed, and he didn't start the fight that led to his expulsion."

"But he finished it in such a violent manner that the kid spent a week in the hospital, and the school kicked him out."

Bo drank from his bottle. "Been doing your homework."

"Oh, yeah. If I were you, I'd learn a little more about your client. He's conning you, Bo."

"The theft stuff will come in, and we'll have to deal with it. None of the rest of it will see the light of the courtroom."

"Maybe not, but doesn't it make you think that Odell could be guilty?"

"I believe that the kid is innocent."

"Did you not see the evidence we rolled out today?"

"Your case has holes. No one saw him do it, and there are no witnesses to Brittany and Odell being together at the bus yard. Someone else could have killed her and framed Odell."

"Is that *really* all you got out of that? You know the jury pool in this county. You really think a bunch of white conservatives are going to buy some kind of conspiracy theory that Odell Champagne was framed?"

"He's a football star. A lot of those conservative types love their ball."

"And his absence from the team cost them a chance at the area and state championship. They haven't won a game since Tullahoma. He's a Black kid on trial for murder in Pulaski, and the circumstantial evidence is staggering. You know how this story ends."

"Are you saying a Black person can't get a fair trial in this county, Frannie?"

"I'm telling it like it is."

"Well, aren't you the one that keeps reminding me that the victim is also Black. Regardless of her celebrity, do you think the jury will be fair to Brittany?" He took another sip of beer. "Do you believe they'll care as much about her as they would if it were Mayor Kilgore's daughter? Or one of Hank's girls."

Frannie gazed down at her drink.

"By the way," he asked, leaning forward and speaking in a lower voice, "why do you think Michael Zannick is dodging your interview requests?"

Frannie abruptly stood and grabbed her glass, draining the rest of it in one sip. "I knew this was a mistake. I thought you were different."

"Different from who?"

"Every other prick in the defense bar. Or the ambulance-chasing plaintiffs lawyers. But you're like all of them. Hell, what am I saying? You're their hero."

Bo stood. "Frannie, I'm doing my job."

"So am I," she said. "I don't want to see the Crutchers dragged through a trial. Theresa is a basket case, Gina barely speaks, and Israel . . ."

"Israel what?"

"Theresa's worried about him. Says he's on the verge of a nervous breakdown."

Bo remembered the confrontation with Israel at his office, knowing that Theresa's fears were well founded.

"Bo, at least make a counter. Do you think Gloria showed all of our cards today?" Frannie spoke the words in a fierce whisper. "All she presented was the bare minimum." She stopped. "Except for Ennis. I didn't agree with calling him, but Gloria wanted to make a dent with that big of an audience there. Leave a mark. With Page's gag order, that'll probably be the last impression any potential juror has before the start of trial."

"Shrewd," Bo said. "Did Page tip her off about the gag order?"

Frannie looked away, and Bo knew she couldn't answer the question even if she wanted to.

"What else do y'all have?" Bo asked.

"No discovery until after the arraignment, remember?"

"Yeah, and I remember you giving me a sneak preview of everything in General Lewis's trial last year."

"That was last year," Frannie said. "No more breaks or shortcuts. Gloria has already told everyone in our department that you get nothing until after the arraignment."

"Playing tough, is she?"

Frannie shook her head. "You have no idea. She sees this trial as a job audition, and she won't be pulling any punches." Frannie leaned close enough to Bo where he could smell her perfume, a pleasant floral fragrance. "You need to convince Odell to plea."

———

Bo stayed and finished his beer. After he paid his tab and began to walk for the door, he noticed a flyer stuck to a bulletin board on the wall. "Fizz Here on Friday, October 21, 9:00 p.m." Bo noticed Brittany's smiling face in the photograph. October 21 was a week after Brittany's murder. Three letters had been handwritten at the bottom of the flyer in red ink. *RIP.*

Bo exited the bar. Out in his car, he called T. J., who said all was fine at the house. He and Lila were both home, and Booker T. and Jarvis had come over to hang out.

"When are you coming home, Dad?"

"Soon, son. I have to see someone first."

"Who?"

Bo started to say, *An old friend*, but stopped himself. "Don't worry about it, OK. I'll be home in an hour."

Bo clicked the phone dead and let out a long breath. In his career as a lawyer, he'd learned that some things couldn't wait. Sometimes the only time was now.

54

Exchange Park was the primary Little League baseball and softball field in Pulaski. It was located near the intersection between Eighth and Jefferson, and the lights of the park were typically on throughout the spring, summer, and early fall. Now, though, in mid-November, it was cold and dark as Bo got out of his Tahoe carrying a twelve-pack of Miller High Life in his right hand.

"Figured I'd get a visit from you."

The voice came from the dugout, and Bo stepped inside and took a seat next to the lone occupant. He tossed the man a can of beer and took one out for himself. "Quite a number you did on me today, Ennis," Bo said. "What? No heads-up?"

"I hope you didn't come here to fuss at me."

"No," Bo said, taking a long sip of beer. "I came to get the rest of the story. I got the feeling that Gloria had you on a pretty tight leash today."

He rubbed the back of his neck. "Not really. I hadn't told her I thought the kid was drunk, but . . ." He took a sip of beer and burped. ". . . I'm pretty sure he was. Investigated a lot of DUIs during my time in the department, and he was definitely not walking or running in a straight line."

"Why didn't you say anything to him?"

"Figured he was blowing off steam. Since he had a six-pack with him, I thought he was probably meeting someone there. Kids hang out at the bus yard all the time. Hell, that's why I stopped sleeping there.

In hindsight, I wish I had said something." He took a long pull from the can. "Another regret in a life full of them."

Silence filled the dugout. "No way you could've known anything was going to happen," Bo said after a moment.

"I'm not sure the kid killed her," Ennis said. "You're his lawyer. Does he have a case?"

"He says he's innocent."

"That's not what I mean."

"I know."

More silence for several seconds.

"Who's your alternative suspect?" Ennis asked.

Bo drank the rest of his beer and popped the top on another one. "Zannick."

"You're kidding."

"No," Bo said. "There's a clear link to the victim."

"Any evidence?"

"Not yet."

"Sounds like déjà vu all over again. Didn't you try to pin Butch Renfroe's murder on Zannick?"

Bo didn't respond. "Had you ever seen Brittany or Odell at the bus yard before?"

Ennis smiled. "Now, you're getting somewhere. That's a question the new General didn't ask. As a matter of fact, yes, I have. I saw Brittany there quite a bit. She and her bandmates liked to meet up and drink there. Sometimes they even played a few jams. Before I started living full time at the park, I'd find a shadowy spot in the yard a fair distance away from them and listen."

"What about Odell?"

Ennis grinned. "Once. Earlier in the summer, I was planning to stay the night in one of the buses, and I heard some noises coming from inside one of them, and the windows in back were fogging up. I stayed clear and saw your client and Brittany emerge from the bus about fifteen minutes later. They both looked pretty happy . . . especially him."

"That's another reason why you might not have thought anything was up on Friday night."

"I still wish I'd said something. Your client was really upset, and he was drunk. Maybe, if I'd engaged him, I could have calmed him down."

"Or maybe he arrived at the bus yard, and Brittany was already dead."

"Maybe that too," Ennis said, squinting at Bo. "Is that what he says happened?"

Bo nodded. Then he stood to go.

"Is it true about the General?" Ennis asked. "Did she quit?"

"Looks like it," Bo said. "Can't figure it out. She seemed fine over the weekend and then poof." He snapped his fingers. "Gone without a word. Not even to her attorney."

Ennis said nothing.

"I told her about the help you gave us in her trial last year," Bo added. "Did you ever talk with her afterward?"

Ennis took a long pull from his can. "Once," he said. "She was very grateful."

"I bet." Bo peered down at the man, sensing there was something he wanted to say. "Can you think of any reason the General would have left without a word to anyone?"

Ennis scratched his chin. "The pressure of that job after all these years—"

Bo's laugh interrupted the former lawman. "The General loved the pressure. She lived for it. Nah, it's gotta be something else."

Ennis gazed past Bo to the shadowy infield. "Helen had a lot to process after her trial. The secrets that came out . . ." He trailed off.

"You mean about her not having an abortion and giving her child up for adoption."

"That . . . and being raped when she was in law school. I suspect she'd buried all that pretty deep. Then everything gets exposed." He whistled between his teeth. "That's a lot for anyone to deal with. Even someone as strong as her."

Bo looked down at Ennis. "Makes sense. Listen, I'm gonna head out now."

"Thanks for the beer."

Bo started to say something about seeing him again but decided to remain silent. Seconds later, he was back in his Tahoe and headed home.

———

Ennis Petrie took the rest of the beer to a spacious storage closet inside the concession stand where he'd been staying since the cold weather had appeared. The shack had an exterior heater that made a hell of a racket during the night but kept things reasonably warm. He knew the president of the park from his days as sheriff, who had agreed to look the other way as long as there were no complaints.

As he sipped the cold Miller High Life, he thought about General Helen Lewis and the secrets she'd disclosed during her trial last year.

And a couple secrets she hadn't shared but which he knew she was struggling to live with.

I believe that good people make terrible mistakes in this world.

Ennis knew that to be true. He'd told Helen so when she'd expressed her gratitude to him after the trial.

But knowing it didn't make things any easier to handle. Not for him.

And not for Helen Lewis.

55

The Grand Hotel Golf Resort and Spa or, as the locals called it, the Grand, was an iconic hotel that sat on the tip of Mobile Bay in the fishing community of Point Clear, Alabama. The hotel originally had opened in 1838 and, over the centuries, decades, and years, had changed management numerous times. But through it all, the iconic vacation destination had lost none of its charm.

Helen Lewis had stayed at the Grand many times for legal seminars and had grown attached to the antique feel of the place, especially the main building, which seemed immersed in the perpetual smell of pine. When you stepped through the doors of the Grand, it was literally like going back in time.

Which is what I would love most to do, Helen had thought when she'd considered where to live out her self-imposed quarantine. Regardless, with the quaint town of Fairhope only a few miles away and the hotel only half-full because it was the offseason, Helen figured there wasn't a better place for her to rest, recharge, and decide what she was going to do. Up until an hour ago, things had been going pretty well. Then her assistant, Trish DeMonia, who had promised to keep her abreast of the Odell Champagne case, had called and given her the play-by-play from the day's preliminary hearing. Though she was interested in the facts that came out and had to admit that Gloria had done an excellent job in her absence, she was much more concerned with what most people would probably consider a minor footnote to the proceeding.

Why hasn't Michael talked with the sheriff's office?

After hanging up with Trish, Helen had scoured all the news websites, reading each of the rundowns about the case but not learning anything further about her son.

Finally, she couldn't stand any more of it and clicked out of her internet browser. She held her iPad against her chest and took in a deep breath, then slowly exhaled. She gazed out at the water and felt a breeze pass through her hair. If she weren't wired on adrenaline and anxiety, she'd probably have a chill.

Helen got up from the bench and walked to the end of the pier. The sun had set, and in the distance, she could see the skyline of downtown Mobile. Out on the water, a couple of boats gave off flickering light. Above her, clouds covered the moon and most of the stars, though she could make out a portion of Orion's Belt. Helen turned and gazed back at the historic resort.

She had to admit she was surprised that Ennis Petrie was a witness, though she knew she shouldn't be. Ennis had been living in the shadows of downtown Pulaski for over a year, and it was very feasible that he might have seen something near the bus yard. But his presence as a key witness further steeled her resolve to stay away from the case. *He knows too much . . .*

She began to walk back toward the shore. The chilly air had finally gotten to her, and she rubbed her arms to warm herself as she walked. She wanted to call Bo and warn him off Michael, but Bo would know something was up if she did so.

I have to stay away, she thought, stepping inside the hotel and breathing in the scent of old pine.

But for how long?

56

Michael Zannick sat on the massive back veranda of his mansion off Highway 31. He sipped from a glass of red wine and enjoyed the feel of the wind on his face. He hadn't attended the preliminary hearing of Odell Champagne, but one of his many employees had. He'd gotten a full report and was perturbed that his name had been mentioned by Bocephus Haynes.

Zannick didn't like surprises.

That's what ended it for me and Brittany. She wouldn't relinquish control . . .

Zannick grabbed his cell phone from the wrought iron table next to him and pulled up a photograph of the young woman who had dominated so much of his time the last three months of her life. Even after her death, he couldn't get her off of his mind. What they could have done together if only she had taken his lead. What they could have accomplished . . .

In the photograph, Brittany was wearing a red bikini bathing suit and lying out by his pool. He knew he should probably delete the image, but he didn't want to lose the memory.

What was it about young women that did it for Zannick? Was it the fact that his own childhood had been stunted by stays in different foster homes? That he had never really grown up and felt more comfortable around naive women whom he could manipulate? Or was he simply a pervert and sociopath? When was he going to learn his lesson? His liaison with the Burks girl had cost him $1.5 million.

Gazing at the picture of Brittany, he knew that his relationship with her had cost him much more.

Zannick felt moisture on his cheek and dabbed at it with his left hand. Looking at the wetness, he wiped his eyes. Was he crying?

He clicked out of the photograph and pulled up his mother's phone number. It had been exactly a month since he'd seen her car off the side of the highway. He hadn't realized how much he had enjoyed those short interludes, regardless of how weird they were. *Where has she gone?* He knew she had taken a leave of absence, but he hadn't called her since. He hovered his thumb over the number but couldn't bring himself to press down.

Zannick had spent so much of his time wondering who he was. He'd known his mother had abandoned him and figured his father had done the same. But last year, he'd learned the bitter truth. His mother had been raped after a football game. That one act—the assault of his mother—had dictated the terms of his life.

Zannick found himself obsessing over who his real father might be and whether he was still alive. He'd come to Pulaski for closure and still hadn't gotten it.

What he had received was the wonderfully pleasant experience of working with Brittany, who'd been destined for greatness and superstardom right up until she walked out of Zannick's home the night of October 14, 2016.

Zannick sipped his wine and stood. The veranda was heated with numerous propane lamps. He shouldn't feel cold, but he did. His thoughts returned to the preliminary hearing.

Was Bo Haynes again going to declare war on him? And if Haynes did come after him, how long would his mother stay gone?

Finally, closing his eyes, he thought of the last time he'd seen Brittany alive. Why hadn't she simply done what he asked her to do? If she had . . .

. . . *she'd still be here.*

Another tear slid down Zannick's cheek. This time, he made no move to wipe it.

57

At the Comfort Inn, Israel Crutcher sat on his bed. He wore the same green scrubs he'd worked in. He'd volunteered for the evening shift after court, and there had been four operations, which was a lot. He should be tired, but he wasn't. It seemed the only time he felt at peace was in the operating room, using his skills to put patients under general anesthesia. Out in the world, all he felt was anger.

Israel held a pint of Jim Beam to his lips and swallowed. Then he trudged over to his suitcase, reaching inside until he felt the cold steel of the pistol. He pulled the weapon out and checked the chamber. Then he pointed it at the mirror, gazing at the reflection of his own bloodshot eyes. When was the last time he'd slept more than four or five hours? He couldn't remember.

After Brittany's murder, he'd thought the only honorable thing for him to do was take his own life. How many times had he put his own gun in his mouth in the last month? But he hadn't pulled the trigger, and now, after watching Bo Haynes in the courtroom today, he was glad he hadn't.

Before he left this miserable world for good, he planned to use this gun for a higher purpose. He imagined his old teammate in his mind. Bocephus Aurulius Haynes had played Division I football for the Bear when Israel had only managed to make small college. Bo had become one of the most famous and feared attorneys in all of Tennessee, when Israel had to scrape out a living as a CRNA despite the fact that he was smarter than every anesthesiologist he'd ever been around. Bo had been suspended twice from the practice of law and yet was still rolling in money; meanwhile, Israel had never experienced any issues with his license but still lived paycheck to paycheck.

Israel scrunched up his face and then relaxed it. Bo had suffered more tragedy in his life . . . *but he still has his kids.*

And I've lost Brittany . . .

He stared around the cold hotel room. *I've lost everything.*

He cocked the weapon and felt adrenaline pour through his veins. His baby girl was dead, and he wasn't going to rest until the persons to blame were six feet under the ground with her.

Michael Zannick.

Odell Champagne.

They were both dead men walking. And if Bo Haynes continued to get in his way, then he would be dead too.

58

Bo arrived at Reeves Drugs the next morning at 8:00 a.m., feeling refreshed, reenergized, and hungry. One of Pulaski's oldest establishments, Reeves had a solid breakfast menu, a great sandwich selection at lunch, and the best homemade milkshake in town.

"You look spry for the ass beating we took yesterday," Lona said, taking a bite of scrambled eggs. "I hope you don't mind, but I ordered for you."

"My usual?"

"Country ham and biscuit, with a side of grape jelly, large coffee, and a small juice."

"You, my dear, are the bomb."

"And get this. I've already reached out to a few of the kids identified by Chief Frannie at the prelim yesterday. Bentley Rogers and Walton League. Both girls were friends of Brittany's and were at Doug Fitzgerald's party. They were around Odell a lot that night, and they don't remember him acting belligerent or violent at all."

"What about the fight with Jarvis?"

"They said it was more of a wrestling match. Horseplay between friends," she said.

"That's not exactly how T. J. and Jarvis saw it. Did they say who Odell left the party with?"

"Both remember him hanging out with Ian Dugan, but neither could remember them leaving." Lona paused. "But both said they had been around Odell and Brittany a lot, and that Odell was always appropriate and kind. Never said a cross word to her."

"Will they be character witnesses?"

"Walton said yes, but Bentley said she'd have to check with her parents."

"Better than nothing," Bo said, taking his hands off the table so that the waitress could set his food and drinks down.

"OK, keep going down the list. We need to find someone who can tell us who Odell left the party with."

"Odell has no idea?"

"Can't remember. He was hammered. Whoever it was, they were friends with Ian. How about Brittany's roommate, Tasha?"

"Still stonewalling. Won't talk to me and hangs up the phone every time I call."

"And Doug Fitzgerald?"

"His parents have thrown a blanket around him. His father told me the last time I rang the doorbell that he was going to call the police if we didn't stop harassing them. You know that T. J. is our best angle to him. Fitzgerald plays basketball. Maybe T. J. could shoot a few baskets with him and ask some questions."

Bo shook his head. "T. J. is already involved in this enough. I'm not going to get him in any deeper." He took a sip of coffee, feeling undeterred. If anything, he was relieved they'd been able to obtain what they had. The testimony from the League and Rogers girls would be helpful, and hopefully they could round up some more character witnesses.

"Here comes Columbo," Lona said, cocking her head to the front of the store as she took in another mouthful of eggs.

Bo turned and saw a plump man wearing a white button-down, khaki pants, and a red-and-white mesh hat with "Roll Tide" embroidered across the front. Albert Hooper sat down in the chair between them and mock frowned at Lona. "What? No food for me?"

"You don't write my paychecks."

"Touché," he said, moving his eyes to Bo and taking a thumb drive out of his pocket. "Here's everything you asked for on Zannick. It has the same historical stuff I did for the Lewis case last year, plus a summary of my surveillance the past thirty days."

"Anything interesting?"

"Not really. Zannick has been holed up in that mansion most every day. Occasionally goes to the Yellow Deli for lunch. Always eats alone. Every so often hits the Sundowners Club strip joint, which he still owns but is now under different management." Hooper held out his hands. "That's really it. Pretty boring."

"What about his muscle?"

"Finn Pusser got out of jail last year, but none of the girls at the Sundowners have seen hide or hair of him in months. Like he's vanished."

Bo remembered the events that had put Pusser behind bars. It bothered him that the criminal wasn't accounted for in some way. "Keep poking around. Hard to believe he could have disappeared." Bo took a bite of his biscuit. After chewing and swallowing, he squinted at the investigator. "What about Zannick's management of Brittany?"

Hooper grinned. "Had to exhaust my contacts in Nashville, but I got confirmation that Brittany had signed a solo deal with ELEKTRIK HI."

"And Zannick negotiated the deal?"

"Yep."

Bo looked at Lona. "As soon as the arraignment is over, I want you to slap a subpoena on ELEKTRIK HI for all documents related to Brittany." He turned back to Hooper. "What about the personal angle?"

"Nothing so far. Zannick's very private, doesn't have any close friends. We really need the surveillance tapes from his house and phone records, but I suspect he'll have purged them by now."

"Can we get those?" Lona asked.

"We should be allowed to seek the discovery of any evidence that might be exculpatory, but who knows with Judge Page," Bo said.

"You've already spoken to the person in town that probably knows Zannick the best," Hooper said.

Bo creased his eyebrows.

"Cassie Dugan. The bartender at Kathy's Tavern. She dated Zannick for several months last year."

Bo put his hands around the back of his neck and gazed up at the ceiling, thinking about his encounter with Cassie at the tavern. Something had bothered him about their conversation even more than the drunken pass Cassie had made at him. *If Brittany signed a solo contract right out from under the band, then every member of Fizz would have had motive to want to hurt her . . .*

. . . including its manager.

Bo lowered his eyes. "We need to speak with all of them again."

Cassie had arranged for Bo and Lona to interview each member of the band at Kathy's after hours a couple of weeks ago. For the most part, those meetings had been fruitless, with neither Ian Dugan, Mackenzie Santana, nor Teddy Bundrick having any knowledge of Brittany's whereabouts the night of her death. Moreover, all of them had said they had no knowledge of Brittany's solo deal until after her murder.

Of the band, Ian was the most important to the case, as he was Odell's friend and the person who'd probably spent the most time with him in the hours before Brittany's murder. During their interview, Ian had said he hadn't seen anything unusual going on with Odell. Like everyone else at the party, Odell had been having a great time and blowing off steam. Because of his own drunkenness, Ian also couldn't remember who'd driven them home either.

"This time alone. Everything about the last meeting was too clean."

"You think someone's hiding something?" Lona asked.

"I don't know," Bo said. "I have a hard time believing that Ian can't remember who they left the party with. My impression from Odell has been that Ian wasn't in as bad a shape as he was and that it was Ian who arranged the ride. It's worth another swing with him and the others. I think Cassie's presence may have buttoned them up."

"I'm on it," Lona said. "What about Cassie?"

"I'll talk with her," Bo said, wondering if that was such a good idea. He bit into his biscuit again and washed it down with juice. Then he looked at Hooper. "I think you've done everything you can do on Zannick for now. While Lona is trying to meet with them, I'd like you to follow each member of the band for a week or so, including Cassie. See if that turns up anything. If any one of them is lying about not being aware of Brittany's solo recording deal, then that person would have motive to want to hurt her. We need to know Fizz inside and out."

"You got it," Hooper said.

Bo took a sip of coffee, and his lips formed a smile. "And I need your help with something else."

"What?"

"It's right up your alley, given your knowledge of the history of Southeastern Conference football."

Hooper raised his eyebrows and leaned his meaty forearms on the table. "What?"

"I want you to find Billy Champagne."

59

Bo arrived at the jail an hour later. When he walked into the attorney consultation room, he saw Odell resting his head on the desk.

"Wake up. Time to go to work," Bo said, taking the seat across from his client.

Odell sat up and rubbed his eyes. If he had slept a wink overnight, it didn't show.

"Ennis Petrie's testimony at the prelim was a surprise. I don't like surprises."

"I'm sorry, Mr. Haynes. I—"

"I don't want your sorry. What I want and what you have to give me is the truth. Otherwise we don't stand a chance in hell of winning. You hear?"

"Yes, sir."

"All right then. Explain what Ennis said he saw."

"I was drunk, still pissed off about the note. I was rehearsing what I was going to say. I wanted to convince her to stay. I . . . I do that sometimes."

"You swear to God that's the truth?" As Bo asked the question, he thought of Odell's three theft convictions and wondered if Frannie was right. *Am I being conned?*

"I swear to God," Odell said.

Bo rubbed a hand over his bald head. "The district attorney general is going to play it like you were planning to murder Brittany. That you were walking toward that bus yard, working up the gumption to kill her."

"Why would I stop and buy a six-pack of beer for us to share on the way to the bus yard if that was my plan?"

"Good point," Bo said.

"Mr. Haynes, have you heard from my mom?"

"Not since she checked into rehab. How about you?"

"She's sent a couple of letters. She says she's doing pretty good." He paused. "Do you know how she's paying for that? She said insurance—"

"I'm paying for it."

Odell's voice began to shake. "Thank you, sir. I—I'll pay you back, I promise. My dad has sent me some money. It's in my account here at the jail. I'm going to give it all to you."

Bo's neck tensed. "Your dad?"

"Yeah," Odell said, his voice bitter. "Guess he's trying to help."

"Has he been here to visit?"

"No, but he sent a letter with the money. Said he was sorry for leaving. Yada, yada, yada. I tore everything but the check up."

"Where's your dad living?"

"I don't know. The letter didn't have a return address. But if I had to guess, I suspect he's staying at the only place where his name means anything anymore."

"And where's that?"

Odell wiped his eyes. "Home."

60

Town Creek, Alabama, was a small town in Lawrence County, Alabama. Known by lawyers as a speed trap between Decatur and Florence, by fisherman for the catfish found at Wheeler Dam, and by farmers for the plentiful cotton crop, Town Creek gained greater notoriety during the 1970s and '80s for being the home of a football powerhouse.

Hazelwood High School was zoned 1A, which was the smallest designation for high schools in the state. But what the school lacked in numbers, it made up for in talent. Many of the names that donned the uniform of the Hazelwood Golden Bears later became etched in the folklore of Alabama football history.

To Bama fans, they were simply known as "the Goode brothers." Kerry Goode, who once had over two hundred all-purpose yards in the first half of a game against Boston College in 1983 and might have won the Heisman Trophy but for a crippling knee injury suffered in the second half of the same game. Chris Goode, the oldest brother, who played defensive back for the Tide in the early '80s. Pierre Goode, the flashiest brother, who started at wide receiver for the Tide in the mid-'80s and caught an eighty-six-yard touchdown pass against Tennessee. And Clyde Goode, the youngest, who played in the late '80s.

A Goode cousin, Antonio Langham, was probably the most famous Town Creek player. It was Langham who iced the 1992 SEC championship for Alabama with an interception return for a touchdown in the final seconds of the game; the Tide would go on to win the national championship.

But before the Goodes, the player whom most people thought of when Town Creek, Alabama, was mentioned was a tailback named Billy Champagne.

Finding Billy hadn't turned out to be very difficult once Hooper confirmed that, as Odell suspected, Billy was still living in Town Creek. After spending the better part of two days in the tiny hamlet and hearing countless citizens tell of the athletic exploits of the great Billy Champagne, Hooper found pay dirt at city hall. The desk clerk there, a fiftysomething lady named Delores Loback, was a Hazelwood alumna who'd been a year behind Billy in school. They still kept in touch and occasionally went out on dates together. She hadn't said the phrase, but Hooper surmised that Delores had a friends with benefits relationship with the man. In any event, Delores had heard of the trouble Odell was in. When Hooper insisted that it was urgent that he get in touch with Billy for information pertinent to Odell's case, she gave him Billy's number. A call and a text later, and Hooper had Billy's agreement to meet with Bo.

———

On November 23, 2016, a week after the preliminary hearing and a day before Thanksgiving, Bo pulled into the gravel parking lot in front of Dot's Diner, an iconic soul food restaurant housed off Highway 31 in Hillsboro, Alabama.

Because Billy was working at the Solutia plant in Decatur, they'd decided to meet at Dot's, which was up the road from the plant a few miles and on the way to Town Creek.

Bo got there first and ordered sweet tea. As he waited, he had to admit that he was nervous. He'd come up in high school a year behind Billy Champagne, but he remembered the name well. Billy had gone to Tennessee and started his freshman year. But, like Bo, injuries eventually ended his playing career before he reached his full potential. Bo had spoken with Billy a few times after games during college and wondered if the man would remember him. He also knew he would have to keep his emotions in check. He was about to meet a man who'd abandoned his wife and son. That didn't hold in Bo's world.

As he took his first sip of tea, Bo saw the door sweep open. A man entered wearing a sweat-streaked blue work shirt, jeans, and dusty boots. He had a boxlike physique with thick tree-trunk legs. He glanced around the place; then the man's eyes fixed on Bo, and he ambled over. As he did, Bo noticed the slightest trace of a limp.

"Bo?"

He stood.

"Billy Champagne," the man said, extending his hand. "Long time."

Bo shook hands and gestured to the seat across from him. "Thanks for coming." He smiled. "And thanks for recommending Dot's. I haven't been here in years."

Billy took a seat. He moved his eyes around the small restaurant. "Hard to beat Dot's for a meat and three."

Before the men could talk further, a waitress came and took their orders. In the awkward silence that followed, Bo sipped his tea and breathed in the pleasant scent of country-fried steak, pinto beans, and mashed potatoes. Billy spoke first.

"Bo, I appreciate what you're doing and what you've done for my son. Odell hasn't gotten many breaks in this world." He cleared his throat. "Meeting you was one of them."

"He's in a world of trouble," Bo said, not mincing words. "The state's murder case doesn't have many cracks."

"But you believe him innocent?"

"Yes."

"Why?"

The question struck Bo as odd for a kid's father to ask, but the answer came to him without much thought. "Because Odell has had to be an adult since he was five years old. Since you left him and his momma high and dry and ran out on them. He's taken some lumps, trying to help Sabrina provide for their family, and gotten into some trouble that he would have never been in if you hadn't disappeared."

Billy stared at Bo as the waitress placed their plates in front of them. When she was gone, he shook his head. "You *are* direct, aren't you?"

"I'm not a bullshitter," Bo said. "I don't think your son is a killer. I do think he was in the wrong place at the wrong time, and I think some powerful people had reason to want to hurt Brittany Crutcher and took advantage of the situation to make it look like Odell killed her."

Billy took his fork and poked at his mashed potatoes. "Why'd you want to meet me, Bo? Surely it wasn't to scold me for being a bankrupt father."

"Odell needs you, Billy. He needs some family in his life. Sabrina . . ." He trailed off.

Billy leaned over his plate. "Sabrina is crazy, Bo. She's a drunk and a druggie and has been for years. We couldn't have a baby after Odell, and she had several miscarriages. After the last one, she turned to the bottle as her solution to everything, and when that didn't kill the pain, she went to harder stuff. The woman I married died with our unborn babies." He sighed. "I wish you could have seen her back in high school. So smart. Sexy. She was the star of the Hazelwood drama team. In *The Wizard of Oz*, she was Dorothy our freshman year, and you wanna talk about singing? When she sang 'Over the Rainbow,' she got a standing ovation from the crowd. When they decided to do the same musical again when we were seniors, Sabrina said she wanted to play a different role, so they cast her as the Wicked Witch of the West. Nailed that too. She followed me to Tennessee and studied acting her freshman and sophomore years. Scored a role in the college's big production of *Rashomon*. You ever seen that?"

Bo shook his head, enjoying Billy's trip down memory lane.

"It's a Japanese play about a samurai, a bandit, and a wife who were involved in the same incident but all describe it different. At the end, a bystander who happened upon the scene shares what really happened." He took a bite of food and pointed his fork at Bo. "It was cool, man, and Sabrina was awesome as the wife."

"What happened?"

Billy frowned and looked down at his plate. "When I blew my knee out sophomore year, I was never the same. I got hooked on painkillers during my rehab and eventually was kicked off the team midway through senior year. We were married at that point, and Sabrina was pregnant."

Bo did the math in his head, and it didn't wash. "Not Odell."

"No. Sabrina stayed and graduated from UT that December, while I licked my wounds and obtained a job working construction. The baby was due in July, and I wanted to go back home so that our parents could help out with the kid. We moved back, and Sabrina had a miscarriage a couple weeks later."

"Did she ever pursue an acting career or use her degree?"

"For a few years she taught drama at Hazelwood, but the job was depressing. She felt like it was beneath her. That by not making more of herself, she had failed. Anyway, when we had Odell, she resigned." He gave his head a jerk. "I think she would have really liked to have been a professor in college. But raising a child was tough, and she never talked about her career after Odell."

"What happened to y'all?"

"Most of it was my fault. I had a hard time holding a job. Started doing pot to ease the pain of not making the league." He looked at Bo. "You know what it's like to have your NFL dreams killed by an injury."

Bo scowled at him. "I didn't quit. On myself or my family."

Billy peered back down at the plate. "Well, I did. And eventually, so did Sabrina. After Odell, she wanted more children, but we weren't able to have any. After her third miscarriage, the drinking really kicked into gear. Then after that, she started smoking pot with me. When that didn't satisfy her, you can probably fill in the rest." He took a sip of tea. "When she became a full-blown addict, I couldn't take it anymore."

Bo felt anger rising within him. "She gave up her career for you."

For a few seconds, Billy didn't say anything. Then he wiped his mouth and peered at Bo with a solemn expression. "Look, I'm everything you think I am. A deadbeat dad. A loser. A has-been. I know I shouldn't have left, but Sabrina got to the point where she was impossible to be around. Every time we had an argument, she would go over the top with it. She'd lie and say I hit her and call the police."

"Your word against hers."

"I was never convicted, not once, on any of the times she pulled that stunt, but Sabrina . . ." He chuckled bitterly. "Like I said, she was an incredible actress."

"Why didn't you seek custody? You could have petitioned the court and taken Odell away from her until she could get her addiction under control."

He looked down at his plate. "I couldn't do it. It would have destroyed Sabrina. Every time I threatened it, she said she would kill herself if I took Odell away. And I didn't want to take his mother away from him."

"So you took his father," Bo said, hearing the sadness in his voice.

"I regret it every day. I've tried to help—I've made every child support payment, and I send cards at Christmas and birthdays—but Sabrina won't have it. She said I made my choice, and she's poisoned the well so much that there's no chance for me and Odell to have a relationship."

Bo looked down at his food, finding that he was no longer hungry.

"Bo, tell me what to do, and I'll do it. I sent some money for your fees—I know it's not near enough, but I'll send more every two weeks."

"He needs more than that."

"I'll come to the jail to visit. I should have done so already. I'm just—"

"You're scared," Bo said. "And I don't blame you. But he's scared too. He's in the foxhole, and he doesn't have anyone right now but me. Sabrina's in rehab."

"I didn't know that," Billy said, averting his eyes from Bo's glare.

"Yeah," Bo said. He stood and threw a twenty-dollar bill on the table. "I came down here to tell you that Odell needs his father, but I'm not sure that's true. He needs someone to fight for him." Bo leaned his hands on the table, looking the other man squarely in the eye. "Not quit on him."

61

Bo's next stop was at his investigator's office loft on the banks of the Tennessee River in Decatur. When he trudged up the steps, he found Hooper doing push-ups as Kenny Loggins's "Danger Zone" played at full blast through his sound speakers. The man was wearing gym shorts, a white Hanes T-shirt, and high-top Air Jordan tennis shoes.

Bo found the power switch for the music system and clicked it.

Hooper looked up from the floor. "Don't laugh."

"You feeling the need for speed?" Bo teased.

"What can I say? I like the '80s. Remember this one. Alexa, play 'Walk This Way,' by Run DMC."

A monotone female voice rang out. "Playing 'Walk This Way,' by Run—"

"Alexa, stop!" Bo yelled. "We have work to do, Hoop."

The investigator stood and took a deep breath. "How'd it go with Billy?"

"Fine," Bo said. "Good job finding him."

"Easy peasy," Hooper said.

"You get the other thing I asked?"

Hooper nodded.

"And?"

"It's bad."

———

A few minutes later, Bo was sitting in Hooper's conference room and looking at a large PowerPoint screen on the wall. A photograph of a kid named Bennett Caldwell took up the whole area, and Bo tensed at the sight. One of the boy's eyes had swollen a purplish red, and there was barely a slit there for him to see. His nose and lip were also red with edema. To say the kid looked like he had had the hell beat out of him was an understatement.

"How'd you get this?"

"I went to high school with one of the Town Creek traffic cops. They still had the police report filed by the Caldwell kid's dad, which had the photos."

"When did this happen?"

"April of 2016. Odell was kicked out of school the next week."

"The police charged him."

"Yeah, but they dropped the charges when several members of the team said that Caldwell threw the first punch."

"Why did the school expel him?"

"Well, according to the vice principal, Hudson Baynes . . . who I happened to have done some investigating for last year . . ."

"I don't want to know," Bo said.

"And I'm not going to tell you. Anyway, according to Hud, this was the last straw. Odell had been convicted of three theft charges, and he'd gotten into several scrapes on and off the football field. Hud said they looked at him like a ticking time bomb."

Bo leaned back in his chair and whistled through his teeth. "Damnit," he finally said.

"None of this will come in. Why did you have me find it?"

Bo stood and looked out the huge window, where several pontoon boats were on the water. "Because I want to know who I'm representing."

"I thought you knew Odell well. That he worked on the farm with you, that he and T. J. were best friends."

Bo gazed up at the ruined face of Bennett Caldwell. "I thought so too."

62

On his way back to Pulaski, Bo made one final stop.

The Madison Recovery Center was a new alcohol- and drug-addiction center in Madison, Alabama. Sabrina Champagne met him outside on a bench under the shade of two trees. Bo peered around and admitted that the place was tranquil. He guessed it would be as good a place as any for a person to face her addiction problems head-on.

"How's my son?" Sabrina asked. Her eyes were tired but clear.

"Not great," Bo said. "This case is bad, Sabrina. If he's convicted . . ." Bo trailed off.

"Thank you for helping him." She grabbed his hand. "And thank you for all you've done for me." She smiled, and there was light in her eyes. For a brief moment, Bo could picture the young woman who'd dreamed of being a professional actress.

"You're welcome." He stood and walked a few steps away from her, gathering his thoughts. "We should have a trial date soon—I suspect it will be in January."

"I'd like to be there," she said. "But I don't want to hurt my son's chances. I know what people think of me."

"We have some time before we have to make that decision."

She stood and approached, again taking his hand. "When that time comes, I want *you* to make the call."

"Regardless of whether you attend the trial, this . . ." He gestured with the hand she wasn't holding to the therapy building behind her. ". . . has to stick."

"It will," she said.

For several seconds, Bo thought about saying more to her. Telling her about seeing Billy and asking her about her college days, but he decided against it. *Too much, too soon.* Finally, he gave her hand a squeeze. "Get well, Sabrina."

63

On Monday, November 28, 2016, a grand jury indicted Odell Jerome Champagne for the first-degree murder of Brittany Crutcher.

A week later, on December 5, 2016, Bo and Odell stood before Judge Harold Page for his arraignment.

"To the charge of the first-degree murder, how does the defendant plead?" Page asked.

"Not guilty, Your Honor," Odell said, and Bo was pleased to hear the firmness in his client's voice.

Judge Page lowered his glasses and looked at the documents in front of him. "Let the record reflect that the defendant has pled not guilty to the crime charged. The court hereby sets this case for trial on January 23, 2017." When he banged his gavel, Bo's heartbeat picked up speed, and he did the math in his head.

Forty-nine days to figure this mess out.

He looked at his client, who continued to stare at Judge Page. Bo swallowed and peered over to the prosecution table, where General Sanchez stared back with fierce determination. He looked past her to Frannie, whose brown eyes held nothing but mystery, the poker player not giving away her hand. Finally, he forced his eyes behind the table reserved for the state and looked at the victim's family. Gina Crutcher had the same blank expression she'd had at the visitation. Theresa Crutcher also seemed numbed by the proceeding. She held her shoulders back and appeared to be staring past the judge's bench to an unseen spot on the wall, perhaps the painting of the former governors of the state of Tennessee, which hung high above His Honor.

Finally, Bo moved his eyes to Israel Crutcher, who didn't appear numb or blank. Israel seemed to be trying to stare a hole into Bo's face, and it was all Bo could do not to break eye contact. But he didn't. Instead, he looked into the bloodshot eyes of his former teammate, which seemed to hold only one emotion.

Hate.

64

Monday, December 12, 2016

At 8:00 a.m., exactly seven days after the arraignment of Odell Champagne, Chief Deputy Sheriff Frannie Storm showed up at Bo's office. "We have your discovery," she said, pointing at the door as four banker's boxes full of documents were wheeled in with a dolly by two deputies. "Right on time," she said. After the arraignment, Judge Page had entered trial deadlines, including an expedited time frame of seven days for the prosecution to produce its discovery responses.

"Thank you," Bo said. "I trust it's everything we requested."

"Everything," Frannie said, her face tense. "Our whole file."

"Something wrong?"

She didn't say anything. Bo turned and saw both Hooper and Lona standing by Lona's desk. They'd been prepared for the shipment and were ready to start going through everything. With a trial date in mid-January, there was no time to spare.

"Want to take a walk?" Bo asked.

"Sure," Frannie said.

———

Out on the sidewalk, the air was chilly and getting colder. Bo wished he had his overcoat but decided not to go back in to get it. There was something on Frannie's mind, and he didn't want to miss whatever it was.

"You going to the Christmas festival this weekend?" she asked, peering up at the courthouse as they passed the old Pulaski Theatre on First Street.

"Haven't thought about it," Bo said. "Maybe if the kids want to go."

"You should go," she said, her voice distant. "It's always so beautiful."

For a while, they walked in silence. Bo didn't push it. Finally, she spoke up.

"Is it OK if we speak off the record?"

Bo hesitated for a second. "Yes."

She sucked in another breath. "You're going to find something in those boxes you can use, and I honestly don't know what to make of it. We didn't catch it in our initial investigation."

Bo felt his skin begin to tingle. "Frannie, what are you saying?"

"I guess I can't say," she finally said, stopping at her patrol car. "You'll know when you see it." Frannie paused. "But also know this. While this new . . . evidence may affect plea negotiations, we aren't going to drop the charges. It is still Gloria's feeling . . ." She hesitated. ". . . and mine that Odell Champagne murdered Brittany Crutcher."

"Why are you telling me this?"

"I don't know," Frannie said. "What have you been saying since the beginning of this?" She looked up at him. "That all you want is the truth."

Bo nodded.

"Well, that's all I want too."

65

If there was a golden nugget in the state's document production, it sure wasn't evident from the beginning. Bo, Lona, and Hooper split up the banker's boxes and worked through lunch and dinner going through everything. Most of the new information they saw was bad.

The report from Dr. Malacuy Ward, the director of the crime lab in Nashville, was particularly staggering. Hair fibers found on the hoodie of Odell Champagne matched the DNA of the victim. Additionally, hair and saliva picked from the T-shirt, sweatshirt, and pants of the victim matched samples provided by Odell Champagne. Strands of hair and saliva taken from the bus seat where Brittany's body had been found also matched Odell's DNA. Finally, the blood found on the base of the bottle was a match for Brittany's. The only good part of the DNA evidence was that there was no DNA link to Odell on the beer bottle. Unfortunately, his fingerprints were all over the damn thing.

Next was a box full of photographs and video. Most of this evidence depicted the crime scene on the morning of the murder. However, there was also the surveillance tape from Slinky's gas station, where Odell had been given the six-pack of Bud Light on his way to the bus yard, and the footage obtained from the SunTrust ATM, where Brittany had withdrawn money shortly before her murder.

By 9:30 p.m., they had filtered through well over one hundred witness statements, several huge stacks of phone records, a box of search and seizure documents, and another container with all the fingerprint evidence. Finally, Hooper, his voice frantic and on edge, whispered, "Roll motherfucking Tide."

"What?" Bo and Lona both yelled across the table. They were in the office conference room. Lona was on the floor going through one box, while Bo was standing at the end of the table looking through another. Hooper was seated at the other end, his hat on backward and shaking a piece of paper in front of him.

"I haven't been this happy since Rocky Block," he said, dancing up and down on his toes.

"What in the Sam hell are you talking about?" Lona asked. "And please stop whatever you're doing with your feet."

"Rocky Block. You know? When Mount Cody blocked the Tennessee kicker's field goal at the end of the—"

"Not that, you moron," Lona said, standing and placing her hands on hips. "The sheet of paper. What's got you yelling Roll effing Tide?"

"Roll *mother-effing* Tide," Hooper corrected. "RFT is good, but RMFT means it's a bigger deal."

"Hooper, can I ask you a serious question?" Lona asked, but her voice dripped with mock sincerity. "When was the last time you got laid?"

"Enough," Bo said. "Let me see it."

Hooper walked around the table and placed the document in front of Bo. Blinking his tired eyes, Bo noticed that it was a printout of the fingerprints identified on Brittany Crutcher's clothes. As Bo scanned the page, Hooper placed his index finger on a particular column in the middle of the page.

Bo looked at the spot and felt a warm tingle radiate down his chest. He peered at his investigator, who had a shit-eating grin plastered to his face.

"Can I get an RMFT, boss?" Hooper asked.

Bo whistled under his breath. "Roll mother-effing Tide."

66

Michael Zannick sat in a table in the back of the Sundowners Club. He was alone except for a glass of vodka. He couldn't remember when he'd stopped bothering with ice. A month ago? Who knew? Since Brittany's death, the days had run together.

Zannick rarely got out of the house anymore. When he did, he came here. Not to enjoy the dancers. He didn't even look at the topless woman gallivanting around the pole on the main stage or the two other strippers who worked at this time of day who'd both offered him lap dances on the house.

He wasn't interested. All he wanted was to be left alone. Hearing more footsteps approaching, he knew that his wish wasn't going to be honored. But these feet weren't adorned with stellate heels but rather black combat boots. Zannick raised his eyes over his glass and almost laughed. "Well, well, well." He slurred his words. "You can't seem to leave me alone."

Bo stuffed a manila envelope into Zannick's hand. "You've been served."

"Don't you have people to do these types of menial tasks?" Zannick asked as Bo started to walk away. "Wait, Counselor. Stay. Have a cocktail on me."

Bo stopped and glared at him. "I'm particular about who I drink with. And it's a little early in the day for me."

"Then sit for a second. Don't you want to interview me?" he asked, opening up the package and beginning to peruse the contents.

A few seconds later, Bo took a seat at the table across from Zannick.

"Phone records, surveillance tapes for September and October 2016, blah, blah, blah, any and all documents that in any way relate to Brittany." Zannick sighed and then cackled as he read. He drank a sip of Grey Goose and winced. "You really think I killed her?"

"The GPS tracking of Brittany's iPhone shows she was using a cell phone tower very close to your house off Highway 31 the night of the murder."

"Is that so? Well . . . you know how finicky cell phone records can be."

"Do you deny she was in your home?"

Zannick gazed at Bo a long time. "No, I don't," he said and saw the expression of surprise on the lawyer's face.

"She was there then."

"She was . . . and then she left."

Bo sneered at him. "And I'm betting that your surveillance cameras show that you left soon after she did."

"You think I followed her."

Bo nodded. "And if for some reason you've lost that footage or it's been destroyed, then that's evidence too."

"Evidence of what?"

"Intent to conceal. To hide something."

Zannick took another sip of vodka. "I've got nothing to hide."

Bo stood and looked down at Zannick. "We'll see."

"You're gonna enjoy this, aren't you?"

"No, dog. The real fun is when I get to cross-examine you on the stand. There's also a trial subpoena in that package. See you in a few weeks."

"And what do you hope to accomplish, Haynes?" Zannick bellowed, rising from his chair, almost spilling his glass of vodka. "I managed Brittany's singing career. She came over to my house after the concert. She was supposed to stay the night, and we were going to leave for Los Angeles in the morning on my private jet." He held out his hands. "But she was upset and having second thoughts." Zannick saw a shadow pass over Bo's face, and he smiled. "I just made this trip worth it to you, didn't I?"

"How long had she been staying the night?"

"About a month." He hiccupped. "You think that raises my motive for killing her, don't you?" He toasted the lawyer with his glass. "But you're wrong. That little nugget only gives your client more reason to do the deed. Your football hero, Odell Champagne, was jealous of my relationship with his girlfriend. He didn't like how much time she was spending with me. And when she dumped him, he snapped and killed her."

Bo blinked at him, as if he were trying to process the words. Finally, gazing at the glass of vodka, he asked, "Do the Hoshima folks know you're drinking like this?"

Zannick waved him off. "Fuck them," he said, burping. "I got them here. They're leasing my land now. The contracts are all signed. I can shit on this floor and you can video it and post it on Facebook, and there's not a damn thing they can do about it. My lawyers drafted that lease, and I'm Teflon, baby." He walked around the table toward Bo. "You hear me, *dog*? I'm untouchable."

"Not for long. Not after I rip you a new one on the witness stand."

"Whatever. I'll take my medicine like a champ. You've got nothing linking me to her murder. Nothing. Nada. Zilch."

"Your fingerprints were on her cell phone and her clothes . . . including her underwear," Bo said. "Did you know that? Only hers and yours."

Zannick blinked.

"How do you think that will play to the jury?" Bo asked.

"Proves nothing other than she spent a lot of time at my house." He grinned. "Probably got her laundry mixed in with mine."

"I think you have that wrong. I think it proves that you tried to force yourself on her just like you did with Mandy Burks, and Brittany was able to get away before you could rape her."

"And I followed her," Zannick said, laughing. "That's your theory."

Bo bared his teeth. "Merry Christmas, Michael."

———

Out in the gravel parking lot, Bo climbed into his Tahoe and took out his phone. As he pulled onto Highway 64, he played back the recording.

He'd gotten all of it. He could call Michael Zannick to the stand now. If Zannick tried to lie about his contact with Brittany the night of the murder, Bo could impeach him with the tape.

After discovering the evidence of Zannick's fingerprints on Brittany's panties and phone last night, he, Lona, and Hooper had decided it was worth it for him to take a shot at getting Zannick to talk. They had to serve a subpoena on him anyway. Why not let Bo do it and take a swing?

And I just got a base hit, Bo thought, gazing at his phone.

The fingerprints on the panties were damning, but they didn't necessarily prove anything. They did, however, taken together with the prints on her phone and what Michael Zannick had just admitted, support the alternative theory that Bo was planning to present to the jury.

Zannick tried to rape Brittany, and she got away. He followed her to the bus station and killed her. Then, after looking at her phone and seeing Odell's texts, Zannick sent Odell a text from her phone as if he were Brittany, asking for one last rendezvous. When Odell woke up, he saw the text he thought was from Brittany, walked to the bus yard, and discovered Brittany on the back of the bus. Gripped with shock, with terrible grief, Odell picked up the broken bottle and Brittany's sweatshirt and left the bus, then blacked out.

Bo nodded to himself as it all came together. *That has to be it.* Still, though, as he turned onto Highway 31 and headed toward downtown Pulaski, something was bothering him. Why had Zannick talked? He had to know that Bo might record him. It didn't make sense. Zannick was a shrewd businessman. Calculating. He didn't make those types of mistakes.

Too easy, Bo thought. A piece that didn't fit.

He's cracking up, Bo told himself, not sure if he believed the words, but it was the only explanation that made sense.

He knows I'm closing in.

———

Inside the Sundowners, Zannick drank from a refilled glass of vodka. Why had he done it? he wondered, going over his exchange with Bo Haynes again and then chuckling softly to himself. He knew why. It was the same reason he hadn't talked to the police yet.

This is a dangerous game, he thought, taking a long sip of Grey Goose.

But I know I'll win.

67

Pulaski's annual Christmas festival took place on Saturday, December 17, 2016. The streetlights were adorned with green wreaths, and there was a huge Christmas tree adjacent to the gazebo on the north side of the courthouse square. Under the gazebo, Clete Sartain, dressed as Santa Claus, greeted children, asking each what they wanted him to bring this year and giving out candy to all the participants. Cassie Dugan had someone covering for her behind the bar at Kathy's Tavern so that she could enjoy a few minutes of the yearly spectacle. In September, there'd been discussion about Fizz playing carols during the festival. What could be better than Brittany belting out all the holiday favorites right on the steps of courthouse?

Cassie felt tears welling in her eyes. Music was playing, but it was being blasted through speakers that had been put in various spots on the square. *Brittany should be here,* she thought, wiping her eyes. *And she would be if it weren't for me.*

"Hey, sis, you cool?"

Cassie turned toward the voice and hugged her brother's neck. "I'm fine. Just sad we aren't playing this."

"I know," Ian said. His curly hair was all over his head, but his eyes radiated fear. "I met with Mr. Haynes today."

"You *what?*"

"He and his assistant dropped by the restaurant. Sat in my section. I didn't have a choice."

"Please, for the love of God, tell me you didn't say anything."

"I didn't. I promise." He paused. "But I think they're onto us."

"How?"

"I don't know. But I got the feeling they aren't buying our story."

"Doesn't matter," Cassie said. "They can't prove anything."

Ian held her eye. "I feel guilty, sis. Don't you?"

"Yes, but I can't risk your future." She paused. "Or mine. We did a terrible thing."

"How long are you going to hold out?"

"As long as it takes."

"Mr. Haynes is a good lawyer, and he's very persistent."

Cassie turned away from him and watched the kids continue to wait for their turn with Santa. Over the loudspeakers, Elvis belted out "Blue Christmas." An appropriate song, she thought. *One that Brittany could have nailed.*

"I've said my piece, Ian. Don't you trust me?"

"Of course. But . . ." He trailed off.

"But what?"

"Don't you want to do the right thing?"

"Not if it costs me every friend I have in this town." She paused. "Or risks putting both of us in jail. I won't do that." She turned away from him and began to walk toward Kathy's.

I can't do that . . .

68

Bo bought hot chocolate for himself and Lila and walked around the square, enjoying the Christmas tunes and trying not to think about the trial of Odell Champagne, which was almost a month away. T. J. was also there, but he was hanging with Jarvis and some of his other friends. Bo was grateful for the quality time with his girl. When she and T. J. were younger, Bo and Jazz used to take them to the annual festival every year, and they would literally have to drag Lila away. Her favorite tradition was telling Santa what she wanted even after she knew the truth behind the magic of Kriss Kringle, nonetheless relishing the excitement that the younger kids experienced while waiting in line. Since Thanksgiving, Lila had been playing Christmas music nonstop throughout the house, and Bo thought he might go crazy if he heard "Silver Bells" one more time. It seemed like every day for the past two weeks had been a buildup for the festival. Even now, at fifteen, she'd volunteered to be one of Clete Sartain's elves and help manage the other kids in line.

"So . . . are you ready for Christmas?" Bo asked.

"I guess," Lila said.

"What do you mean, you guess? You've talked about nothing but for the past two weeks. Something wrong?"

"You know how much Mom loved Christmas. I love it, too, some- times it just . . . makes me sad."

Bo felt a lump in his chest and drank his cocoa. She was right. Jazz had loved every minute of the Christmas holidays, insisting that they get a tree on Thanksgiving night and then always overdoing it with too many presents, too much food, and too many family gatherings. It was hectic, stressful, and . . .

. . . *wonderful*, Bo thought, his eyes beginning to mist over.

"I'm sorry if I upset you, Daddy."

"It's fine, sweetie. I miss her too."

Lila pointed. "Look, there's Frannie." She then said, "I'm going to go help Santa, OK?"

Lila ran off, and before Bo could protest, Frannie had stopped in front of him.

"Merry Christmas," she said, an edge to her voice.

"Same to you," Bo said. "Something wrong?"

"Oh, I love getting subpoenas on Friday afternoon in cases that are over a month out."

"It'll take time for the records to come in," he said, stepping around her and beginning to walk toward his daughter. He didn't want to discuss the case here. Alas, Frannie followed him.

"You've subpoenaed almost every company owned by Zannick. Isn't that a bit excessive?" she asked, catching up to him.

Bo continued to walk. "We found the item you mentioned when you dropped off the box."

"I don't have any earthly idea what you're talking about."

"Fine," Bo said. "Let me ask you something, Frannie. Do you ever not talk about work? It's a festival. Have some hot chocolate. Live a little."

"Do you really think Zannick killed her?" Frannie asked. "Or is this just smoke and mirrors, trying to drum up reasonable doubt wherever you can find it? Striving to help another guilty client go free."

Bo felt his blood beginning to boil. He stopped and glanced toward the gazebo, where Lila was helping a young toddler sit in Santa's lap. He took a deep breath and peered at Frannie. "Are you done?"

Frannie shot daggers with her eyes and started to walk away, but Bo called after her. "Hey, Frannie. Hey!"

She looked back at him.
"Merry Christmas."

———

An hour later, as he turned left on College Street to head home, Bo called his son and asked what take-out dinner T. J. had in mind. Lila had said pizza, and when T. J. agreed, Bo pulled into Little Caesars and picked up two Hot-N-Ready pepperoni pies.

As he traveled the remainder of the way home, his thoughts drifted to the case. The evidence they'd discovered of Zannick's fingerprints was great. It would leave open questions that the prosecution would have to explain. Set up enough questions, and doubt would begin to creep into the jury box.

Another inquiry for the state involved the murder weapon. The broken beer bottle. Odell had been seen with a six-pack of Bud Light, but in the crime scene photographs produced by the state, all six bottles were unopened and intact.

Where did the seventh one come from? The bottle of Bud Light used to bash Brittany's skull had to have originated from somewhere else. *Where?*

He figured that the state would argue that Odell had brought a spare from Doug Fitzgerald's party or from his apartment and decided to stop for more on the way. Based on the state's investigation, Odell wasn't the only person to leave Doug's party with a sixer. After the keg was blown, Doug had gone and bought more beer. The closest gas station that would take his fake ID had been running low on cases of beer, so after buying three cases, Doug had bought several six-packs as well. It would have been easy for Odell to have grabbed a bottle or two before leaving with Ian Dugan. He could also have taken one from the fridge in his apartment, which did have Bud Light in it based on the inventory produced by the state in its search of the place.

Bo surmised that a jury would probably buy either theory, but he didn't. Odell said he remembered grabbing a six-pack but didn't take a single. When he got to the bus yard, he discovered Brittany's body and didn't have time to drink any of the beer he'd brought, which was consistent with the carton being full when the authorities arrived.

Where did the extra come from? The forensic analysis of the bottle showed that it had been opened, and saliva had been taken from what was left of the broken opening. But, unlike the definitive findings of all the other DNA, the results had been inconclusive. Dr. Malacuy Ward's report concluded that the saliva on the opening had likely been contaminated by the dirt on the bus floor after the bottle had shattered. It could also have been sipped on by multiple people.

A mystery, one that Bo thought he could use at trial. Taken with the evidence of Zannick's fingerprints on Brittany's underwear, Bo felt like he had a fighting chance to establish reasonable doubt.

And if Zannick looks as pitiful as he did at the Sundowners last week, even better.

Tapping his fist on the steering wheel, Bo felt hope rise within him.

We have a chance . . . Based on how the case had begun, that was all they could ask for.

———

Upon arrival home, Bo hugged his kids and let his dog out. He, T. J., and Lila ate pizza on the back porch, and Bo drank a cold beer. When they were finished, he gave the bread scraps to Lee Roy and stayed out on the porch while his children played Xbox. Finally, he heard the ring of his cell phone. On the screen, a name popped up that he hadn't thought about in a long time.

"Was wondering when you might call me," Bo said. "Just couldn't stand it?"

"How are you?" Helen asked.

"Honestly, not too bad. Went to the Christmas festival tonight. The kids had a good time." He took a sip of beer. "So what gives me the pleasure? You aren't one to call to shoot the bull."

There was a long pause. Bo heard the sounds of Lee Roy's snoring below him. Finally, the General spoke in her firm voice. "Do you think Champagne is innocent?"

"Yes," Bo said. "Until proven guilty."

"Seriously . . . you don't believe there's a possibility that he could have killed Brittany."

"I don't," Bo said.

"Well . . . do you have an alternative theory yet?"

Bo peered up at the moon. "I would have figured you would have talked with Gloria about the case."

"No, I've stayed away. Want to give her full rein and not interfere. But . . ."

"You're curious."

"Yes, damnit, I guess I am. Are you going to answer my question?"

"Zannick," Bo said. "And I think I've got him this time. He's acting weird, General. Almost like he wants to get caught. He's lost a lot of weight. Won't talk with the police. And he actually did talk with me and gave me some nuggets that I can use at trial." Bo paused. "Crazy all the terrible things that have happened since Michael Zannick moved to Pulaski."

"Yeah," Helen said. "Crazy. Look, Bo, I have to go, but thanks for filling me in. I made the right call by taking a break, but I miss the action."

"I know you do," Bo said.

They said their goodbyes, and Bo went inside the house. He checked all the locks and walked upstairs, where Lila was already in bed. He kissed his daughter's forehead and started to pull away from her, but she grabbed his arm. "Daddy, is everything fine?"

"Yeah, baby girl."

"I'm worried about you. Everyone seems so mad." Bo had actually thought folks had been fairly respectful at the Christmas festival, but perhaps his expectations had been low. Other than Frannie Storm, no one had spoken to him the whole time he was there.

"I know, but don't you worry." He brought her in for a hug. "We're going to be all right."

He walked into T. J.'s room. His son was sitting at his desk, reading a book.

"What you got there?" Bo asked.

"*To Kill a Mockingbird*," T. J. said. "I read it last year at Huntsville High, but we're reading it again for AP English at GCH."

"A classic," Bo said.

"Yeah. It's good. You know, the lawyer in the story kind of reminds me of you."

"Atticus Finch?"

"Yeah, you know. How Atticus takes Tom Robinson's case when he knows he probably can't win. He expects the jury will probably convict Robinson because he's Black but still takes the case."

"Why does he do that?" Bo asked, remembering reading the story himself many years ago and watching his son, whose expressions reminded him so much of Jazz.

"Because it's the right thing to do. A person shouldn't be convicted of a crime because of the color of their skin." T. J. furrowed his brow. "Or because they did some bad things in the past."

Bo felt a ripple of pride pass through him. He pushed himself off the bed and kissed his son on the forehead. "Proud of you, big 'un." He walked to the door and looked back at T. J. "Since you're rereading it, I guess you know how it ends. Didn't work out too well for Tom Robinson."

"Doesn't make what Atticus did any less right."

Bo smiled. "Love you, son."

"Love you too."

Bo went downstairs and poured himself a glass of water. Then he walked around the house, checking the locks on the doors and gazing at the stockings for Lila and T. J. that he'd hung on the mantel. He peered at the fake tree he'd bought at Walmart, which Lila had decorated with the ornaments that her mother had spent a lifetime collecting. He touched the cardboard cutout nativity scene ornament that T. J. had made as a preschooler, where he'd drawn a crimson number 12 on Joseph's robe. Bo giggled, knowing that the stunt had earned the boy some grief from his teacher at school but had made for a lifelong story. He moved his eyes to the angel that adorned the top of the tree, which had been Jazz's great-grandmother's and passed down through three generations. Lastly, as always, he took a few seconds with the ornaments that Jazz had bought from the places they'd visited as a family. The one of Mickey and Minnie Mouse wearing Santa hats with "Disney World 2008" printed across the two characters' chests always made Bo think of the four of them riding down Space Mountain, his kids and wife laughing and screaming their heads off and Bo squeezing his eyes shut and praying they'd get to the bottom before he puked. The miniature of the Grove Park Inn in Asheville, North Carolina, where Bo had attended a legal conference in the summer of 2004. The kids had been so young. Jazz had wanted to see the Biltmore, but they'd only gotten halfway through the tour before Lila had thrown a fit about being hungry.

Bo's gaze finally landed on his favorite ornament, and he cradled it in his palm. A crystal ball with a painted beach and the words "Saint Lucia 2005" written in the sand. He and Jazz had gone to the small Caribbean island to celebrate their twentieth anniversary. The ornament always got him to thinking about Piton beer, emerald water, and incredible sunsets. Mostly, though, it made him see Jazz as she had been then and always: funny, intelligent, and intoxicatingly gorgeous. Despite the beauty of the island, they'd spent most of those four nights and three days in their room . . . catching up on lost time.

In some ways, Bo knew his love for the Saint Lucia ornament was self-destructive. There should have been more trips like that one. They shouldn't have been playing catch-up. The decoration brought him happiness and a flood of regret.

Eventually, he ended up back out on the porch. For all the success he'd found in the last year, there were times, like when he was watching the Giles County versus Tullahoma football game, when he was gripped by a powerful sadness. He was fifty-five years old. He missed his wife and knew that it wouldn't be long before it was just him and Lee Roy in the house together.

Before he went to bed, Bo went to his office and entered the password on his gun case. He took out his Glock, checked the chamber, and then put the gun on the nightstand. He liked to keep the weapon by the bed at night just in case. Then he got on his knees by his bed and prayed. He'd had an on-again, off-again relationship with the good Lord over the years, but he'd found himself praying more and more since regaining custody of his children. He didn't want to screw up their lives or the new life they'd made together. He prayed for their health and safety, and he prayed for strength and guidance. Before sleep mercifully took him, he thought of Odell Champagne and how odd life could be.

T. J. had compared Bo to Atticus Finch, and Bo was gratified by the comparison. Yet if he were honest with himself, he wanted more than what Atticus had wanted. Of course, he wanted Odell to receive a fair trial. He desired that justice be done. In that regard, Bo, like Atticus, was a servant of the law.

But underneath it all, Bocephus Haynes wanted something more primal. Something that Atticus Finch hadn't achieved in the famous literary trial.

I want to win.

69

Helen alternated between gazing at her cell phone and at the dark waters of Mobile Bay. After hanging up with Bo, she'd needed to move and decided to take a walk along the path that skirted the bayside mansions to the west of the Grand Hotel. When she returned, she decided to take a last stroll down the pier. She knew the water held no answers for her but stared down at it anyway. Sometimes, she wished she could just jump off and have the bay swallow her up. A fitting, perhaps appropriate end.

She moved her eyes back to the screen of her iPhone. She'd pulled up the familiar number and finally decided she could hold out no longer.

He answered on the second ring. "Mother."

"What are you doing talking with Bo Haynes? Have you lost your mind?"

A long pause and then a few bitter chuckles. "I thought you were on an extended leave of absence."

"I am."

"Then why are you calling me about an active case that your office has charged someone else with."

Helen found that she couldn't breathe. She hadn't heard his voice in over a month. "Why are you doing this, Michael?"

"I didn't kill her," Michael said. "But Bo is a good lawyer—you should know that better than anyone. Look at what he helped you get away with last year. I suspect he's smart enough to get Odell off. Hell, he's probably good enough to get me charged with the crime."

Helen couldn't believe her ears. "Michael, what are you—"

The phone clicked dead in her hand. She started to call back but then thought better of it.

What's wrong with me? She closed her eyes and breathed in the salt air coming off the bay. She'd hoped that coming to Point Clear would help clear her mind, but if anything, she felt even more jumbled and confused than ever.

I got away with murder, she thought.

I have a son.

What in the world am I gonna do with the rest of my life?

Helen felt tears brimming in her eyes, and she fought them back. *This isn't working,* she thought. *How can I stay away?*

Eventually, she walked back toward the lights of the Grand. *I have to make a decision. I can't go on like this. I either need to get on with my life and job . . .*

. . . or turn myself in and face the music.

Helen entered the hotel and took a seat at Bucky's Birdcage Lounge, the Grand's late-night bar. She ordered a whiskey sour and took a seat by the window. A man was playing the piano and singing Billy Joel songs, but Helen paid him no mind, lost in her own torturous thoughts. *He's forcing my hand,* she realized, taking a long sip and grimacing as the sour concoction slid down her throat. *I have to decide.*

After another taste from the glass, she gazed again at the waters of Mobile Bay.

Soon . . .

70

On New Year's Eve, Bo had no plans. Lila was spending the night with a friend, and T. J. was going to the movies with Jarvis and would stay at Booker T.'s house.

Around 6:00 p.m., he was toying with the idea of seeing if Frannie Storm had any plans, but then he thought better of it. Frannie had been livid with him at the festival. Besides . . . *I'm too damn old for her.*

An hour later, as he was about to put a frozen pizza in the microwave, he received a text from his investigator. Happy New Year and Roll Tide. Got something for you. Call me.

Bo did, and Hooper answered without the phone fully ringing once. "I know who Odell left Doug Fitzgerald's party with," he said.

"Well, Happy New Year to you too," Bo said, his pulse quickening. "Who?"

———

Four and a half hours later, Bo sat in one of the back tables of Kathy's Tavern next to Cassie Dugan. The bartender was stunning, dressed in a low-cut burgundy cocktail dress that highlighted her purple charm necklace, which Bo recognized as the one she had shown him the night of the funeral. Bo, on the other hand, wore dark jeans, a white shirt, and a gray blazer. They'd already split a couple rounds of beers. On the stage in front of them, a man with an acoustic guitar was belting out Kenny Rogers's "Love Will Turn You Around."

"You look great," she said as the song wound down and the guitar man said he was taking a ten-minute break. She ran a finger down her neck and winked at him.

"You too," Bo said. "Nice to see you wearing your grandmother's necklace again."

She moved her head from side to side as if she was unsure whether to agree. "It looked better on Brit . . . but I figured it was time." She hesitated and looked at him. "It is a new year, right?"

This time it was Bo who winked. "Yep. And it's nice to have something to do to celebrate. I hope you don't mind us coming here."

"No, it's comfortable," Cassie said. "I have to admit I was surprised to get your text. I kind of figured you'd be staying home tonight."

"That pitiful, huh?"

Cassie shook her head. "Not at all. There's nothing sexier than a man who loves his wife. I'd give anything to have someone love me like you loved her."

Bo peered down at the table, unsure of what to say. She sounded genuine, and he felt guilty for what he was doing. But, after all, she'd lied to him.

"I'm sorry about coming on to you so hard the last time we were together."

"Don't worry about it. Happens to me all the time," he joked.

"I bet it does," she said, reaching her hand out and putting it on top of his.

It looked like she was about to say more, but a waitress put two glasses of champagne on the table. "It's on the house, y'all. Happy New Year."

"Right back at you, Jules," Cassie said, winking at her replacement tonight, a forty-seven-year-old part-time employee named Julie Hurd.

Bo took his champagne and clinked it against Cassie's glass. "Here's to good timing," he said and drank his glass down.

But Cassie didn't touch her champagne.

"You know, there's a saying my momma used to use."

"Oh, yeah. What's that?"

"I may be stupid, but I'm not *fucking stupid*."

Bo blinked his eyes. "I don't understand."

"You didn't ask me out tonight for a date or to have a New Year's fling, did you?"

His face broke into a tiny grin, but he kept his eyes fixed on her. "Guilty as charged."

She pushed her champagne aside and took a long sip of beer. "So what do you want?"

"I want to know why you failed to tell the sheriff's office about how you picked up your brother . . . and Odell Champagne from Doug Fitzgerald's party the night that Brittany Crutcher was murdered." He let the words hang in the air and stared at Cassie until she averted her eyes. "And I also want to know," Bo continued, "why you lied to me about it."

"I'm not sure I understand what you're talking about," Cassie said, but her tone was terse, and her arms had tensed to the point where Bo could see veins.

"One of the partygoers, a sophomore named Katie Joliff, a JV cheerleader who was one of the few who wasn't stoned or drunk, remembers Odell leaving in the back of an old blue Mustang GT. I have the names of every single person who attended that party, and none of them drive that kind of car . . . but you do."

Cassie stared off into space.

"Your brother called you to pick him up, and Odell asked for a lift. Isn't that true?"

"I can't believe you set this meeting up as a New Year's date and would spring this crap."

"I can't believe you would lie about something so important."

"Happy New Year, Bo," she said, standing and grabbing her purse.

"Cassie, wait," Bo said, also standing. "Please . . . tell me what happened."

Cassie was already heading for the door.

71

On January 1, 2017, at 8:00 a.m. sharp, Cassie Dugan walked into the Giles County Sheriff's Office. She told the deputy at the front desk that she had information related to the murder of Brittany Crutcher and wanted to speak with Chief Deputy Sheriff Frannie Storm.

Fifteen minutes later, Frannie arrived and led Cassie into a tight interrogation room. Once she'd set up her tape recorder, she asked for Cassie to state her name, which she did.

"Ms. Dugan, you said that you wanted to give a statement. Please proceed."

Cassie inhaled a large gulp of air and exhaled, trying not to be sick to her stomach. She hadn't slept since Bo Haynes had accosted her at Kathy's Tavern. "After the concert at the Brickyard on October 14, 2016, I went back to work out the rest of my shift at Kathy's. At midnight, I closed up and headed home. On the way, my brother, Ian, said he was at a party and was too drunk to drive. He asked if I'd come get him." Cassie hesitated. "When I arrived at Doug Fitzgerald's house, Odell Champagne approached my brother and asked for a ride home. Ian asked me if that was OK, and I agreed. On the trip to his apartment, Odell was very angry. He said that Brittany Crutcher had broken up with him, that he was distraught. I knew Odell personally because he had hung around a lot of Fizz's concerts and practices." She again paused and drank from a cup of water that Frannie placed in front of her. "Before we got to his apartment, I told Odell something I wish I hadn't." Her lip began to tremble.

"What did you tell him?" Frannie asked.

"I told him that he was better off without Brittany . . . because she'd been cheating on him. It was a lie. I didn't know whether Brittany was being unfaithful or not, but I was so mad at her."

"Why were you mad?"

"Because she'd signed a solo deal and left the band holding the mail. My brother was mad too."

"Go on," Frannie said, and Cassie could tell she now had the chief deputy sheriff's undivided attention.

"At first, I don't think Odell believed Brittany was cheating, but when I told him it was with Michael Zannick, he went berserk. He said he knew it and started punching the back of the car seat. I had to stop my vehicle a couple blocks before I reached his place." Cassie licked her lips. "I hadn't even come to a complete stop, and Odell was opening the door to the back seat and hopping out. He was so upset."

"Did he say anything else that you remember?"

"Yeah," Cassie said. "He said, 'That bitch is going to pay.'"

———

"Why didn't you tell us this when we took your statement the first time?" Frannie asked after giving Cassie Dugan a few moments to collect herself. Frannie was trying to steady her own breathing, as what Cassie just said could be the final nail sealing the case against Odell. They could use her testimony to further prove motive and to show that Odell had acted with premeditation when he killed Brittany. A dagger to the heart if Cassie was telling the truth.

"Because I wasn't sure if I'd committed a crime. I knew something bad was going to happen, and I didn't do anything. I thought Ian and I might be considered accessories. Either way, I felt so guilty." She put her face in her hands. "I should've called 911 after I dropped him off."

"Why didn't you?"

She wiped her eyes. "Because I was mad at Brittany."

"You wanted her to die."

She shook her head. "No. I didn't think he'd go through with it."

"Why are you coming forward now?"

"Because Bo Haynes told me that he and his investigator had figured out that I was the driver. I knew it was time to come clean." She squelched a sob. "Am I going to be arrested?"

Frannie didn't think what Cassie had described was sufficient to prove that she was an accessory to murder, but she wasn't about to tell her that now. "Let's talk with General Sanchez about that."

72

Twenty-four hours later, Bo stormed into the attorney consultation room of the Giles County Jail and flung Cassie Dugan's statement on the table in front of Odell. "Tell me if that's true."

Odell read the document and looked up from the sheet with terrified eyes.

"I haven't said one word in our talks about any alleged affair between Michael Zannick and Brittany. Nothing came out at the prelim, either, and the gag order prevents there being any press about it. Did Cassie Dugan tell you that Brittany was cheating on you with Zannick while she drove you home?"

"I don't remember Cassie Dugan."

"Did anyone in that car you left Doug Fitzgerald's party in tell you that Brittany was cheating on you?"

"Ian did," Odell said, his expression pained. "I didn't kill her, Mr. Haynes. I swear to you."

"Odell, before you got to the bus yard that night, did you think she was cheating on you?"

He hung his head and stared at the table. "Yes, sir, I did."

"And did you say that she was going to pay?"

He held out his palms and gazed at Bo with anguish. "I can't remember."

PART FOUR

PART FOUR

73

On the Friday before trial, at 11:00 p.m., after poring over every document in the case ten times, Bo had finally had enough. The pages were
beginning to blur. He'd started putting together his opening statement,
which was always important in a trial but would be especially significant in this case. How could he set the tone for his theory that Zannick
had killed Brittany Crutcher and framed Odell? How could he get
around Odell's powerful motive to do the deed, which the state would
prove through Brittany's handwritten breakup note and the testimony
of Cassie Dugan, Ian Dugan, Ennis Petrie . . . *and my own damn son*?

How would he emphasize the state's one glaring hole in its physical
evidence: Where had the seventh beer come from?

Beyond his opening, he was also sweating whether he should put
Odell on the stand. At the pretrial hearing earlier that day, Judge Page,
over Bo's objection, had said he would allow the state to introduce evidence of Odell's prior convictions for theft as impeachment evidence if
and only if Odell chose to testify. That was the right call, but it didn't
make Bo feel any better. If Odell testified, the state could show the jury
through his prior convictions that he was dishonest and lacked credibility. If he didn't take the stand, the jury would never hear him deny
that he killed Brittany, which was something Bo deemed as necessary
in defending a murder case.

He rose from his seat and walked toward the front of the office, calling Booker T. on his cell. "All good at the house?"

"Yeah, cuz. All good. T. J.'s still up studying for a chemistry quiz, and Lila's already in bed."

"Thanks for doing this."

"You got it. Ain't nobody going to get in this house, and if they do, they're leaving with a ton of buckshot up their ass and a really angry English bulldog's teeth on the rest of them."

"Lee Roy's riled up."

"Yeah, man. He's doing that low growl thing he does when his world ain't right. You know what I'm talking about?"

Bo did and couldn't help but smile. He'd inherited Lee Roy from Professor Tom McMurtrie, and there were times when he could almost feel his old friend's presence when he was around the dog.

"Frannie's outside patrolling the street too."

"Frannie herself?"

"Yeah," Booker T. said.

For a few seconds, neither man said anything. Then Booker T. cleared his throat, and when he spoke, his tone was grave. "You OK, Bo?"

"Yeah, just tired."

"This case has you down, doesn't it?"

"It's kicking my ass."

"You remember something, cuz. You don't make up the facts. All you can do is deal with them. You still need to come to terms with the fact that Odell may be guilty."

"I can't do that, Booker T. I . . . can't."

Booker T. was silent for a half of a beat and then chuckled. "That's probably why you're so good in the courtroom."

"Thanks again, man. I'll be home soon."

Bo put the phone in his pocket and looked around the office. It would all still be here in the morning. What he needed now was some rest. Tapping his pocket and making sure he had his Glock, Bo stepped outside. He was about to climb inside his Tahoe when he saw a familiar face across the street that caused his stomach to twist into a knot.

Israel Crutcher wore green scrubs and held a paper cup in his hands. He glared at Bo and then gestured with his finger for Bo to cross the street.

Bo hesitated, but only for a second. Then he walked across First Street, where Israel was leaning against a light pole in front of the Bluebird Café. At this time of night, the Bluebird had long since closed.

"Israel."

"Bo."

"Something I can do for you?"

"Yeah," Israel said, tossing the cup at Bo.

Instinctively, Bo reached for the container, seeing Israel's punch and reacting too late to block it. He caught the cup with both hands at the same time that Israel's fist connected with his right eye socket.

Bo fell hard onto the sidewalk, spilling the brown liquid in the cup all over him. The smell of bourbon overwhelmed him, but he was able to roll and avoid being kicked in the chest. He jumped to his feet as Israel started to swing another haymaker. Bo dodged this one and threw his own punch. A straight right hand that landed square on Israel's nose, busting it open and causing blood to splatter onto Israel's scrubs. Before Israel could hit the ground, Bo grabbed him and flung him against the brick wall. Israel swung a weak punch with his right hand, and Bo caught it and put his knee in his former teammate's stomach. He felt the air go out of Israel's lungs, and the other man dropped to the ground.

Bo looked around and saw no one in sight, which wasn't surprising at this time of night. He knew the sheriff's office and the Pulaski PD were out patrolling, but Israel had timed his attack to miss them.

"What the hell are you doing, Iz?" Bo asked, squatting over him.

"You still trying to one-up me, Bo," Israel said, rolling over on his side and gasping for air. "Just like you did in high school."

"I'm doing my job, Iz. That's it."

"And would you be interested at all in this case if it was someone else's daughter?"

"Yes," Bo said. "I would. I believe that Odell Champagne is innocent." Bo saw a police car in the distance. "Look, Iz, I'm going to forget this little encounter happened. But if you *ever* come at me again, it'll be the last time, you understand?"

Israel Crutcher pulled himself to his feet, holding his rib cage.

As Bo started to cross the street, Israel called after him. "Hey, Bo."

Bo looked back at him but continued walking.

"We're not done." He spat the words, and blood ran from his nose down his neck. "Remember that."

74

Bo pulled into his driveway a few minutes later, his eye throbbing. As he parked, he saw a police car pulling in behind him. *What now?* he wondered. Had someone reported his fight with Israel? Bo hopped out of the car, feeling another adrenaline surge, but he relaxed a tad when he noticed Frannie behind the wheel. He walked over as she rolled down the window.

"Just wanted to check—hey, what happened to you?" She climbed out of the car and leaned toward him. Again, Bo smelled the floral scent of her perfume that he'd first noticed at Hitt's Place. "You run into someone's fist?"

"It's nothing," Bo said. "I had a disagreement with someone."

"Who?"

Bo thought about lying but was too tired. "Israel Crutcher. He sucker punched me on the sidewalk on First Street." He gave a weary smile. "He's in worse shape than me now."

Frannie reached inside her vehicle for the CB, but Bo put up his hands. "Please don't, Frannie. I'm not going to press charges, and I doubt Israel is going to make any more trouble before trial. He got what he wanted."

Frannie hung up the microphone and squinted at him. "And what was that?"

"My attention."

"You need to put some ice on that bruise. You might have a shiner."

"Won't be my first. And probably not my last either. I've always had a nose for trouble."

Frannie took a step closer to him. "Did you try to get Odell to take the new deal we offered? Fifteen years, Bo. Odell would be out in his early thirties. That's as good as it is going to get with this type of evidence."

"I informed him of the offer, and he refused."

"Make him see reason."

"He's innocent," Bo said.

"He's a liar, Bo. A serial liar. And because of how the motion hearing went today, Gloria will be able to prove that fact if you put Odell on the stand. In your heart of hearts, you know he's got no chance unless he testifies. You'll have to call him, and when you do, Gloria will destroy him."

Bo glanced up at the sky, collecting his thoughts, before turning his attention back to the lawwoman. "Look, Frannie, we both know that Gloria wouldn't have lowered the amount of jail time in her offer if she wasn't worried about an acquittal. Now, I'll admit, in my heart of hearts, I wish this case wasn't going to trial. But it is, and come Monday, you can rest assured that your new General is going to have a fight on her hands."

She peered at him for a long time, and finally a tired smile came over her face. "Bocephus Haynes is a bad man," she said, speaking in a teasing voice reminiscent of her aunt Ellie's. "You take care of yourself."

"You too."

Bo walked back to his car but noticed that Frannie still hadn't moved. He turned toward her when he reached the side door to the garage. "How is it that you got stuck with patrol duty tonight? The chief deputy sheriff. I would have figured you would have assigned this job to one of your minions."

"I didn't get stuck with it," she said, sticking her chin out.

"Oh?"

"I volunteered," she said before climbing into her squad car.

75

Israel woke the next morning in his hotel bed, still wearing his scrubs from the previous day. His head pounded from a hangover, and his nose hurt almost as bad. He stumbled into the bathroom, examining himself. He didn't think his nose was broken, only split open. He figured a few stitches would do the trick. He called a general surgeon friend who owed him a favor and got it fixed up that afternoon.

Afterward, he took a long drive, eventually ending up at Maplewood Cemetery. He put flowers on his daughter's grave and sat on the grass beside the headstone for what must have been hours. As the sunlight started to fade, he finally left, but not before kissing his hand and placing it on the concrete marker. "I'm so sorry, baby girl, but I'm going to make amends this week. I swear, as God is my witness, I will."

When he was back in his vehicle, he unclicked the glove compartment and took out his pistol. He'd moved it here yesterday and had thought about bringing it out on the square last night for his confrontation with Bo. He could have ended things once and for all.

Not yet, Israel thought. His mouth began to quiver as he peered out the window to the hill where his oldest daughter was buried. Then, returning the gun to the glove compartment, he peeled back onto the road. *Not yet,* he thought again, as the last vestiges of the sun slid down the western horizon.

Not until I've made amends . . .

76

"ALL RISE!" The voice of Sundance Cassidy rang out over the courtroom, and Bo and Odell stood together as the Honorable Harold Page strode to the bench. Unlike at the preliminary hearing, the only seats that were filled in the courtroom were by the parties and the victim's family. Bo shot a glance behind the state's table, where Israel Crutcher looked a bit worse for wear with a couple of stitches over his nose. For Bo's part, while his eye was still sore, the swelling was gone. As he gazed around the nearly empty courtroom, Bo knew the scene tomorrow would be much different. While Judge Page wasn't allowing any spectators to be present for jury selection, the trial was fair game, and Bo expected it to be standing room only.

"State of Tennessee versus Odell Jerome Champagne," Judge Page announced, once he was seated in his chair. "Are the parties here?"

"Yes, Your Honor," Gloria Sanchez said. Instead of General Lewis's customary black suit, Gloria wore a navy suit with matching heels. Next to her stood Frannie, who looked trim and sleek in her khaki uniform.

"Yes, Your Honor," Bo said.

"Are we ready to bring the jury venire in?"

After Bo and Gloria had both answered in the affirmative, Harold turned to Sundance. "All right, go get 'em."

———

The next seven hours were an arduous affair where both Gloria and Bo asked the assembled forty-five potential jurors a series of questions, trying to get at their predispositions and biases. Typically, plaintiff's lawyers and criminal defense attorneys preferred younger jurors with a more liberal slant, a hard combination to find in Pulaski, Tennessee.

At 4:30 p.m., they had their jury. Twelve people. Eight men, all white and ranging from age thirty-two to seventy-four. Four women, three white and one African American. The three white women were ages twenty-four, thirty-eight, and fifty-six.

The Black woman was eighty-two-year-old Edna Couch, a retired teacher who had spent thirty-five years teaching third graders at Pulaski Elementary. Gloria had tried to strike her, but Bo had objected under the landmark *Batson v. Kentucky* decision handed down by the United States Supreme Court in 1986, where the court held that a lawyer in a jury trial couldn't use a peremptory strike to exclude a potential juror if the reason was solely because of race.

In a surprising reprieve for the defense, Judge Harold Page agreed with Bo, and Edna Couch was now on the jury.

After giving the members of the jury a long summation of the importance of their service and instructing them to not discuss the case outside of the jury room or to do any research on the case while home, Judge Page dismissed them for the day. When the last juror had filed out, he turned to the lawyers.

"So there's no chance for a settlement?"

Bo wondered if Page's decision to uphold his Batson challenge was to see if he could convince the state to soften the terms of their plea deal.

"None, Your Honor," Gloria said.

"None," Bo echoed.

Page took off his glasses. "All right then, opening statements tomorrow morning at nine."

77

On Tuesday morning, Bo arrived at the courthouse at 7:00 a.m. He sat in the alcove outside the courtroom and watched through the window as the Giles County Courthouse Square began to fill with people. He glanced at the notes for his opening statement, but by this time, he knew what he was going to say. Around 8:45 a.m., as he gazed out the window, he heard a familiar sound from behind him. The clicking of high heels on tile. He turned.

"General?"

Helen Evangeline Lewis, wearing her trademark black suit and heels, stood before him as if she'd never left. "Bo."

"So . . . are you back or just here for a visit?"

"Not sure," she said.

"You going to watch?" Bo asked.

Helen gazed down the hall toward the district attorney general's office and then back to Bo. "I'll be around, but I don't want to be a distraction to Gloria. I'm mainly here for moral support."

"For who?" Bo asked, wrinkling up his face.

"The state of Tennessee, of course," Helen said. Then she winked at him and strode down the hallway.

"This is so messed up," Bo whispered to himself. Then he heard a voice call his name from the courtroom.

"Bo?" It was Sundance.

"Yeah?"

"Starting in five minutes. You ready?"

Bo made a show of shrugging his shoulders. "We'll see." Then he followed the bailiff into the courtroom.

78

The opening statement of Gloria Sanchez was almost clinical in its deliberate precision. She first went through the physical evidence. The fingerprints, blood results, hair samples, and other DNA that all pointed to Odell Champagne as Brittany Crutcher's killer. Then she addressed motive, first showing an enlargement of the breakup letter and then summarizing the testimony establishing that the defendant had been angry about the split and, in the words of Cassie and Ian Dugan, had threatened to make Brittany Crutcher pay, less than two hours before her murder.

Gloria ended with the state's bottom line. "Ladies and gentlemen of the jury, the defendant, Odell Jerome Champagne, had the means, opportunity, and motive to commit this crime. Motivated by anger and jealousy, the defendant unlawfully and with premeditation caused the death of Brittany Crutcher. I'm confident that when you've heard all the evidence in this case, you'll reach the only verdict that justice demands." She paused. "Guilty."

———

Bo's opening focused on the holes in the state's physical case. While Odell Champagne's fingerprints were found in a lot of places, there were other prints on key pieces of evidence, including the prints of Brittany's new manager, Michael Zannick, on the victim's underclothes and cell phone. There was also no evidence from any witness establishing that

Odell Champagne had anything more than the full six-pack of beer that had been found when he was taken into custody. Finally, where did the seventh bottle, the one that killed Brittany Crutcher, come from?

He told them he expected Judge Page to instruct them at the end of the trial that the burden of proof rested with the prosecution to prove beyond a reasonable doubt that Odell Champagne intentionally and wrongfully caused the death of Brittany Crutcher. If any of them had even one doubt, the prosecution would not meet its burden, and the only verdict they could render would be not guilty.

Bo ended with a plea for justice. "I ask you to keep an open mind and do what you think is fair."

79

The prosecution's first witness was county coroner Melvin Ragland, who opined consistent with his testimony at the preliminary hearing that the cause of Brittany Crutcher's death was blunt force trauma to her forehead, resulting in a fracture to the victim's skull.

Bo moved his eyes beyond the bench to the gallery, where Theresa Crutcher was crying softly. As had happened at the prelim, many of the spectators were also wiping their eyes at the graphic nature of the testimony. Next to him, Bo could hear his client's rapid breathing. He wrote, "Keep it together," on his notebook and slid it over to Odell.

Ragland concluded as follows: "In my opinion, Ms. Crutcher was struck on the forehead with the broken bottle of Bud Light found at the scene. The force of the blow caused the glass to shatter, which left specks of glass on the victim's clothes."

Finally, Ragland confirmed that, based on the condition and temperature of the body and the amount of rigor mortis that had set in, his estimated time of death was between 1:00 a.m. and 3:00 a.m. on October 15, 2016.

On cross-examination, Bo obtained Ragland's admission that, while the clothes of the victim contained a lot of glass, there were very few microscopic shards of glass found on the defendant's clothing. In fact, the only specks of glass had been located on the defendant's right sleeve.

Ragland argued that he would certainly expect that to be the location where most of the glass would be found since the defendant was right handed and presumably hit the victim while holding the bottle in his right hand.

Bo fired back that given the force of the blow and the glass found on various parts of Brittany's clothing and person, wouldn't he expect to have seen more glass on the defendant?

"Yes," Ragland conceded.

Next up for the state was Dr. Malacuy Ward, the director of the crime lab in Nashville, a veteran of many trials over his twenty-five-odd years in forensics. Dr. Ward testified that the blood found on the broken beer bottle matched that of the victim. He also testified that the blood on the victim's and the defendant's clothes was a positive match for Brittany's. Additionally, hair follicles and saliva discovered on the victim's clothes and on the bus seat where the victim's body had been discovered matched samples provided by the defendant.

On cross-examination, Dr. Ward admitted that there were other hairs found on the clothes that didn't match the victim's or the defendant's. He also admitted that saliva taken from what was left of the opening of the broken beer bottle couldn't be conclusively matched to the defendant.

Unfortunately, there wasn't much else Bo could do with Ward's testimony.

The state's next witness was Frannie Storm, who took the jury through her entire investigation from the time she arrived on the scene the morning of October 15 up until the present. She described finding the body on the bus and how the police dogs had located the bloody broken bottle and a passed-out Odell Champagne. Through Frannie, Gloria was able to introduce the fingerprint evidence, showing Odell's prints on the broken beer bottle and the back of the bus where Brittany's body had been found.

On cross, Frannie had to admit that the fingerprints of Michael Zannick had been identified on the victim's underclothes and cell phone.

The state's next witness was, at least in Bo's opinion, intended to be a slap in his face.

"Your Honor, the state calls Mr. Thomas Jackson Haynes."

There was a murmur in the crowd as T. J. strode into the courtroom and took the stand. It wasn't every day that a key prosecution witness was also the son of lead counsel for the defendant. Once seated, T. J. shot his father a glance, and Bo nodded at him. He had told T. J. last night that all he expected of him was to tell the truth.

Now, Bo watched as his son was sworn in and taken through the preliminaries of the ball game and the concert. After several minutes, Gloria got to the heart of it. "How was the defendant acting at the party after the concert?"

"He had a lot to drink and was angry because Brittany had broken up with him with a note. He was acting obnoxious, which wasn't like Odell." She then had him describe Odell's altercation with Jarvis and T. J.'s pleas with Odell to leave the party with them, which Odell refused.

"T. J., before you left the party, did you hear the defendant say anything about Brittany that you remember?"

"He said there was no way he was going to let her leave him like that."

"Anything else?"

"Yes, ma'am." T. J. glanced at Bo, who nodded for him to continue. "He said no one was going to treat him that way and get away with it."

"Thank you, T. J."

"Cross-examination, Bo?" Judge Page asked.

"No, Your Honor."

The state's final evidence on Tuesday was introducing the text messages sent by Odell Champagne to Brittany Crutcher the night of the murder. They did this through the testimony of Deputy Ty Dodgen, who testified that the defendant's cell phone had been found on his person when he'd been discovered and identified lying on the ground at the bus yard the morning of October 15, 2016. Gloria took the cell phone out of the plastic evidence baggie and handed it to Ty. "Is this the cell phone you found on Odell Champagne's person?"

"Yes, it is."

"And were you able to capture all of the text messages that the defendant sent to Brittany on the night of the murder?"

"Yes."

"If it pleases the court, will you please read those to the jury."

Dodgen took the phone and read in a deliberate voice as Gloria displayed the texts on the screen to the right of the jury box.

11:07 p.m. Great concert, babe. Me, T.J. and Jarvis are at Doug's house. Please come. I got your note, and I want to talk with you before you leave.

11:22 p.m. Hey, Brit. Please respond. I can't handle this breakup. Not like this. I need to see you.

11:59 p.m. Where you at? You really going to blow me off like this? Meet me at the bus yard later. Please Brit.

Dodgen paused before he read the next text. "This one has some language."

"Just read it, Deputy," Judge Page instructed.

Dodgen nodded and looked back down at the phone.

12:16 a.m. Fuck you then.

There was a rustle of murmurs from the gallery. Judge Page banged his gavel for quiet.

"Are there any more texts from the defendant to the victim, Deputy?" Gloria asked.

12:31 a.m. Where are you? How can you do me this way, Brit?

Dodgen stopped. "Those are all of his texts to her."
"Are there any messages from Brittany?"
"Yes . . . one."
"What does it say?"

1:02 a.m. Odell, I'm at the bus yard. Please come. I'm sorry. I want to see you.

Gloria let the last message hang in the air for several seconds. "Thank you, Deputy Dodgen. No further questions."
"Cross-examination, Mr. Haynes."
"Yes, Your Honor," Bo said, striding toward the evidence table. "Deputy Dodgen, I'd like you to look at the victim's phone. May I?" he asked Gloria, and she gave a curt nod. Bo retrieved the baggie with the iPhone and handed it to Dodgen. "Now that's the cell phone of Brittany Crutcher, correct?"
"Yes."
"And all of those text messages that you just read from Odell Champagne are on there, correct?"
"Yes."
"But Odell wasn't the person who texted her the most that day, was he?"
Dodgen adjusted himself in his chair. "No."
"Who sent her the most messages?"
"Michael Zannick."
"How many?"
Dodgen took out the phone and counted. "Ten from him and five from her."
"Can you read those to the jury?"

Dodgen did, most of them dealing with the contract that Brittany had signed earlier that day with ELEKTRIK HI and the concert that night. As the deputy began reciting the messages, Bo turned to the defense table, where Hooper had set up his laptop. Bo gave the OK sign, and Hooper brought up an enlargement of the texts on the screen adjacent to the jury. Before Dodgen reached the final and most significant message, Bo interrupted him.

"Officer, for the jury's benefit, we've created a blow-up of this text chain. Can you look at the screen and confirm that these are the messages exchanged between Michael Zannick and Brittany Crutcher on October 14, 2016?"

Dodgen squinted at the display. After a few seconds, he leaned forward and spoke to the jury. "Yes, those are them."

"Who's the last text from?"

"Mr. Zannick."

"And can you read that one to the jury?"

"Yes sir." He cleared his throat and spoke in a flat voice.

11:17 p.m. Am I going to see you tonight?

"Thank you, Deputy," Bo said, making sure to look at as many jurors as he could. "No further questions."

"Redirect, General?" Page asked.

"No, Your Honor."

"OK," the judge said, looking at his watch. "Since it's almost five o'clock, we will adjourn for the day."

As the jury filed out, Bo took in a deep breath and exhaled. They'd taken their licks, but the last evidence the jury had heard supported his alternate theory that Zannick was the true killer. It was rare to score any points for the defendant in a criminal trial on the first day.

I'll take what I can get, Bo thought.

80

Bo arrived home dog tired and hungry, but there was a surprise waiting for him. In the driveway, he saw Helen Lewis's black Crown Victoria. Once he was inside the house, T. J. confirmed what Bo already knew. "The General is waiting for you out on the porch."

"Thanks, son," Bo said. As T. J. began to walk away, Bo called after him. "Hey."

"Sir?"

"You did good today."

"I hope I didn't hurt the case too bad."

"You told the truth," Bo said. "I'm proud of you, son."

"Thanks, Dad."

Bo grabbed a beer and found Helen sitting in one of the two rocking chairs and rubbing Lee Roy behind the ears. T. J. had started a fire in the fireplace, and it felt nice and toasty on the porch despite the January chill. Bo sat down and popped the top on his bottle. He took a long sip and squinted at Helen. "General, you're full of surprises this week."

Helen shook her head and peered down at the ground. "I'm about to drop three more on you."

"Three what?"

"Surprises."

"Bigger than you taking a leave of absence for several months and then showing up out of the blue right before trial?"

Helen peered at him with sad eyes. "Unfortunately so."

———

Bo sat and watched the fire for a long time after the General finished talking. He said nothing, focusing on the orange flames and, every so often, taking another sip of beer. Though he rarely drank during a trial, he'd already downed four Yuenglings while listening to Helen's story.

"I know it's a lot to take in at once," she said, her voice soft.

Bo scoffed. He cleared his throat and peered at her across the porch. "Zannick is your son."

"Yes."

"Your *son?*" Bo repeated, still not quite believing it.

"Yes."

Bo shook his head and looked back at the fire. "That would be enough to shell shock anyone, but killing Butch too." Bo let out a manic giggle that he stopped. "So Frannie was right all along. I *did* help exonerate a guilty client."

"I killed him, Bo, but I didn't murder him. It was an accident. He begged me to finish him off after the fatal shot, and I obliged."

"You obliged," Bo said, hearing the utter incredulity in his voice. He took another pull off the bottle and began to pace around the porch. "Those two bombs would have been more than enough, but you had to go and sabotage my defense of Odell too."

"It was going to come out at trial."

"How?"

"Through me. Michael didn't kill Brittany Crutcher. He may have tried to mess around with her that night, and he clearly touched her underwear at some point, but after she left his house, he didn't go after Brittany." She paused. "He went to find me."

"And he did," Bo said, still not believing it. "You're his mother . . . and his alibi."

———

An hour later, Bo walked the General to her car, still reeling over the revelations she'd made.

"What are you going to do?"

"I don't know yet," Bo said. "Gonna have to think about it."

"If you turn me in, I'll understand."

"I'm not going to turn you in," Bo said. "I can't. I'm your attorney . . . or at least I was. Regardless, everything you just told me would be protected by the attorney-client privilege."

"I'll waive it if you want to turn me in."

"I won't waive it," Bo said.

"I'm sorry, Bo. I know you had developed your whole case around Michael being your alternative killer. I should have told you sooner. I just didn't know what to do. When I heard your opening statement and saw what you did with Michael's text messages to Brittany, I knew I had to come forward."

"Am I the only person who knows about you killing Butch?"

She shook her head. "Michael knows. And there's one other."

Bo thought he knew who she meant but wouldn't say his name. "Good night, General."

"Good night," she said, kissing his cheek. "I'm truly sorry."

81

On Wednesday morning, the state called its final three witnesses. Ennis Petrie took the stand and testified consistently with what he had said at the preliminary hearing. He saw the defendant, Odell Champagne, walking down Eighth Street at approximately 1:15 a.m. on October 15, 2016. While walking in the same direction and just ten yards away from the defendant, he saw Odell talking to himself, and a couple of times, the defendant had beaten his chest with his fist. His demeanor had been agitated. Upset.

On cross-examination, a sluggish Bo, fighting fatigue and a hangover after the General's bombshell the night before, was able to get Ennis to concede that Odell had appeared to be inebriated by how he was walking. Also, Ennis hadn't seen any beer in Odell's possession other than the six-pack of Bud Light that he had been holding in his right hand.

Cassie Dugan was the state's next witness. She described picking up her brother, Ian, and Odell Champagne at Doug Fitzgerald's party. While driving Odell back to his apartment, she testified that she'd told the defendant that Brittany was cheating on him with Michael Zannick.

"And what was the defendant's response?" Gloria asked, watching the jury.

Cassie wiped tears from her eyes and stuck her chin out. "He said, 'That bitch is going to pay.'"

On cross, Cassie admitted that she hadn't initially told the sheriff's department about Odell's comments, nor had she disclosed that she had driven Odell to his apartment after the party. She also admitted that she wasn't sure whether what she told Odell about Brittany's infidelity was true. "You misled the sheriff's department during their initial interview, and you lied to Odell Champagne about Brittany Crutcher's relationship with Michael Zannick."

"I'm not sure if it was a lie or not."

"You spoke to him as if it were the truth, didn't you? You didn't waffle any with Odell, did you?"

"No, I didn't."

Bo hoped the questions might at least scar Cassie's credibility with the jury.

The final witness for the state was Ian Dugan. Ian wore a navy suit and had slicked his long curly hair back. He testified to hanging out for a couple of hours at Doug Fitzgerald's party and said that Odell had been very upset about the breakup. He'd been in the car when his sister had said that Brittany was cheating on Odell with Michael Zannick, and he hadn't said anything to the contrary. Ian, too, remembered that Odell had lost his temper, though he wasn't exactly sure what he'd said. Something like, "I'm going to get her back," was all he could remember.

On cross, he admitted that he hadn't been forthcoming in his initial statement to the police.

On redirect, Gloria asked him why he and Cassie hadn't told their full story earlier. Looking right at the jury, Ian said that they were scared they would get in trouble. "We should have come forward sooner," he said, looking down and shaking his head. "And we should've called the police and warned them about Odell."

At noon, as Ian descended the witness stand, Gloria stood and spoke in a loud, firm voice. "Your Honor, the state rests."

82

"Is the defendant ready to proceed?" Page peered over the bench at Bo.

Bo stood and buttoned his coat. After asserting the customary motion for judgment as a matter of law that the state's evidence had failed to make a prima facie case, which Page denied, Bo put his hand on his client's shoulder.

"The defense calls as our first witness the defendant, Odell Champagne." Bo's original plan had been to put Zannick on as his first witness, but he'd scrapped those plans after his conversation with Helen last night. He was trying this case now off the cuff, making things up as he went. Helen had taken his alternate theory, and he'd now have to wing it.

Odell took the stand and was sworn in by Sundance Cassidy. "Odell," Bo began, calling him by his first name in order to highlight his youth for the jury. He decided to proceed with the question that every member of the jury had waited for since they were put in their respective chairs three days ago. ". . . did you kill Brittany Crutcher?"

"No, I did not."

"Did you hit her with a blunt object in the forehead?"

"No."

"How was it that you ended up at the bus yard on the early morning of October 15, 2016?"

"Brittany texted me to meet there. That was a special place for us."

"Why was it special?"

"It was the first place we ever made love. I—"

There was a smattering of murmurs, and Judge Page banged his gavel for quiet. Then he gestured for Odell to continue.

"I'd texted her earlier to meet me there, but she hadn't responded. When I got home after Doug Fitzgerald's party, I got her message. She said she wanted to see me."

At this point, Bo backtracked and had Odell describe to the jury how he had ended up in Pulaski and about the troubles he'd had with the law in Town Creek, Alabama. He'd learned early in his legal career that, if there was bad news to be shared about a client in front of the jury, it was better if the client testified about it first. *You never want a jury to be surprised about something bad your client did,* Professor McMurtrie had taught.

After Odell explained that his theft convictions had resulted from a need for food, Bo took Odell into his senior year at Pulaski and had him describe for the jury meeting and falling in love with Brittany almost at first sight during his lap around the track with her during summer workouts. The nights they'd spent studying, first at her house and then at Tasha Ferguson's apartment. Finally, Odell admitted that the bus yard had become a sort of ground zero for their relationship. "After that first time, we met up there a lot. Brittany didn't live at home, and I didn't like being at home."

"Why didn't you like being at home?"

"Because my mom's an alcoholic."

Finally, Bo directed Odell to the night of the murder, starting with him finding the breakup note in his pocket and then the party at Doug Fitzgerald's.

"Did you regularly drink alcohol?"

"No. Hardly ever."

"How much did you have to drink that night?"

"At least five beers at Doug's house. Probably more."

"Why did you drink so much?"

"Because I was angry and hurt. I guess . . . I guess I wanted to kill the pain."

"Were you drunk?"

"Yes, sir."

"Do you remember going home after the party?"

"Vaguely," Odell said. "I remember being in a small car with Ian, and I remember him saying that Brittany had been cheating on me with Michael Zannick."

"Did you know that Michael Zannick was Brittany's new manager?"

"Not exactly," Bo said. "I knew Mr. Zannick had given a lot of money to the band, but that was it."

"Did you like Mr. Zannick?"

"No, I did not."

"Were you jealous of him?"

Odell looked at the jury. "I was jealous of the time that Brittany seemed to be spending with him. I knew she had been to his house a few times because she'd told me."

"Did you know she had spent the night in one of Zannick's guest bedrooms on several occasions?"

"Yes."

"What did you think of that?"

"I didn't like it."

"Did you tell Brittany how you felt?"

"Yes, I did, but she didn't have much choice. Tasha had a boy-friend, and there were times when she wanted her privacy. When that happened, Brit needed a place to stay, and I didn't want her with me, because we didn't have the room, and even if we did, I was afraid my mom would fly off the handle."

Bo felt all this background was necessary so the jury got the full picture. Now he got back on point. "When Ian told you that Brittany was cheating on you with Zannick, how did that make you feel?"

"Betrayed. Hurt."

"Angry?"

"Yes, sir."

"The prosecution has introduced several text messages that you sent Brittany that night." Bo pulled up the messages on the PowerPoint used during the state's case in chief. "Did you send these texts?"

"Yes, sir."

"Did you want to kill Brittany?"

"No, sir."

"Did you tell Cassie Dugan or anyone else that you wanted to make her pay for what she had done?"

"I don't remember saying anything like that," Odell said. "If I did, I was lashing out. I admit I was angry and probably said some things I wish hadn't." As they had rehearsed, Odell looked at the jury. "But I would never lay a hand on Brittany. Didn't matter how bad she might have hurt me. I loved her." Odell's voice was thick with emotion, and he wiped his eyes.

"When you got home from the party, what did you do?"

"For a while, I laid on the couch. Drifted off to sleep. I woke up after about half an hour and saw that I had a text from Brittany to meet her at the bus yard."

"What did you do next?"

"My mom wasn't home, so there was no car. Even if there was, I was too drunk to drive. So I walked."

"Do you remember seeing a man named Ennis Petrie, who testified earlier in this trial, on your walk to the yard?"

"No."

"Did you stop anywhere along the way?"

"Yes. I stopped at the Slinky's on College Station and got a sixer of Bud Light."

"How? You're underage."

"The guy at the station gave me the beer for free."

"Why?"

"Because I scored three touchdowns and ran for a hundred and fifty yards against Tullahoma." Odell's delivery was so matter of fact that several people in the gallery actually chuckled, as did two jurors. *A laughing jury doesn't convict,* Professor McMurtrie had said, when Bo had been a second year on the trial advocacy team at Alabama. It was advice that Bo had always thought was well taken, and the sight of the smiles in the jury box sent a sliver of hope through him.

"Were you talking to yourself on the way to the bus yard?"

"Probably."

"Why?"

"I was rehearsing what I was going to say. I wanted to try to convince her to stay."

"Were you still angry?"

"Yeah, I was, but intense and nervous is probably more like it. I was afraid this was the last time I was going to see her, and I was still a little drunk. I didn't want to say the wrong thing."

"Did you ever beat on your chest with your fist?"

"Yeah, I was trying to psyche myself up and sober up. I wanted to say the right things."

"Did you bring anything else with you to the bus yard other than the six-pack of Bud Light?"

"No, sir."

"Did you drink any of the beers?"

"No, sir. I was planning to share them with Brit. Bud Light was about the only beer she would drink."

Bo walked over to the exhibit table in front of Sundance Cassidy and pointed at the evidence bag containing the broken beer bottle. "When was the first time you saw this broken bottle?"

"When I found Brittany on the back of the bus."

"Was she already dead?"

"Objection, Your Honor. Lack of foundation."

Bo almost thanked Gloria for the interruption. "When you walked down the aisle of the school bus, describe what you saw."

Odell took a deep breath and exhaled into the microphone. His voice was shaky as he began to talk. "I n-n-noticed her feet first. They were hanging out of the aisle, and she had on socks. When I got up to her, she was just staring back at me, and her eyes weren't moving." He gripped his hands together. "She had a massive bruise on her forehead, and the broken beer bottle was on the ground next to her. I leaned toward her and could tell she wasn't breathing."

Bo walked to the edge of the jury railing and looked back at his client. "Is there anything else you remember?"

"Yes," Odell said.

"What?"

"Brit loved to chew gum. She'd put lots of pieces in her mouth. She always smelled like bubble gum." He swiped at the tears in his eyes, and his lips and hands trembled. "I saw a big wad of pink gum on the ground by her face." Odell let out a sob.

Bo glanced at the jury and saw that tears were falling down the cheeks of Edna Couch as well as Retta Colson, a thirty-eight-year-old teacher at Pulaski Elementary.

"Does the witness need a break?" Judge Page asked, frowning at Odell and then at Bo. "Should we take a short recess?"

"No, Your Honor," Odell said, straightening up but not wiping his eyes. "I'm OK."

Bo again looked at the jury, deciding it was time to wrap things up.

"Are you telling the truth today, Odell?"

"Yes, sir."

Bo looked at his client. "Did you kill Brittany Crutcher."

"No, sir. I loved that girl."

Bo turned and looked at the jury and then Judge Page. "No further questions, Your Honor."

———

On cross, Gloria impeached Odell with his prior convictions and then ended with motive.

"You were angry that Brittany Crutcher broke up with you with a note, weren't you?"

As Bo instructed, Odell kept his hands to the side of the witness chair and held his shoulders back. *Your body language must convey that you have nothing to hide and these answers don't hurt you.* "Yes, ma'am, I was," he said, his voice calm and matter of fact.

Perfect, Bo thought.

"And you were jealous of her relationship with Michael Zannick," Gloria continued.

"Yes."

"And when Ian Dugan told you that Brittany was having a sexual relationship with Zannick, you got even angrier, didn't you?"

"Yes."

"And this was about an hour before you headed to the bus yard."

With his back straight, arms out, voice never wavering, Odell answered. "Yes."

Gloria glared at Odell and then looked at the jury. "No further questions."

Odell walked with a steady and unrushed gait from the stand to the defense table. Once he was seated, Bo touched his arm. "Excellent," he whispered.

———

"Mr. Haynes, call your next witness," Judge Page asked.

"Your Honor, the defendant calls Rufus Slinkard."

Bo looked toward the double doors just as Lona opened them and escorted Rufus into the courtroom. Rufus, or "Slinky," as he'd been called since he was six years old, was a wiry man with arms so long they hung almost to his knees. In 1974, he'd opened a gas station and convenience store on College Street. Though he'd become affiliated with Wavaho about a decade ago, he'd never changed the sign on the front, which simply read, SLINKY'S GAS. For a man approaching ninety years old, Slinky looked fit and alert.

"Please introduce yourself to the jury," Bo said.

"Slinky," he said, and there was a smattering of laughs.

"Can you give your full name for the record?"

"Sorry. Rufus Elihue Slinkard." He smiled at the jury. "You can see why I prefer Slinky."

More laughs, and even venerable old Harold Page cracked a smile. It had been a long, tense day, and it seemed everyone was grateful for a reprieve, even His Honor.

"Did you see the defendant on the night of October 14, 2016?" Bo asked.

"Hell, yeah," Slinky said. "Scuse my language, Your Honor."

"Where did you see him?"

"On my television. Kid scored three times, and we whupped the snot out of Tullahoma."

"Yes, sir. I'm talking about after the game," Bo said, grateful for Slinky's slow speech and failure to get to the point. Bo was buying time, as he needed to decide if he was going to call any more witnesses. "Did you see Mr. Champagne in your store?"

"Yes, sir. He came in around one in the morning."

"And how was it that you were open that night?"

"We're open twenty-four hours, Bo, and have been since 1974."

"Did you sell the defendant a six-pack of beer at one in the morning on October 15?"

"No, sir, I didn't."

"Did you give him any beer?"

"Your Honor," Gloria stood. "As an officer of the court, I would remind the witness of his rights under the Fifth Amendment to not incriminate himself."

"Thank you, General," Page said. "Slinky, you don't have to testify. You can take the Fifth Amendment."

Slinky ran a hand through his matted-down silver hair and guffawed. "Harold, I'm eighty-nine years old. I had a lapse in judgment that I'd probably make again." Then he turned to Bo. "Yes, sir. I gave Odell Champagne a six-pack of Bud Light."

There were murmurs through the crowd.

"Why'd you do that?"

"'Cause he's the best damn football player I've ever seen," Slinky said. "No offense, Bo. And because I saw him approaching on foot and knew he wasn't driving."

"Did he seem angry?"

"No."

"Is there anything about his demeanor that you can remember?"

"He was acting nervous," Slinky said. "Bouncing on his toes."

"Did he say anything to you?"

"He thanked me for the beer. That was it."

"Thank you, sir." Bo walked to the defense table and pulled up the surveillance video from the gas station on his laptop, projecting it on to the screen. "Mr. Slinkard, you produced the surveillance video of my client's time in your store the morning of October 15 pursuant to the state's subpoena, isn't that correct?"

"Yes, I did."

Bo pointed toward the screen. "Is that you on the tape?"

"Yep. Ugly all day."

Bo suppressed a grin. "What time is that in the lower right-hand corner?"

"One oh eight a.m."

Bo pressed play, and the video showed Odell Champagne enter the store and walk to the cooler, returning to the counter seconds later with a six-pack carton of Bud Light. Though the picture was fuzzy, Slinky appeared to be talking to Odell, and then Odell waved at him and left with the carton.

"Does that video fairly and accurately depict your interaction with Odell Champagne?"

"Yep," Slinky said.

"Did Odell act angry, agitated, or upset in his time with you?"

"No, he did not," Slinky said, pointing at the screen. "He was a perfect gentleman."

Bo glanced at the jury and then back at the witness. "No further questions."

"Cross-examination?"

"Yes, Your Honor," Gloria said. "Mr. Slinkard, based on the video, you were in Odell Champagne's presence for about forty-seven seconds. Is that correct?"

"Yes, ma'am. About a minute."

"Not even a minute, was it?"

"No, guess not."

"Thank you. No further questions."

"All right, Mr. Slinkard," Judge Page said. "You're dismissed."

"Should I just go to the jail?" Slinky asked, and there were a few more chuckles from the gallery.

"Uh . . ." Harold threw up his hands. "I'm sure the sheriff's office will be in touch."

"Okeydoke," Slinky said, climbing down from the stand.

Seconds later, Page turned to Bo. "Any more witnesses today, Counselor?"

Bo looked at the clock on the wall: 4:20 p.m. and he had no other witnesses to call. He thought about having some of Odell's teammates testify as to his overall good character and that he wasn't prone to violence, but he didn't want to open the door to Odell's assault charge in Town Creek. Bo envisioned the beaten face of Bennett Caldwell that Hooper had shown him on the PowerPoint screen. "Your Honor, the defense would ask for a recess for the rest of the day."

"Do you have any more witnesses, Mr. Haynes?"

"Possibly, Your Honor," Bo said. "If it pleases the court, can we recess for today and let the court know tomorrow?"

Page frowned. "That doesn't please the court, but I'm old and tired, so I'm going to allow it." He banged his gavel. "We are recessed until tomorrow morning at nine. Mr. Haynes, be prepared to either call your next witness or rest, understand?"

"Yes, Your Honor," Bo said, giving Page an appreciative nod. "We'll be ready."

83

Bo, Hooper, and Lona gathered around the conference room table an hour after Judge Page's recess. All three were exhausted, but Bo needed his team now more than ever. After they had wolfed down sandwiches that Lona had picked up from the Yellow Deli, Bo peered at both of them and decided to disclose his dilemma.

"Michael Zannick has an alibi."

"No, he doesn't," Hooper said. "His surveillance cameras show his car leaving his mansion at eleven fifty p.m. Exactly five minutes after Brittany left in her 4Runner."

"And Zannick didn't go to the bus yard to kill Brittany," Bo said, his voice teetering with exhaustion. "He went to Helen Lewis's house."

"What?" Lona said.

"He went to the General's house."

"Are you sure?" she asked.

"Unfortunately I am. The General told me herself. So . . . if we call Zannick, he'll say he was with her, and then I'm sure the state will call Helen, and she'll confirm it."

"And there goes our alternate theory," Hooper said.

"And any chance of an acquittal," Bo said.

Lona's face was twisted in confusion. "I don't understand. Why the hell would Zannick go to the General's house, and why in God's name would Helen Lewis talk to him in the middle of the night?"

Bo let out a ragged breath. "Because she's his mother."

———

It took a while for that to sink in. Bo didn't reveal Helen's other bomb-shell—that she had actually killed her ex. He would hold on to that secret, as it did no good to tell them. But he trusted his team. Even so, he swore them to secrecy, telling them both that as employees of his law firm they were obligated to uphold the same attorney-client privilege that he was bound by.

"I think I'd still call him," Lona said. "Have him admit that she was at his house. That she was upset and was thinking about reneging on the deal he had negotiated for her. You have him dead to rights on that with your recording."

"What if he says he has an alibi?" Bo asked.

"Don't ask him whether he went to the bus yard; just plant all the seeds leading up to Brittany leaving the house."

Bo had considered that approach but couldn't get his mind right about it.

"I wouldn't call him," Hooper chimed in. "There's nothing he's going to add to the story if you can't challenge him on his lack of an alibi. Since he has one . . ." He shook his head. ". . . and it's a damn good one, I would not call him. Too much risk for not enough gain."

Before Bo could agree, Lona chimed in. "I hate it when you're right," she said, scowling at the investigator with a playful tease in her tone and eyes. "I changed my mind. I'm with Columbo. Screw calling Zannick."

"So we rest?" Bo asked.

Lona and Hooper both nodded. Then Hooper leaned back in his chair. "And you get prepared to give the closing argument of your life."

Bo closed his eyes. "It's going to take that."

84

After dismissing Lona and Hooper for the night with plans to meet back at the office at 7:00 a.m., Bo spent the next two hours going over every pertinent crime scene photograph and all the video evidence, looking for any possible angle. Finally, at 7:30 p.m., he resolved to go home and eat with the kids and Booker T. But as he was climbing into his Tahoe, he got a phone call from a number he didn't recognize. Thinking it was probably a solicitor, he answered it anyway. "Yeah?"

"I need to talk with you."

"OK," Bo said, recognizing the voice. "When?"

"Now."

"Where?"

"The church sanctuary."

"Does Israel know about this?"

The phone clicked dead without an answer.

———

Ten minutes later, Bo walked into the sanctuary of the Bickland Creek Baptist Church. Theresa Crutcher sat in the choir, looking at the stained glass windows on the opposite wall. As Bo approached, she didn't look at him.

"Theresa, what can I do for you?"

"I'm scared, Bo."

"Why?"

"I want my baby to have justice."

Bo climbed the steps into the pulpit and took the chair next to Theresa. "I want that too. Why are you scared?"

"I'm terrified of what Israel is going to do if that boy gets off." She sighed. "I'm also afraid of what he might do if Odell is found guilty and not sufficiently punished."

Bo thought about Israel's threats over the past few months and the altercation he'd had with his former teammate last Friday night. "What do you want me to do?"

For several seconds, Bo watched her. Then, finally, he leaned close. "Theresa? Tell me."

She wiped tears from her eyes. "I don't know, but I'm worried. This case is probably going to be over tomorrow, isn't it?"

"Probably."

"Israel left today without speaking to me or Gina. He was so mad after Odell testified. You know how he's always been. Israel is a good man, but . . . he's volatile. And something inside him has broken since Brittany's death. He's not the same person." She began to cry. "None of us are, I guess."

Bo felt sick to his stomach. "Theresa, what can I do?"

"I don't know," Theresa said. "I just . . . wanted to tell someone, and I didn't want to tell the police. I hope my instincts are wrong. I hope Israel is all bark and no bite."

Bo rubbed his eye where Israel had punched him.

"But you don't think so, do you?" Bo asked.

Theresa turned and looked at Bo with heavy eyes. "No, I don't."

85

Israel Crutcher sat on the concrete floor in the nurse's lounge of the hospital and stared at a spot on the cinder block wall. The pistol was in the pocket of his pants, and every so often, he put his hand on the grip. *This circus ends tomorrow,* he thought.

It had been all he could take today listening to how Odell had molested his daughter. He was going to end this farce. It was obvious to him that there would be no justice for Brittany. There was no law that was going to make this right.

"But I will," I whispered. "As God is my witness, I will."

Tomorrow . . .

86

Bo wasn't sure what to do as he pulled away from Bickland Creek Baptist Church. His whole case had been built around the theory that Zannick had killed Brittany and set up Odell. If Zannick didn't do it, then who did? As he drove the streets of Pulaski, a terrible thought kept creeping into his subconscious.

Am I about to help another guilty client go free?

Bo eventually parked outside of Kathy's Tavern. When he walked through the door, Cassie's reception was anything but welcoming. "No interviews tonight, Bo. No talk. No nothing. If you want something to eat or drink, Julie will be right out."

Bo managed a curt smile and found a booth in the back. He ordered a beer from Julie but decided against the burger. His meeting with Theresa had killed any appetite he'd had. *What am I missing?* he thought, rubbing his temples hard with his knuckles. *There's got to be something.*

After ordering another beer, Bo stood and tried to clear his mind by peering at the many photographs on the wall of the bar. There was the country music star, Billy Dean, who'd shot to fame in the '90s, and many others, including of course Fizz. Bo admired the photograph of the band, taking a few seconds looking at each of them. Brittany Crutcher. Mackenzie Santana. Teddy Bundrick. Ian Dugan. Bo then saw a small banner reading "New Year's 2017" with a number of photographs under it. He squinted and eventually found the one of him and Cassie. He smiled, thinking how attractive she had appeared in her dark-red dress. He looked again at the photo and felt the tiniest tickle in his brain. He walked back to the photo of the band and eyed it closer, moving his face to within a few inches of the page.

"Closing time, Bo."

He turned and saw Cassie glaring at him. He took a long sip of beer, and the tickle he'd felt became stronger. "I'm leaving," he said.

———

Bo drove straight to the office, calling Hooper on the way. When he arrived, Hooper pulled up what he wanted in a matter of seconds on his laptop computer.

"Oh my God," Bo said, pointing at the screen. "Check the inventory," he said. "Go through every page."

"I will," Hooper said. "But we both know damn well it's not in there. How did you—?"

But Bo was already walking for the door. Five minutes later, after speeding all the way there, he was knocking on Theresa's door.

"Bo, are you—?"

"I need to see your living room."

"Wh—?"

"Please, Theresa. This won't take one minute."

She opened the door, and Bo ran through the house to the living room, stopping when he saw the photograph on the wall. The one that captured an image that a billion people had watched on TV.

"Oh my God," he whispered again.

87

At 8:30 a.m., Bo walked into the courtroom and did a double take at the person seated behind the defense table.

Sabrina Champagne wore a conservative black dress, her dark-brown hair permed into a stylish but subtle curl. She looked beautiful, and Bo couldn't help but smile. The woman's eyes were clear. Gone was the haze of alcohol.

"Sabrina, you look . . . fantastic," Bo said, meaning it.

"Thank you," she said. "I know we talked about me staying away, but today may decide my son's future. He's been abandoned his whole life by his parents." Her eyes glossed over. *"But not today."*

———

When Odell was ushered into the courtroom, he couldn't contain his emotions when he saw his mother, hugging her tight and crying on her shoulder.

"Momma, you look so . . . *good*," Odell said, wiping his wet eyes. "Why are you here?"

"To stand by my wonderful son."

88

Thirty minutes later, after the jury had been escorted into the courtroom, Judge Page looked down his nose at Bo. "Will the defense be calling any additional witnesses?"

"Yes, Your Honor. The defendant recalls Ms. Cassie Dugan."

Page raised his eyebrows as if he were surprised by this news. "OK, is Ms. Dugan here?"

"Yes, Your Honor," he said. After visiting Theresa, he'd sent Cassie a text saying, Be at the courthouse tomorrow at nine. You're my first witness in the morning and you're still under a subpoena.

Seconds later, Lona ushered Cassie in through the double doors. Bo glanced to the defense table, where Albert Hooper, dressed in a navy-blue blazer, khaki pants, and a houndstooth tie, was seated behind his laptop. He nodded at his investigator, and Hooper returned the gesture. Once Cassie was seated in the witness chair, Bo wasted no time.

"Ms. Dugan, are you familiar with the SunTrust ATM machine on College Street?"

She wrinkled up her face. "Yes. I've gotten cash there many times."

Bo gestured with his arm at Hooper, and the screen to the side of the jury lit up with an image of a silver Toyota 4Runner parked under the overhang protecting an ATM machine. It was dark outside, but the machine was well lit. Bo pointed at Hooper, who paused the video.

"Recognize that car?"

"It's Brittany's," Cassie said, confusion in her tone.

Bo hooked a thumb at Hooper, and the image changed to a close-up of the young woman in the SUV. Though she was in profile, it was obvious who she was.

"And is that Brittany Crutcher?"

"Yes."

"And can you read the numbers on the lower right-hand corner of the screen?"

"Yes, 10/15/16, 12:41 a.m."

"Date and time, right?" Bo asked.

"Correct."

Slowly, Bo moved his index finger in a circle, and the screen began to move. The woman in the car was fiddling in her purse. Then she leaned forward and began to push buttons. Once she had extended herself out the window, Bo said, "Now."

The screen paused with an image of Brittany Crutcher looking at the digits on the machine with fierce, determined eyes. She wore the black GCH sweatshirt that Odell Champagne would later be found cradling on the ground at the bus yard. There was one loose strand of brown hair hanging in one of her eyes, but that wasn't what Bo was looking at. "Zoom in, Hooper."

Seconds later, the screen showed only Brittany's neck. Above the letters of the high school hung a purple charm necklace, barely visible but yet there.

Bo peered into the eyes of Cassie Dugan. "Recognize that piece of jewelry."

"Oh . . . no." Cassie choked the words out.

"Hooper," Bo said. Seconds later, the screen held two images. The paused picture of Brittany Crutcher's neck at the ATM, just minutes before her murder, and another photograph of Brittany, this one from *America's Got Talent*. It was the photo in Theresa's living room, which Bo had snapped several shots of himself on his iPhone before leaving the Crutcher home last night. Brittany wore a black cocktail dress and the same necklace with the purple charm.

"Is that the same piece of jewelry there, Cassie?" Bo asked.

Cassie Dugan's face had gone pale, and Bo saw a sheen of sweat on her neck. "Yes," she croaked.

"Hooper," Bo said again, and a third image joined the others.

An audible gasp emerged from Cassie's throat. It was the photograph of Bo and Cassie from Kathy's Tavern. Hooper had found it on Kathy's Tavern's Facebook page last night. Bo in his button-down and sports coat. Cassie in her burgundy dress, and around her neck . . . the necklace with the purple charm.

"*Oh, no,*" Cassie said again. *"No."* She put her hands on her face and began to sob.

"The sheriff's office didn't find that necklace at the crime scene, Cassie." Bo pointed at the prosecution table. "All this evidence they gathered," he said. "All these photographs of Brittany Crutcher's dead body. And not one single mention of a necklace that she was wearing exactly twenty-one minutes before she texted Odell Champagne that she was at the bus yard waiting for him."

Bo looked at Frannie Storm, and the chief deputy sheriff was half off her seat, her body coiled as if she might need to move at any second. She gave Bo a slow and powerful nod.

"Brittany didn't stop by your house and give you that necklace on the way to the bus yard, did she, Cassie?"

She shook her head.

"You'll need to answer out loud, Ms. Dugan," Judge Page said.

Bo peered around the courtroom, which was filled to capacity, not a single seat vacant. And he could not hear a sound. The silence was wonderful, energy burning within him.

"No. She didn't."

Bo knew that asking an open-ended question on cross was usually ill advised, but there were times when it could be effective. "How did you get that necklace, Cassie? The one that Brittany Crutcher was wearing just minutes before her murder."

Cassie's face was blank, her voice now almost monotone. "It's mine. My grandmother gave it to me when I was seven years old." She coughed out another sob. "I always thought it was lucky. I gave it to Brittany before she went on *AGT*. After she made the finals, I told her she could keep wearing it."

"How did you get it back, Cassie?" Bo pressed.

"I told her . . . when she said she was signing with ELEKTRIK HI that she had something that belonged to me." Her whole face started to quake, tears falling down her now-red cheeks. "No," she whined again.

"How did you get the necklace back?" Bo asked for the third time.

Cassie's voice was nothing but a croak. "He told me she gave it back to him after the concert."

"*Who?*"

Cassie closed her eyes. "My brother."

89

Ian Dugan sat on the back row of the school bus.

It wasn't the same one, but close enough. He'd known something was wrong that morning when Cassie had said that Bo Haynes was putting her back on the stand, so he'd skipped school and left his car at the Legends Steakhouse. Then, like Odell had done three months earlier, he'd walked here.

To where it all began.

And where it all ended . . .

So many good times the band had experienced in this yard. Him, Mack, Teddy B., and Brittany. They'd been a team. They were going to make it all the way to LA. The new Alabama Shakes. They had a song on the radio. They were so close.

But Brittany had ruined everything.

Ian hadn't meant to kill her. He figured she might visit the yard one last time. After all, that was where Odell had wanted to meet her, and other than the small garage studio at his and Cassie's house, it was where the band had spent most of their time. Ian had forgotten to get his grandmother's necklace and needed to get it back before Brittany left town. His sister would be furious with him for not remembering to get it after the concert. Or at least that's what he'd told himself, trying to rationalize his wish to see Brittany again, to express the anger he felt over her decision.

Once he and Cassie had arrived home, he'd waited a few minutes and then snuck back out. He'd taken his sister's Mustang and driven around town, passing by Brittany's apartment and eventually seeing her 4Runner parked near the bus yard.

When he'd seen her standing by the bus, sipping on a Bud Light, seemingly without a care in the world, twisting the necklace around her finger, he'd just lost it. He'd started screaming at her, telling her she'd busted up the band. She told him to calm down, but that only made Ian madder. He was a solid musician but knew his odds of making it big without Brittany were low. He said that she was conniving and no good, destroying dreams, that someone needed to teach her a lesson. She ran up the steps of the bus and tried to shut the door on him, but he blocked it and pushed through. He'd completely forgotten about the necklace at that point. All he'd wanted was some acknowledgment from her that she was wrong.

He hadn't planned on hitting her. He'd never hit a girl in his life. Hell, he'd barely been in any fights. But as he'd followed her down the corridor, she'd thrown her shoes at him. He'd ducked and dodged one and actually laughed.

But the other one almost caught him in the mouth, and as it whizzed by his head, a switch flipped in his brain. He walked toward her. When Brittany pointed the beer bottle at him and told him to stand back, Ian snatched it out of her hands. He turned his back as she screamed for him to go fuck himself.

He'd wheeled on her, intending to throw the bottle into the far window and scare her, but she'd walked right into the blow.

"It was an accident," he whispered, remembering his panic when he'd noticed that Brittany wasn't moving.

In the shock that had followed, he'd paced the corridor of the bus, trying to figure out what to do. The adrenaline rush of the fight had made him stone sober and hyperalert. Ian was a smart guy. A talented gamer. How could he get himself out of this mess?

The only answer that came to him was to set someone up. His friend.

Odell had been so angry about Brittany blowing him off.

He'll come, Ian knew. *If he's nudged at all, he'll come down here.*

As he worked through the problem, Ian knew he couldn't call Odell or send the text himself. Finally, as the seconds began to tick off in his mind, he'd taken off his shirt and wiped down the beer bottle, which had shattered. Then, wrapping his hand in the shirt, he'd reached into Brittany's pocket and pulled out her cell phone and texted Odell.

When he'd descended the steps of the bus, he'd seen his grand-mother's necklace lying on the ground. Brittany must have dropped the jewelry when she'd run up the stairs. Ian had hesitated, but only for a second. He'd grabbed the necklace and put it in his pocket. There might be questions about why it was lying on the ground.

How could I have been so stupid?

He'd then walked back to his car, which he'd parked up the hill toward the college, and had driven home.

———

Ian hung his head as the memories flooded back to him, and he wiped his eyes. He gazed out the window of the bus. It was dark now. How long had he been here? He'd lost all track of time.

But he knew he'd been outed. He'd checked Twitter a few hours ago and seen the news. One tweet after another declaring the dismissal of the charges against Odell Champagne and the search for the presumed killer, Ian Dugan.

"We should have known you'd come here," a strong female voice rang out from the other end of the bus. "This *is* where the band liked to hang out."

Ian blinked and he rose to his feet. "I—"

"Shut up, Ian," Frannie said. "Hold your hands out in front of you."

He did, numb, and Frannie cuffed him. "Ian Dugan, you are under arrest for the murder of Brittany Crutcher. You have the right to remain silent . . ."

———

Three minutes later, Frannie escorted Ian down the steps of the bus. On the ground below, Deputies Ty Dodgen and Bradley McCann waited along with Sheriff Hank Springfield. As they led him away, Frannie saw a man leaning against a silver Chevy Tahoe on the curb. She walked toward him, her legs feeling like jelly.

"You were right," Bo said, a tired smile forming on his mouth.

"We'd checked everywhere else," Frannie said. "The school. His house. Legends Steakhouse. It's not that surprising to think he'd come back here." Her voice cracked on the last syllable as emotion finally overcame her. She leaned into him, and after a brief hesitation, he wrapped his arms around her. "But Brittany is still gone," she whispered. "That beautiful girl is gone."

90

An hour after Ian Dugan was arrested, after Bo had granted several interviews to local and national press outlets, he parked his car outside his office. When he arrived inside, he was met with balloons and noisemakers. Lona and Hooper were wearing party hats, and Odell and Sabrina Champagne sat on the couch in the lobby. Bo noticed that Sabrina was clutching tight to her son's hand.

After the sound died down, Lona sprang forward and handed Bo a glass of nonalcoholic champagne. Then she kissed him full on the cheek. "Last criminal trial?" she asked.

"I guess I should never say never," Bo said. He took a long sip from the glass, relishing the sweet taste. "I said that last year, and look at me now."

"Roll Tide," Hooper said, extending his own glass to Bo.

"Roll motherfucking Tide," Bo corrected, slapping the investigator on the back as laughter filled the room.

But seconds later, the sound of the door squeaking open made them all stop and turn.

Israel Crutcher stood in the opening.

Bo felt his whole body tense, but he managed to take a step forward. "Iz," he managed.

"Bo . . . this is hard for me to say."

"You don't have to—"

"Thank you," he managed. He opened his mouth, and then he bit hard on his lip. "She was my baby, Bo. You know . . . my girl."

Bo set his glass down and stepped closer. He touched his old team-mate's shoulder. "I know, Iz. And I'm so sorry." He heard his own voice crack, and then he turned to see Odell standing in front of them.

"Mr. Crutcher . . ." Odell's voice was strong and firm.

Israel wiped his mouth and eyes and blinked at Odell. "Yes?"

"Would it be OK if I saw her?"

Again, Israel seemed to struggle to find the words. Finally, he managed a nod.

91

That evening, the town of Pulaski lifted the law on visiting Maplewood Cemetery at night.

Israel, Theresa, and Gina Crutcher stood on one side of Brittany's headstone, while Odell and Sabrina Champagne were positioned on the other. Bo, T. J., and Lila, along with Lona, Hooper, and Booker T., filled out a circle, which grew as more people arrived.

Eventually, candles were lit.

The circle grew until there were hundreds of people. Members of the Bickland Creek Baptist Church. Students from Giles County High School. Mackenzie Santana and Teddy Bundrick from Fizz. Most of the Pulaski Police Department as well as the majority of the Giles County Sheriff's Office, including Frannie, who Lila insisted take a place next to her.

Finally, a voice rang out above the crowd, and Bo turned to see Sabrina Champagne, arching her head toward the heavens.

"Amazing grace, how sweet the sound . . . that saved a wretch like me . . ."

Bocephus Haynes held tight to the hands of his children as they all began to sing with Sabrina.

Is justice possible in the world? Bo wondered, looking around the group of people who'd assembled to celebrate the life of Brittany Crutcher. Bo wasn't sure, but one thing was certain.

We have to try.

EPILOGUE

June 16, 2017

Helen Evangeline Lewis parked in front of the Yellow Deli. Her heart was pounding as she entered the restaurant and climbed the steps to the table where he had told her to meet him. As she approached, Michael Zannick rose to his feet.

"Hello . . . Mother," he said. There was no tease to his voice.

"Hello, Michael." She hesitated. "Happy birthday."

He grinned. "Thank you."

They took their seats as the bearded waiter, whose name was Henry, came up to them with menus. "Ah, General Lewis, are you having lunch with Mr. Zannick?"

"Yes," Helen said, looking at Michael as she spoke. "He's my son."

Once they'd placed their orders and Henry had walked away, Helen leaned back from the table and crossed her legs. "Well, Mr. Millionaire Businessman. What do you want for your birthday?"

Michael's face broke into a toothless smile, and he leaned his elbows on the table. When he spoke, his voice was just above a whisper. "To know who my real father was."

THE END

ACKNOWLEDGMENTS

My wife, Dixie, was my first ever reader many moons ago. Over the years, she has been a bouncing board for story ideas, and I'm not sure the plot twist with Michael Zannick and General Lewis at the end of *Legacy of Lies* would have happened without her encouragement. She is my wife, my best friend, and my everything.

Our children—Jimmy, Bobby, and Allie—continue to inspire me to write every day. I'm so proud to be their father.

My mother, Beth Bailey, is always one of my first readers. Perhaps I'm biased, but I'm fairly certain that I have the best mom in the world.

My agent, Liza Fleissig, has helped make my dreams come true as a writer, and she continues to push me forward to places I never thought were possible.

My developmental editor, Clarence Haynes, has been on this journey since my second novel, and his guidance kept this story from going off the rails. During our time working together, Clarence has become a good friend and trusted confidant. Our conversations and email exchanges during the editing process are something I look forward to with every book.

To Megha Parekh, Grace Doyle, Sarah Shaw, and my entire editing and marketing team at Thomas & Mercer, thank you for your continued support. I'm so proud and honored to call you my publisher.

My friend and law school classmate, Judge Will Powell, as he has done for all my legal thrillers, provided helpful advice on criminal law matters and was one of my first readers.

Thank you again to my friends Bill Fowler, Rick Onkey, Mark Wittschen, and Steve Shames for being early readers and encouraging me along the way.

My brother, Bo Bailey, was an early reader, and I am grateful for his help and steady presence in my life.

My father-in-law, Dr. Jim Davis, continues to be a source of positive energy and, as always, gave me an insightful read of the story.

My friends Joe and Foncie Bullard from Point Clear, Alabama, have provided tremendous support, and I'm so grateful for their help, encouragement, and friendship.

My friend Cindy Nesbitt, who is the director of the Giles County Public Library, was a valuable source of information for local places in Pulaski.

My friends Kristen Kyle-Castelli and Tom Castelli were again helpful in explaining the nuances of Tennessee criminal law and responded on a dime to my last-second questions.

Winston Groom, legendary author of *Forrest Gump*, died on September 17, 2020. When I was trying to break through with *The Professor*, a blurb from Winston was the one extra push that I'm convinced helped me land a contract. I was an unpublished author at the time, and I didn't know Winston other than through his incredible stories. I queried over a hundred bestselling authors, begging for a blurb. All said no except Winston. This great man taught me two lessons that I have shared with prospective writers and readers in my book talks over the years. First, you never know what someone will do for you unless you ask. Second, in the writing world, which is full of a thousand nos, all it takes is one yes that can change your stars.

Thank you for saying yes, Winston. Thank you for being so gracious to me and my family.

You will be missed.

ABOUT THE AUTHOR

Photo © Erin Cobb 2019

Robert Bailey is the bestselling and award-winning author of the McMurtrie and Drake Legal Thrillers series, which includes *The Final Reckoning*, *The Last Trial*, *Between Black and White*, and *The Professor*, as well as the Bocephus Haynes series, which debuted with *Legacy of Lies*. He is also the author of the inspirational novel *The Golfer's Carol*. *The Wrong Side* is his seventh novel. For the past twenty-one years, Bailey has been an attorney in Huntsville, Alabama, where he lives with his wife and three children. For more information, please visit www.robertbaileybooks.com.